Barrie Mahoney worked as a teacher and a head teacher in the south west of England, and quickly fell in love with the area. Later, he became a school inspector in England and Wales, and had the privilege of visiting many different schools. Barrie's work in schools enabled him to witness many amusing incidents, and to listen to children's views about life and the world in general.

A new life and a career as a reporter in Spain's Costa Blanca, led Barrie and his partner to launching and editing an English language newspaper in the Canary Islands, where he now lives enjoying life in the sun as a freelance journalist and author.

Journeys and Jigsaws

Book 1

From Teacher to Drag Queen

Barrie Mahoney

Journeys and Jigsaws

Book 1

From Teacher to Drag Queen

Vanguard Press

VANGUARD PAPERBACK

A CIP catalogue record for this title is
available from the British Library

ISBN 978 184386 538 4

Vanguard Press is an imprint of
Pegasus Elliot MacKenzie Publishers Ltd.
www.pegasuspublishers.com

First Published in 2009

Vanguard Press
Sheraton House Castle Park
Cambridge England

Printed & Bound in Great Britain

This novel is dedicated to David Hicks, my life partner, without whose endless love, support and encouragement this book would never have been written.

Acknowledgements

I would like to thank my family and friends for their love and support and to David for his well-honed proofreading skills.

To the children in the many schools where I have worked as a teacher and inspector, for their laughter, openness and natural insight into life.

To professional colleagues in schools throughout England and Wales whose skill and dedication I have been privileged to witness and I have so often admired.

To my publishers, Pegasus Elliot MacKenzie, for their professional help and support and the peace of mind that comes with knowing that you are in the right hands.

Chapter 1

The Interview

The shiny blue sports car sped its way through the narrow, winding lanes into a sleepy village one sunny Tuesday morning and screeched to a halt outside the Old Rectory. Prior's Hill was a traditional 'picture postcard' village, with its golden-brown stone buildings and thatched cottages clustered together around a small church at the bottom of a majestic hill of the same name and providing the backdrop to this idyllic scene. A large manor house to the right of the church was clearly intended to be the focus of the village, and in scenic competition with the church, with the small stone cottages gathered alongside providing a mere reflection of the grandeur of the main building.

To the less well-informed observer it might have seemed a little strange that the entire collection of cottages looked almost identical with their rich golden-brown stone and dark thatch roofs. Even the windows and doorframes were of the same colour – with the occasional 'renegade' cottage sporting a front door of a slightly different shade of green. The morning sunlight enhanced the rich golden stonework of the cottages, creating a hazy glow that indeed was fit for a picture postcard. Prior's Hill was very much a feudal estate – even in the 1980's – with all the property and adjoining land belonging to its local wealthy landowner. Even the small church blended into the scene perfectly. There was no one to be seen, only the occasional dog barking in the distance.

The blue sports car turned sharply to the right of the church and went down a small dusty lane where a small school building, schoolhouse and Rectory completed the idyllic scene. It was as if the school had been deliberately hidden from view, so as not to spoil the visitor's initial impression of the village. Outside the school and Rectory were parked a number of cars and bicycles, and children's voices could be heard from inside the school building.

The dishevelled young man in a smart grey suit leapt out of the car clutching a brand new briefcase and looking nervously at his watch. He started fiddling with the latches on the car's soft-top and, deciding that he didn't have time to pull up the hood, started walking towards the old iron gate. Damn, late again, he thought. He had left his friend Tristan's flat in Bridgehampton in good time but, as usual, he still managed to be late. Why, oh why, had he come all this way for an interview with the Spitfire's soft-top down? His usually dishevelled long hair had caught the worst of the wind on Prior's Hill and was desperately in need of a good comb, if not a good cut.

"Mr Young?" enquired the friendly middle-aged woman who answered the door. She looked like a little bird, with a thin and delicate bone structure. "We received your message. You are a little late, aren't you?" James mumbled his apologies, adding that he had had trouble with the car that morning. "Never mind, the Governors are waiting for you. I'm June, by the way, the Reverend Doctor's wife," she announced formally, adding as an afterthought, "He is the Rector and Chairman of the Governors."

James mumbled yet another apology and, stumbling over the worn rug in the hallway, as well as an equally worn yet very friendly golden retriever dog, was led into a small room where the other candidates were waiting. They were an assorted bunch – three men and two women – all in very smart suits. The very sight of this group made James feel very grateful that he had taken Tristan's advice and visited Burton's two days earlier to buy his. He didn't usually bother with suits, much preferring to wear a sports jacket, which he considered to be far more practical day-to-day clothing for working with children. As he had explained to Tristan the night before, why go to the bother of wearing a suit when it would be covered in glue, paint and vomit within a few days of buying it? James now, however, had joined 'the game', one where image and first impressions were important; a new briefcase and the removal of his goatee beard were all part of the recent transformation of this sincere young man.

The assembled gathering nodded to James as he entered the room, clutching his brand new briefcase. The new suit and unused briefcase made him feel a little ostentatious as he sat down in an upright chair at the side of the young woman and he was anxious to appear unruffled and 'cool', as befitted his years. One of the other candidates, a bald man with a thick black moustache, whispered gently, "We didn't think you were coming. Thought you had been scared off." The others smiled knowingly and nodded.

James began to explain, somewhat unconvincingly, about the troubles that he had had with his car that morning. Unconvincing, because the truth was that when Tristan, his friend in Bridgehampton, had heard that James was going for an interview, he had invited him to stay at his flat for the night. Tristan was James' oldest friend and they loved spending time together. A good 'booze-up' with his mates was something that James had not had time for recently and Tristan's invitation was very appealing. "Great idea," James had said. "We can go out for a meal and then I can get an early night. I must be up early and in good time in the morning. No late nights, Tristan!"

But one drink had led to another and it was the early hours of the morning before James had managed to get to bed. In the morning he had awoken – late – with a very sore head and with a potentially difficult interview for the head teacher of a rural school to face. Tristan was still in bed by the time that James left. James left a note on the kitchen table and crept out of the apartment. He was already wishing that he had stayed in a hotel, as the school Governors had suggested, nearer to the school.

The elderly Triumph Spitfire sped happily from Bridgehampton city centre and seemed to be enjoying a long journey at last. The smart little car may have been elderly – 1967 vintage – but it had barely covered 20,000 miles in the last twenty years. The Spitfire meant a lot to James. It had been his brother's pride and joy. Bought from new, the little car had hardly left the garage that had been especially built for the purpose. Simon, his brother, was somewhat fastidious, and couldn't bear to risk the car being damaged and so preferred not to use it unless it was a really special occasion. He would keep it clean and polished in the garage while he used another vehicle for day-to-day use. Several years later, when Simon had been diagnosed with a terminal illness, he had begged James to take the car and to look after it 'for the future'. James was happy to do so, but for many months, he too couldn't bear to use it as it brought back too many painful memories of his brother's last days. It was only after Tristan had intervened and told him how ridiculous it was to buy a car, tax and insure it and never use it, that he decided that enough was enough and that he would start to use the little car again.

"Well, we've all been in. Just you they are waiting for now," said the short, bald man, who later introduced himself as Peter. "I don't think I stand a chance anyway. They are really looking for a good Anglican and I'm a Catholic." James nodded thoughtfully, wondering why it was that men who cannot grow hair on their heads bothered to have a chin full of the stuff. It had always puzzled him. He only ever had a beard when he couldn't be bothered to shave. He had been told that it rather suited him and made him look 'less boyish'.

Wendy, the shy young woman at James' side, added, "Aren't they a dry lot? Something from the last century. I find the whole thing a bit creepy – I didn't think this sort of thing went on any more. What do you make of that Lord of the Manor and his strange wife? I don't think she liked me – she asked me some dreadful questions and then didn't want to know the answers. I am sure she was drinking gin all the time. I could smell it on her breath."

James and the other candidates began to laugh at these remarks until they saw that Wendy was indeed seriously concerned about the interview process. Jean, one of the other candidates, added, "Seemed a very strange interview to me as well. They didn't seem at all interested in my educational theories and ideas, just wanted to know if I played the piano! I don't play any instruments and that wretched woman just snorted when I said so! Anyway, I get the feeling that Wendy and I are just here to make up numbers. They want a 'Headmaster' really. Have you noticed, Wendy, that they keep referring to 'Headmaster' and not 'Head teacher'?"

"They asked me if I had ever sung in a choir!" added the short, tubby man next to 'James'. I gather they are looking for someone to lead the church choir as well! Maybe someone should tell them that the curriculum is priority nowadays."

"That Reverend Doctor seems a bit pompous as well, doesn't he?" added Wendy. "He was the one who was in the papers a few years ago, you know."

The group of candidates turned to listen as Wendy whispered the gossip that she was obviously desperate to share with them. “Yes, he was the Rector who, during his induction service, had to pull on the bell rope as part of the service. Apparently he forgot to let go of the rope and shot up to the belfry whilst hanging on for dear life!” The group tried to stifle their laughter as they all pictured the pompous priest getting his just desserts – hanging on for dear life during his ‘big moment’!

Wendy went on, warming to her theme, appreciating the reaction from the group. She added, “It seems the Bishop just briefly glanced upwards and said something like, ‘I see that our dear brother is destined for higher things’! It brought the place down apparently. I hear that the Rector is still angry about it and no one is ever allowed to mention it. The press had a field day! So whoever gets the job – just heed my warning. Don’t ever mention it – if you want him on your side, that is! Anyway, I’ve never heard of anyone calling themselves a Reverend Doctor before!”

James had heard about this strong camaraderie amongst applicants for jobs in teaching before. Teachers are strange beings – they love to talk, gossip and challenge each other, but they look after their own if a member of the group has a problem or is in any kind of crisis or adversity. He had noticed this before at other interviews. The group that he was now with was a good example of team bonding – they were talking to each other as if they had known each other for years. James had heard many times that lifelong friendships were often made waiting for interview. He had already warmed to Wendy, Jean and Peter, but was still not too sure about Eric, a tall man in a bottle-green suit, or, indeed, the short tubby man in the corner who refused to make eye contact with him.

“The only one who asked any sensible questions at all was that man from the Education Department,” whispered Peter.

"Being a church school, he has no say at all, purely advisory. It's all up to Sir What's-His-Name and that batty wife of his, I guess."

The others nodded, but Wendy added thoughtfully, "I think that the Rector is a force to be reckoned with. Not sure I would like to cross him. He seems more academic than religious, if you see what I mean?"

"How long is all this likely to go on for?" James enquired. "I only received my envelope a couple of days ago and it didn't really say anything. Does it take place over two days or will it all be over today?"

"It will all be over today," said Peter, confidently. "I have had several interviews with this lot down here. They like to take us out to lunch to see if we handle our knives and forks properly, then they ask half of us to leave and have a second round after lunch. Last time I had an interview like this I didn't get home until late evening! It is a bit like the election of a new Pope, except they don't have smoke. Mind you, this lot probably have that as well," he added wickedly.

Peter's last comment concerned James. He had hoped to meet up with Tristan again that evening before his long trip back to the North. Oh well, he just would have to wait and see what happened. James, a gregarious man by nature, had tried to catch the eye of the tubby man with a wispy beard and moustache sitting in the corner, as he was the only one of the candidates that he had not spoken to. The tubby one studiously avoided eye contact with him and this made James even more determined to speak to him.

"Hello, I'm James," began James brightly, as he held out his hand to shake the tubby one's hand. "Very pleased to meet you. Where are you from?"

“Good morning,” replied the tubby one, still seated and looking up at James for the first time. “I’m Michael Jones, I’m from South Wales.”

Michael did just glance at James as he too proffered his hand and gave what James considered to be a very limp handshake. Michael reminded James of a Chinese Mandarin, without the robes. He had the facial hair, the air and the distant supremacy that would not have looked out of place in *Madam Butterfly* or, indeed, the cast of *Aladdin,* thought James, wickedly.

James had not really intended to go for the job. He had been quite happy in his role as deputy head teacher of a large primary school just outside Manchester. The families were a rough-and-ready lot and the kids were tough, but he really liked them and felt that he was doing a worthwhile job in the school. Although he had a full-time class responsibility, he had ended up running the school for much of the time recently, because his head teacher had been drawn into other duties. Marion, a gifted and inspired woman who had successfully led the school for many years, had been drawn into the national debate about the quality of teaching and learning in literacy and numeracy. It was also rumoured that she would shortly be joining the new National Inspectorate for Schools.

For years, the national tabloids had screamed that national standards had been falling, but the results of St. Nicholas’ Primary were commendable, given the catchment area and the background of many of the children. Marion had gradually been drawn away from the school to talk about her methods to the local authority inspectorate as well as HMI, the government inspectors. Evening courses in neighbouring authorities had also taken their toll and Marion was spending less and less time in her own school. The school Governors, teachers and parents were becoming increasingly concerned about her regular absences and it was up to James to pour oil on troubled waters and to keep the good ship St. Nicholas afloat. James was doing a good job and staff, Governors and parents alike regularly praised his efforts. Indeed, one of the local authority advisers had confided to James, during one of his less discreet moments, that should Marion leave, as she surely soon would, it was likely that James would get the job as head teacher of St Nicholas; if that was what he wanted.

James was horrified. He was only twenty-nine and had taught in just two schools. He felt that he needed much more experience before the weighty responsibility of being a head teacher landed upon his shoulders. He enjoyed being with children and he enjoyed teaching. He did not want to become purely office-based, as Marion was. Surely the whole point was to keep good teachers in the classroom? No, the thought of what might happen and the decisions that he may have to make in the very near future worried him.

James was not one to worry for long. He was still often in the party mode that befitted a young man of his age and he still had many friends of his own age whom he had met at university. He sometimes found it hard to adjust to 'adult responsibilities', although he was meticulous in his preparation and attention to detail in his classroom. He liked and respected the children he taught and they adored him. It was a strange and heady mix. Indeed, one local education authority adviser had told him that his classroom manner was 'exemplary'. However, James was puzzled by the comment at the end of the very detailed feedback following one science lesson that the 'children learned successfully alongside him and sometimes in spite of him'. Those who really knew James would have identified this comment right away. Sometimes his enthusiasm and heady spontaneity just got in the way of the planned curriculum.

James had decided to apply for the job in the Bridgehampton area after his best friend, Tristan, had told him that his sister, who lived in a village a few miles from the school, had heard that Prior's Hill was looking for a new head teacher. "Seems the other one couldn't keep his flies zipped up," said Tristan. "Patsy says he was being a little too friendly with some of the mothers on the Parent-Teachers Committee." Several scandals later and the Governors had decided to dispense with his services. James had lost his parents a few years earlier and had recently lost his brother, and felt that he needed to move closer to his best friend. Tristan too had his fair share of personal problems, as well as difficulties at work, and was talking about moving to the same area to be nearer to his elder sister, Patsy, who was the only real family that he had left since the death of his mother. His father was preoccupied with his new family since his marriage to a much younger woman and had little time for Tristan since his own mother had died. Tristan hoped that he and James could even share a flat together. All in all it seemed like the right time for a change and a new challenge for both of them.

"Mr Young, the Governors are ready to see you now," said June, the Rector's wife, who entered the room carrying cups of yet more coffee for the remaining candidates.

"Good luck," said Wendy, and the others nodded their heads in friendly agreement. June too smiled at him as James left the waiting area. James was shown into a very large and dark study. Red and gold flock wallpaper adorned walls that were heavy with portraits of people in clerical collars as well as those of saints and other religious pictures. The room was so dark it was difficult to see the faces of the Governors clearly until his eyes became accustomed to the darkness.

"Do sit down," boomed the Rector, a tall yet portly man with a very red face.

The single wooden chair in the centre of the room faced a row of tables behind which sat the most important members of the school's governing body – Sir Toby Peatwhistle and his wife, Lady Lotitia Peatwhistle, George Cole, the Clerk to the Governors whom James had met before, and six other Governors sitting around the room, who nodded to him as they were introduced. James noticed the representative from the LEA seated quietly on one chair at the end of the row – Paul Jones. James recalled having met him before somewhere on a course about something called 'Accelerated Learning', which seemed yet another bandwagon to evaluate. Paul Jones smiled with recognition when he saw James and nodded.

"Thank you for driving down to see us today," began Sir Toby, an elderly, quietly spoken man with a strong public school accent. "We know it has been a rush for you, but you have done well to travel from Manchester this morning."

James didn't correct his mistake and nodded appreciatively. The group seemed friendly enough; there were plenty of nods and smiles, and James began to quite enjoy the interview. After all, like all good teachers, he too rather enjoyed performing and being 'centre stage'. Perhaps it wasn't going to be as bad as he had thought?

"I see that you play the piano with one hand, what?" began Lady Lotitia. "Delightful, I am so pleased. Tell me, with which hand?" Lady Lotitia was a tall, elderly, yet dignified-looking woman with wispy grey hair that appeared to be fighting back any attempt at serious styling. She wore a dark green tweed suit and a large ceramic brooch. The brooch stuck in James' mind – he remembered that his grandmother had one very similar.

James didn't think he had heard the question correctly and paused for a moment. "Yes, I do play the piano a little – enough to bash out the odd hymn in assembly anyway. I also play the keyboard. The kids love that."

Lady Lotitia leaned forward and peered over her half-moon glasses disapprovingly.

"Mr. Young, we do not teach young goats at Prior's Hill Primary, what? Not one of those nasty electric things? Can't abide the damned things. That is not music, what?"

"Er, well, the kids, sorry, I mean children, seem to like it." James was clearly rattled by the first of the broadsides from the local gentry. "It seems to give them confidence."

"James, do tell the panel about all the work that you have been doing in English teaching at your present school. Your head teacher tells us that you have achieved some remarkable results in a very short time."

James turned towards Paul Jones, the Local Authority adviser, and smiled, grateful for the questioning to be brought on track again by 'someone who knew' and that he could talk confidently about his subject. Paul Jones, for his part, had heard it all before. How he hated these interviews at church schools. He had to attend and give his advice on behalf of the Local Education Authority, but was rarely listened to. Indeed, of all the schools on 'his patch' it was the church schools that caused him the most problems. If only the Governors would listen to his advice in the first place.

Paul Jones had been part of the Prior's Hill interviewing panel for many years and, indeed, he had developed a soft spot for Sir Toby over the years, whom he liked and respected, but he was continually irritated by Sir Toby's quirky wife, Lady Lotitia. On a bad day she could be just plain rude, while on other occasions, like today, she was just tolerable, mainly because of her love for a gin and tonic. He wondered whether she would ask

THAT question again, and smiled as he reflected upon the answers that previous candidates had given to one of Lady Lotitia's questions and her subsequent outspoken reaction once the candidate had left the interview room. It was almost worth attending the interview just for that! He recalled with horror Lady Lotitia's stated wish for one of the candidates at an interview for another headship in the area to be "horse whipped in front of the parents and pupils" and that it was socialist headmasters collectively who were responsible for the current ills of the nation. "All this socialist nonsense and loss of the Empire started with headmasters," she had proclaimed loudly as she had swept out of the room clutching a glass of her favourite tipple. Paul reckoned that he spent at least two days a week on this less than rewarding task when he could have been out directly supporting schools. It was a very frustrating job, but someone had to do it.

"Well, it is a joint project between the parents and staff. Marion, my head teacher, and I believe that if children are to learn successfully, we must work with their parents. Many of our parents have poor literacy skills themselves and so we have devised a programme to help them work with their child at home – to give them confidence that they are doing the right thing. We have found that reading standards have improved greatly over the last few years and parents seem to enjoy helping their children both at home and in school."

"So, Mr Young, you are telling me that you have found a cheap way to teach children by getting the parents to do it themselves. Why send them to school in the first place, then? Surely your job is to teach children and not the parents?" interrupted Lady Lotitia, smiling sarcastically at her husband. She sat back in her chair, confident that she had made her point.

"Hear, hear," added her husband, nodding gravely, who until this point had said nothing. "What you seem to be suggesting is a cheap way of getting people in to teach the children."

"You a Christian, Mr Young?" interrupted the Rector. "I see that you are a baptised member of the Anglican Church. Do you attend church regularly?"

"I believe in God, but I am not exclusively a Christian," replied James. "I also try to appreciate the truths of other religions as well. I go to church from time to time, but not exclusively to an Anglican church. I am still trying to find out more for myself." He sat back in his chair with a not unnoticeable sigh of relief. James thought that his answer was rather good.

"Hmm, so you are not a Christian, what? You listen to all that socialist mumbo-jumbo from other religions as well?" interrupted Lady Lotitia with a snort.

"That's not really what Mr Young said," challenged the Rector, who appeared to be somewhat annoyed at Lady Lotitia's interruption. "I think he is simply expressing his view that other faiths have much to contribute to our own. Is that what you were saying, Mr Young?"

"Quite so," James replied, anxiously trying to steer the questioning away from this line of enquiry. He began to fiddle nervously with the button that he had discovered was loose on the cuff of his new shirt. "I also run a guitar club and the children and I often play during morning service at the local church."

"Hmm, more nasty non-instruments, what?" grumbled Lady Lotitia. "You'll be telling us that your children play those nasty whistle things during morning assembly next. Can't abide the damned things – not proper instruments. The previous head teacher was always on about them, and wanted the Governors to pay for them – recorders, what?"

James thought it best to bite his tongue and wait for the next question.

"Tell me, do you get the children to clear up at the end of an art lesson and when they make a mess or do you leave it for the cleaners?" This question came out of the blue from a tall woman with tight curly hair seated next to George, the Clerk to the Governors. James later discovered that her name was Angela and she was also the school's caretaker and cleaner.

"I believe that children should be taught to care for themselves and their environment. If they make a mess, then they are the ones responsible for clearing it up," answered James, who had now regained his composure. Angela nodded and smiled appreciatively.

"Mr Young, thank you so much for coming to see us today. My name is Dawn Edwards, and I represent the Diocesan Education Committee. If appointed, you will see quite a lot of myself and my colleagues as we try to work closely with all the Church schools in our area." Dawn Edwards leaned forward, fixing James with steely grey eyes. She continued, "I have listened to your answers to Governors' questions with great interest. Tell me, what are your views about the introduction of the new Diocesan syllabus for religious education? We are very proud of it."

Dawn Edwards was an imposing woman – tall, slim and with a commanding presence. She was clearly not someone to be trifled with and, judging by her well-rounded vowels, was someone who was used to the finer things in life.

James thought for a moment and decided that he had better come clean about the issue of the syllabus. "Well, I haven't had the opportunity to read a copy of the new syllabus yet, but yes, I would welcome any guidance that the Diocese could give."

Dawn Edwards nodded, initially looked puzzled and then looked irritated as the implication of James' answer became clear to her. She turned towards the Rector. "Surely copies are already in the school. I am surprised that the Governors did not make them available to the applicants. It is a most important document."

"Quite so, dear lady," replied the Rector, looking slightly taken aback. "I am sure that this was an unfortunate oversight. It has been a difficult term and these interviews were arranged in haste, were they not, Mr Cole?"

He glared at the Clerk to the Governors. George nodded and shrugged his shoulders.

Dawn Edwards was clearly not at all happy with the responses given, and closed her folder with a sharp click and sat back in her chair once again. She looked across to Lady Lotitia, who clearly had another question for James.

Lady Lotitia leaned forward, her swollen steely grey eyes piercing menacingly over her half-moon spectacles. "Mr Young, if you had a child that ran away from school, what would you do when he was brought back?" Paul Jones could be seen sighing deeply at the side of the room. He knew what was coming...

James had the sinking feeling that this dreadful woman did not like him at all and that whatever he said would be the wrong answer. The interview was not going well and he knew it. He felt that he should just say what he believed and enjoy the day out. After all, he would see Tristan later and they could commiserate over a few drinks together.

"Well, if one of the children in my care ran away I would feel that I had failed and I would want to know why he had run away. When he came back to school, I would talk to him about what made him unhappy about school and try to help him to overcome it. I would also try to ensure better supervision so that this could not happen again."

"Would you beat him? What?" interrupted Lady Lotitia.

This comment made James very angry.

“Certainly not, and I am appalled at your suggestion. Violence of any kind has no place in school and certainly not in any that I am in charge of. It is an admission of defeat and only makes matters far worse. I am surprised, no, horrified, at your suggestion.”

“Thank you, Mr Young, that will be all.” Lady Lotitia nodded, smiled at her husband and sat back in her chair, taking a large sip from a rather large glass of clear liquid in her hand.

Chapter 2

Lunchtime

It felt as if it was time for lunch. James was longing for the opportunity to escape from the ordeals of the morning's events and to have a wander around the village. Maybe he and the other candidates would be able to visit the local pub, the Prior's Arms, for a sandwich? However, this was not to be the case. First, the candidates had to endure a lengthy wait in the waiting area, where they shared breathless accounts of their own interviews and remonstrated with themselves for not answering questions more effectively than they had. A warm feeling of camaraderie was already developing between most of the candidates, as James had noticed during the few interviews that he had previously experienced. It seemed strange, and indeed maybe unique amongst teachers, that a group of people all competing for the same job should behave in such a supportive way to each other, but James felt that was just the nature of most teachers. They all loved talking about their schools, their jobs and their pupils. It was a kind of invisible fraternity. Anyway, children can be so amusing and teachers can immediately appreciate and share the fun of many classroom experiences with each other. It is the hidden glue that binds all teachers together.

Rather unnervingly, the candidates' hushed discussions were continually interrupted by howls of laughter and deep guffaws from the interview room. After a while, the uncontrollable laughter became disturbing and the candidates looked at each other in embarrassed silence. The reflective silence of the candidates was only broken when Peter, who was clearly not amused by this frivolous turn of events, suddenly blurted out, "Well, I am so pleased we gave them a good morning of entertainment. They obviously enjoyed it as much as we did! Maybe they thought they were interviewing for a circus."

"Well, I think it is plain bad manners," huffed Wendy. "Surely they are aware that we can hear everything they say."

Eric, a tall sallow man sitting in the corner of the room, and who had only entered into the briefest of conversations until this point, suddenly surprised the others by joining in the discussion. He took off his dark-rimmed glasses and laid them pointedly upon the coffee table in front of him, together with the magazine that he had been clutching since he arrived.

"What do you expect from this type of people? They clearly don't care about anyone else's feelings. It's just like stepping back in time – a feudal village with feudal attitudes. Why would any of us want to come to work in a place like this anyway? I really don't like it and I am appalled at the attitude and behaviour of these people. I really must consider my options before this nonsense goes too far."

The others were clearly shaken by Eric's sudden outburst and nodded silently in agreement with what he had said. Eric, whose overall appearance was not improved by the wearing of a well-worn, creased, bottle-green suit, was now sporting a bright red face as a result of his anger. He gathered his spectacles from the table in front of him, sighed deeply, picked up and continued reading his copy of *Bridgehampton Life*.

Michael too was now entering fully into the banter with Jean, Wendy, Peter and James. James began to like the stocky

Welshman as he began to talk excitedly about his passion for rugby and how he intended to bring the sport to this rural village.

"I tell you, start them young, forget this soccer nonsense and teach them a real sport that they can be proud to be part of. It will open doors for them and change their lives."

James was none too sure about this. He hated most sporting activities, although was happy to have a knock around on the tennis court with Tristan from time to time and the occasional swim in really hot weather. As for football, be it rugby or soccer, well, he could take it or leave it.

"Did you see the wonderful sports facilities at the school, Michael?" asked James. "They certainly have done well to keep such a large playing field, haven't they? Pity the swimming pool looks such a mess, though."

"Yes, I noticed that," replied Michael. "I think it's because it is a Church school and they have some sort of charitable endowment that provides all the extras that council schools don't often get. Seems a bit unfair, really. If it was a Council school they would have sold the land off by now and built a housing estate on it. You should see the school that I'm at. We have to get a coach once a week to take us three miles to the nearest green space for outdoor games. Children need a large outdoor playing space. If it's wet, we can't go. Sometimes, it is weeks before my class gets a decent game."

Then followed a discussion about sports facilities in each of the candidates' schools, and the merits of teaching rugby and football. There was also much discussion about the swimming pool, which nearly all the candidates agreed was currently a health risk.

"I would fill it in and turn it into an environmental area," announced Jean. "Who needs a pool on site nowadays anyway when there are perfectly good ones that can be used throughout the year in most towns. Anyway, with a small staff you can guess who would be responsible for maintaining it, can't you? It would be one of us! All those nasty chemicals as well."

The others laughed as Jean recounted tales of life at her present school. She was already a head teacher of an even smaller school than Prior's Hill. It was under threat of closure, and Jean and her Governors were having difficulties in convincing the Education Department that a twelve-pupil school was still viable and desirable to maintain. It appeared to be a losing battle.

"Of course, in my heart of hearts, I know that the school should be closed and merged with others in the area, but how can you say this when you are the head teacher? My school has been at the heart of village life for years and everyone expects me to back it, so I do!" Jean learned forward and whispered conspiratorially, "It was dreadful trying to come here today. My Chair of Governors knows, but no one else. They would think I was a traitor to the cause and I would possibly be tried and convicted for witchcraft." Jean giggled as she made gestures of being helplessly tied to a ducking stool. Now it was the candidates' turn to be concerned that their exuberant laughter would disturb the interviewing panel next door.

James tried to picture this well-rounded, bubbly lady as head teacher of a twelve-pupil school. Her pragmatic and trivial account was an attempt to hide the views of someone who cared deeply about her village and school. James correctly saw through this and was impressed with this dedicated and amusing teacher.

"Anyway," Jean went on, enjoying the attention that her story was receiving, "there is just myself and Molly, the infant teacher. Even the caretaker left last month and we cannot get another. So, each evening after school I have to do the cleaning as well. Sometimes one of the Governors comes in to help, but I do get so fed up with cleaning the boy's toilets. Why is it that little boys' pee just smells so bad?"

"That is quite out of order, Jean," interrupted Michael, who had been listening carefully and whose eyes had gradually narrowed as Jean was telling her story. "That is quite out of order. Surely the Education Department, the Diocese or your union could do something?"

"Tried everything, but no one wants the job, particularly as our future is uncertain. Either I do it or we close because it is a health hazard. Anyway, it doesn't really bother me, but my husband does complain that I now always smell of disinfectant! Not good for the sex life, you know!" Jean rocked in her chair as she happily realised that she had now been appointed as chief entertainer to the group.

Wendy, who had sat silent until now, was clearly horrified about her colleague's predicament. "What is happening today? Surely someone will be doing the cleaning for you. What about Molly, the other teacher?"

"Oh no, I cannot ask poor old Molly. It is as much as she can do to get to school nowadays. She retired once, but came back to help me out. No, I shall do it first thing tomorrow morning. The Chair of Governors says that he will lock up and put some disinfectant down the toilets, but he has an important meeting to go to and cannot do anything else today."

The lengthy wait came to an abrupt end when June scurried back into the room to tell them that they were shortly to be collected by the Governors and taken to a nearby restaurant for lunch. "The Governors' treat" was how she put it with a nervous laugh. This "treat," according to June, was to be followed by the Governors' deliberation of the merits (or not) of each candidate before entering into a second round of the contest. This was not what James had wanted to hear. He had planned to have some time by himself. It was not that he was not hungry either – he had not eaten since the previous afternoon. It was just that James was a vegetarian.

"Excuse me," said Eric suddenly. The bottle-green suit suddenly stretched itself to its full height as he towered over June. "I shall not be attending lunch. Indeed, I am withdrawing from the interviews and no longer wish to be considered for the position. Would you care to pass the message on or, out of courtesy, maybe I should have a word with the Chair of Governors?"

"Er, well, I am not sure about that." Eric's announcement took June completely by surprise. "Lunch has already been booked for you. Why not decide after lunch, maybe? I am sure you are hungry after such an early start this morning. Let me have a word with the Reverend Doctor." June went off, looking troubled, into the interview room, returning a few minutes later with Paul Jones, the LEA Adviser. "Let's have a word together about this Eric, and see if we can sort it out," said Paul calmly as he led Eric outside into the garden.

Minutes later the front door could be heard closing heavily and Eric was seen striding down the path clutching his copy of *Bridgehampton Life*. A few minutes later, Paul Jones returned to speak to the remaining candidates. He sat down in the place where Eric had spent the morning.

"Mr Stone has decided not to proceed further. It was not for him. Well, now we are down to five – let's have lunch." He stood up, beamed broadly and led the remaining five candidates into the Rectory garden.

James' vegetarianism was often a sore point with his family and some of his friends. This was not a fad or fashion, but something that James really believed in from the bottom of his very being. Quite simply, he loved animals and couldn't bear to eat them. As a young child he had always hated the taste of meat and fish, and from a very early age had quickly associated meat with the animals that were his friends. Growing up in a remote country area with mainly animals for company, James had quickly become very close to the many creatures that were both his pets and his friends. These sincerely held beliefs and ideals often led to problems for James when he went out socially. Few people really understood and it was often an issue at university, where his peers delighted in arguing and debating the point with him. Unaware of the benefits at the time, these arguments had honed James' skills of debating an issue intelligently, calmly and rationally. He never brought up the issue unless others did and, nowadays, James always won the debate. Tristan was the only person in James' life who never questioned or made fun of his views and this sensitivity was not lost upon James. However, one thing that James was not aware of until much later was that Sir Toby and Lady Lotitia owned and ran one of the largest intensive pig farm operations in the area. To compound the felony, Peter, one of the other candidates, had a father who owned one of the largest chains of butchers' shops and farm retail outlets in the region.

The remaining five candidates and ten Governors entered the dining-room of a nearby country house hotel. Governors had been detailed to transport each candidate in their personal vehicles to the restaurant – no doubt part of the modern day interview process, thought James. James had been fortunate and had managed to get a lift with Paul Jones. James liked Paul and felt that he was a decent, if harassed, member of the Education Department staff, and had been impressed with his contribution to the recent 'Accelerated Learning' course, which they had both attended. Much of the conversation was about James and his present school. Paul knew Marion a little and clearly admired her work and her approach to working with parents.

"You may think this is a sleepy English village, James," announced Paul. "But I am pleased to say that this County is brimming with initiatives that will help to improve what we are doing in local schools. It is a difficult area as we have so many small schools. Some will no doubt have to close to make the whole service more efficient, but we have some hard-working and dedicated people working in this Authority."

"Where does this leave Prior's Hill?" questioned James anxiously. Jean's recent troubles flashed back into his mind – particularly the account about having to clean out the toilets. The possibility of closure had not even occurred to him. However, he was aware of the school's falling roll and did not want to preside over a 'sinking ship'.

Paul thought for a moment. "This is off the record, James, but my view is that Prior's Hill, with the right person in charge, has a very bright future. True, parents have removed their children in droves because of past events, but, in my experience, many parents are a fickle lot and will bring their children back to the school as soon as they see that it is a good and happy place to be. Prior's Hill, as a result of recent events, is now a sad place, but it was not always like this. It used to be one of the best schools in the area – yes, even with more than its fair share of eccentric Governors." He laughed jovially as his car swept into the restaurant car park. "You'll love this, James. They do one of the best steaks around! Go for the mushroom sauce option, it's delicious."

One large circular table had been placed in the centre of the grand and impressive dining room. It was like something from a stately home with its wood panelling and impressive paintings in gilt frames. Name cards were already in place, adorning the crisp white tablecloth. James' heart sank when he saw that he had Lady Lotitia seated to the right of him, but Peter was seated to his left. He liked Peter, so that should help with the lunchtime conversation. He caught a glimpse of Jean beckoning to him and mouthing something to him silently from the far side of the table. She clearly didn't want to sit next to the Rector and was hoping that James would sit next to her. It was not to be and Jean too suddenly realised this when she caught sight of the white place cards that were already set out. The seating plan had obviously been thought about carefully before lunch.

Before James sat down, he had a quiet word with one of the waitresses, who was scurrying past carrying a large silver bowl of soup. "I am a vegetarian," he whispered. "Any chance of something without meat or fish?"

"No chance of that here, me duck," was the reply from the diminutive waitress. "We only do meat." Then she added as an afterthought, "I can do you a bit of cheese if you like and you can have that with some vegetables. We had a nice bit of Stilton come in yesterday. Maybe you would like some of that?" She scurried off to remove the spare place setting that was to have been Eric's.

James sat down, now desperate for a glass of wine. Sadly, there was to be only water to drink. The Rector put his hands together, bowed his head and said grace. Jean caught James' eye and winked. This brought James close to disgracing himself and he pretended to develop a sudden cough in order to disguise his stifled giggle. The Rector also took the opportunity of expressing his appreciation to the remaining five applicants for attending this "most fortunate of gatherings," as he quaintly put it. A little over the top, James thought, and winked back to Jean who, by now, was thoroughly engrossed in conversation with Angela, the cleaning Governor – no doubt repeating the tale of after-school cleaning of the boy's toilets. Jean spotted the wink and it was now her turn to disguise her sudden need to laugh with a hasty sip of water following a pretend fit of coughing.

At last, the warmed crusty bread rolls were passed around. It was a time for small talk and even Lady Lotitia seemed to be beaming contentedly at everyone as she appeared to listen intently to the conversations around her. James did happen to notice that she had another large glass of clear liquid with a slice of lemon in her hand. They talked about the price of property – houses and land, the village, the market price of milk, and the perceived evils of the Labour Party opposition.

Plates of hot steaming beef were passed around and James was given a large plate containing a small slab of cheddar and a piece of Stilton. "What's this?" exclaimed Lady Lotitia. "Are you ill or on a diet, what?"

Oh dear, here we go, thought James. "No, I am a vegetarian. I just don't eat meat or fish."

An uneasy silence descended upon the gathering. It seemed to James that everyone in the dining room had stopped talking and all were now glaring at him. He fiddled with his napkin. Predictably, it was Lady Lotitia who broke the silence.

"Oh, you young people and your silly fads," she snorted. "My niece said that when she was at college and then said she ate chicken! Grew out of it. I expect you will too when you grow up, what?" she guffawed loudly and then took a large swig from the half-empty glass clutched tightly in her hand.

"I expect you eat fish. I just don't understand you young people. You say you don't eat animals, but eat eggs and fish. Damned stupid and symptomatic of some of the half-baked theories of 'do-gooders' in our country today, if you ask me," blurted out Peter, anxious to make a good impression on the gathered group.

This outburst greatly surprised James. Until this point he had rather liked Peter and they had been getting on very well together. Why had he suddenly made an issue of James' dearly held beliefs?

"No, I don't eat anything that has a face or had a mother." laughed James, anxious to lighten the conversation. He was well aware of where such conversations could lead – with him losing his temper and thumping on the table. His father had warned him about such outbursts in the past.

"Don't give me that nonsense. What about eggs? Surely they have a mother?" continued Peter, warming to the theme and suddenly well aware that he had the full attention of everyone seated around the table. If he played his cards right, surely a good debate would count very much in his favour?

This predictable old chestnut began to annoy James, who was well-used to debating the subject in the University Debating Society. This was then followed by statements such as, "If we all stopped eating meat there would be no more cows and that would destroy the English countryside," and so on. James had heard it all so many times before and he was tired of it. Before he knew what he was doing he had launched into a debate about animal rights, cruelty, vivisection and all manner of issues that he felt strongly about. He didn't care. He felt that he had already blown the interview and that he may as well as enjoy lunch and say what he truly felt. After all, Eric had said and did what he believed, so why shouldn't he? He was also painfully aware that all other conversation at the table had ceased and he was leading, somewhat alone, a very heated debate with four competing candidates and ten Governors who, from their dismissive comments, appeared none too pleased to hear his radical views. James noticed that only Paul Jones from the LEA remained silent. Even Lady Lotitia sat quietly for once, gently swaying from side to side in her seat. James noticed that she now had a fixed smile playing on her lips and seemed rather distant.

Lunch eventually came to an end. James felt exhilarated, but knew that he had destroyed any chance that he may have had of the headship of Prior's Hill. Even so, he had been true to himself and he was only twenty-nine years old after all. He still had plenty of time on his side. As he walked soberly and alone out of the room, the diminutive waitress sidled up to him.

"Good for you, young sir," she whispered conspiratorially. "My daughter, Carol, is a vegetarian as well and she is doing all right. It was not a choice for her, but because of a medical condition. You stick to your guns, me duck."

"Thank you," replied James gratefully. "That is very kind of you. Thank you very much for the cheese as well, by the way. What is your name?"

"Peggy, Peggy Skinner," whispered Peggy. "We shall meet again, me duck. Carol goes to your school."

James was confused. He couldn't remember any Skinners at Marion's school, and what would this woman's daughter be doing in Manchester anyway?

"Which school did you say your daughter goes to, Peggy?" asked James, seeking some clarification of this confusing conversation.

Peggy beamed. "As I said, me duck, your school, Prior's Hill."

"Well, we shall see," laughed James. "You are a bit premature, Peggy. I am still being interviewed."

Peggy sidled up to James again, pulled him closer to her and whispered in his ear.

"As I said, me duck, we shall meet again very soon. My daughter goes to your school."

It was six o'clock. It had been a long day and James was anxious to get back to see Tristan. Well, it had been a day out and an experience of sorts. He had watched all the other candidates in action over lunch and had concluded that it was Peter who would get the job. In this chauvinistic environment he was sure that, as good as both Jean and Wendy were, a woman would never get a job in this school with the present governing-body's attitudes, and had probably only been invited to make up gender balance requirements anyway. Judging from the nods of approval and words of support over lunch, the Governors clearly liked Peter. Yes, it was he who would surely get the job. Wendy and Michael had both been told after lunch that their presence was no longer required. Eric had already left and now it was down to Peter, Jean and James to enter the final round. James had reached the stage where he was tired, fed up and wanted to get away as quickly as possible. He had had enough.

The door to the study swung open. "Would Mr Young step this way, please?" boomed the Rector with a stern look on his face. Silently, James stood and followed the Rector back into his study. James suddenly felt very hot – this wasn't the envisaged outcome at all.

"The Governors would like to offer you the post of Headmaster of Prior's Hill School. Are you in a position to accept the offer?" asked the Rector, with a faint smile on his lips.

James could not believe his ears. They were really offering him the job after all that business at lunchtime and that dreadful interview? Initially, James was stuck for words and just looked at the Rector and Sir Toby in disbelief. Sir Toby nodded and smiled kindly. "Yes, er, yes, thank you very much. I am pleased to accept the position. I will try to do my very best for the school and for the children."

"Welcome, Headmaster," beamed Lady Lotitia, firmly stuck in her seat. "Welcome to our little community. We do hope you will be very happy here, what?"

James cringed. He hated that term, 'headmaster'. It sounded so fatuous – old, crusty and boring, and had nothing to do with the real world and with educating the young. First and foremost, he was a teacher; he just happened to be leading what he hoped was a professional team of teachers. James smiled and said nothing. That battle was for another day.

"When will you be moving to the village?" asked Angela enthusiastically. "Will you be moving into the school house? It hasn't been lived in since Mr Charter was here many years ago and it needs a bit of work doing to it, but I am sure we can make it habitable again. It would be very handy to get to work, no travel."

James could think of few things more horrendous. As much as he loved his job, he had no intention of sharing his private life with the community – any community, even if a house did come with the job.

"No, I am hoping to share a flat with a friend in town," James replied with hesitation, and then added with a laugh, "Probably better for the kids if they don't see me all the time!"

Lady Lotitia visibly cringed and coughed, rather falsely James thought. He was well aware of her thoughts about goats…

"What will Mrs Young think to a move to Prior's Hill?" asked the Rector, "Would she be willing to restart the Young Wives Group, do you think?"

"There is no Mrs Young," James replied. "I am not married. I hope that doesn't cause the Governors a problem?"

There was an embarrassed silence and a shuffling of papers as James was led out of the room.

Many weeks later, when James had an opportunity to speak to Paul Jones, the LEA advisor, he asked the question that had been burning in his head since the interview.

"Paul, why me? Why did they appoint me after that dreadful interview and that embarrassment over lunch?"

Paul slapped James on the shoulder. "Don't worry about it. You were simply the best man for the job. First of all, the quality of your debate about being a vegetarian left them all in no doubt that you have a passion and force in the quality of your arguments that this school needs, and secondly, you answered THAT question correctly."

"Which one was that?" asked James, running a replay of that dreadful day in his mind.

"You know, the one about the child running away from school. Lady Lotitia has been asking that question for over twenty years since her own boy, Giles, ran away from school and was given such a beating that she never forgave or forgot the incident. She asks everyone the same question. You just happened to give the right answer! She's not a bad old girl really. Her heart is in the right place, James!"

Chapter 3

The Prior's Arms

The interview was by no means James' first visit to the school. When he had first heard about the job, he had driven to Prior's Hill on one of his frequent visits to see Tristan. As they turned off the main road and negotiated several tiny lanes in Tristan's battered Mini, James was immediately taken with the village as it came into sight. Prior's Hill seemed to have slipped into a time warp all of its own. It was hard to believe that here he was in the 1980s. The silence of that Sunday morning visit was something that James had never experienced before and would never forget. It was certainly unlike anything that he had experienced in the tired Manchester housing estate where he lived. James assumed that the villagers must all be in church. Tristan had accompanied James on this visit, and indeed offered to drive, curious to know what his friend was letting himself in for, although very unhappy that he had to get out of bed before midday on a Sunday morning.

When they had arrived at Prior's Hill, Tristan's first helpful comment had been, "This place is spooky! We have slipped onto the cover of a posh chocolate box!" The pair walked around the school, admiring the old horse-chestnut tree in the centre of the playground and the golden-yellow stone building before heading to the picturesque pub that was, James thought, so very conveniently placed at the bottom of the school's football field. Tristan looked much happier as they strode down the lane circling the field on that sunny, silent Sunday morning, heading towards the pub.

The pub didn't match the style of the other buildings in this picture postcard village at all. Although attractive in its way, the Prior's Arms was a traditional whitewashed building, not golden-brown stone, and with a thatched roof that had been patched recently. Several wooden tables and chairs were placed in the beer garden outside, although most of them were empty.

James pushed open the heavy wooden door in the entrance porch. An ancient, smoky-grey cat strolled out and blinked as it caught sight of and felt the warming midday sunshine. James, who was very fond of cats, bent down to stroke it. The cat hissed at him viciously and leapt out of the porch into the lane outside. Immediately the heavy oak door creaked open, James and Tristan could hear loud talking and laughter as they peered into the relative gloom and smoke of the Prior's Arms.

It soon dawned upon James and Tristan that the reason why the village was so quiet was that most of the villagers were inside the pub and not the church. The landlord, a friendly Irishman with bright blue twinkling eyes and a ready smile, beamed at them and asked what they wanted. Tristan ordered the drinks and James managed to find an empty table tucked away in the far corner of the bar.

"Surely there is a mistake in the spelling? This place should be called 'The Prior's Alms', as in almshouses," mused James. Tristan knew what was coming next and made a sharp exit to the bar. James was likely to spend ages now reflecting upon the meaning and derivation of the pub's name. Maybe they just couldn't spell around here?

“Well, this will be OK for you, Jay, won’t it? Just look at the veggie selection on that blackboard!” beamed Tristan, returning with the drinks. He whispered darkly, “And just look at some of the characters here. Are they real, do you think?”

James looked round. Yes, they certainly looked an odd bunch. Some of the characters reminded him of the Thomas Hardy film, *Far from the Madding Crowd*, that he had seen at his local cinema recently. There were four old men, all with flat caps and tweed jackets, arguing at one table. The conversation was certainly heated and animated. Two of the group were smoking cigarettes, whilst another was sucking lovingly at an old clay pipe, which was neither filled with tobacco nor lit. James and Tristan tried to listen in to the conversation, but it was quite difficult to understand the local dialect. There was a group of plump women in white aprons at the next table having another animated, but more friendly, conversation. There was raucous laughter and much nodding of heads. “Bet they’re on about the men at the next table, Jay,” whispered Tristan with a laugh. It seemed to both of them that not much had changed in the last hundred years or so.

There were also a few well-behaved children sitting at the far end of the bar, some with cans of cola or glasses of orange squash in their hands. James was almost surprised that they were not wearing traditional smocks, but modern jeans and T-shirts instead. Maybe they went to the local school? Although James would have like to have chatted to them to find out more he decided against it. James had learned from past experience that the one person that children do not like to see out of school is their teacher. James was convinced that most children up to the age of nine or so expected their teachers to work and live in the school all day and all night, and only be let out for special occasions. They had no concept of their teachers having a home life or doing such day-to-day things as washing the car, shopping and certainly not drinking in a pub. That was one step too far for the average child.

"Two ploughman's – one with ham and one with Stilton!" beamed Les, the landlord, as he put two massive plates in front of the strangers. As well as the ham and cheese, there was salad, pickles and a huge piece of warm crusty bread that smelled delicious. "Where are you strangers from then?" said Les. "Just out for a Sunday drive? Not many folk find us down here."

James explained that he and Tristan were first-time visitors to the village. He had intended upon being cautious at this stage and not saying too much to anyone, as he certainly hadn't made up his mind to apply for the job anyway. However, it was too late. Tristan had decided to tell Les everything.

"Jay may be applying for the job as head teacher here," blurted out Tristan, taking a liking to this friendly Irishman. "We are doing a reconnaissance of the village before James applies for the job. We may even come to live here."

"You sound like a military man to me," laughed Les.

The conversation then became serious and went from one of polite chatter to visiting tourists to one where Les was listening and watching James very carefully. Les was interested, very interested in the conversation. He pulled a chair over and sat with them. "I see," he said with a sigh. "We certainly have had a fair few headmasters in the last few years. I just wish we could get one of them to stay."

"Why is that?" replied James, hardly disguising his curiosity and anxiety to know more.

"Well, it's not really for me to say. I'm no expert," began Les. "Our two kids go there. The teachers are friendly enough, but there is no working together. The kids say it is boring. There is never any money to do anything and I know the Governors are worried about the school. We've also had our fair share of scandals as well recently..."

"Les, are you coming over to help or leaving me to do it all?" bawled a bad-tempered woman at the other side of the bar. "I cannot cook and serve as well. Get your butt over here – now!"

"That's Jill," explained Les with a wink. "My beloved. Got a heart of gold, but the temper of the old man himself. She's from Dublin, you know," he added as if that explained everything. "Must go, hope to see you again soon." He shook hands, first with Tristan and then with James. "Good luck – you'll need it," he added ominously, grinning at James. "My wife used to be one of the school Governors!"

"What did you tell him all that for?" said James crossly as they left the Prior's Arms. "You didn't have to tell him all that, did you? Now everyone will know."

"Can't see the problem, Jay," replied Tristan defensively. "I liked Les and at least it got him talking. You going to apply for it then?"

"Not sure," mused James, after a pause. "I feel I want to, but I haven't even been inside the school yet. What did he mean about all the problems there? The scandals?"

"Well, you know what these villages are like," snorted Tristan, with a grin. "All having fun and games with each other, wife-swapping, village romps and the like. That's all they have for entertainment out here! I think it's great. This place will be a doddle. Anyway, you always told me you wanted your own school eventually. Maybe now is the time and this is it."

"Come off it," grumbled James. "I have to make a big decision and I cannot make it based on a pretty postcard village, a bunch of yokels in a village pub and a very friendly Irishman! This could be one of the biggest steps that I will ever take. It means giving up a job in a school I like, teachers I work well with and kids that I am very fond of. Get real."

"Well, that's up to you, Jay. Only trying to help. It does mean that we can see more of each other though. I thought that was important to you as well. You must decide for yourself," said Tristan quietly.

The pair hardly spoke to each other during their journey back to Bridgehampton. Tristan drove, whilst James sat thinking about his future, or was it their future?

James′ next visit to the school came one week later. Marion had given him part of the day off and it was late one Friday afternoon that James drove, this time alone, to the school. It was four o'clock, the time that the Clerk to the Governors had suggested that he arrive at the school. James walked into the playground and was immediately met by a small, friendly, but frail-looking man who had obviously been waiting for him.

"My name is George Cole," he announced quietly. "I am the Clerk to the Governors. Have you had a good drive from Manchester? I see you have arrived right on time."

James hated being late for anything and this comment rather pleased him. He rather took to this man – a real gentleman, quietly spoken, but someone whom James felt comfortable with right away. Pleasantries over, the pair walked through the side door of the old stone building and down a narrow corridor, littered with PE kit and clothing strewn over the floor. The building looked tired and desperately in need of a coat of paint.

"The children have gone home now," said George, after a period of silence. "The caretaker has yet to arrive but, as you can see, tidiness is not a strong point in this school." James sensed that George too was embarrassed at what he saw around him.

"I will take you to the staff-room. You can meet the teachers. They are waiting for you."

James entered what seemed to have been a small living-room. It was obviously part of the schoolhouse. The walls still retained flowery wallpaper and there were four old leather armchairs gathered around an empty, yet dusty, fireplace. A battered coffee table sat in the corner, holding an array of chipped mugs and an empty vase. Apart from a few copies of the *Times Educational Supplement* and a BBC Radio and Television for Schools wall chart, the room was empty. The seated teacher stopped talking and looked at James.

"This is Anne Armstrong," said George pointing to a young woman sitting in one of the worn leather armchairs. "Anne is deputy head teacher and has been acting head teacher since the previous incumbent suddenly left."

James and Anne exchanged pleasantries, with James particularly noting the words "since the previous incumbent suddenly left".

"Are you enjoying the job, Anne?" asked James. The young woman shook her head. "No, not really. I shall be pleased when a new headmaster is appointed. It's not what I really want to do, but there was no one else available."

"When did the previous head teacher leave?" continued James. "Did he move to another school in the area?"

There was an initial silence and the young woman seemed lost for words. James began to regret asking the question.

"No, not in this area. He left about a year ago," replied George, stepping in to reply for Anne and obviously sensing the awkwardness in the flow of conversation.

George then introduced James to the infant teacher, Vanessa Sprigg. Vanessa was a tall, gaunt-looking woman who found it difficult to maintain eye contact. She stood and shook James' hand feebly, whilst continuing to delve into a plastic bag and eat grapes as she spoke.

"I hope you would not make too many changes if you get the job, Mr Young. We are doing really well here at the moment.

Lovely children, and the parents work very closely with us," Vanessa added defensively.

"Quite so," smiled James, adopting his vague response routine, and wondering what that conversation was all about. He turned to the last member of the team. An elderly-looking woman, with a firm jaw, glanced upwards briefly, yet remained firmly seated.

"Cook, Emily Cook. I teach the Upper Juniors," she stated firmly, and then added, "Where did you train? You seem very young to be a headmaster."

"Young by name and Young by nature," retorted James with his usual flippant and well-rehearsed response, and then added when he saw the glare that was coming his way, "Er, Goldsmiths." He was somewhat taken aback by the directness of the questioning and thought he ought to make a bit more of an effort. "I just look young for my age," he added, beaming awkwardly. "You should see me with my beard," he added, trying to lighten the conversation.

"I would rather not, young man," responded Miss Cook in a forthright manner. James assumed that she was a 'Miss,' although he was later to discover that it was, in fact, Mrs Cook. "I cannot abide beards, such a scruffy thing for young men in the teaching profession, and such a bad example for the children. Don't you agree?"

It was hard for James to find words at this point and he was grateful when George intervened. "Come and meet the school secretary, Doris. Now she really is a tyrant," he added with a twinkle in his eye.

James bid his farewells with a "Good to meet you all" to the staff as he was led through another doorway into a dark dingy corridor. "Take no notice of Emily," added George. "Her bark is far worse than her bite. She only teaches two days a week normally as the head's relief, so she is not too much of a burden to bear. She can be a rather awkward sort, but the children rather like her, I am told."

James rather doubted that anyone would like that old dragon, but nodded in agreement as he followed George to the next room. He was led into a very tidy room – the tidiest of the rooms that he had seen so far. The school office. Even so, James could see that it was desperately in need of a good coat of paint and a new carpet, judging by the threadbare patches that he saw. He peered inside. The office looked as if it meant business. There were two grey filing cabinets, two desks and paperwork sitting in neat basket trays on both desks. He could smell the familiar smell of the spirit duplicating machine and smiled as he saw the familiar purple letters that it had just produced. So many schools had relied upon these machines in the past, although most had upgraded them to ink duplicators and, indeed, some of the better-endowed schools even had one of the new photocopiers. James had often wondered how many school staff were high on duplicator fluid before the school day began...

"This is where Doris, the school secretary, works. It is also the headmaster's office," added George, smiling as he held open the door. "Doris is our most troublesome member of staff."

"It will be when I get you home, George," snapped a voice. "Hello, Mr Young. I am pleased to meet you," came the voice from the side of the door. James turned to see a tiny, yet smiling, middle-aged woman perched on a stool, peering at him through thick spectacles. She looked a little like an owl perched on a log, James thought. "I am Doris, George's wife, if you hadn't already guessed."

"Pleased to meet you, Doris," smiled James as they shook hands. Doris beamed at him through her owl-like glasses. He took an immediate liking to this little lady. She also reminded him of someone he had met before somewhere.

"Yes, Doris is my wife," smiled George. "As you can see she is small, but beautifully formed, aren't you, my angel?" Doris slipped off her stool and gave George a playful smack on his bottom. "See what this vixen is like? All we ever seem to talk about nowadays is school. Doris has been here forever and even roped me in as a Governor when things became a bit difficult recently."

James felt uncomfortable at this point. Another reference to 'difficult' that was not fully explained. It reminded him of that Sunday lunch with Tristan at the Prior's Arms. He was curious to know more, but then remembered that he was here for a courtesy visit and must not outstay his welcome, or ask too many awkward questions at this stage.

"Do you like dogs, Doris?" asked James suddenly, trying to change the subject. He did not know why he asked that question so soon after their initial meeting.

"Yes, I do. Very much, why do you ask?" replied Doris, puzzled.

"Er, no reason, really. I just thought that you seem a doggie person." James felt himself going pink as he realised that what he had just said may not be interpreted as a compliment. "Er, I love dogs and I just sense that you do too."

"Yes, I do, Mr Young. We don't have one at the moment because George is allergic to fur, but I would love to have one of our own. One of our neighbours has a beautiful Labrador that we take for a walk most Sundays," smiled Doris, sensing James' discomfort.

"How many pupils are there on roll at the moment, Doris?" asked James, anxious to find out a little more without appearing to be too pushy. "By the way, please call me James, Doris."

"There are fifty-eight children on roll at the moment, but it looks like the numbers will be dropping to forty-five or so at the beginning of September. We seem to be losing some of the pupils to local private schools as well as some of the other local County schools. We have had a few problems with some of the parents recently and I guess they are voting with their feet."

George looked at Doris and frowned. Doris, sensing that she had already said too much, returned to her stool and carried on typing her letter. James too felt uneasy and that it was now time to leave. He went back to the staff-room, but by now the other staff had left. George saw him to the front door and said quietly, "Don′t let what you have seen or heard this afternoon put you off, James. This is a great little school, but it just desperately needs help to move it into the next century. I came to school here myself, and so did Doris, and it had a wonderful reputation in those days. Both of our children also came here as well. It would be such a pity if they closed it, which we fear they will if pupil numbers continue to fall. We have just hit a bad patch and we need someone to lead it forward again. I know the Governors would be right behind anyone who was to be appointed. Give it some thought, won't you?"

James assured George that he would, then they shook hands and James thoughtfully closed the heavy iron gate behind him. One thing was clear to him; if he did decide to apply and get the job, it would certainly be a challenge.

Chapter 4

The First Visit

It was the first week of August and an impatient young man was fiddling with the lock that secured the old iron main gate to the school. The gate eventually swung open and James stood for a moment, glancing at the scene that lay before him. There was no smart grey suit to be seen this time, just a bright yellow sweatshirt, a pair of faded blue jeans and a beige pullover tied casually over his shoulders.

It was a very attractive looking school that had a 'lived-in', although neglected, feel about it. A large playground with one of the most majestic horse-chestnut trees that James had ever seen graced the front of the building. He pictured children playing 'catch-and-chase' games around its enormous apron. He could almost see and hear the time-honoured games of conkers, which left many a sore set of knuckles at the end of a lunchtime break, being played by generations of shouting children. This stately golden-brown stone Victorian building was adorned with a set of the most beautiful arched windows, together with two equally beautiful arched doorways and solid wooden doors at each end of the building. A perfect symmetrical balance that James' tidy mind appreciated. No doubt these two doorways used to be separate entrances for the boys and girls, thought James as he headed towards one of them. The yellowing paintwork on the windows and doors was flaking, and James tried a number of large keys in the impressive bunch that he had collected from the Rectory until one particularly impressive iron key finally turned the lock.

It was rare for James to take much time off for himself during the long summer holidays. Contrary to the popular belief that teachers did nothing during their six-week break, James was usually hard at work preparing lessons and his classroom for the new term. Before his parents had died, James usually took a week off to see them at the beginning of the school holidays, but after a day or two of living once again within a tight-knit, smothering, although loving family, he always wished he were somewhere else. The highlight of his summer holidays was usually a week or so away with Tristan. They would usually go biking or hiking. Sometimes they would stay in Youth Hostels but, more usually, they would go camping. Last year they had spent a wonderful week in the Lake District – one of James' favourite parts of the country, although more often than not it rained. Last year was different – it was brilliant sunshine for the whole week and they had an unforgettable time. James chuckled as he recalled some of the antics that they had got up to in Kendal. He doubted there would be time to go anywhere this year.

A grubby stainless steel sink and a collection of dead plants were the first things that met James' eye. This, together with grubby, cracked and in some cases missing floor tiles and a curling coconut mat, completed the scene. Paint from the end of many an art session was splattered around the sink area. One of the doors of a kitchen-style cupboard unit was hanging on one hinge. James shuddered at the sight of clothes pegs bearing torn or peeling nametags from several generations of children. James was used to organisation, tidiness and good order, and found these scenes offensive to the eye as well as conflicting with his view of a pleasant learning environment. Marion, his previous head teacher, was a stickler for the 'quality of the learning environment', as she put it, and had drummed this philosophy into James, which he had made his own. This whole area needed gutting, thought James, and it would take more than colourful drapes, flowers and colourful displays to put right. Much more.

James opened the large door to the left, which led into the main classroom – this was to be his classroom, for some of the time anyway. It was, in fact, at the bottom end of a very large traditional Victorian school hall with a folding glass screen at one end. The classroom end was huge and housed a collection of battered desks with lift-up lids that must have been there since the war. James looked despairingly at some of them. Names were carved or scratched on the lids by past generations of pupils and the inkwells still bore the stains of their many occupants' labours.

James sighed – this was even worse than he remembered from his first visit. The walls were bare, but punctured with the holes left by countless generations of drawing pins and staples. He shuddered as he noticed the remains of dried sticky tape on the painted walls, together with the remains of paper chains from one long-forgotten Christmas party. The wooden floors were unpolished, scratched and uncared for. Two old cupboards sat in one corner. James opened the double doors and was immediately faced with an assortment of protractors, compasses, boxes of chalks, old exercise books and rubbers. He closed the door quickly. A second cupboard revealed a collection of reading books. He could not believe the age of some of them. Old annuals, comics, copies of reading schemes such as *Janet and John*, *Through the Rainbow* and *Old Lob* greeted James. He shut this door quickly.

A brand new television set and Betamax video recorder beamed at him from the far side of the room, together with a large box that proudly proclaimed 'BBC Computers' underneath the TV stand. The box looked unopened and James decided that he would leave this for further investigation on another day. Looking around at the chaos before him, James suddenly felt sick and sighed, "What have I done?"

He slid back the heavy wooden screen which divided this classroom from the rest of the hall. This part of the hall housed a very large stage standing nearly three feet above floor level. More tables and chairs were on the stage. Surely this was not used as a classroom as well? In the area between 'his classroom' and the stage stood another new television on a large metal stand and another Betamax video recorder, together with two sets of wall bars, and jumping boxes, together with a pile of tangled skipping ropes and assorted hoops. This area obviously functioned as a small gym as well, but James was puzzled as to how it could be used with his classroom at one end and another classroom at the other. Questions needed to be asked about this one. Yellowed peeling paint and dirty walls completed this depressing scene.

James followed the route into the next room. This was a tiny room housing an enormous central heating boiler and safety cage. Piles of small tables were stacked in one corner, as well as four stacks of small chairs. A grubby threadbare carpet completed this dismal scene. Surely this was not used as a classroom as well? James recalled seeing a group of children in this room being read a story by someone, but had assumed that it was used for small withdrawal groups. An old television timetable stuck to the wall was the finishing touch to this dismal picture.

During James' first visit to the school he had been given a whistle stop tour by George, the Clerk to the Governors. James had focused more upon the staff than the actual fabric and condition of the building. Anyway, he told himself reassuringly;

schools always look bad at the end of term-time. Children's paintings, stories and posters would soon have the place looking bright and colourful once again.

He moved through into a small kitchen area. A stained ceramic sink, stacks of unwashed coffee cups and mugs, and an old refrigerator greeted the new head teacher. Broken floor tiles and peeling paintwork were the least of James' concerns. Another room to the right looked like the small living room of the old school house. A worn and dirty carpet, a fireplace and four grubby armchairs completed the scene. James recognised this as the staff-room. Old union notices adorned the walls together with piles of yellowing copies of the *Times Educational Supplement* heaped on an old wooden desk. Copies of the 'BBC Television and Radio for Schools' programme lay on one of the torn leather chairs. A sad looking cheese plant sat dried out, mournful and unloved in the corner of the room. James poured a glass of water over its parched soil. Surprisingly, yet another brand new colour television, together with a Betamax video recorder stood gracefully in the corner of this depressing room.

James smiled as he recalled a recent heated staff-room debate at Marion's school several months earlier. The PTA had given the school some money to buy a new video recorder. Should they purchase the VHS or Betamax system? Marion, who was not at all interested in "such learning diversions," as she put it, had delegated the job to Henry, the earnest science co-ordinator, who was keen to purchase a VHS model. There had been a heated argument involving all of the staff, with Sharon, the young and enthusiastic teacher of the third years, who "knew about such things as her father was a TV repair man", was firmly of the opinion that Betamax was best and that "anyone who bought VHS needed their heads examining as it was outdated technology!" After much debate they had finally decided to go for VHS. James couldn't help wondering what Sharon would make of this lot!

James pulled on the heavy fire door that led to a small hallway with a narrow staircase and which he correctly assumed was the rear entrance to the schoolhouse. One door, with an equally heavy fire door, stood before him. James peered around the door and rediscovered the office, neatly arranged with a large desk in one corner with a stack of papers, letters and documents in the centre and a well-organised desk to the right, complete with typewriter, telephone and a small stack of registers. The room also housed two new grey metal filing cabinets. James recalled his first meeting with Doris, the school's capable secretary. This was the best equipped and organised room in the school so far.

The staircase looked uninviting; indeed, the stairs themselves looked positively dangerous with the torn and threadbare carpet that was coming adrift. James decided that he would have to go upstairs to fully discover 'his new empire'. Cautiously, he walked up the narrow flight of stairs and turned to the room on the left. He opened the door gingerly. Piles of old textbooks, nativity costumes, broken desks, swimming floats and punctured footballs met his gaze. A collection of sad and stuffed small birds in a broken glass case were dumped unceremoniously on top of a pile of old atlases. The room smelled musty and damp, and James was concerned to see huge stain marks spreading down the walls from the ceiling. The roof was obviously leaking and would have to be an early priority.

A smaller-sized room to the right of the staircase presented James with a similar picture, except in this room one of the windows was broken and a large brown damp stain disfigured the far wall. Small fungi were growing on the lower section of the dingy wall. James was horrified. The roof, or maybe the water tank, was leaking and needed fixing. He made a mental note to get that repaired immediately as well. He looked at the window with the broken glass and was heartened to see a huge expanse of well-maintained playing fields and a second, smaller playground in one of the most beautiful settings that he had ever seen, nestled in the hillside. A small overgrown garden with flowerbeds wreathed in weeds and a good-sized raised swimming pool completed the scene before him.

The swimming pool contained at least three feet of dark green and very unhealthy-looking water and it was obvious that it not been used for some time. James remembered one of the candidates at the interview mentioning the pool, but he had forgotten to ask more about it. Let's hope it is a village thing and has nothing to do with the school, thought James. He had very little sympathy for, or understanding of, swimming pools and was of the firm belief that they spread disease and were the most unsanitary of creations. He had never forgotten a television programme that focused upon the chemical analysis of swimming pool water after young children had used it. Over a period of time the pool in the documentary had become almost 100 per cent urine. This, then, was why young children looked so happy and 'relieved' when they were in water – they were using it as a giant community toilet! Little did James know then that this feature would prove to be one of the many difficult challenges that he would have to face at Prior's Hill.

A small dark corridor led to one of the most untidy rooms that James had ever seen. To him, the room was filled with pure junk. James, who was tidy and well-organised by nature, always found it hard to deal with when he had to work with a less than tidy and organised colleague. In his experience, most teachers tended to be the most untidy of species, often complaining loudly when threatened with the possible disposal of stacks of old books, charts, cardboard, Christmas cards and yoghurt pots in their cupboards and stockrooms as "they will all come in useful one day". In this room, torn atlases of a long-forgotten British Empire, cardboard boxes, remnants of ancient reading schemes were all put to rest. A tiny brown mouse scurried across the room as James attempted to release one of the blinds that darkened the worst excesses of the room. He gave up, because in place of the old blind lay cobwebs so thick that it made little difference whether the blind was up or down. The room smelled damp and unwelcoming. James decided that he had seen enough for one day and shut the door quickly. One of his first jobs, after the repair of the roof, would be to order a skip and dump the lot. What had he done? Why, oh, why had he left the ordered sanity of Marion's school? This place was a pure nightmare. Where was he going to begin?

James suddenly became aware that someone was watching him. He looked at the cottage that was next to the far end of the playground. It was the end cottage of a block of three very pretty sandstone cottages that perfectly matched most of the other buildings in the village.

"Good day to you, sir," came a voice sporting a rich rural accent. James gave a friendly wave as he strode across the playground and came face to face with his new neighbour.

"Jack Sparrow at your service, sir. You'll be the new headmaster?"

Jack Sparrow leaned forward over the wall. James smiled as he looked at the elderly man who had just saluted him. He was a man in his mid seventies, although an exact age was difficult to determine because of his weather-beaten face and toothless grin, that is, with the exception of three stumps at the front. He beamed another toothless smile.

"That's right, Mr Sparrow. Good to meet you," replied James, shaking the hand that was offered to him. "You are our nearest neighbour then?"

"That's right," replied Jack. "Born and bred in this village and lived in this 'ere cottage all my life. Father was born here too. Us Sparrows have nested in this village for many a year," Jack laughed. This was obviously a well rehearsed joke.

James laughed, taking a liking to the old man. "Did you work in the village as well?"

"Still do, young sir," replied Jack. "I work for Sir and my Lady up at the Manor House. I help look after the dogs. I don't do as much as I used to as my legs are not so good nowadays, but he has always been good to me and I wouldn't want to let him down. I like the dogs and the job suits me fine. I goes when I wants and I comes home when I wants."

James nodded, suddenly realising the implication of the conversation. Yes, he should have known, Prior's Hill would be a hunting area and no doubt 'the dogs' that Jack had referred to were part of the local fox-hunting scene. James abhorred fox-hunting and he had been on demonstrations against it with other students when he was at college. He decided to keep his more radical thoughts on the subject to himself on this occasion.

Jack gave another toothy grin. "Came to this school, I did. It was a good school when I was here. Mr Foster, the headmaster then, was a tyrant though. Firm but fair, but if you crossed him – well, you couldn't sit down for a week!" Jack laughed and continued, "It was just Mr Foster and his wife in them days. They lived in the schoolhouse and they treated us like part of the family. They had no children of their own, you see. There's been many changes since my time. Headmasters have come and headmasters have gone – three in the last seven years, or maybe it was four?" Jack stopped for a moment as he began mentally counting and recollecting recent headmasters.

This background information was helpful to James. He loved the idea of continuity of education through these old village schools, and was intrigued to know more about his predecessors – without looking too inquisitive at this stage. He had plenty of time today and decided to let the old man carry on with his recollections.

"There was Mr Edwards, a real gentleman. People spoke well of him and he really got things moving here. It was he who built our swimming pool. Villagers loved him for it. Said as we were close to the sea, every child should learn to swim and so they did. Swimming champions were brought up in this pool. My boy even won a cup for swimming in that pool over there, you know. It's very much the heart of the village. Us Sparrows could always swim like fishes! 'Sparrow the fish' they called me!"

Jack gave another wheezy, toothless laugh as James tried hard to visualise this old man in his prime. This last comment was not what James had wanted to hear. His thoughts of closing the pool and turning it into a nature conservation area as soon as he had the opportunity began to evaporate before his eyes as Jack continued.

"Then there was Mr Pearce. He was a strange man. Lived with his sister here for a couple of years. He ran the church choir and was a brilliant organist, you know. She had a lovely singing voice and they did quite a bit for the village, but there was just something that I didn't like about him. I had left school by then, but there were rumours." The old man stopped talking as he looked around him. "They say that he did away with his wife," Jack blurted out suddenly.

"What happened?" questioned James, anxious to know more about this as well as more recent history. No doubt Jack would get there in the end.

"Police came and took Mr Pearce away one afternoon. The children were still in class and they had to get the Rector to come and take charge. The following day they came and took her away as well. It was a real scandal for the village and many said they couldn't sleep at night knowing what he did. School was closed for a week whilst everything was taken away and a temporary headmaster came from County Hall for the rest of the term. We never did really hear what happened. They did say that she helped to poison his wife. That's all we heard. It all seemed to go wrong after that..."

"That was dreadful," responded James, fascinated by this account from the school's past. "But how long ago was that? In the last few years?"

"No, sir, that was a good while ago. I had just left school and started working for Sir's father." Jack paused briefly. "How many pints would you like each day?"

"What do you mean, Jack?" James looked puzzled.

"The milk, how much milk should I bring you each day for the staff?"

"Are you the milkman as well then, Jack?" laughed James, still puzzled, but accepting the need to just go along with some things in this strange village.

"Maybe I am, young sir; I am for you anyway. Brought milk to this school for years. I have a key and I leaves it in the kitchen. Just you tell me what you need when term starts and it'll be there. Never missed a day in sixty-odd years!"

"That's a remarkable record, Jack. You must have been bringing it as a boy? Thank you, that is very kind of you. I will let you know what we need in September and then we must arrange to pay you, maybe each month or at the end of each term?"

"Never mind that, young sir, I have my ways and I does what I have to do. No need to pay for the milk. Don't mention it again, I don't like to talk about money, young sir. It always brings problems." The old man winked and nodded and then wandered back to his cottage, giving James a brief wave as he left.

What a nice old man, thought James. He was pleased that had met one friendly face and was relieved to have Jack as a neighbour. Maybe Jack would be able to fill in the school's missing history for him one day? He liked the old man and felt that he had a heart of gold and could be relied upon. He would have liked to have found out more about his predecessors, though.

A good-sized portable classroom tucked in the corner of the rear playground was the final nightmare to be explored. James climbed the short flight of stairs and unlocked the door. Yes, it was what was known as an old Hebditch-style classroom, which he recognised from a school where he had been on teaching practice. James recalled that these buildings were made by a local firm and were well-known for their good quality. The only problem was that many schools continued to use them long after they had reached the end of their working life. Schools that had grown rapidly often grew clusters of them in their playgrounds, when an extension to the main school building was the real solution. Sadly, most Local Education Authorities seemed to lack the finance and, James often thought, the political will to replace these temporary buildings with more permanent structures.

This classroom was a light and airy room, and the overall condition inside looked quite good and gave James some hope. He remembered that this room was home to the small number of infant children attending the school. The bright red tables and chairs were of the 'wipe down' metal and Formica variety, and looked quite new. James looked around and was concerned to see very little in the way of equipment – no sign of sand-and-water play equipment, home play area or, indeed, not a carpet in sight. Marion was a great believer in carpeted classroom areas, with bright cushions and, more often than not, an armchair for the teacher. This, she believed, aided the speaking and listening process and added a degree of comfort and informality to the school day. There were boxes of books from assorted, yet ancient, reading schemes, beads, Lego building blocks, and a box full of old and broken abaci. A sad group of unloved dolls looked at James forlornly from a plastic box in the corner. Arms, eyes and hair were missing from most of them. These nightmare objects would have to go. Long-forgotten plants in pots, dried out broad beans in jam jars, and sweet jars cluttered the tops of the working surfaces around the perimeter of the room. James felt a little more optimistic – at least the classroom was sound, all he would have to do was to get it equipped properly, but that would cost money.

James had had enough for one day. He would return the following day with a clipboard and begin to make a detailed record of what was needed. He might even manage another conversation with Jack Sparrow. However, his first job was to find a builder who would repair the roof quickly. He locked the heavy side door, secured the gate and fled to the safety and security of his blue sports car and sped out of the village.

Chapter 5

The Benefactor

James worked alone in the school for most of August. True to his initial intentions, a large skip was waiting outside the school for him on his next visit. A huge quantity of old and damaged books, broken furniture, boxes and even slate boards were soon emptied into it, and the skip became full much more quickly than James had intended. James thought that once he had cleared a decent space for storage in what was to be the new stockroom, then the real work of preparing his classroom and other areas could begin in earnest. During this time, James was travelling each day to the school from Bridgehampton where he had been staying with Tristan, giving little thought to the need to find some accommodation for himself, and maybe Tristan as well, much closer to the school.

James had to admit to himself during the lonely hours of many recent mornings that he might have taken on too much of a challenge. Would he really be able to breathe new life into the school? He was a determined young man and once he had set himself a challenge, he was not one to give in easily. He had drawn up a list of priorities, and overall planning for the new school year was prepared for discussion with staff at the first staff meeting in early September. Now all he had to do was to make the school fit for purpose – within the limited resources at his disposal.

He would liked to have met and talked to staff much earlier than September, but all had made it clear to him that they would either be away or unwilling, in Emily Cook's case, to interrupt their long school holidays. James found this difficult to understand, as Marion had always insisted that planning for a new school year took place before the end of the previous year and that a series of meetings took place well before the start of a new year.

"We usually come in and have a chat the day before term starts, James," Emily had told him clearly. "That is usually more than enough."

James was worried about equipment for the new school year. Reading material, schemes and quality books for older pupils were in short supply. He had oddments of exercise books and paper, but nothing was standard. He would have to ask Marion if he could borrow some until he could find out if the school had any money left. Maybe the local library in the large town would also help?

Tristan felt sorry for James. He could see how hard his friend was working and how worried he was about the start of term, and he was concerned for him. Late one evening, when James stumbled in from yet another day of sorting, cleaning, carrying and throwing, he collapsed on the sofa beside Tristan. Tristan poured him a large glass of wine and went to get his meal, prepared hours earlier, from the oven. When he got back with a tray, James was fast asleep. Tristan didn't have the heart to wake him, but took off his shoes and threw a rug over him, put his head on a cushion, and left him to sleep.

The following morning James was still asleep when Tristan was preparing breakfast. James awoke with a start. "Why didn't you wake me up?" he shouted at Tristan, who was in the kitchen preparing some toast and coffee. "You know I have a lot to do today."

"You are working too hard, James. You need to sleep as well sometimes," replied Tristan firmly. "We are halfway through August and you haven't taken a day off since you left your last school. Have breakfast and a long, hot bath, and then we will talk a few things through. I have a few ideas that may help. Anyway, are we having a holiday away together this year?" Tristan already knew the answer to that question.

James stumbled out of the bathroom dressed in an old pair of jeans and a clean white vest. "That feels better," he said, beaming at his friend. "Sorry about last night. I can see you cooked me something again. I was just so tired. Amazing how a good sleep and a bath can get you going again though, isn't it?"

Tristan nodded and pushed over a cup of coffee to James. "I've been thinking. I am due a few days off, you need help, and so I am coming to give you a hand." Seeing James starting to protest, he added, "Don't even try to argue. I have made up my mind and I have called in to say I am having a few days off. This is the nearest thing that we are going to call a holiday together this year, isn't it?"

James knew when he was beaten. There were times when Tristan could not be argued with. This slim and handsome ex-soldier could also be very stubborn once he had made up his mind, and it was this tenacity and loyalty that were two of the things that James liked so much about him. He could certainly do with some help. Every bone in his body ached and he still had so much to do. "OK, OK, no arguments. It's just that I am buying dinner tonight – OK?"

Tristan nodded and gave his friend a wry smile.

"Don't forget the sandwiches, Headmaster," laughed Tristan, knowing how much James hated that title, pointing to the kitchen table.

James walked over to the kitchen table, opened the plastic bag and peered inside. Two neat packs of sandwiches, wrapped in transparent film, two apples, a box of apple tarts, a large pack of chocolate biscuits and two cans of cola had all been prepared for the day. Tristan had prepared something similar for James each day that he had gone to school, knowing full well that his friend would never stop to take a break. He smiled appreciatively at Tristan – a typical soldier, always so well prepared, he thought.

"I don't know what I would do without you, Tristan. Off we go then."

Over the next few days, the pair began to make inroads into the clearance of rubbish in several rooms. What James was already calling the 'stockroom' was now empty of rubbish and in its place stood neat piles of exercise books, paper and card that James had discovered in the downstairs office and in classrooms. James had ordered the fifth emptying of the skip, when there was a loud knock at the door followed by a shout. "Are you there, Mr Young?" came a commanding voice from below.

James peered downstairs and was surprised to see Sir Toby Peatwhistle standing by the back door. James ran downstairs and opened the door to his surprise guest.

"Sir Toby, good morning, it is nice to see you again."

Sir Toby and James shook hands.

"Well, James, I know you have been working here for many days during your holidays. I also know that there is much to do and so I was anxious not to disturb you. You arrive early and leave late. However, I thought the time had come to see if there is anything that we can do to help you?"

"That is very kind of you, Sir Toby," replied James, who was pleasantly surprised by this offer of help. "Let me show you what my friend and I have been doing."

Sir Toby came up the stairs, nodded to Tristan, and viewed the near-empty stockroom. "My goodness, you have been busy," he said. "The villagers have been wondering what you have been doing. Are you sure you meant to throw out all of those things?" He smiled wryly. "I have seen villagers leaving the skip with armfuls of goodies each evening when you have left, and so I wondered if you really meant to throw all of it out?"

James nodded and gave a brief description of what had been disposed of.

Sir Toby laughed and nodded. "Yes, I thought as much. Lotitia and I have been guessing about its contents. We were sure you wouldn't throw anything out that was valuable."

James continued with his explanation, concerned that he may have gone just a little too far without discussion with the Governors. Sir Toby waved a hand and interrupted his flow of conversation.

"Well, you are the headmaster. That is up to you. It is your decision and judgement. What are you going to replace all this with though? At the last Governors' meeting we discovered that the school is very short of money. Indeed, we are in deficit. There is just no money to buy new things. You had better be careful. The villagers are already asking questions."

James' heart missed a beat. He had not asked detailed questions about money so far. He had just assumed there was enough – for the essentials anyway. How could he have been so foolish? He looked at Tristan, who pulled a face. It seemed a fair assumption that as nothing appeared to have been spent in the school recently, other than on new televisions and Betamax video recorders, there would still be some money to play with.

"It seems to me than you need a bit of help in sorting out this room," began Sir Toby after he had cast his eyes around the mouldy walls. "Are you here tomorrow? I will send one of my men over to seal and repaint the room for you. I will get him to put some shelves up for you and then you and your friend can begin to make a start on sorting this lot out. We need your kind of enthusiasm, Mr Young, but a few words of advice. Don't upset the villagers. They are a tough lot and don't take to newcomers very well. Try and take them along with you. They make bad enemies, but once you get to know them, and they know you, they will be your friends for life. Is there anything else I can do for you?"

"I am concerned about the roof. It is leaking badly in two or three of these rooms, as you can see. I have tried to get hold of someone at County Hall, but they say it is a Diocesan matter. I have called the Diocesan Education Office, but the people that I need to talk to are on holiday."

"Yes, that too is another issue we discussed at the last meeting," nodded Sir Toby. "We really need an architect's advice, as I suspect we may need a new roof. That could take months to sort out." He paused and thought for a moment. "I will send one of my men, around tomorrow. He used to be a roofer, but mainly thatch. I am sure he could do something as a temporary fix until we can get the Diocese involved."

With that, Sir Toby nodded and retraced his steps down the narrow staircase. "By the way, this may help a little." He pushed a crumpled piece of paper into James' hand and strode out of the door.

"What was that all about, James." whispered Tristan. "Which planet is he from?"

"I don't care where he comes from," grinned James. "What a good man. Look what he has just given me." James passed over the crumpled piece of paper to Tristan. It was a cheque for one thousand pounds.

Sir Toby's visit gave James and Tristan a great boost of enthusiasm, and the following day they were joined by Jack Sparrow, as well as two more of Sir Toby's employees, Bert and Eddie. The three local men stripped, sealed and painted walls in the new stockroom as Sir Toby had promised, and began to make a start on cutting and fixing wooden shelves. Jack Sparrow surprised James with his skills as a carpenter. "You didn't tell me that you were a carpenter, Jack," laughed James.

"There's many a thing folk don't know about Jack," replied Jack, suddenly referring to himself in the third person. "Jack has many skills that folk don't know about."

"Well, Jack, I am very grateful to you all for your help. We couldn't have done all this without you."

"As I said to you, young sir, the school needs someone like you to put it back on the rails. I am happy to help and, with the right approach, you will find that other villagers will too."

By the end of the week, James and Tristan, together with employees from Sir Toby's estate, had cleaned, washed and painted the three upstairs rooms. Rubbish had been disposed of and the new stockroom was now graced with Jack's shelving, already laden with sugar paper for painting, ancient exercise books, drawing paper and other assorted stationery. Sir Toby had visited each day, enthusiastically inspecting the work that had been done and giving the go-ahead for further work. James' thinking was that throwing away and tidying the upstairs rooms in the school house would not only make way for storage of unwanted and occasional items from the downstairs classrooms, but might, in time, provide additional accommodation for small groups of children requiring special help with their reading, music lessons and the like. James was wise enough to realise that he would have to get permission from the school Governors as well as County Hall for pupils to use the upstairs rooms because of insurance and safety requirements, but it was a possibility for the future.

Now that James could clearly see what stock he had available to use, he was concerned to see how limited it really was. True, he had enough paper and pencils to see them through to the end of the century. However, where was the paint, glue, sticky tape and all manner of items that James would normally consider to be essential? He was also concerned that even the exercise books seemed to be designed for older children, with no provision for the plain paper and wide lined books that are usually the stuff of infant classrooms.

James had already tried to get to the bottom of school finances by speaking to Doris, the school secretary, one afternoon in early August. Puzzled by what seemed like a serious situation he had telephoned Doris, who had invited him to have tea with her and George. He had left Tristan painting the walls and called at Doris and George's neat little cottage just outside the village. James was struck by the beautiful garden in front of their home. Someone obviously liked gardening and was very good at it too. He was also amused to see one of the largest collections of garden gnomes that he had ever seen gracing the side of the path, together with toadstools, grottos and all manner of artefacts, no doubt all designed to make a gnome's life an even happier one, thought James.

Doris greeted James with a warm smile and led him into the cosy kitchen where there was a delicious smell of cakes baking. "I have just baked a chocolate cake, James. I thought you would like to have a piece. Tea or coffee?"

"Who is the gnome fancier, Doris?" asked James, grateful for an opening topic of conversation unrelated to the reason why he had really called for tea.

"Oh dear, that's George," laughed Doris, wincing. "Cannot abide the things myself, but George collects them from wherever we go. He even brought one back from France with us last year. Lucky we were on a ferry and not a plane, it was so heavy. Anyway, it does make present-buying easy. If we are stuck for an idea, we just buy him a gnome. It keeps him happy."

A large mug of tea was placed before James, and a very generous slice of chocolate cake, laced with fresh chocolate icing and large red cherries on the top. Doris poured herself a mug of tea and sat before him, perched on a stool, her large round glasses making her look even more like an owl than when they had first met, thought James.

"George had to go out and sends his apologies," said Doris. "You didn't bring your friend with you. I expect he could have done with a cup of tea as well?"

James wondered how she knew that Tristan was in school as well. "No, I left him finishing off the painting. He has helped me so much. I have been so pleased with the help that Sir Toby and his men have given us as well."

"Yes, he is a good man," replied Doris. "He looks after his workers as if they were part of his own family. Lady Lotitia is a strange one, as I expect you have found out already. She has a heart of gold though, but it is her liking for the drink that is her undoing. Takes all sorts, I suppose."

"Doris, this is the best chocolate cake that I have ever tasted," began James generously. James liked cakes and this was certainly one of the best that he had tasted for a long time.

"I am a bit worried because the school doesn't really have any stock. We shall need quite a few things before September and time is getting on. Do we have any money left?"

"Not really," began Doris. "Peter Wright, the previous head teacher, did all that sort of thing himself and didn't involve me. Since he left, I have tried to make sense of it, but it seems that we have a very large overspend, although I am not sure why. The Governors had a meeting recently about it and the Rector had to go to County Hall. He may know more than I do."

"Yes, but surely the school would have had a new budget from April and the previous head teacher had left by then. Surely not all of it has already been spent?"

Doris grimaced. "Just before he left he ordered several video recorders – the staff were against it, but he insisted that they were a good buy. There was also a large order for gym equipment and I think a lot of money had to be spent on the swimming pool. Also our numbers have fallen so much recently that some money from the previous year had been taken back. That's really all I know. Another piece of cake, James?"

"Yes, I see," replied James thoughtfully, brushing away crumbs from the last piece of chocolate cake from his mouth. "Yes, please, Doris, another piece would be lovely. It is delicious."

"Pleased you like it," smiled Doris, showing pleasure at the compliment that she had been given. "Charlie, my youngest, loves my chocolate cake and that's why I always have one ready. Why don't you speak to that man from County Hall, Mr Jones, I think his name is. You must have met him at your interview. He may be able to give you some more money."

"Yes, good idea, I will. Tell me, Doris, did anyone ever check or question the spending? Was there ever an audit?"

"No, not really," replied Doris, after careful thought. "Peter didn't like me being involved, so even though I was the school secretary he used to get me to go and hear the children read. He used to like to do anything with money and ordering himself. I know the Governors were concerned and kept asking questions, but nothing ever happened. I don't ever remember an audit taking place, although we once had a letter saying that there would be one, but nothing ever happened."

James decided not to pursue the questioning any further for fear of sounding as if he was blaming Doris in some way. “Well, thank you, Doris. This has been lovely, but I really must go now. You make the best chocolate cake. It really is melt-in-the-mouth stuff. Charlie’s a very lucky boy.”

"Well, he’s a grown man now with a wife and a baby, but he still likes his chocolate cake."

By now, Doris was cutting another two slices of the now much-reduced cake; she wrapped them in tin foil and thrust them into James’ hand as they walked out of the front door.

“Another piece for you and one for your friend – just to keep you both going. I will come over in the next few days and if I can help just say the word.” Doris beamed at him as they walked together to the gate.

“Prior’s Hill has some problems, James. You know that already, but it is not easy to talk about. This is a close-knit community and we all have to watch what we say. Give it time and you will begin to make sense of it. I know you can do it. George and I will help you all we can.” Doris waved, turned and went back into the cottage.

James walked towards the gate, glanced to the side of the pathway and caught a glimpse of a large garden gnome grinning at him.

It was early Friday evening as James and Tristan walked briskly towards The Prior’s Arms.

“It has been a good week. Thank you for helping me out. I don’t know what I would have done without you, Tristan.”

“That’s what friends are for, James. Anyway, it wasn’t just us, was it? Look how Sir Toby and his men helped. They have been amazing. I just wanted you to get a good push and then you will be able to carry on under your own steam. You have taken on a huge challenge, but it feels good and I know that you are the man for the job."

"What about you, Tristan?" questioned James. "We haven't really talked about where we are going to live and what you are going to do. You are not going back into the Army, are you?"

"No, James, I am not. I have done my years and although I enjoyed it I don't want to do any more. I don't really want to stay as a supermarket security guard either. There must be something else I can do. I am pleased you said 'we', by the way. Where are we going to live?"

James thought for a moment and nodded. "Why don't you think about starting your own business? You seem to be able to do anything. You are good with your hands and you have many skills."

"That's just it, James, I don't. OK, I can fix things and blag my way through, but I am not as clever as you. I wouldn't know where to begin starting a business. I like to work outside. I am more physical and I would hate sitting at a desk all day."

James didn't pursue the conversation any further. He had had similar discussions with Tristan before and his friend's lack of self-esteem always annoyed and surprised him. Tristan was capable of far more than he thought, but convincing him was another matter. He was also worried about where they were going to live, but didn't want to think about that now as well. He changed the subject deliberately.

"By the way, you know that one thousand pounds that Sir Toby gave me? Well, I had a chat with the man who owns the bookshop in town and he is going to give us a really good deal if we buy some of his excess stock. I had a look yesterday and I can get some really good deals. Even though it was a lot of money, and most generous of him, it still doesn't stretch far enough. I can get new books for the young children, but not the older ones." He paused. "I really must find out why it is called 'Arms' and not 'Alms'," he continued, trying to fill a gap in the silence.

"James, does it really matter?" laughed Tristan. "I am starving and I could even eat one of your veggie burgers! Three days ago you promised that you would take me out for a good meal if I helped you. Now's your chance, but for goodness' sake, stop going on about that damn name!"

Chapter 6

Getting Ready

To many people, clearing the stockroom may seem a very strange way of getting ready for the new school year, but for James it was a statement – a statement of intent. He already felt overwhelmed by the overall task and getting just one small area organised to his satisfaction gave him the encouragement that he needed to continue with his challenge. James was deeply grateful for Tristan's help and between them they had cleared and cleaned the room. Bert, Sir Toby's friendly odd-job man, and his friend, Eddie, had spent nearly a week cleaning the walls, sealing, undercoating and repainting the room. Bert was a man of very few words, but James gathered that he too had been a pupil at the school, as had his father before him. Bert communicated with James mainly through a series of grunts and one-word answers. However, James quickly felt that Bert was a friend of the school and would do what he could to help. Eddie, on the contrary, was a real chatterbox and quickly filled any gaps or awkwardness in conversation. He also liked to smoke and often disappeared to a space behind the kitchen building for a cigarette.

Working together during that week, Tristan and Bert developed a strong bond – mainly through their shared weakness for chocolate digestive biscuits. James was always irritated that

Tristan somehow managed to retain the figure of a model. Whatever he ate seemed to have no effect upon his size and shape, whereas James had to watch his diet carefully and chocolate biscuits were certainly banned as far as he was concerned. True enough, on the second day of the major clean-up, when Bert had just finished rubbing down one wall, Tristan appeared with mugs of coffee as well as a plate of chocolate biscuits. Since that time, the two had got on very well and Tristan made sure that chocolate biscuits were a regular feature of the next few days work.

Later, Eddie arrived to help fit shelving in every available space in the room. James and Tristan had spent their time sorting out paper of all types, shapes and sizes, exercise books, textbooks, boxes of chalk and all manner of items that would come in useful – as long as it could be found easily. James confidently felt that he wouldn't need to order exercise books and basic stock for the next year or so, and particularly for such a small school roll. Sir Toby had also paid for the timber and shelving brackets, as well as providing the skilled labour. James had already spent Sir Toby's one thousand pounds on two large boxes of new books, although, according to James, many more were needed for the older pupils.

The next major task was James' classroom. It was a huge space at the end of the main school hall. A large folding glass-and-timber Victorian screen separated his class from a space that was intended to be used as a small hall for indoor PE and for watching television. At the far end of the room was a large stage about three feet above the main school hall floor. James had already managed to talk the caretaker, Angela, into resurfacing and polishing the timber floor, which now gleamed, but it was the stage that really concerned him most.

"See that, Tristan," he said to his friend. "A class of kids spend most of their day on that stage. It is their classroom. They are all about seven to nine years old. I can see them falling off and hurting themselves. What crazy idiots decided to build a stage here and put the kids on it?" The situation troubled James whenever he saw it and he knew that he would have to find a way of resolving the problem before long.

The next few days saw James stapling brightly coloured backing paper to the cracked and mouldy walls, repainting blackboards that had ceased to be true to their name for many years, mounting pictures, wall charts, multiplication tables, word lists – anything in fact to disguise the poorly finished walls and to transform the room into something that resembled a modern classroom. He managed to find all the pieces for the new BBC computer languishing in the storeroom, and connected the monitor and the brand new cassette recorder, which had been rebranded as a 'data recorder'. He held his breath and switched the equipment on. After a short delay, the start-up screen appeared and a green cursor started flashing at him. Thank goodness, he thought. At least we have a working computer, a television and video. Not a lot else, but at least it would go some way towards introducing his new pupils to the wonderful new world of computers.

The lack of books worried James. He was not too concerned about the lack of textbooks as he had many work cards that he had made over the last few years that he could use. He had a blackboard and a voice, so he would use those, he reasoned. Anyway, with such a wide age range in one class he wouldn't need that many textbooks at the same level anyway. Marion had already offered to let him borrow a selection of books from her school and maybe one of the local schools would help him out until he could afford to get some more. No, what he was most worried about was the lack of attractive reading books for the older pupils. There were oddments of old reading schemes such as *Old Lob* and the *Ladybird* series. There was even a handful of

Janet and John reading scheme books, which James remembered from the time when he was at school as a pupil. What he lacked were modern, interesting and colourful reading schemes, as well as graded reading material for what he assumed, and hoped, would be needed by his more able readers. The furniture in the classroom was of the old desk-and-lid type that James reasoned had been there for centuries. How he would have loved to scrap them all and replace them with bright colourful tables and drawer units. He would have to wait for that. There was no bookcase, but some old crates that would look quite smart once they had been covered in bright fabric.

Over the next few days, James bought a new and colourful carpet square for the reading area for twenty pounds from the carpet shop in the nearby town. It was originally priced at thirty pounds, but when James explained that it was for his classroom at a school in the next village, the shopkeeper had agreed to give him a generous discount. Mr Penny even delivered the carpet free of charge the following day.

Mr Penny was the owner of the long established family-owned shop, Penny and Son, in the nearby town of Abbotsford. A large sign loudly proclaimed this fact, adding that it was 'Established in 1910'. This statement gave the business an air of superiority that set it apart from the other 'more ordinary' shops in the High Street. Mr Penny, a short bald man with the shiniest of heads that James had ever seen, presided over the operation. Indeed, James found it very difficult not to stare at the head's highly polished surface and, after a lengthy wait, came to the conclusion that Mr Penny had very much a 'hands on' view of running his business. Although there were two sales assistants it was Mr Penny who advised, sold, wrote out the order forms, took the money and finally arranged to deliver the carpets.

"My father used to come here, and his father before him," Mr Penny told James proudly as he rolled out the new carpet square in James' classroom. "Many a Penny has been spent here." He guffawed loudly, showing great pleasure at his well-rehearsed joke. I have never been inside the school before today though. Father sent me to a private school in town. This is a lovely old building, but I can see it needs some work doing. You just let me know if you need any more carpets. I can always give you a good deal and maybe even put some offcuts your way. Just you let me know. I try and help local schools when I can and it would please me to help in memory of my late father. It would be a tragedy if lovely old schools like this were ever closed. I hear that Skudder Bay School is going to close next year."

James, who only just managed to stop himself staring at the shiny head before him and resisting the urge to polish it further, nodded as he listened to Mr Penny's views on why County schools were rapidly being closed and the virtues of private education. James quite liked the man, but found Mr Penny's views on private education disturbing. Still, if the shopkeeper was willing to help him to carpet the school at a reasonable price, James was willing to bite his tongue and listen to what he considered Mr Penny's more extreme political views on the value of private education.

James was grateful to Mr Penny and was already thinking about carpeting all of the classrooms, but he would need to talk to the other teachers and the Governors first and see what they wanted. He knew from past experience that carpeting classrooms could be controversial. James could never understand why, if schools put on a practical mathematics workshop evening for parents, very few would bother to attend. However, if it was to discuss carpets in classrooms, the school hall would be full of controversial voices and opinions. He suddenly remembered a similar battle that Marion had had with the Parent-Teacher Association when she had tried to carpet one of the infant classrooms. Certainly James had heard all about Skudder Bay and was concerned because it was not that far from Prior's Hill. He just hoped that the Local Education Authority would not get too carried away with the idea of closing small schools throughout the County.

"This one should be alright," continued Mr Penny. "In its day it was always full and often very difficult for outsiders to get a place. It had a good reputation. My father and uncle only managed to get in here because grandfather knew the Squire well socially through the hunt. Seems that the school fell out of favour a few years back, but I don't know why. I am sure you will soon turn it around again."

James thanked Mr Penny and showed him out of the building. "Yes, I like this school, Mr Young; I know father was happy here. Mind you let me know if there is anything that you need."

James also managed to find two old, but sturdy, bookcases for sale in a nearby junk shop. Again, he managed to get the price reduced to thirty pounds for the two – delivered. By the end of the week, the walls of the classroom had been transformed, the floors were bright, shiny and clean, and a new carpet was placed in the corner of the room, together with the two bookcases and an old armchair that used to belong to his mother. He had even arranged a meeting at very short notice with the local librarian.

On impulse, James called into the small library in the centre of Abbotsford at the end of one very busy day of sanding and re-varnishing some of the old desks in his classroom. Tristan had already completed several desks, but as he had to go to work had left James to finish the job. James felt tired and decided to call into town on his way home to get a bottle of wine as his contribution to the evening's meal. He spotted the library next door to the supermarket and decided to have a closer look. Later that evening, when speaking to Tristan, James was horrified when he realised that he had not been appropriately dressed for the occasion. His varnish-stained denim jeans, torn green sweatshirt and worn plimsolls were not of James' usual standard of dress. James was also smelling very strongly of varnish, which did not blend well with some of Tristan's spicy aftershave that he had liberally splashed over himself many hours earlier.

The small town library was empty of readers, with the exception of a tall woman in her early forties who was studiously looking at and replacing books upon the shelves in the children's section. She "tut-tutted" as she discovered yet another book with a torn cover and carefully placed it in a plastic basket labelled 'For Repair'. James stood patiently at the counter waiting for the librarian to finish her task. He was in no great hurry to leave and rather enjoyed watching someone else working for a change.

Jasmine De Valle was the town's librarian. A single woman, she had already begun to accept that, in common with the books that surrounded her, she too was destined to be left on the shelf. It was not that Jasmine was unattractive. A true beauty she certainly was not, but on a good day she could radiate the enthusiasm and raw charm of a pubescent schoolgirl, but only when she could talk about her beloved books or classical music. Some would call her abrupt, others would say she was rude, whilst others would simply classify her as 'a little eccentric'. The truth was that Miss De Valle was thoroughly frustrated with her lot in life, impatient with the readers whom she was employed to serve, and she longed for something new to happen in her life. She spent her days in the library with Carol, her talkative, yet dilatory assistant, who lacked the enthusiasm and spark for the life that Jasmine craved.

Jasmine finally finished replacing the books on the shelves, spotted a scruffy young man leaning on her polished counter, looked at her watch and sighed. Crossly, she marched back to her desk and glared at James.

"We close in five minutes. You had better be quick."

Not one to mince her words, Miss De Valle was even snappier than usual. Her curt welcome took James by surprise. Oh dear, he had met this type before, he thought; major charm offensive needed here.

James listened, waited for the outburst to finish and looked Miss De Valle directly in her eyes. He smiled gently before he spoke.

"Well, I am sorry, but I have been here for a few minutes waiting for you to finish. I didn't like to disturb you. You seemed so engrossed in what you were doing."

"Well, as I said, I am going to close shortly. It has been a long day," Jasmine responded, not quite so sharply. "What can I do for you?"

"I should introduce myself. My name is Young, James Young, the new head teacher of Prior's Hill School. I need some help and I wondered if I could talk to someone."

Jasmine listened carefully and shook the hand that James held out to her. She gave just a hint of a smile.

"I am so sorry, Mr Young. It has been a long day and my assistant has been off sick. Let me just lock the door and then I will try to do what I can to help you."

James nodded and walked with Jasmine to the door and waited while she slid the brass bolt across.

"Now we won't be disturbed. Let's sit over here. Now, what can I do to help?"

James began to tell the librarian his problems in getting books for his pupils in the short time that he had before term began. He told of his beliefs in providing children with only the best books available, and the way books should be displayed and treated. He spoke her about his views on storytelling and getting parents to read with their children and share the experience together. He talked about his love of books and how he wished to share this world of knowledge, laughter, joy and excitement with children. All this was music to Jasmine's ears and she listened intently to the sincere young man who was seated in front of her.

By the time that James left the library two hours later, he had talked the librarian into agreeing to double his book allowance for not only his class, but for the whole school for the next two years. In addition, Miss De Valle agreed to personally select and deliver a range of suitable books for the age range that James was teaching. Miss De Valle also agreed to loan the school a further selection of books that would help with their current projects and topics, as well as giving advice on how to develop a quality reference library. She also found herself volunteering to talk to parents about a home-school reading partnership. As a final gesture of support, she offered to visit the school twice a month to hold story-telling sessions for pupils.

Later that month, Tristan took an afternoon off work to see how James was getting on, as well as to help him to deliver the old armchair. Tristan didn't usually give praise easily and James glowed with pleasure when Tristan praised his friend for what he had achieved. He put his arm around James' shoulder and gave him an affectionate hug.

"This looks like a classroom now, Jay. Not a bit like the dump that I saw on my first visit. You have worked so hard. I am so impressed with what you have done in such a short time. Well done!"

This was just what James had been hoping Tristan would say. Praise from Tristan meant more to him than from anyone else he could think of.

Tristan also had a surprise of his own. He gave James what looked like a huge round ball covered with a large orange curtain. “Here, this is my contribution,” he announced proudly.

James removed the curtain to find a huge globe. It had been in Tristan’s family for many years, but he had no use for it.

“My uncle gave it to me when I joined up,” explained Tristan. “I have no use for it – it is far too big for my flat, but I thought it would look rather good over there.”

Tristan took the globe to the far corner of the room and proudly placed it on an old coffee table, which he first draped artistically with the curtain.

“You see, Jay, you are not the only one who can make things look nice,” he said with a laugh. In later years, James thought back to this moment with a warm glow of pride, and realised just how reliable and special a friend Tristan had been to him during those very difficult few weeks at Prior’s Hill. Indeed, at a later time, James realised that it was at this moment that he knew how much he loved Tristan.

It was the beginning of September and James was becoming increasingly concerned that apart from himself and Tristan, and many visits from Doris, no one else had been in the school to prepare for the new term. There was less than a week to go and although he had arranged a staff meeting for the day before term started, he knew from experience that it required much more effort than a couple of hours after a staff meeting to prepare for a busy new term. He wasn’t sure whether he should telephone the other staff to check when they were coming in or to leave them to it and see what happened. He was particularly keen to talk to Emily, his part-time head teacher’s relief, as they would need to plan the timetable and curriculum carefully for the new term. He mentioned this dilemma to Doris as they were taking a short coffee-break from sorting out old papers in the office.

“Do you think they will come in before term starts, Doris?”

“Well, they usually do, James. They are not as well organised as you, but it usually happens. Just wait and see – I think you will find that everything is OK. Let them get to know you first and see what you expect from them. You can always make changes after that. Be warned though that Emily can sometimes be a bit, shall we say, awkward.”

“What about the cleaning? I have only seen Angela once since term ended. Surely she should have been in giving the place a good clean before the new term starts? I put some disinfectant in the toilets the other day as they were smelling so bad.”

“They have their own way of doing things around here, James. It will happen, but it may not be when you expect. I know that Angela is away at the moment, but I expect she will be back before Tuesday.”

“I hope so,” exploded James. “Term starts on Tuesday.”

It was Friday afternoon and term was due to start on the following Tuesday. James was coming to the end of his preparations and by mid-afternoon he felt that he had done as much as he could. His classroom was ready for business. He had covered the walls in brightly coloured sugar paper, hung cheerful wall charts and posters, and had even stuck name labels above the clothes pegs in the corridors. It was the naming of these, as well as exercise books, that troubled James, because he was still uncertain as to who would be in his class and, indeed, the school. Doris had class lists ready, but she knew that a number of pupils who were registered wouldn’t arrive, whilst others who were not expected would hopefully turn up during the first week of term.

Cupboards had been emptied, cleaned and rubbish thrown away, and items that were to be kept were stored away neatly.

The children now had a reading area with bookcases, carpet and a range of colourful books provided by Jasmine from the library. James had managed to find, buy or borrow a reasonable range of mathematics and science equipment that was now displayed or stored neatly in different parts of the room. Tristan had repainted the elderly blackboard, as well as some of the walls where mould and scuff marks had won and the battle to clean them had been lost. Tristan's globe now proudly graced a corner of the classroom next to the nature table that James had enjoyed setting up with Tristan. Yes, James was pleased with their efforts – there was still much to be done, but he had now created a good working environment for his pupils. He just hoped that Emily would approve and work well with him, but he would need to see her to find out.

Doris and James had jointly reorganised the office, which was now much more to her liking. Although reluctant at first, Doris had really got into the swing of throwing rubbish away. James chuckled to himself when he remembered that Doris wanted to keep dozens of bottles of ink and typewriter ribbons for a machine that they no longer had – just in case. Now each time she came into school she would ask him if she could move this or throw away that, and she was becoming more confident in making the office work for her. On the Friday afternoon, Doris arrived with an armful of bright flowers.

"I bought these cheaply in the market today. I thought we could have some in the classrooms and in the hall. It will make the children feel welcome. Here are yours – and a new vase to keep them in."

Doris placed a new glass vase containing a bunch of assorted brightly coloured blooms on James' desk.

"That's perfect, Doris. What a lovely thought!" beamed James gratefully.

"Your classroom looks great, James. You and Tristan have worked so hard. The stockroom is perfect and I can now find everything that I need. I see that you have set up the hall ready for Tuesday morning. You have even tidied the staff-room!"

"Yes. There is a lot that I would like to do in there, but I thought we could talk about that as a staff together on Monday. You will be there as well, won't you?"

"Are you sure? I have never been asked before. Do you think the others would mind me being there?"

"Of course you can, Doris. Stay for as long as you like. You are part of the team and so I would like you to be there, if you can manage it, that is. Can I just ask you for another big favour?"

"Of course, James, just say the word."

"How about another chocolate cake?"

James arrived at the school early on Monday morning. The staff meeting was not due to start until ten o'clock, but James wanted to make sure that everything was ready. He had bought a jar of coffee, sugar and milk for the meeting. As he was placing the bottle of milk in the fridge, he noticed that a new bottle was already there. He suddenly remembered Jack Sparrow and his promise of a daily milk delivery – he was obviously a man of his word and had started his duties early. Doris had agreed to make a chocolate cake for the meeting. James had prepared an agenda, together with other documents for the staff to look at.

He wandered into his classroom and, to his delight, noticed that the classroom on the stage looked very different to the last time that he had seen it. Anne Armstrong had clearly been in to prepare it. Tables and chairs had been set out, there were now colourful posters and wall charts on the walls, new pencils and crayons had been placed in newly decorated tins and the free-standing drawer unit had children's names clearly written on with labels stuck to the outside of each drawer. A vase of Doris' flowers also stood proudly on the teacher's desk. Yes, the room looked cheerful and ready for action. The small hall, which was the space between the two classrooms, looked as if the floor had been given another coat of polish, as had the entrance halls and kitchen. Even the toilets were smelling fresher and Angela had finally cleaned the basins and sinks – they were now gleaming.

James went to look at the outside classroom. He opened the door with some excitement, but was immediately disappointed to see that nothing had been done inside since he was last there. It had been cleaned, but the boxes of forlorn and unloved toys still remained as he had last seen them. Tables and chairs were still stacked in the corner of the room and the walls were still bare. It was obvious that Vanessa had not been in school since the last day of term. He frowned.

It was ten o'clock, and James and Doris went to the staff-room for the meeting. Anne was already there and greeted James and Doris warmly. Vanessa suddenly appeared in the doorway, kissed Anne and nodded to James and Doris before sitting down in one of the well-worn chairs. Doris began handing out mugs of hot coffee and slices of her chocolate cake. She had even brought forks and paper napkins. James had never known staff-room 'eats' to be served in such a delicate manner before. Doris was in her element.

"Has anyone seen Emily?" asked James, concerned that his part-time classroom teacher had not appeared.

"I met up with her for coffee a few weeks ago," replied Anne. "She seemed alright, but I doubt she will come to the meeting today as she is now part-time. She said she wasn't sure if she would have the time to come today."

"Hmm, I had assumed that she would be here. That was the impression she gave me when we last met. How else will she know what we are doing this term?"

There was an embarrassed silence. After a brief welcome and general discussion about holidays, James began to outline his vision for the school, the need to increase pupil numbers and above all, improving the accommodation and equipment in the school. As the meeting progressed, James became increasingly aware that, despite animated conversation and ideas from Anne and contributions from Doris, Vanessa said nothing.

"What do you think about school visits this term, Vanessa? Do you think your children would like to go to explore the sea-shore with Class 2? Will it link to your theme this term?" asked James directly to Vanessa.

"Hmm, what's that?"

"I was wondering if you would like to visit the sea-shore this term. If two classes go together we can get a cheaper deal with the coach company. Will in fit with your theme this term?"

"Erm, yes, maybe so. I am not too sure of the detail yet. May I let you know later?"

James nodded and the discussion focused upon class lists. Certainly the question of who would be arriving on Tuesday was a matter of great concern.

"Have you had any contact with any of the local playgroups, Vanessa?" asked James. "Did they give any idea of who would be coming?"

There was no reply from Vanessa. She was fast asleep.

Chapter 7

New Beginnings

James liked the beginning of a new school year. It was always exciting for him because it was the time for a new start and everything looked so clean and fresh. This year was to be no exception and James had worked very hard during the summer break preparing for this day. He stood in the playground beneath the old horse-chestnut tree looking at his new domain with some pride. It was by no means perfect, but he was pleased with what he had achieved so far and he was now looking forward to meeting the children and their parents.

It was still very early in the morning. James had been excited about the first day of term and he had not slept well. He had left long before Tristan had awoken and began writing a note for him on the kitchen table. However, Tristan had beaten him to it and on the back of an old envelope was written a note for James in Tristan's familiar scrawl.

"I knew you would leave long before I got up. Look in the fridge. Good luck – I'll be thinking of you. Love, Tristan."

James opened the door of the fridge to find a plastic carrier bag containing a packet of cheese and pickle sandwiches, a bag of crisps and an apple. There was also a Mars bar, a can of fizzy drink and even a paper serviette. A lump came to James' throat – what a thoughtful thing for Tristan to do! James began to feel a little guilty. He had not managed to go away for a few days' holiday with Tristan as he had promised. Tristan had been in school helping him during most weekends and he had even taken time off work to help. He had never complained or made hard work of it. What had he given Tristan in return? James tiptoed back into the bedroom and saw Tristan still fast asleep. His long blond hair lay spread around his handsome, tanned face.

"Thank you for my packed lunch, Tris," he whispered gently in his ear.

"Think nothing of it, Mr Headmaster. Have a good day," grunted Tristan, still partly asleep. James leaned over his friend and kissed him gently on the forehead.

James glanced towards the side door of the school building. There was a small boy sitting on the step outside. James walked over to him, looking at his watch. It was still only a quarter to eight.

"Hello, what's your name?"

The small boy looked away from James – whether it was with fear or embarrassment, James couldn't tell.

"Andrew Pickles, sir," replied the small boy, still not looking at James.

"Well, Andrew, it is nice to see you. You are my very first pupil here. Why are you so early? We don't start for another hour and a quarter."

"Dad's got to go to work, he drops me off on the way to the farm," replied Andrew. "He drives a tractor," he added with pride as an afterthought, and turned towards James.

"I see," said James, concerned to see this small boy waiting alone in the playground. "Did you have any breakfast?"

"No, there wasn't time. We had to leave quickly."

"Was mum still in bed, Andrew?"

Andrew looked away again and didn't reply. James noticed the cheap torn and worn dark blue anorak that the neglected little boy was wearing. It was dirty and he could see from the stains on his overlong grey trousers that they had not been washed recently either.

"Perhaps she will bring you something later, Andrew. How old are you?"

"Seven."

"Well, Andrew, that means you will be in Mrs. Armstrong's class, but she won't be here for a while. Why don't you come and help me get ready in my class? I'm Mr. Young, by the way, your new head teacher."

James sensed that there was something wrong and decided not to ask any more questions for the time being. He led the small boy into the school by the hand and into his classroom. There were still a few things to be done, but James was more concerned about Andrew. By now, Andrew had taken off his worn anorak and placed it on the table beside him.

"Tell you what, Andrew. I made too many sandwiches this morning. Can you help me out and eat a couple for me? I hate wasting food. Do you like cheese and pickle?"

Andrew nodded and smiled at James.

"Are you thirsty? I am going to make myself a cup of coffee. Would you like a glass of milk?"

"Milk, yes please."

"Good, I'll go and get one. You get started with those sandwiches, Andrew."

James hoped that Jack Sparrow had carried out his milk delivery promise and was relieved to see that a fresh bottle of milk was already sitting in the fridge. He poured a large glass of milk for Andrew and switched on the kettle to make himself a cup of coffee. By the time he had returned to the classroom with the glass of milk and mug of coffee, Andrew had eaten Tristan's sandwiches and was now looking much happier.

"How about a Mars bar, Andrew? I'm not too keen on them."

Andrew nodded and James smiled as he watched the boy drinking his milk and eating the chocolate bar at the same time, smearing chocolate over the outside of his mouth.

"You were telling me about your mum, Andrew. I am just going to get some new pencils and then, when you have finished, perhaps you could put them on the tables for me."

"She's gone."

"Oh dear, what do you mean, Andrew? Gone for a holiday somewhere?"

"No, she's just gone."

The small boy put his head on his arms on the desk and started to cry. James was alarmed.

"I'm sorry, Andrew. What's the matter?"

The small boy sobbed and sobbed, a mixture of tears, milk and chocolate smeared all over his face. James put his hand kindly on the boy's shoulder.

James was relieved when a cheery, "Good morning, Mr. Young," came from the end of the hall. It was Anne Armstrong.

"Good morning, Mrs. Armstrong. It is really good to see you," said James with more than a hint of relief, as he walked towards his deputy. They shook hands warmly. "Andrew here has been helping me with a few things. He arrived very early this morning."

Anne nodded and gave James an understanding look.

"Hello, Andrew. My, you are early, aren't you? Did dad have to go off to work early again?"

Andrew nodded, his crying now stopped.

"Will you come and help me to get ready? The other children will be here soon. Maybe just go and wash your face and then I will find where you are sitting. You are on the stage this year, Andrew. That'll be fun, won't it?"

James winced when he heard a mention of the stage. It was a very sore point of concern for him.

"I'm helping Mr. Young first," replied Andrew proudly, picking up the box of pencils that James had left for him.

"Well, that's alright. You finish helping Mr. Young and then come over to me. You can help both of us. How's that?"

Andrew smiled and nodded, and walked off to the boy's toilets to wash his face as Anne had asked.

"It's a problem, James," began Anne when Andrew had disappeared. "A strange family. There's Andrew, a baby and an older brother, Chris, I think he is called, who goes to the secondary school. Mr. Pickles works at a farm a few miles away. Mum walked out a few weeks ago, leaving the two boys and the baby with the father. We don't know why, but some say she was depressed after the birth of the baby and couldn't cope. Money was a problem as well as she could no longer work at the farm. Dad began to drink away his troubles and started shouting a lot. We all noticed that Andrew began to look very neglected last term and often began to cry for apparently no reason – before all this happened. The other children also began to tease him, because he is also very smelly sometimes and I don't think he washes very much. My guess is that he wets the bed."

"So dad is looking after the two boys and the baby on his own?"

"Well, I think social services took the baby to the mother's sister, the baby's aunt. She lives in town and she agreed to look after the baby, but couldn't take on the boys. No-one knows where the mother is. She just disappeared one morning and nothing has been heard from her since. There were rumours that Mr Pickles did away with her when he came home drunk one night, but that is just village gossip. I just don't believe it for a moment. He's not a bad man, just a bit rough. The police and social services were involved, but they found nothing. The two boys have been left with their father. No doubt about it, that family is under a lot of pressure at the moment."

"Did they have problems before the baby or has this all happened since?"

"They seemed alright before, James, but as I say, there were signs of neglect with Andrew last term. I didn't really know that much about them as the boys were not in my class. They rarely came to anything held in school, but they sometimes came to a jumble sale or bring-and-buy sale. Money was always tight for them and the children often had no money for school trips and the like. The mother was very quiet and dad always did the talking. He seemed alright – a hard-working man by all accounts. Vanessa may know more as I think she taught Chris, the older boy, a few years ago."

"Hmm, well, we will have to do something about this. Andrew was here when I arrived at half past seven this morning. He hadn't had any breakfast either. Does he get free school meals?"

"No, although he's entitled. We tried that last term. Mr Pickles said he wasn't accepting charity from anyone and that Andrew would bring his own lunch, but sometimes Andrew brought nothing at all, or maybe just a bag of crisps or some plain biscuits. One of us used to go to the village shop to get a filled roll for him. Often there was a spare lunch going and so we would give him that. Once Andrew told his mother about the cooked lunch we had given him and Mr Pickles came in shouting the odds. He was furious and told us not to do it again."

"I see," replied James. "I'll give social services a call and see what we can do. Meanwhile, we need to keep a close eye on him. We cannot have him arriving so early as there is no one here until much later. If it was raining, the poor lad would be drenched."

By now, James could hear the familiar sound of children shouting in the playground. The school bus had arrived bringing about twenty children from outlying villages. A group of parents stood with their children near the infant classroom and others were chatting outside the school gate. James walked outside and was soon surrounded by many children, all anxious to meet their new head teacher. The chatting from parents outside the school gate stopped as the eyes of both parents and children fell upon the stranger to their school.

"You Mr Young?" enquired a portly lad in a bright red pullover and smart grey trousers.

"I am," replied James, smiling at the sea of happy faces in front of him. "My goodness, have you all arrived on the bus? There are more of you than I thought."

"Yeah, most of us, but that lot walked from the cottages," replied the red pullover, pointing to a large group of boys and girls at the other end of the playground.

"Are you good at football?" enquired a tall, athletic-looking boy. "We like football, but Mrs Cook only lets us play netball, and that's a girl's game," he added with a disparaging frown.

"Er, yes, I like football," lied James. "I am sure we will have a few games and maybe we can play some of the other schools – football and netball."

A whoop of joy came from the group of children in front of him. James was pleased that he had said the right thing, but wondered if he had been just a little too enthusiastic about a game that he personally disliked so much. Maybe he shouldn't have said quite so much so enthusiastically.

"Which team do you support, sir?"

"Liverpool," replied James quickly. It was the only team that he knew anything about as Tristan followed them and he would sometimes watch a match with Tristan to keep him company, although it bored him rigid to do so. He felt that Tristan appreciated the gesture.

Cheers followed from some of the children, with a few boos from the others. James decided that it was time that he changed the subject, but before he could, a tall, slim girl thrust herself forward.

"Are we going on any school trips?" enquired Ruby who, judging from her size, James was sure would be in his class.

A woman in a long raincoat approached and interrupted James, thrusting a bottle and a teaspoon contained in a sticky plastic bag into his hand.

"This is for Eddie's cough," she croaked. "We've all had it and Eddie's cough has kept us up all night. Just make sure he has a teaspoon at break, one at lunch and another at afternoon play. OK?"

"Right, but if Eddie is on medication, surely he should be at home?" asked James.

"He's alright now, it's just a cough. I'm off to work. Give me a call if he throws up again though. Number's on the bottle." With that briefest of introductions, Eddie's mother was out of the gate before James could raise further words of protest.

"Yes, I hope so. Where would you like to go?" James finally answered Ruby, who was standing impatiently at his side with her arms folded. James found it easy to imagine Ruby as a mother herself, standing in that very same playground in maybe twenty years' time.

"London," replied Ruby without hesitation. "Coombe School always go to London in the fourth year."

"Oh, is that so?" replied James, taken aback. He thought there would be far more appropriate and closer things to see locally. He was not at all sure about London as a suitable place for primary school children, and particularly for those who may never have left their village.

"Yes," interrupted Louise. "They go every year and stay in a hotel. My friend Mandy says they have burgers, go to Madam Tussauds and see the Houses of Parliament. Mr Wright said we could go as well last year, but we didn't in the end because he was sacked. Our parents were very cross and my Dad came and shouted at the Rector. Can we go this year, because it's my last year? If we don't, we will all be very cross as well," she added with a just a hint of menace in her voice.

"We shall see. I guess it all depends upon how hard you work and how well you behave, doesn't it?"

The school gate creaked open and in staggered Doris, carrying the familiar two large bags, balancing a large cake tin in her left hand and her car keys gripped firmly between her teeth. She staggered over to James, removed her car keys from her teeth and smiled.

"Good morning, Mr Young. I see that you have already met some of our rising stars." Doris smiled at the group of children in front of her.

"Yes, I certainly have. Would you two girls mind helping Mrs Cole with those bags? I think she could do with some help."

"Thank you, children. Yes, if you could just take the bags and put them in the office and I will bring the tin."

"Is there something in there for us, Mrs Cole?" came a voice from a small child who suddenly appeared at Doris' side.

"Maybe a little something to have with your milk later, Josh," smiled Doris. She whispered to James, "I always make them some special biscuits for their first day back."

James groaned with mock disappointment. "And there was me thinking it was my chocolate cake and cherries."

The church bell from the tower opposite the school chimed nine o'clock – it was time for the day to begin. The first few hours of the new school term were, to put it mildly, chaotic. Few of the junior schoolchildren appeared to know which class they should be in and many stood around looking confused and unhappy in the school hall. The infant class appeared to fare rather better, as James could see from his window – all the children went into the outside classroom, many with parents. He would check what had happened at break time, but meanwhile he had to sort out where the junior children should be. Doris appeared with class lists and it seemed that a number of children had arrived that had not been planned for. Doris sighed and whispered angrily to James.

"He was always doing that. Parents would just call in or phone up and he would just tell them to bring them along on the first day of term. No records were transferred from other schools, not even a name or address noted down. He was just so desperate to get more pupils back, he would take anyone. I have a list, but it seems that there are several names missing and a few others that I have never seen before."

By "he," James assumed that Doris was talking about his predecessor, Peter Wright. He smiled, but made no comment. He already had his own views about his predecessor, which he felt would be better kept to himself.

"Well, looking at ages, it seems as if I have twenty-eight pupils and Anne has twenty-six. If the original estimate of around sixty pupils in total is anywhere close, that means that Vanessa should have only six children in the infant class and I am sure that I saw more than that go into the classroom this morning. It looks as if we have rather more pupils than we had planned for, Doris."

"I'll go and check now, James. You get started and I'll tell you at break time. I would like to have come to your first morning assembly, but I think I am better off going to the infant class."

With that, Doris scurried out of the classroom and across the playground, and James settled down with a provisional paper list which acted as a register, for the first week anyway and until these important documents arrived from County Hall.

The first school assembly of the new year was equally chaotic. Children seemed to arrive from all parts of the school and others were brought in late by their parents. This was just an assembly for the junior children – the infants would be far too traumatised by such an event on their first morning, James had reasoned. Eventually, the assembled gathering sitting on the newly polished wooden floor settled noisily to listen to a welcome from their new head teacher and a well-prepared story about 'New Beginnings' that James had used before at Marion's school. The story had gone down rather well there, but at Prior's Hill few children seemed to be listening to what he had to say. After a feeble rendition of 'All Things Bright and Beautiful,' sung without music because James had forgotten that no one at the school was a pianist and that he had not planned for any music, which he had always been used to. James had rarely heard such dreadful singing in any school and wondered if music had previously had any place in the school curriculum.

James was also disturbed to see how generally scruffy the children seemed to look. He had not expected this. True, there was no school uniform at Prior's Hill, which he would have preferred, but usually on the first day of term pupils tended to arrive looking their very best. New clothes and children washed and scrubbed sporting recent short haircuts were what James was used to. These children, although there were exceptions, generally looked untidy with many clearly wearing hand-me-downs.

James was not too happy with the way his first assembly was going, and decided to cut it short and ask the children to return to their classrooms. He was horrified to hear the cacophony of noise and to see pushing and shoving as the children returned to both his and Anne's classrooms. Children were running up and down and sliding down the banister of the staircase leading to the classroom on the stage, and James could easily see an accident happening. James had had enough and cried, "Stop!" in the loudest voice that he could muster. He clapped his hands and insisted that all the children came and sat in silence before him once again. When silence had finally been established, James resumed his usual quiet manner of speaking to children. He was horrified with himself for shouting. James never shouted and usually remained calm, and it was because of this approach, Marion had told him during one of his school reviews, that children listened so well to him.

"Well, children. That was quite a display of very poor behaviour this morning that will not happen again. I am not happy about it and you should be ashamed for letting yourselves down so very badly on your first morning back to school. When you come into the hall for morning assembly you will do so in silence and you will return to your classroom in silence. Our assembly, our morning service, is meant to be a calm and reflective start to the school day. It's meant to be an opportunity for us to say 'Good morning' to Jesus, as well as to each other. I expect you all to listen and sit quietly. Do you understand what I am saying?"

Most of the children nodded and some fidgeted uncomfortably.

"Yes, sir," they chanted.

"Mrs Armstrong, would you take your children first please?"

Anne Armstrong stood up and her class climbed the staircase to the stage beside them quietly and sat down at their desks.

"Now my class."

James' class stood up and his new pupils led in silence through the doorway of the partition screen and sat quietly at their desks.

James managed to catch up with Vanessa at break time. Anne was on playground duty and Vanessa wearily came into the staff-room clutching a cup of coffee. She sat down heavily in the old armchair.

"You look exhausted already, Vanessa. Have you had a good morning?"

"Yes, I think so, but more children arrived than I expected. I think Doris said it was eighteen. I was only expecting six, or maybe seven."

James nodded. "Well, I guess that is good news, but you are the only one over there, Vanessa. We need to get someone else to help you, particularly as you are in the mobile classroom. Have one of Doris' biscuits. They are delicious. She made one for each the children as well, would you believe?"

Vanessa smiled. "Yes, she is a wonderful cook, isn't she? You know, James, I have been promised more help for the last six years. It never happens. No money, always no money. Mrs Scott, Sam's mum, comes in to help me a couple of times a week for an hour or two on her way home from the hospital. That helps a bit."

"Yes, I know, Vanessa, and it is good to have parents helping, but you really need a trained full-time classroom assistant with that age group. What happens if someone is ill? You don't even have a telephone or intercom over there, do you?"

Vanessa shook her head and smiled wearily. "Well, I'll believe it if it happens, James. I'm used to it. The little ones are never treated as being important in the school and I always have to make do. I'm not really complaining, James, but it does get me down sometimes."

James nodded. He had a few ideas of how to make things better for Vanessa, but he would need to get approval from the Governors first. Everything he wanted to do seemed to cost money. He was also concerned about Vanessa; she didn't look like a well woman and this was just the first day of term. What would she be like by the end of term?

The morning went quickly. Despite continual interruptions from parents bringing their children late to school, suppliers, builders and delivery men all wanting to see him, James managed to establish some order in his new class. Doris had done a magnificent job of fielding off callers until after school. Once James had made it clear that on no account was he to be disturbed if he were with a class, unless it were a matter of life or death, Doris had no problem whatsoever in adapting to her new and enhanced role.

"Just as long as I know, James. Peter Wright never minded who came and went and often he would just leave his class to it. Sometimes I had to go in and get them under control again. He never seemed to worry."

"Well, I do, Doris. It is not a perfect arrangement, but I am their class teacher first and foremost, and I will do just that whilst I am in the classroom. Anything else will just have to wait until after school or when Emily is covering for me."

"What about Governors and the Friends' Committee, James? They seem to just come and go as they please. What should I tell them?"

"The same rule applies, Doris. I am happy to see them, but at the end of my teaching day, and preferably with an appointment."

James' class was now settled and busily writing about their holiday experiences in the new pristine exercise books that

James had just given them. He wanted to see what they could do before he could really decide what he should be providing for them. Initially, there seemed to be some confusion about what the children had to do. When James had finished speaking to the class, several hands immediately shot up into the air.

"Yes? It's Sally, isn't it?"

"Yes, sir, Sally Watson, sir. You mean we have to write about it?"

"Yes, that's right, Sally, I would like you to write about your holiday. The things that you have done, where you have been and the people that you were with."

"Didn't do nothing, sir. Didn't go anywhere. Mam had no money."

"Well, it doesn't mean you have to go away, Sally. Surely you did something at home? Playing with your friends or perhaps a trip into town?"

"Didn't do nothing. Didn't go anywhere. I watched TV."

"Right, Sally, then write about some of the programmes that you enjoyed."

"Didn't like any of 'em," Sally persisted.

James ignored the last comment and the continually waving hand. He could certainly see Sally as an awkward parent in a few years' time.

"Yes, I'm sorry, I haven't remembered all your names yet. Can you remind me, please?"

James turned and nodded to a slight, pasty-faced boy in the corner and smiled at him.

"Neil, sir. How much should I write, sir?

"As much as you want, Neil. You have about forty minutes now and then we can spend a little more time on it later this afternoon. If you want to, you can take it home for homework."

A hand shot up.

"Yes, Sally?"

"I can't do homework, sir. My mum says we shouldn't do it because we are too young. She told sir that last year as well," she added threateningly.

"Thank you, Sally. We will talk about that later," replied James. He had never had parents saying that they didn't want homework for their children before this and usually it was just the opposite.

James suddenly caught sight of Neil gathering up his new exercise book and pencil and heading towards the classroom door.

"Neil, where are you going? You don't need to take your exercise book and pencil to the toilets."

"To Mrs Sprigg's, sir."

"Why are you going to Mrs Sprigg?" questioned James.

"I always goes to Mrs Sprigg's when I writes, sir."

"But why would you do that, Neil? You are in my class this year."

A hand shot up. Sally had another announcement to make.

"He always goes to Mrs Sprigg's when he writes, sir. See, he's slow, sir, and Mrs Cook says she hasn't got time for him and so he goes to Mrs Sprigg's and works with the infants."

Sally looked triumphantly around her, as she loved to be the first with any kind of news.

This last comment made James angry, very angry indeed. How dare any child be humiliated in this way? He would be having words with Mrs Cook and Mrs Sprigg about this issue. He walked over to Neil and put his hand on the bemused boys' shoulder and spoke quietly and kindly to him.

"Sit down, Neil. I am your teacher and from now on it will be me helping you all the way. I'll come over to you in a moment and we can get started, can't we?"

Neil nodded gratefully and sat down at his desk.

"Sir, I've finished."

"You cannot possibly have done, Thomas. We have only just started."

"I've finished," announced Thomas defiantly, placing his pencil on top of his closed exercise book.

"Well, let's have a look at it, Thomas," replied James, walking over to the small boy sitting in front of James' desk. "You must be a very quick worker!"

James opened the exercise book and read the words carefully written at the top of the page – "My Holiday. The End. By Thomas Jones."

A hand shot up.

"Yes, Sally, what is it?"

"He's not a quick worker, sir. He's just stubborn. Mrs Cook says."

"Thank you, Sally."

Chapter 8

Cooks and Dinner Ladies

Prior's Hill School was one of those fortunate village schools that still had a kitchen and cooked lunches on the premises. James had heard that some local education authorities were thinking about stopping cooked lunches in small schools and replacing it with either a container delivery from the nearest secondary school or, in some cases, sandwiches for the free school meal children. The new Minister for Education had recently stopped free school milk for primary-age children and there were many teachers, James included, who were concerned about the nutrition that many primary school pupils were getting.

When James applied for the job he had been relieved to see that the school still had its own small kitchen tucked away in the corner of the playground and an adjoining dining-room. 'Dining-room' may have been too glamorous a word to use as it looked like, or indeed may have been, an old wartime Nissen hut, painted white on the outside. It was a most unpleasant building and James remembered the disgust he felt the first time that he had stepped inside. Apart from the smell of stale food, the room was stark and unwelcoming. Some of the windows were cracked and had been temporarily repaired with pieces of hardboard. No doubt this was the result of many seasons of stray footballs and rounders balls hitting the glass. Condensation poured down the walls leaving a mouldy trace of grime in its place. The tiled floor was cracked and in places, some of the dark maroon tiles were missing. James wondered about the health implications of the floor's surface in a food area. The tables and chairs scattered around the room were haphazardly arranged, but although the Formica-covered tables and wooden chairs were old, they looked clean enough. This room was very neglected and something would have to be done about it.

In contrast to this, James was delighted to see a clean and well-organised kitchen adjoining the dilapidated dining-room. George Cole had introduced James to Mrs Monica Hilary, the school cook who had reigned supreme over her territory for many years. She had seen head teachers come and go, and she initially greeted James with a brief look of disdain that revealed her intense dislike of 'change' in general, and new head teachers in particular.

"So's you the new headmaster, then? Other one didn't last long," sniffed Mrs Hilary over the noise of the electric potato peeler. She didn't bother to acknowledge James' outstretched hand.

"My hand's covered in flour. That over there's Jean."

"That over there" nodded towards James, wiped her hand on a nearby tea-towel and walked across to greet him.

"Hello, I'm Jean Sparrow. I think you have already met my grandfather."

"So, you are his granddaughter!" exclaimed James. "Jack is a wonderful man. He has been very welcoming and one of the first people that I met in the village. He delivers our milk, you know."

"Yes, he's very proud of that little job," beamed Jean. "He loves the school. Knows everything about it, past and present. I always tells him he's a nosey old codger."

"Well, it is very useful for me, Jean," laughed James. "I have so many questions and it sounds as if Jack would have the answers to most of them."

"It's just the two of us, Mr James," interrupted Mrs Hilary, impatient with all the small talk so close to lunchtime. "Forty-odd dinners a day plus meals for the 'meals-on-wheels' service. It gets busy, but I does it my own way."

James thought that the comment that "I does it my own way" contained words of warning clearly intended for him.

"What about menus, Mrs Hilary? Do they come from County Hall?"

"They gives me menus. Sometimes I does it, sometimes not. It's all frozen this and tinned that nowadays. If I has it in my garden, fresh cabbages and beans, then I brings them in and cooks them instead. I'm not being told to open tins when I have all this fresh stuff rotting in my garden. Doesn't make sense, Mr James, does it?"

James was rather taken aback by this outburst, but nodded in agreement, not bothering to repeat his correct name to Mrs Hilary. He doubted she would listen anyway.

"So do you have to order the food that you need from County Hall or do you order from the suppliers direct?"

The determined cook paused for a moment and said mysteriously, "Well, they does and they doesn't, if you sees my meaning."

It was lunchtime. The first indication of it was the arrival of the three 'dinner ladies' whom James had met during his first visit to the school several weeks earlier. The trio arrived together and James could hear them talking loudly in the corridor outside his classroom. Judging from all the laughter, it seemed that they got on very well indeed with each other. That helps, thought James, as he briefly remembered the odd run-in that he had had with dinner ladies in the past. It always seemed strange to James that so many dinner ladies in the land were well-meaning mums anxious to help their local school and earn some money at the same time, and yet most seemed so undervalued. Most dinner ladies were untrained and inexperienced, yet they had full control of pupils and their welfare for at least an hour at lunchtime each day. They were responsible for discipline, health and safety, first aid, and hygiene, as well as being judge and jury during many pupil disputes. James had realised very early in his career that a good dinner lady was worth her weight in gold. One of the best that he had worked with was Mrs Ellis at Marion's school. She had the most amazing repertoire of children's games up her sleeve and could keep large groups of children entertained and amused for hours. James smiled as he remembered the first time that he had met Mrs Ellis – French skipping in the playground. For all of her sixty years, Mrs Ellis was not one likely to give in gracefully to growing old.

James opened the door from his classroom and looked into the corridor, and the group of dinner ladies immediately went silent.

"Good morning," exclaimed James, cheerily. "Good to see you all again. Is there anything that you need? Anyway, I expect you are well-used to the routine by now."

"I should be," laughed Anna, a large lady with a very round, smiling face. "I've been here for twenty-odd years now. I say 'odd', because I stopped counting long ago," she laughed again nervously.

"Hello, I'm Gloria," announced a small, yet equally rounded lady to her left. "Oh yes, there's not much about this job that you can tell our Anna. Getting her to stop yakking is the main problem, Mr Young."

"James, please do call me James," said James, turning to the last member of the team. "I'm so sorry, but I have forgotten your name."

"I'm Heather. Pleased to meet you, James. I'm Sophie's mum. She is in your class. I only stepped in at the end of last term because they were desperate to find someone. I've stayed on to see if you want me this term, but if not I will quite understand. I don't need to work you know, I'm just helping out."

"I'm sure we need you, Heather. We have three dining-staff on the payroll and if you are happy with the job please continue and we can have a chat about it at the end of the month. You ladies will have to tell me what you expect of me and who does what."

"You don't have to do anything, James. Mr Wright mostly went out at lunchtimes. It is usually just us and the kids. Anna is kind of in charge and sorts it out if we have a problem."

James was horrified. "You mean there are some days when no teacher is on duty?"

"Oh yes. Happens often, but we don't mind. The children are usually pretty good and if it gets too bad we send them all into the hall for a quiet moment," beamed Anna. "Works well with most, just as long as we don't cross young Sally in your class."

"Hmm, and what happens if there is an emergency or any first aid needed?"

"Well, Anna usually does that," interrupted Gloria. "She used to be a nurse, you know."

"That was many years ago, Gloria," interrupted Anna, "but I like to think I know what to do in an emergency. Anyway, Doris is brilliant. She always helps us when she can or if we have a crisis."

"Well, I like to eat with the children on most days," said James. "On the odd occasion when I am not here, either Anne or Vanessa will be here. A member of the teaching staff should always be on the premises as well."

"Just as you like, James, but it is not necessary," smiled Anna. "You teachers work hard enough and deserve a break at lunchtime. Will you be eating a cooked lunch with the children?"

"I would like to," began James. "However, I am a vegetarian and I imagine that would be difficult, so I will bring my own."

"Yes, young Carol Skinner in Class 2 is a vegetarian also," nodded Gloria. "Her mum wanted her to have a vegetarian cooked lunch as she's entitled, but was told they couldn't cater for just one child. Have a word with Mrs Hilary. I am sure she will do something for you if you ask nicely. She's a funny old thing. Heart of gold though, so you make sure you butter her up, James."

The three dinner ladies chuckled at the thought of Mrs Hilary responding to being "buttered up", and James thought that he detected a wicked wink from Gloria, but he wasn't sure.

"I don't know about that," smiled James. "I am sure she is not the only vegetarian here. Anyway, there are two of us now and so I will see what I can do for both of us. I will have a chat with Mrs Hilary about it."

James became increasingly aware that the noise level from his classroom had risen. He wondered what was going on.

"Look, if you will excuse me, the children seem to have finished their work and are getting restless. I will see you again at lunchtime."

James turned to see what the noise in his classroom was about when Simon one of the older boys, ran up to him.

"Sir, come quickly. It's Eddie. He's been sick."

Lunchtime was an 'experience' and it had been a long time since James had witnessed such good-natured chaos. Children seemed to be running around everywhere – both inside and outside the school building. James was also very concerned about the supervision by adults. Both Anne and Vanessa had disappeared. Anna was supervising the meals in the dining-hall, whilst Gloria was with the infant children in the outside classroom. Heather was nowhere to be seen, whilst children were roaming around both the large playground areas and in the school building. The chaos that James was watching was an accident waiting to happen.

James had just had his first confrontation with Eddie's mother. Eddie had been sick and was not at all well. Eventually, after a number of telephone calls, Doris had managed to track down his mother at work. Mrs Flanagan was none too pleased at having to take time off work to come to collect her son.

"It's only phlegm, Mr Young. You call me at work to take him home? It's only phlegm. I'll have my pay docked for this, you know."

"That's as may be, Mrs Flanagan, but Eddie is sick. He has not been well all morning. Just feel his forehead – if I'm not mistaken he has a fever. Anyway, you told us to call you if he was sick again."

"Rubbish. I tell you it's just a bit of phlegm. I'm not happy. I will lose pay, thanks to you. You wait till I tell my husband."

With that, Mrs Flanagan grabbed the poor Eddie, who looked as if were about to vomit again, and propelled him out of the school gate and down the lane.

Suddenly, Heather appeared from down the lane with a child at her side.

"Sorry, Mr Young. It's Richard. He forgot his PE kit and he was worried. I just popped home with him. I have his mum's key as we are neighbours. She won't mind. There we are, Richard, off you go. Take your bag and hang it on the peg."

"Yes, thank you, Heather, that's very kind of you. However, it's not a good idea to leave the rest of the children on their own. Please don't leave the premises when you are on duty. If there had been an accident, no one would have been around to help."

Heather glared at James. "I was only trying to help, but if that's what you want. I know when I am not wanted."

With that, Heather flounced off across the playground and out of the gate and James never saw her again.

James had not seen his part-time teacher, Emily Cook, since that first visit when he met the staff. Emily was working full-time then as they had no head teacher and Anne was acting head teacher. Since James' appointment, Emily would revert to her part-time role of just one day each week. James was surprised and disappointed that she had not appeared for the staff meeting before term began, as she had indicated that she would. He had assumed that she would still want to be involved in the preparation for the term since they were both teaching the same class. Indeed, as far as James was concerned, she had to.

He caught a glimpse of Emily walking through the school gate with a basket in her hand. Several of the older children ran to greet her and James walked briskly to catch her before she disappeared around the side of the building.

"Good afternoon, Emily. Good to see you again. Have you had a good holiday?"

"Good afternoon, Mr Young. I hear you have been working very hard in school. Now, I thought I would take my class for a game of netball this afternoon as the weather is so nice. There is also a useful TV programme I thought we would watch. It is a lead-in to the year's sex education programme for the older children."

“I think we need to have a chat about the timetable, Emily, when you have a moment. Games are later in the week when I can get some help from parents. We can then give the children a choice of football or netball. I think they would like that.”

Emily glared at him. “We always have games on Tuesdays. We don’t have football here. The children are too young. They can play that at secondary school.”

“As for sex education,” James continued, undaunted. “We need to share this with parents and get their agreement before we start a sex education programme. The new County guidelines tell us to be very careful about this. Remember too that we have eight-and nine-year-olds in the same class – the sex education programme is only for the ten-and eleven-year-olds.”

“Stuff and nonsense, Mr Young. We always start sex in September. I have been doing this for years and the younger children enjoy it as well.”

James felt himself wanting to laugh at what Emily had just said, but bit his tongue instead.

Emily’s thin lips became even thinner. “Well, if that’s the change on my first day back we will need to talk.”

“There are many changes, Emily. That is what I had hoped to talk to you about at the staff meeting we had yesterday. As you didn’t attend the meeting, I had to make some decisions and this is one of them.”

“Meetings? We’ve never bothered with meetings before. My work was always acceptable to Mr Wright and the children were happy.”

With that Emily swept off around the corner of the building.

“Yes, Sally?”

“Mr Young, should I ring the bell?”

After his brief encounter with Emily, James retreated to his office for a much-needed cup of coffee. Doris was already perched on the new typist's chair that James had bought her and was busily typing a letter.

"Let me get you coffee, James. Have you eaten?"

James shook his head. "Thank you, Doris, but I had forgotten all about lunch. To be honest I didn't fancy eating in that dreadful dining-hall. I feel sorry that the children had to eat in there, in the state it is."

"Yes, it is grim, isn't it? Let me get you that cup of coffee. Did you bring any lunch with you?"

James nodded and remembered that he still had a packet of crisps left from Tristan's packed lunch.

A short time later Doris appeared with a mug of coffee and a cheese sandwich neatly cut up on a plate with a salad garnish.

"I had a word with Mrs Hilary. You made quite an impression in the kitchen this morning, it seems, James. Your predecessor never bothered to speak to her before. You actually spoke to her about menus and where she gets food from. She was quite impressed."

James was taken aback. "It was only a courtesy visit, Doris. Five minutes at the most. It was the least that I could do. She is on the payroll after all."

Doris continued, "Mrs Hilary is a good old thing, but not one to cross. Anyway, she made you these sandwiches and asked why you didn't have a cooked meal, as you were on duty all lunch hour? She saw you. I told her you were a vegetarian."

"Oh dear," grimaced James. "What did she say about that?"

"She said she quite understood and that she has to prepare special meals for some of the 'meals-on-wheels' people, and said she could quite easily cook a meal for you if you would like it. Seems she went on a special-needs catering course last year and I think she would rather like to try it out. I think you made a friend with Mrs Hilary."

"That's brilliant, Doris. Thank you. Maybe she would also cook one for Carol Sparrow in Anne Armstrong's class as well? I'll have a word with her tomorrow."

"Have you had words with Emily?"

James nodded. "She is not happy with me."

"I gathered that, James. She came storming into the staff-room, threw her basket on the floor and muttered something about girls playing football."

"Well, I told her that we have a new timetable and we now have games on Thursday. That's the only day I can get help from a couple of the fathers for football. It's their day off. Tristan says he may come in and help as well."

Doris nodded. "Yes, I thought it was that. Problem is that Emily has always had it her own way. She's always done netball for girls and boys on Tuesdays. Yes, I know most of the boys hate it and want to play football."

"Well, this afternoon I have asked her to let the children finish their writing and then it is supposed to be History, but goodness knows what she will do then as she wants to start her sex education programme. I told her we were not doing that until the parents have been consulted."

"Well, at least she's only in for two afternoons a week, James."

By now James was hungrily tucking into his cheese sandwich and Doris returned to typing her letter.

"Doris?"

"Yes, James?"

"I think Heather has walked out."

After his brief lunch, James wandered to the infant classroom. He was grateful to get some air. It was a lovely day, crisp but sunny. He caught a glimpse of Mrs Hilary putting the rubbish in the bin and strolled over to her.

"Thank you for those sandwiches, Mrs Hilary. It was really kind of you and much appreciated. Doris tells me that you don't mind giving me a vegetarian lunch."

Mrs Hilary gave him what passed for a slight smile. "Well, I does what I can. Do you eat eggs and cheese?"

James nodded.

"What about fish?"

"No, I don't eat anything that's had a face or a mother." James had read this rather snappy quotation somewhere recently and despite it not having gone down well at his interview lunch, he still thought it summed up his position rather well.

"What about eggs then?"

James entered the untidy hut that served as the infant classroom. Briefly, he watched Vanessa reading a story to a group of six children sitting on the floor in front of her. James was pleased at the response that Vanessa was getting from the children. They were mostly attentive and several were joining in with the hand actions that were demanded in the story, *The Three Billy Goats Gruff*.

When Vanessa caught sight of James, she stopped and put down her book.

"Hello, Mr Young. Children, this is Mr Young, the headmaster of our school. Say hello to Mr Young."

"Hello, Mr Young," the children shouted.

"Hello, children. I am sorry to interrupt your story. I just wanted to see that you were all happy here and that you were looking after Mrs Sprigg for me? Are you?"

"Yes, Mr Young," chorused the children.

"Just a small group of part-timers in this afternoon, Mr Young. The morning group is larger and we may have to adjust who comes when. There were several this morning that I was not expecting."

"Yes, Doris mentioned it to me. Well, that is good news. By the way, Mrs Sprigg, what is young Neil doing over here?"

James had just spotted Neil from his class sitting at a table and on a chair that was far too small for him, trying hard to write a few words with the help of a worn copy of *Collins Infant Dictionary* that lay in front of him.

Vanessa stood up and walked across to James.

"Just a moment, children. I need a quick word with Mr Young."

Vanessa whispered to James, "I wanted a word with you about that. Emily always sends Neil over to me when he has to do his writing. She cannot cope with him and feels that I am better placed with the equipment to help him. That's as may be, but I don't really have the time to help him as these little children are so demanding. It's not good for Neil either. I know he hates coming over here. It's not my place to say anything to Emily, but could you do something about it please, James?"

"Of course I will, Vanessa, but you should have said something to Emily long before now. It really is not good for Neil's self-esteem. If he needs help, then we will do it another way."

"Thank you, James. You will learn that Emily is not one to be told, sadly. She's a good teacher but, shall we say, she is headstrong."

"Neil, how are you getting on? I have just had a word with Mrs Sprigg and she tells me that you don't need to come here anymore, so you must be making good progress."

Neil smiled at James. "I hate coming here. I like Mrs Sprigg though, but what will Mrs Cook say?"

"You leave that to me, Neil."

The afternoon raced by. Between sorting out interviews with parents and visitors and dealing with many queries from Doris, James had managed to arrange for someone to come from

County Hall later in the week to inspect the dining-room on the grounds that it was a health hazard. James smiled to himself as he remembered the words of advice that he had received from Marion on his last day at her school.

"Always remember, James, that whatever you want doing from County Hall, just remember that if you mention it is a health hazard or anything to do with health and safety, they will be along like a shot. They are all afraid of being sued nowadays. It works!"

Marion was a wily woman and a redoubtable head teacher. A single woman, she was a true professional. Her pupils always came first and woe betides anyone who stood in her way. James did not always approve of her way of doing things, but he did admire her and had to accept that she got results. The lessons that she had taught him over the last few years were now proving to be invaluable.

He tried yet again to contact someone in the Social Services Department. James had been greatly disturbed by Andrew that morning and felt that he should discuss the problem with someone who knew more about the family. James was annoyed with himself when he had declared to the duty officer it was "non-urgent" and expressed his irritation at the duty officer's response.

"You'll have to speak to Mark Tyson about this. He's the casework officer for your area, but he had to go to the dentist today. I will tell him you called and he will get back to you. You did say it was not urgent, Mr Young."

It was already four o'clock and most of the children had either been collected by the school bus or their parents. James, Vanessa, Anne and Emily finally gathered in the staff-room and were drinking tea or coffee and eating large slices of Doris' chocolate cake.

"I don't like the classroom layout at all, James," began Emily. "That carpet in the book corner is ridiculous and will get covered in clay and paint. Those desks with the gloss varnish look dreadful. You have taken away that antique feel of the school – they had names of some of the children's parents and grandparents carved on them. You have destroyed local history, James. Also, I cannot find a lot of my old books and materials. Have you thrown them out? Why didn't you discuss it with me?" Emily demanded, her thin lips now looking even thinner than at lunchtime.

James bit his tongue, feeling a huge wave of anger rising within him. He looked at the bitter woman in front of him, the pursed lips and the straight combed grey hair.

"I'm sorry you feel like this, Emily, but you need to realise that it is my classroom too now – I am in there for four days a week and you are there for just one day. Although we may have different ways of doing things, I am sure we can work together."

Emily snorted. "I think your changes are ill-considered and you should have consulted me."

"I would have done if you had been at the meeting," retorted James.

"I think the desks look lovely," intervened Anne. "James and his friend worked very hard during the summer to make them look nice, Emily."

"Nice? Carpets, curtains, fabric and flowers don't make a classroom, Anne. It's what the children are taught that matters."

"I quite agree, Emily," replied James, suddenly realising that Emily was about to talk herself into a corner. "Now, I am pleased you mentioned that as I haven't seen your termly planning yet. Do you have a copy for me to look at, Emily?"

"What planning?" snapped Emily. "I have never handed in any before, although I have my own, of course."

"Well, let me have a copy of that then," replied James, calmly. "I need to see what you are planning to cover this term so that I can fit my planning around it. We need to make sure that we don't repeat the same thing every year, Emily. In Class 3, for example, we have four year groups and it would be nonsense to do the same thing every year."

"I've never had to hand anything in before."

"Well, from now on I would be grateful if you would let me have your termly planning before term starts, as well as completing a record book at the end of each week."

James handed each teacher a blue Teacher's Record Book similar to those he had used at Marion's school.

"This is a good idea, James," exclaimed Vanessa. Emily glared at her. "This will be very useful – it has class lists, timetables and even a record to keep of any money collected. It will save all my bits of paper. Where did you find these?"

"Thank you, Vanessa. Yes, we used them at my last school and I thought they would be useful."

"So that's the way it is now, is it?" snapped Emily. "All paperwork and no time to teach."

"Come off it, Emily," interrupted Anne. "All James is asking us to do is what we should be doing anyway."

"I'll see what my union says about this. We were warned about all the extra paperwork coming."

The staff meeting was an uncomfortable experience for James, although as time passed the group managed to discuss a number of less controversial items. Emily even responded positively when James suggested taking part in the area netball tournament, even though he added, "We also need to enter the football one as well."

This was a comment that Emily ignored and she made a point of picking up the copy of the *Times Educational Supplement* from the table in front of her.

“We also need to look at what we can do to improve the infant classroom, Vanessa,” began James. “I think you need a classroom assistant or nursery nurse in there. You are on your own over there with no telephone. What happens if there is an emergency?”

James received no reply, because Vanessa had already fallen asleep.

Chapter 9

All the World's a Stage

"You cannot possibly remove it. It is part of village life," stated Emily firmly at the end of one of James' more controversial staff meetings. The main point for discussion had been the school stage – yet again. The area at the far end of the school hall was where the children of Class 2 and their teacher, Anne, spent most of their school life, perched above the main floor of the school hall. James winced every time he saw it. Young children worked on tables and chairs and, despite endless warnings from their teacher, were often perched at the very edge of the stage. It was an accident waiting to happen.

This issue was one of the very first that James had raised, with both the School Governors and the Parent-Teacher Association shortly after he had been appointed as head teacher. The Governors had promised that it would be thoroughly discussed, but it was left to the Rector, who was also the Chair of Governors, a sombre and unamused individual, to explain the situation to James during one of their regular Friday lunchtime meetings. James occasionally found the weekly meetings helpful, when he had the time to spare, and irritating when he did not. The Rector, a large and haughty individual with a permanently red face, always arrived right on time, which James appreciated. After initial courtesies the two would make their way to the school office, Doris would make her excuses and leave, whilst James and the Rector sat side by side on the uncomfortable chairs in the corner of James' office, with James usually staring out of the window in front of him during the inevitable long silences that would follow.

James would always offer the Rector a cup of coffee, an offer which would always be declined, but Doris would make one for James anyway. After all, it was his lunch break and it was usually the first drink that he had since leaving Bridgehampton early in the morning, particularly if he had been on morning playground duty. James was grateful to have a few minutes of relative peace and calm, and although he often found the Rector irritating he was often pleased to have someone to share his problems, issues and, indeed, successes with. The Rector rarely smiled, but always listened intently to what James had to say and nodded from time to time, which James took as approval. However, there were no such nods of approval forthcoming when James began to touch upon the thorny subject of the school stage. The Rector's countenance hardened and his lips became pursed as James yet again gave his reasons for the immediate removal of the stage on the grounds of health and safety.

"Impossible, quite impossible," began the Rector. "The Governors have had a lengthy discussion about it and we think it unwise to remove the stage in the interests of village harmony."

"Village harmony?" exploded James. "What about children's safety? Have you seen the tables and chairs on that stage recently, Hubert? It is an accident waiting to happen. We have no other space. The little room with the boiler is far too small to use as a classroom, if we use the hall section that would be the end of PE and, besides, it is far too close to Class 3. There is nowhere else to go."

James often made a point of calling this pompous priest 'Hubert', when he remembered. No-one else did and the Rector had never invited him to do so. However, it was James' way of levelling the odds that were stacking up against him. After all, he was usually referred to as 'James' and he didn't see why he should not return the favour.

"You completely miss the point, James. This school is also at the centre of village life. If we remove the stage, we are casting a blow against community and co-operation. Let it be. No-one has fallen off the stage since it was built. Just tell the children to be careful and to move further away from the edge, would be my advice."

James bit his tongue and didn't reply. Now it was his turn to be the cause of an awkward silence which, in normal circumstances, he would have been anxious to fill. After what seemed a long passage of time the Rector continued.

"It was nearly eighty years ago. The Village Players had nowhere to rehearse and perform and they wanted a space in the village. One of their members, Miss Lucy Lane, bequeathed a considerable sum of money to the school when she died and so a stage was built in her memory. Since that time, and every Christmas since, the Prior's Hill Players have staged a pantomime in her memory. The school hall is always packed with villagers. It really is wonderful to see the village coming together on these occasions."

"Yes, but how long has a class shared that area as well?" enquired James. "Surely parents aren't happy to see their children perched on the stage like this and having to negotiate a steep staircase every time they want to go to the toilet or go to the playground? These are young children, Hubert."

"No-one else seems to mind," huffed the Rector. "There have been no problems so far and most of the children are sensible, I should think. They wouldn't fall off the stage – they know it will hurt them."

"Yes, and we would be to blame for negligence," snapped James, appalled at what he had just heard. "Surely an annual pantomime cannot take precedence over pupils' safety? Surely the stage has to be removed?"

"Quite out of the question," replied the Rector firmly, standing up and preparing to leave. "You must learn to work with the village and not against it, if you don't mind me saying so. You are making far too much of this issue, James. Now I really must get on, if you will excuse me."

The Rector gathered up his cassock and swept grandly out of the room, leaving James, mouth open, appalled at the Rector's abrupt manner.

"I just don't believe that man," exploded James to Doris, as she quickly returned to her typewriter. "He seems oblivious to the needs of this school. Why is he a Governor anyway?"

Doris smiled. "Calm down, James. It's not you. He is always like that. He doesn't want to upset his parishioners, that's all." She paused. "I probably shouldn't say this, but there was an accident a few years back. One of the children, a boy called Simon Cook, fell off the stage and broke his arm. His parents were furious. His mother, Carol, was a good friend of mine. We thought they would take it further as her brother is a rather well-known London lawyer. In the end, despite threats, they didn't follow it up. I think they thought it would make life difficult for me. They had a big row with the Rector and the previous head, and then the boy was suddenly taken out of the school and sent somewhere else. The head was very angry with the Governors and threatened to resign over the issue."

"What happened, Doris? Was it followed up with the Governors and the Education Authority?"

"Nothing happened after that, James. It was near the end of the summer term and the school began to be faced with other problems. Your predecessor was under pressure to leave anyway and it was all somehow swept under the carpet. I agree with you that something needs to be done and I know George and a few other Governors think so too."

This was an interesting insight, thought James. He had been told it was a unanimous response by the Governors. This obviously wasn't the case.

"Too right it does," snapped James. "It is an accident waiting to happen. I will call the LEA and the health and safety people right away."

"Steady on, James," interrupted Doris, her bright eyes beaming through her owl-like glasses. "If you want my advice, you will do nothing. Just bide your time. You have achieved a lot in a few months here and I know that the parents support you so far. Don't upset them or the village now. Just wait. Your time will come to sort out this problem."

Doris was quite right. James' time would come – but not in the way that he would have liked.

It was a very wet Monday morning. The children had to come in from the playground early as it was too wet for them to remain in the playground. School assembly had just finished and the children had filed back to their classrooms. In James' class it was time for the weekly spelling test, which also gave time for some of the stragglers to arrive before the main lessons of the day began. James was just about to launch into the third spelling when there was a very loud crashing noise that came from Class 2 at the end of the hall, followed by a loud cry and several piercing screams. James ran to the dividing screen door to be met by Alice, one of the children in Class 2.

“Mrs Armstrong says please come quickly, Harold has just fallen off the stage!”

Alice, a small confident girl of eight, delivered her message in a very loud and clear voice and then, overcome with the seriousness and importance of what she had just said, burst into tears. James grabbed Alice’s hand and the pair ran across the hall to the end of the stage to be met by the portly Harold in a crumpled heap on the floor beneath the stage with a distressed Anne Armstrong kneeling by his side, administering a wet paper towel to the cut on Harold’s head. As Harold’s chair lay overturned at his side, James could imagine exactly what had happened and he feared the worst. Several children were crying and others sat in stunned silence at their desks. There was not a sound or movement from Harold.

"Is he dead, Mr Young?" whimpered Alice.

"No, no, of course not, Alice. Harold has just had a bit of a bump," replied James, not at all confident that this was the full extent of Harold’s condition.

“Ask Mrs Cole to call an ambulance urgently, please,” said James to Alice, who was still standing beside him. “Mrs Armstrong, please take all your children into my classroom and keep an eye on mine as well. I will deal with this.”

Fortunately, by now Harold was moaning and saying that his head hurt. James ran another paper towel under the cold water tap and placed it on his head.

“It’s alright, Harold. You are OK. You have just fallen off the stage. We are going to get a doctor to have a look at you. Your mum will be here soon as well. What happened?”

“Er, Sonia threw me her rubber. I tried to catch it and I fell backwards, I think,” replied Harold. James could have hugged him. He was so pleased to hear the boy talking to him. “My head hurts and I feel dizzy. I think I am going to be sick.”

"You are OK, Harold," repeated James, but as he said this, Harold vomited all over his jacket and lapsed into unconsciousness once again. James held Harold's hand and wiped the vomit away from his mouth. By now Doris had appeared at the door, very concerned to see the scene before her.

"The ambulance is on its way and I have also called Harold's mum," she whispered to James. "I'll go and sort out your class for you. Just shout if you need me."

"Thanks, Doris. Anne is with them, but I think she could do with a bit of help. I will stay here with Harold until the ambulance arrives."

Within minutes, the two ambulance men had arrived and Harold was lifted onto a stretcher and taken out of the school hall. James decided that as Harold's parents had still not arrived, he would go to Abbotsford Hospital with him. Before James left, he called Anne into his classroom. Doris had already taken the vomit-covered jacket from him and placed it into a bin liner for cleaning and brought in his track suit top to wear to the hospital instead. His children, as well as those from Mrs Armstrong's class, sat in silence. Anne looked as white as a sheet and James feared that she too would be sick.

"Mrs Armstrong. May I have a word with you before I go with the ambulance?"

Anne walked very unsteadily across the room to James.

"I'll keep an eye on things here while you go to the hospital with Harold, James. I think Harold slipped on the wet floor. It is so wet outside and I think that was the problem."

"Yes, I wondered about that. I noticed some wet leaves on the stage floor. The children must have brought them in on their shoes. Anne, you don't look at all well. Just go and have a glass of water and a sit down in the staff-room for a few minutes. Doris will keep an eye on things here and Vanessa will be in the hall with the infants for their PE lesson very shortly. I'll be back as soon as I can."

It suddenly occurred to James just how vulnerable they all were in a crisis. A school with very few adults around could be a very dangerous place and he was putting his school secretary in a position of huge responsibility. This must never happen again.

Fortunately, after tests at Abbotsford Hospital, Harold was declared fit and well enough to return home, although he was advised to spend the rest of the day in bed. Harold's parents arrived shortly after James and Harold had arrived in Casualty, with Harold's father smelling strongly of manure and Harold's mother, who had come straight from the local bakery where she worked in the mornings, smelling of freshly baked bread. It was quite a heady combination when combined with the usual disinfectant smells of a hospital.

"It's not good enough, Mr Young," shouted Mrs Freeman angrily. "I always knew there would be an accident on that stage one day. It's up to you to get rid of it. If you don't, I will make sure that someone in authority does. Call yourself a headmaster? My Harold could have been killed and it would have been all your fault."

With that she grabbed Harold by the hand and led him to their small pick-up van that was parked outside the main door. John Freeman just glared at James and added, "She's right, you know."

James went home that night feeling both sad and angry.

"The worst thing is that I know they are right. It is my fault and I should have done something about it, Tristan."

"Well, do something about it then, Jay," replied Tristan, handing James a glass of wine. "You had a serious situation today and a child was hurt. I'm sorry for the boy, but isn't that just what you need to get things moving?"

James knew that Tristan was right and he sat down with him on the sofa to plan his strategy.

The following morning James made two telephone calls. The first was to the Rector asking that an urgent Governors' meeting be called with the proposal for the removal of the stage at the top of the agenda. The second call was to the Chairman of the Parent-Teacher Association, Simon Tucker, asking for an urgent meeting.

"No, I am not calling a meeting, James. As I told you before, the removal of the stage is out of the question. You are overreacting. One clumsy child fell off it in eighty years. That doesn't warrant upsetting the village. Just wait and see. It will all blow over. You wait and see," replied the Rector defensively.

"To the best of my knowledge it is more than one child that has fallen off the stage. What about Simon Cook?" blurted James, immediately regretting that he had betrayed Doris' confidence. "That stage must be removed and I must request an urgent meeting."

"That is all I have to say on the matter, James. We can discuss the possibility of a handrail at the Governors' Meeting next month if you wish. Now, if you will excuse me, that is all I have to say on the matter. Good morning to you." The phone went dead.

"I don't believe that man," exclaimed James. "He will be in the pulpit on Sunday imploring his flock to 'Love one another'. What a self-centred hypocrite!"

"Calm down, calm down, James," said Doris softly. "Look, I know it is frustrating, but that is how this village works, sometimes at a snail's pace. Why don't you have a word with George and a few other Governors – off the record? They may be able to help. I'll make you a cup of coffee."

As Doris left the room, the phone rang.

"I'll get it," shouted James.

"Hello, James, it's Simon. You wanted to talk to me?" came the voice of the effusive chairman of the Parent-Teacher Association.

"Good morning, Simon. Thank you for calling back so promptly. I need your help. Can you call around to see me as soon as possible? I need to discuss something urgently with you."

James had only met Simon a few times before, but they had got on well. James was relieved that Simon was so enthusiastic about the school and willing to help in any way that he could. Simon was about James' age, an insurance broker, and was already a father of three children. Simon had married a much older woman who already had two children by her first marriage, and she and Simon had just had a baby boy. Both stepchildren came to the school and Simon was determined to make a good impression and to offer what help he could. Recognising that something serious was going on, Simon agreed to leave work early that afternoon and see James when he had finished teaching for the day.

"Simon, you have a daughter in Class 2. You must be aware of the problems with the stage and that a child fell off it yesterday?"

"Yes, Sarah told me all about it. She was very upset. Is the lad alright now?"

"Thankfully, yes, this time," replied James. "The next time it may not have such a happy ending. Simon, I need the Association's help – to remove the stage."

Simon paused before replying. "Yes, I thought that would be coming up sooner or later. Yes, I agree with you, but if you remove it, it will cause one hell of a row in the village, you know. Have you cleared it with the Governors?"

James lied. "Well, they are considering my proposal. They agree with me that something should be done, but they are worried about the cost as we have very little money to repair the plaster and such-like once the stage has gone."

"Well, that shouldn't be too much of a problem," replied Simon. "We have one or two of the fathers who would help with taking it apart and I can do the plastering myself. Yes, I used to be a plasterer, James. It shouldn't cost too much if we do the work ourselves. I guess we will need an electrician, but we can always sell the timber to pay for that if we can't find anyone to do it free for us. It must be worth something."

James hadn't thought of the electrical issue and had completely overlooked the electrical and television sockets on the stage that would be needed in the classroom afterwards. At least the timber would be worth some money; he could sell that to pay for the electrical work.

"When do you want this doing, James?" continued Simon. "Maybe during the summer holiday would be best. At the end of the school year maybe?"

"No, no, Simon," interrupted James. "It is essential we do it right away before we have another accident. How about this coming Saturday afternoon?"

"Are you quite sure about this, James?" asked Doris, as Simon left the room. "You are going to get into a lot of trouble over this one."

Saturday afternoon came and James and Tristan stood in the empty school hall.

"Where are the others then, Jay?" asked Tristan. "We need more help than this. It is too big a job for just the two of us."

A few minutes later, Doris and George arrived together with the class teacher, Anne. Doris glared at James. "I am not sure that this is the right way to go about it, but we will back you all the way."

The door opened and Simon strode in. He looked worried and walked over to James.

"We have a few problems, James. Most of the parents I have asked are against the idea. Many of the members of the PTA are also in the Prior's Hill Players. They are upset and angry at the suggestion. There is talk of a petition to the Education Authority and the Governors to stop you. Some parents are also frightened about what will happen to their jobs and the tenure of their cottages if Sir Toby and Lady Lotitia find out that they were involved. Those are all tied cottages, you know. They come with the job. Folk are not prepared to jeopardise their homes and jobs for the sake of the school stage. You can drive away from here James and get another job, they cannot."

"Oh, I see," said James, disappointed, and casting a glance at Tristan, who was shaking his head with concern. "When did you tell them we were going to take out the stage?"

"When I began to sense their response, I told them I thought it was during the summer holidays," replied Simon with a grin. "Best get on with it now then, hadn't we? It will be too late if they complain later."

There was a brief pause as the group considered the implications of what they were about to do. Tristan broke the silence, picked up a saw and said, "Let's get on with it then." The others nodded and the work began with the wiry, yet strong, Tristan effortlessly lifting up the first large plank of wood. Plank by plank the school stage began to slowly disappear.

Later during the afternoon they were joined by Jack Sparrow and Sir Toby's man, Bert. "He will be an angry man when he finds out what I've done," replied Bert. "Harold's mum is my sister and she is really upset about what could have happened to young Harold and so am I. Family comes first. That stage is a bad 'un."

Shortly afterwards there was a knock at the door. Doris disappeared, returning shortly afterwards with Mr and Mrs Freeman, Harold's parents, and two older, even stockier versions of Harold. These, presumably, were his brothers.

"Sorry we were so hard on you the other day, mate," grunted Mr Freeman to James. "We were upset. We are here to help you. You are doing the right thing and we know it won't be easy for you afterwards. This is not going to happen to another bairn at this school. Others think the same, but they won't come and help because they are frightened. We don't care. We have our own caravan and don't live in one of them tied cottages. We can do what we like."

James nodded appreciatively and shook John Freeman's hand. Already, Harold's brothers were getting stuck in to the job with the tools that they had brought with them. Indeed, Harold's mother seemed to be quite an expert as well with the large iron jemmy that she was ferociously wielding.

In the months ahead, James would come to value and admire Jack Sparrow and Bert even more than he did now. They were two stalwarts who knew right from wrong and would not be threatened by the feudal attitudes that were so rife in Prior's Hill. The village hierarchy controlled not only jobs and homes, but what they could and could not do. He was to learn that the group of people working so hard before him were to become some of his closest friends and allies. He threw off his jacket and grabbed a large hammer.

Over the next few hours, the stage gradually disappeared. Plank by plank it was gradually taken apart, and the hefty timbers stored outside the back door. The area beneath the stage was full of pantomime costumes, fur and feathers from the many pantomime productions. Broken scenery, boxes of makeup and stage lighting were all crammed underneath. James suddenly realised that all the costumes and paper and card scenery also constituted a fire hazard, and shuddered when he thought what could have happened. Part of him felt some guilt, as he was also sensitive enough to realise how much activities of this kind meant to any community. He would store all the items carefully until he had made contact with the secretary of the Prior's Hill Players. He foresaw a difficult meeting ahead.

"Ugghh, just look at this," cried Doris from somewhere beneath the stage. Her husband went to look. "Looks like some kind of rodent has been nesting here."

"Well, it's not mice, that's for sure," laughed George. "Looks to me as if we have been giving free board and lodging to a family of rats here as well." Doris screamed and moved as fast as her little legs would carry her.

By late on Saturday evening, the group stood back to survey their handiwork. The stage had now gone. The hefty main beams supporting the structure were now placed neatly at the side of the hall, ready to be taken outside. Boxes of costumes, scenery and stage-lighting equipment were strewn over the floor. All that was left now was an ugly, unpainted and mouldy area of wall and dusty wooden floorboards that formed the original school floor.

"Hmm, this is going to take a bit of time to tidy before I can bring children back in here," mused James. It was far too late to do any more work and so James thanked the group of helpers, and he and Tristan were left surveying the scene before them.

"Well, you did it, Jay," murmured Tristan. "You have really done it. My guess is that hell is about to break loose. Have you thought about the consequences of all this? You did join a union of headmasters, I hope, Jay?"

"Well, it's too late for that now," snapped James, tired and irritable. Yes, he knew only too well what was coming, but felt that his actions were certainly justified. "Let's go home. I've had enough of this place."

Sunday morning saw James and Tristan brushing, scrubbing and sanding the desolate area that was to become the new classroom. Simon arrived shortly afterwards and started plastering parts of the wall that needed attention. Bert and Jack came in at lunchtime and immediately started sanding and painting the walls that had been damaged during the removal of the timbers.

During the afternoon, Doris put her head around the door. "I thought you boys would still be here. Have you been home at all? Look, I've brought you some chocolate cake and some freshly-made coffee."

"Doris, you are a treasure," beamed Tristan, and gave her a big hug and kiss. Tristan had already met Doris a few times and was already very fond of her. Doris glowed with pleasure.

"Yes, she certainly is," agreed James. "I just don't know what I'd do without her."

Doris now looked embarrassed and went pink, but beamed.

"Well, you are stuck with me, I'm afraid. This place and I go together. Now, what do you boys want me to do?"

After several cups of coffee and large chunks of Doris' delicious cake, the workers continued the day's task, ably assisted by Doris, who amazed the men with her boundless energy. By mid-afternoon, the stage area was looking respectable and by the time they were ready to leave, tables and chairs were in place. It began to look something like a classroom.

"I said that I would take Anne's class tomorrow morning so that she can tidy up this area and get some posters and wall charts on the walls," explained James. "She wanted to come in today, but her back is playing up again and the last thing I need right now is for her to be off sick. Besides, there is nothing that she can really do until we get this finished. Her work starts tomorrow."

"Yes, she is a good girl," said Doris. "You give her plenty of support and encouragement, James. It is just what she needs to build her confidence. She has had far too little of that in the past. She is a good teacher and the children and parents adore her."

James had already recognised Anne's talents and was delighted with the way that she had followed his suggestions and worked with him. He also appreciated that she had come in to help him to remove the stage yesterday. That meant a lot to him as well. He had hoped that Vanessa and Emily would also show their support, but it was not to be. James needed friends and allies right now. He also realised that Anne too lived in one of the tied cottages and may have placed herself in a difficult position.

By the end of Sunday afternoon, an exhausted and rather grubby group followed James out into the main playground pulling and locking the heavy oak door behind them.

"So this is headship, Jay?" mused Tristan, looking at his friend with a grin. "You told me it was all about having staff meetings, drinking coffee with Governors and writing policies!"

James punched him playfully.

"No, I didn't. I knew it was going to be hard, but maybe not quite as hard as this."

"Have you ever asked yourself why your predecessor left?" interrupted Doris suddenly. "Headship of a small village school is about everything, your whole life, it just takes you over. You become part of the village. You are the best teacher, caretaker, cleaner, decorator, anything that needs doing. You have to do it or get it done. Some just don't realise this and cannot hack it. It takes a very special type of person. Don't worry, James. I know you can do it. I would say you proved it this weekend, but the next bit won't be easy either. But I think that once you have ridden out the storm, people will look up to you for this."

James felt awkward at Doris' philosophical outburst, but smiled and nodded, grateful for her approval. He now knew what she meant, but his immediate priority was ensuring that there would be no more Harold incidents.

With that, Doris opened the school gate, carrying her usual blue string bag with a cake tin perched on top and placed it all carefully in the back of her blue Fiesta. "Have a good night, you two. Make sure you go home and no more talking of school tonight either. See you in the morning, James."

"That little lady is worth her weight in gold, Jay. You have a real treasure there."

"Yes, I know," replied James, as he locked the gate. "And Doris isn't the only one, is she, Tris?"

Chapter 10

Consequences

James awoke early, looking forward to starting the new week. It was a strange mixture of feelings because, on the one hand, he felt elated at what he had achieved during the weekend but, on the other hand, he knew that there would be repercussions. However, a major problem that had been troubling him had been solved and he was ready to argue his case to anyone who challenged him.

Tristan too was concerned for his friend and had given James a pep talk and a big hug before he left for school.

"You tell them, James. That stage was dangerous, an eyesore and a fire risk. Your main responsibility is towards the children and not to a bunch of would-be actors. You did the right thing and don't let anyone tell you otherwise."

James had planned to teach Anne's and his own class jointly that day to give Anne the opportunity to get her new room ready. As soon as he could find some money, he would get that area of the hall fully decorated. Yes, he was sure there would be problems to deal with this week, but he was convinced that most reasonable people would see the sense of what he had done. He also made a mental note to make contact with the secretary of the Prior's Hill Players as a matter of urgency. Whatever wrath was waiting for him, he had ensured that no more children were going to fall off the stage.

When he arrived at school, he was surprised to see the Rector waiting outside the gate for him.

"Good morning, Rector," said James cheerily. "What brings you here so early? I thought you were at St John's this morning?"

"Certainly I was due to be, but I felt that I had to see you urgently before my next appointment."

The Rector frowned and ignored the friendly hand of greeting that James held out. James unlocked the gate, and the pair walked in silence to the rear door of the school. James unlocked the door, cancelled the security alarm and showed the Rector to his office.

"Can I make you a coffee, Hubert?" enquired James. "I usually have one when I arrive."

"No, thank you, and I would be grateful if you would save yours until I have left. James, it is important that you realise the seriousness of what you have done, and the possible serious consequences. I have been receiving complaints from many villagers, the Priors Hill Players and the school Governors all weekend. Indeed, I can think of no issue in recent times that has sparked off such venom and hostility in our community towards the school. I too am very disturbed, particularly in view of our last conversation and my request that you should not proceed with your ill-considered plan."

James listened and remained silent. During his limited contacts with the Chair of Governors, he had learned that it was better to let the Rector speak when he had something to say. Hubert wasn't usually interested in the reply anyway. This man was someone who liked to be listened to, but did not wish to listen to the views of others.

"Furthermore, I have received a telephone call and an apology from the Chairman of the Parent-Teacher Association, saying that he was misled into helping you on Saturday and that he would not have done so had you been truthful with him about your discussions with the school Governors. He has made it clear that any further financial support from the Parent-Teacher Association will be dependent upon his decision of whether or not to support your future projects."

James could not believe what he was hearing.

"You say that you have received complaints from villagers and Governors. Have you received any negative comments from the parents of children in Class 2?"

The Rector ignored James' question.

"I am now on my way to County Hall this morning to discuss the situation with the area inspector. There will be an emergency Governors' meeting on Friday afternoon when the matter will be fully discussed. We will expect you to make yourself available at the end of the meeting at around six o'clock, James," he added pompously.

"I think that you are forgetting that I too am a school Governor, Rector and, as such, surely I have every right to attend all Governors' meetings and not just the end of the meeting," James blurted out defiantly.

"That may be so, but not in the case of possible disciplinary action against the headmaster, James. You would be best advised, for once, to follow my advice on this matter. Now, if you will excuse me, I must be on my way." With that, the Rector swept out of the school office, not bothering to close the door behind him.

After a few minutes, Doris' head appeared around the door.

"Is it alright to come in now? I'm sorry, James, but I heard the last part of that conversation. I am so sorry about what is happening. He can be such a pompous man, can't he?"

James stood up from his chair where he had remained seated after the Rector had left.

"Good morning, Doris. I have no secrets from you. Of course, come in. It is time that I was on playground duty."

"No, James, you are not doing that this morning after such a nasty meeting. I will ask Vanessa to do it for you. Have a cup of coffee and sit and relax a little before assembly."

Although James was a teaching head teacher, with a four out of five days' class teaching responsibility, he always made a special point of being in the playground each morning to welcome the children and staff. Experience at Marion's school had taught him that likely problems were often easily dealt with directly with parents when they were delivering their children to school in the morning. It was a strategy that, although time-consuming, worked well and many parents took the opportunity of seeing him about their problems, issues with their children, difficulties at home and many other problems. However, on this occasion, he felt that Doris' advice was sound. He had another cup of coffee before lessons started instead.

That week was not a good one for James. The words "disciplinary action" kept reverberating in his head. He tried to put it out of his mind until Friday, but Tristan sensed what was wrong and tackled him about it when he arrived home late on Monday evening.

"You think you may lose your job, don't you?" he said. "So what, James? You have done your best for that place and if they don't like it you can easily get another job. You are a great head teacher. You have ideas, you put the children first and everyone likes you. It's just a silly power game they are playing. Have you checked with your union about this yet? What exactly can they do? Surely it's just a rap over the knuckles and you will be told not to be a naughty boy and not to do it again!"

"Thanks, Tristan, but I doubt it would be that easy to get another job if I have had disciplinary procedures recorded against me. No, I haven't checked with the union. To be honest, I have not had time to join one yet. I know I should. Maybe I should have a word with one of the other head teachers in the area or maybe that inspector from County Hall, the one who interviewed me, Paul Jones?"

"For goodness sake, Jay, for an intelligent man you can be so stupid at times. I think it is now time to put yourself first. Get some advice and find out where you stand before it is too late."

James nodded and returned to marking the pile of exercise books in front of him. He really didn't know what to do and, James being James, he had a tendency to bury his head in the sand and not to face up to problems, believing that they may go away.

Late on Tuesday afternoon, James walked determinedly to the Manor House. In the early days he wouldn't have even considered giving any explanation to the gentry who ran the village, but already James was seeing that the village functioned in a certain way and he too would have to play by the rules. The main reason that James wanted to see Sir Toby was to give him an explanation of his actions before he heard too much from other people. James liked Sir Toby and was genuinely touched by his kindness and support during his first few weeks at the school. It was the least that he could do. He walked up the long well-manicured driveway to the Manor House with all manner of flowers and shrubs adorning its borders. He strode to the main door and pulled on the heavy old chain that activated the bell. After a few seconds, the heavy wooden door creaked open. James was amazed to see Peggy Skinner, the waitress from his interview lunch, standing before him.

"Hello, Peggy. My goodness, this is a surprise. What are you doing here? I thought you were a waitress at the restaurant?"

Peggy smiled. "Hello, me duck. I usually do for Sir and my Lady, but sometimes I help out in the restaurant as well. By the way, my Carol loves your school now and she has settled very well this year. It's all down to you, Mr Young. You have so many new ideas!"

James smiled. "Thank you, Peggy. That is very kind, but I am not sure if I am the flavour of the month with many people at the moment. Is Sir Toby in?"

"No, I'm sorry. He has gone to a meeting at the big school. Lady Lotitia is in the rose garden, though. Would you like to see her instead?"

James knew that he didn't really want to see Lady Lotitia. It was not that he disliked her. It was just that he found her irritating and couldn't understand how her mind worked. But James decided that it would be impolite not to see her.

"Thank you, Peggy. If she can spare me a few minutes, I would be grateful."

Peggy led James around the side of the old mansion house, through a heavy iron gate that was set inside a gap in an ancient privet hedge and into one of the most beautiful rose gardens that James had ever seen. Lady Lotitia could be seen in the distance, sitting in a large comfortable chair alongside a white-painted iron table and wearing one of the largest and floppiest of sun hats. For once, she had a pen and not a glass in her hand. She smiled when she spotted James, and waved her hand imperiously.

"Good afternoon, Mr Young. How nice to see you again. Do sit down."

James shook Lady Lotitia's hand and sat down on the less comfortable iron seat beside her. Lady Lotitia had no intention of standing to greet her visitor and continued.

"What a wonderful day," she sighed. "I have just been writing my diary. A gel likes to keep a good diary you know, Mr

Young. My mother always told me to write a diary every day and I have done as she asked ever since I can remember," she laughed. "She always told me to live my life as if it were an open book that people would read one day after my death. What? I think she meant that I should live my life in a way that I would not be ashamed of. Well, I have tried, but I am not often very successful, but I do keep writing the diary anyway. Who knows, I may get better at life as I get older."

Lady Lotitia gave James a tired smile and stared at him with her piercing grey eyes.

James smiled. "I think that is wonderful, Lady Lotitia. A diary is a good thing and you have done well to keep it up all this time."

He began to see this strange woman in a new and more sympathetic light.

"I am forgetting my manners. Can I get you a drink? What would you like? I am having my afternoon gin and tonic, would you like one?"

"Well, I would, but I had better not as I am driving home afterwards," replied James. "I really would love a cup of tea though. If that isn't too much trouble?"

Lady Lotitia rang the ornate bell that was placed alongside her on the table. Peggy appeared from the main building shortly afterwards. She scurried through the rose garden.

"Yes, ma'am?" she enquired.

"A pot of Earl Grey for Mr Young and my usual, Peggy. Maybe Cook still has some of those yummy scones she made earlier?"

"Of course, ma'am. I'll check, ma'am," Peggy curtsied and scurried back to the house.

"So you want to see me?" smiled Lady Lotitia. "Now, let me guess. You want something for the school jumble sale, a donation to the new school library, what?" Her voice began to trail away as if speaking to herself. "They all want something. They never come to see me. Always want something."

"No, it is nothing like that," replied James. "I just called in to see you and Sir Toby. I feel I owe you both an explanation. Sir Toby has been very kind in helping me during my first few weeks at the school and I wanted him to find out what I have done from me rather than from village gossip."

"Young man, this sounds serious. Do I need to sit in a higher chair and put on my cross face? Do tell, it sounds so intriguing, what?"

"Well," began James, hesitantly, knowing that he was already sporting a bright red face and already annoyed at himself for his obvious nervousness in confessing to this strange, usually inebriated, woman.

Peggy appeared, carefully carrying a large wooden tray. She placed on the table a very large gin and tonic with a slice of lemon, a pot of tea and a large plate of scones that were brimming with jam and cream.

"Do tuck in, James," beamed Lady Lotitia. James noticed that she had called him James for the first time that afternoon. "Thank you, Peggy, you may go now."

Peggy curtsied and nodded to James. "Very good, ma'am," she said, and disappeared through the privet hedge.

James poured himself a cup of tea, and began his story.

Lady Lotitia sat watching him carefully. Between sips of the clear liquid in her hand, she rarely took her steely grey eyes off him. She let him tell his story without any interruption. When James had finished, she paused and passed James the plate of delicious-looking scones.

"Do take one. They are delicious. Cook makes the most divine creations, but I think she excels herself with these. The cream is from our own cows, of course, and I picked the strawberries for the jam myself. I'm having one, but not sure one should with gin, what?" she added with a wry smile.

"Thank you, I will, they look delicious," replied James gratefully. He was relieved to have shared his troubles with a willing listening ear, and felt strangely unburdened when he had done so. There was silence between the two. James waited for a response, but a response never came. Lady Lotitia's steely grey eyes seemed to bore into his very being as she delicately ate her scone and sipped her gin. She rarely took her eyes off him.

After what seemed like an eternity, James stood up. "Well, it is time for me to go. Thank you for seeing me and thank you for the tea. Please tell Cook that the scones were delicious. Would you please pass on what I have told you to Sir Toby? I will try to see him myself as soon as I can."

Lady Lotitia waved her hand and nodded, but declined to stand up to see her guest out of the garden. "Very well, James."

James turned to leave. He felt awkward and that he should say something more, but thought better of it.

"James?" Lady Lotitia enquired quietly. "Does this mean that I won't have to sit through hours of those damned silly pantomimes every year? Can't stand them, and those chairs of yours are so hard."

"Well, not in the school hall now anyway," smiled James, confused at this strange woman's reaction once again.

"Good man," exclaimed Lady Lotitia, taking another sip of gin with a smile of immense satisfaction upon her face.

James once again felt that his interview with Lady Lotitia was one of the strangest conversations that he had had in a long time. He felt that he had somehow caught a glimpse of a more vulnerable side of this complex and confused woman, and felt ashamed that he had dismissed her and her views so lightly in the past. During this conversation, he had witnessed a more lucid and sensible side to her personality, but he still couldn't quite work out how she thought, although there was no doubt that she could be a good listener when she wanted to be. James walked through the iron gate in the privet hedge and made his way along the long driveway. As he reached the corner of the magnificent golden stone building, Peggy appeared from the main doorway. She was carrying a large plastic box, which she thrust into his hand.

"Mr Young. These are for you. Lady Lotitia asked me to give you some scones to take home for you and Mr Tristan to enjoy later, duck." She smiled and added, "You see, she is not such a bad old thing, is she?"

James was overwhelmed. "Peggy, that is very kind of her. Do please thank her for me. She didn't seem to hear what I had come to tell her though. I thought she was angry with me."

"Mr Young. You forget that my Carol is in Anne's class. I knows all about young Harold and the stage and what you did last weekend. Good for you, duck. If I had known what you were doing I would have helped as well. Should have been pulled out years ago. Lady Lotitia already knows all about it, duck. I told her yesterday after my Carol got home and told me."

Friday afternoon finally arrived. James was relieved. He wanted to get the matter resolved and, yes, he had made a decision that he had not even shared with Tristan. The very thought of it worried him. It had been a very bad week. When he was with the children, it had been alright. They helped him to forget his troubles and, as usual, he had just buried himself in his work. Relations with the staff had been difficult. Both Vanessa and Emily had made it clear where they stood over the issue and made a point of not being in the staff-room when he was there. Anne had gone out of her way to help him and seemed to sense the times when he too needed some support, but it was clear that she was also very troubled about what was happening.

"You just go off now, James. I am taking both classes for a story," she would say at the end of the day. James smiled and gratefully accepted the offer. He was proud of the way that Anne was developing professionally and she was no longer afraid of taking control when it was needed. During the week, James had often caught Anne and Doris talking together quietly in the staff-room, but they would cheerily change the subject whenever he appeared.

Doris too had been nothing but helpful and supportive. Her husband, George, also a school Governor, had been to see James on several occasions and although not wishing to appear to take sides, he had made it perfectly clear that the children's safety must come first. After all, he told James, there was another perfectly good venue in the village, the Scout Hall, and he could not see why the Prior's Hill Players could not use that. Doris had also seen to it that tins of her very special chocolate cake – the dark one with layers of cherries – were always on hand and James was getting seriously worried about the increasingly tight stretch of his belt.

He walked to the Rectory door and rang the bell. He was greeted warmly as usual by Lockett, the very fat and friendly golden retriever, although only a brief, "Oh, it's you, Mr Young. Good afternoon," came from June, the Rector's wife.

This was not such a warm welcome as he had had the last time that he had entered the Rectory, James thought.

"Just wait in the lobby for a few minutes, will you? I will let you know when the Governors are ready to see you."

Eventually, James was asked to go into the Rector's study. A small group of Governors were gathered, together with Paul Jones from the local education authority, and Dawn Edwards, from the Diocese. He was shown to a chair. Apart from George, no one smiled. It looked as if he was in for a serious meeting.

“Mr Young, you know why we have called this meeting. The Governors have been very concerned that you have destroyed one of the school’s assets and, if I may say, one of the major assets of the village, without consultation and discussion.”

James’ heart was beating rapidly. Should he say his resignation speech now or save it for later? He decided to continue to listen.

“In any community, it is important to work together for the sake of the whole community and not to take pre-emptive action that may jeopardise the harmony and well-being of the whole community,” the Rector continued, rather taking to what he was hearing himself say.

“James, what the Rector really wishes to say,” interrupted Sir Toby suddenly, showing obvious irritation at the Rector’s ramblings, “is that although we would have preferred that you discussed your plans to remove the stage with the school Governors, whom you should regard as your allies if not your friends, we feel that your decision following Harold’s accident two weeks ago was, on balance, the correct and responsible one. As headmaster of the school, you are responsible for its day-to-day safety, and the interests and well-being of the pupils and indeed the staff. This must come first and is the reason why we Governors delegate these responsibilities to you as headmaster of the school. In short, the Governors fully support your decision.”

James could not believe his ears, “You mean, you don’t want me to leave?” he blurted.

“Certainly not. Whatever gave you that foolish idea?” replied Sir Toby with continued irritation. “This is stuff and nonsense and the sooner we all move on to what is really important for the school and its pupils and to support you in your work the better. Incidentally, I have asked the Governors to approve an immediate emergency funding allowance of five thousand pounds from the Down and Jones Memorial Fund to help you to tidy up the stage area, repaint the whole hall and the two classrooms and maybe get some new furniture. The chair I used as a pupil is still there and that was some seventy years ago!"

All James could think of saying was a hasty "Thank you" as he was led out of the Rector's study by Paul Jones, the LEA inspector, who had a broad grin on his face.

"That was touch and go, James. Why ever didn't you tell me what was going on? It has been a difficult week for me as well you know, and I really thought we were going to have to move you somewhere else quietly at one point. This lot can be very difficult if rubbed up the wrong way," he added with a whisper.

"I still don't know what happened," mused James. "I was certain that they were going to throw the book at me."

"And so they were," replied Paul. "It was just that this morning the Governors and the Authority received a claim for negligence and substantial damages from a London lawyer acting for the injured pupil, Harold. It seems that Harold's family have someone in high places who knows exactly how to get what he wants on their behalf."

"I see," said James thoughtfully. "But why the sudden change of heart?"

"Well, it seems that Sir Toby's lawyer spoke to the London lawyer and discovered that the lawyer's own nephew, a previous pupil of the school, also fell off the stage a few years ago. The whole thing was hushed up at the time and the boy suddenly left the school. Somehow, the lawyer found out that the same thing had happened once again and that this time the pupil, Harold, was badly concussed and it could have been more serious."

"I still don't see," said James who was, by now, even more confused.

"The lawyer made it clear that unless something was done immediately to remove the stage, he would proceed with a legal financial claim against the school Governors and the Local Education Authority. As it turned out, your action in removing the stage let the Governors and, if I might say, the Authority, nicely off the hook."

Paul grinned conspiratorially, slapped James on the back and continued. "What have you been saying to Lady Lotitia? Seems that you have made quite a friend of her as well. She was very vitriolic about the stage and came out with all guns blazing in support of you at the meeting. I don't know how you managed that one, James. No one dares cross her when she is like that!"

James suddenly remembered the conversation with Doris that he had had earlier during the week. He recalled that one of her best friends was the other injured pupil's mother. It now all became perfectly clear. Somehow a word in the right ear... Just wait until he saw Doris again!

Paul continued, "The other piece of good news, James, is that the Rector has resigned as Chairman of the School Governors over the issue and Sir Toby will take over as the new Chair of Governors from next term. He's not a bad old boy, assuming you keep on the right side of him and touch your forelock from time to time. He is also Chair of Governors of the local secondary school in Abbotsford, so I doubt you will see that much of him anyway."

"It just gets better and better. I cannot tell you how relieved I am. Thank you, Paul, for your help."

"That's alright, James. Just try to work more closely with us in the future and tell us what is going on. On a more serious note, you need to be aware that you have made a number of enemies here."

"What do you mean?" replied James, rather taken aback by this comment. "I know I have had a few problems with the stage, but I thought that most parents were behind me and supported me with the other changes that I have already made."

"It's not really the parents, James. Well, not many of them anyway. Look, I am not sure how to say this or indeed if I should, but you are an unmarried man of thirty who has no girlfriend nor shows any sign of interest in one."

"So?" replied James defensively. "I am far too busy sorting out Prior's Hill School than to have any kind of a social life. For Christ's sake, that is my business anyway. Besides, I am only twenty-nine!"

"Calm down, James. Don't make this any more difficult for me. Just listen. You seem to spend all your spare time with your friend. Tristan, is it? You live with him and it appears he is often in school helping you. It's just that, people talk you know and jump to conclusions."

"As I said, the little piece of private life that I have is my own business," snapped James.

"Well, take it as well-intentioned advice from a friend – whatever you want to call it, James. It doesn't matter to me what you do as long as you are effective in your job here, and from what I have seen you are. However, make no mistake, there are some unpleasant and determined characters in this village. They could run rings around the Mafia. Remember what happened to your predecessor? You have already crossed the Rector and he is certainly not on your side. If they want to get rid of you, they will find a way of doing so and you have already stirred the hornet's nest and made enemies. Be careful, James, just be careful."

Chapter 11

The Librarian

Jasmine De Valle was not content with her lot in life. Although she had been working as the town's librarian for many years she felt unwanted and, indeed, unloved. Although she adored books and was content working amongst them, she did crave for intelligent and meaningful conversation. She did not include her chatty assistant, Carol, in this category and got impatient with Carol's endless 'twitterings' about her nights out and her latest boyfriends, fashion, pop music and, to Jasmine, other trivial issues. Jasmine would smile politely, nod, and sometimes say, "Of course, Carol," or "That's bad form, Carol."

There were few visitors to the Abbotsford library. Saturdays were generally busy, but only because many parents realised that if they dropped their children off at the library early, they would get a couple hours of peace to get on with their shopping. Jasmine was, in all but name, a baby-sitter, providing a free service for Saturday morning shoppers.

During weekdays, there would be a steady trickle of callers until lunchtime. Elderly men would come out of the rain to read the daily newspapers and middle-aged women would call in to collect a copy of the latest romantic novel. Jasmine felt sorry for these women, many of whom were trapped in their homes for long hours at a time, with little money and children to look after.

Their only escape was often the predictable romantic novel that bore no resemblance to their own unfulfilled lives. Jasmine did not want to become one of these women.

As a result of the lack of adult company and stimulation Jasmine would make the most of any opportunity when it arose. In company she would tend to talk too much, laugh too much and, increasingly nowadays, drink too much. Sadly, these social indiscretions would mean that Jasmine was invited to fewer and fewer events, other than the formal 'work occasions' that she was expected to attend. Indeed, it had been well over a year since Jasmine had been invited anywhere – the last being to Carol's birthday party, which both she and Carol preferred not to talk about and would rather forget.

Jasmine sniffed as she recalled the unhappy event and gave *Gulliver's Travels* another hearty 'bonk' with her date stamp as an outlet for her recalled annoyance. After all, how was she to know that the young man whom she had been getting very friendly with in the hallway was, in fact, Carol's older brother, John, who had recently become engaged to a local nurse. There really was no reason at all for the appalling scene that the nurse had caused when she had caught her fiancé and Jasmine kissing heartily at the side of the coat stand. Her screams had brought the rest of the partygoers into the hallway to see what was happening. Jasmine recalled the bitterness that she had felt when Carol's father had asked her to leave, but it was the comment that "As an older woman, you ought to know better" that really hurt her pride. After that event, Carol and Jasmine didn't speak for nearly two weeks. This seemed like an eternity to Carol, yet provided welcome relief for Jasmine.

It was as Jasmine was recalling the horrors of her last evening out that she spotted a good-looking, badly dressed young man standing by her counter. As Jasmine would recall later, it was not the aura of the young man that drew her attention, but the strong smell of varnish that wafted from his direction. He did look scruffy in his torn green sweatshirt and stained jeans, but what can you expect nowadays? thought Jasmine. When she glanced at the earnest young man a second time, she was taken by his boyish features and the fact that he was waiting so patiently. He had a lovely smile and beautiful dark brown eyes, she noticed.

Jasmine was taken aback when she later discovered that the young man, with whom she had been so abrupt, was the new head teacher of a local primary school. She had already heard from Carol that a new head teacher had been appointed to Prior's Hill, but other than this she knew very little about him.

Several hours later, after Jasmine had taken James to a quiet seating area and he had told her all about his views on children's reading and story-telling, Jasmine felt that she knew this young man intimately. She had agreed with him because he perfectly echoed her own deeply held views. By the time he had left, Jasmine remembered that she had offered, and he had agreed, for her to select and deliver regular changes of library books to the school as well as holding story-telling sessions for pupils and their parents. She had also agreed to help him plan and set up a new school library. How Jasmine liked a challenge!

The next few weeks were to be some of the most fulfilling that Jasmine had known. As she carried out her day-to-day tasks in the library, Jasmine reflected upon their chance meeting. At last she had an excuse to talk to someone who was intelligent and passionate in his beliefs. Here was a man whose views on literature reflected her own. Maybe she had found her soulmate?

"Is that woman in again today, James?" snapped Emily over coffee one morning.

"If you mean Miss De Valle, yes, she is. She is bringing in that set of books about Shakespeare that you asked for, Emily, and she is reading a story to Class 1. I don't know why you are so against her."

"Oh, she's always in here interfering with something or other," grumbled Emily. "Why do you let her come into the staff-room? This is for the staff, not helpers."

"Come off it, Emily. She has reorganised our books, culled everything that is out of date, advised parents and comes in on her day off to read to the children. Don't you think we should welcome her and at least give her a cup of coffee?" replied James, weary of Emily's constant criticisms.

"A mug of coffee, yes, but in our staff-room, no," snapped Emily. "That woman gets in the way and has an opinion about everything."

"Well, she does rather remind me of someone else in the room," laughed James.

Emily glared at James and, for once, said no more.

It was true that Jasmine was loud, very loud. When she laughed, it was as if she wanted the whole world to share the joke, it was so hearty. James recalled that the first time she had laughed in his class, all the children had stopped talking and looked at Jasmine in amazement.

"She laughs like a horse," Timothy Blossom had confided to James, later in the morning.

"Horses don't laugh, Tim," replied James.

"Mine does," insisted Timothy, looking surprised that James had doubted him.

"Emily does have a point," Doris had said to James one morning as he signed the parents' newsletter that she had just typed.

"Emily has a point about what?" enquired James defensively.

"About Jasmine De Valle."

"Oh, it's just Emily being awkward as usual."

"Well, I am not so sure. I grant you that Jasmine has done a huge amount for the school over the last few weeks, but she now seems to be here every day. Not only does she spend her day off here, but have you noticed that she is now coming in at lunchtimes and even after school?"

"Well, she has been busy cataloguing all those new books and remember that she has just launched the library club. She is training the kids to run the new library when it is finished. I admire her dedication."

"It's not that I don't like her, because I do, James. It's just that she is spending so much time here I am wondering what's in it for her?"

James looked up from his letters. "I am surprised at you, Doris. What a thing to say about her. I thought you were more generous than that?"

Doris went pink, bit her bottom lip and carried on typing.

"James, darling, do come over here," boomed Jasmine one afternoon as she was feverishly covering a set of new reading books with sticky-back plastic.

James blushed. "Maybe call me Mr Young when there are children about, Miss De Valle," he said quietly, ignoring the snigger coming from a group of junior girls who were working on a nearby table. Sally pointed and sniggered.

"Oh, so sorry, Mr Young, I didn't think," giggled Jasmine using what she thought to be her 'quiet' voice.

"Just look at these drawings? Aren't they a scream?" laughed Jasmine, pointing to a set of cartoons on one of the books.

James laughed and nodded. "You are certainly getting through a lot of books, Miss De Valle. Thank you for helping us like this. I cannot believe how well this library is coming on."

"Say no more, Mr Young, I am delighted to help. After all, it is my speciality, amongst other things," she added, giving James a flirtatious look and then laughing loudly.

James, now flushed with embarrassment, left the room and retreated to his office to start his marking. He liked Jasmine, but he just wished she were quieter, much quieter.

There was a knock at the door. It was Jasmine.

"Just off now, James. I've covered all those books and I've asked young Sally to start on the next set first thing tomorrow. I'll be over later to catalogue them."

"That is so kind of you, Jasmine, but you really mustn't spend so much of your time here. You have other things to do at the library, I know."

"I enjoy it, James. It is wonderful to see all the good things that you are doing here and I feel that I am part of it."

"Well, thank you. We all appreciate it, but we don't want to take advantage of your good nature," James smiled.

"James, what are you doing this weekend? It is my birthday and I am having a few friends over for drinks. Would you like to join us on Saturday evening?"

James thought for a moment. He and Tristan had nothing planned. Surely Tristan wouldn't mind if he had an evening by himself?

"That would be lovely, Jasmine. What time should I come?"

"About eight-ish. That is wonderful, James. It will just make my birthday!"

"James, I need to talk to you," announced Doris abruptly as soon as she arrived in the playground.

"Good morning, Doris," beamed James. "You seem a bit stressed this morning. Is everything alright?"

"Good morning, James," replied Doris. "I'm sorry, James, I was forgetting my manners. I just need to talk to you as soon as I can. We have a problem brewing."

"I understand," said James, looking alarmed. "Look, let me see if Anne will cover playground duty now, and I'll come into the office and we can talk about it over a cup of coffee."

A few minutes later, James and Doris were sitting in the school office drinking cups of coffee. James was concerned as he had not seen Doris so agitated and serious before.

"Well, what's the problem?"

"It's Jasmine De Valle," began Doris.

"Oh, not this again," exclaimed James, impatiently. "I really don't know why you and Emily are so against her!"

"It's not that, James. I don't mind her, but I do see what Emily is getting at. It's just that George heard something unpleasant last night."

"Go on."

"Apparently, the village is alive with gossip about you and Jasmine De Valle. They say that you and she are having an affair."

James listened in silence, paused and put down his coffee.

"Are you serious, Doris?" James began laughing.

Doris didn't laugh. She sat in silence, looking at James.

"It's not possible. Jasmine and I are just friends."

"Well, apparently some of the older children have been going home saying that Jasmine and you are having an affair in school, when it is closed. You and she have been seen here together later after school. People have just put two and two together..."

"Well, for your information, Doris, and please pass this on to anyone who wishes to know, Jasmine and I have been working here after school to catalogue new books, fit shelving and trying to get our new library into some sort of shape. Why don't people just mind their own business?" shouted James.

"Please don't shout at me, James. I am only telling you this for your own good. Peter was suspended for his affair, if you remember. It is a sore point in this village. I thought you ought to know."

James paused, smiled and put his hand on Doris' shoulder.

"I know," he said quietly. "I am sorry that I got angry with you. It's just that Jasmine is helping me so much, helping the school, and all people can do is gossip and say hurtful things about us. It is all so destructive."

"James, you know how much I admire what you are doing and I like you. George and I and a few others are looking out for you, that's all. Prior's Hill is a strange place. Gossip is rife here. For some people, it is all they have to talk about. I guess it is human nature in a place like this."

"Look, Doris. I will be totally honest with you. What you are saying is not true. It cannot be true."

"People talk, James. A good-looking young man and a frustrated older woman. It happens."

"Look, Doris, if you haven't guessed by now I will tell you. I am gay. I live with a man, Tristan, and he is my lover. I have no place in my heart, my life or my bed for Jasmine De Valle."

James looked troubled. He hadn't said much all evening and Tristan was worried. Tristan knew that James hated fuss and particularly when he had something on his mind. It was usually better to leave him be and wait for him to talk and share a problem in his own good time.

"Lovely meal, Tris. Thanks," began James, giving Tristan a hug. "Sorry I haven't said much over dinner, but I have a few things on my mind."

"Yes, I guessed. Let me know if I can help. Fancy a drink?"

"Yes, I could really do with one tonight," replied James, falling onto the sofa. Tristan poured two large glasses of red wine and sat beside him. After a few minutes James began.

"It's Jasmine De Valle."

"The librarian lady? She's been a great help to you, hasn't she? You've done nothing but sing her praises recently."

"Have I? Well, yes, she has been a great help."

"What's the problem then?"

James paused and sighed. "Well, according to village gossip, I am having an affair with her."

Tristan paused and looked at James. "And are you?"

"What are you saying, Tristan?" exclaimed James. "Of course I'm not. I'm gay, in case you haven't noticed, Tris."

"So? What does that mean, Jay?"

"It means I fancy men and not women, Tris. Come off it, don't you believe me?"

"It's not as simple as that, Jay, is it? I told you what happened to me in the Army. I am gay, but I still fell for that girl in Belfast and look at the trouble it got me into."

"Yes, but that was different," said James.

"How was it different, James? OK, I was younger then, but it doesn't mean that I didn't fancy her. I did. I so wanted to be 'normal'. It's just that it wasn't quite the same as...as with you."

"Come off it, Tris. Jasmine De Valle is nearly old enough to be my mother!"

"What's that got to do with it, Jay? For an intelligent guy you can be very thick sometimes. Age is irrelevant. It's how you feel inside about someone that matters."

The two sat in silence for a few minutes.

"So you are saying it is possible to fancy men as well as women?"

"For some people, yes. I think it can be sort of halfway for some. I think there are many straight men who fancy other men although they are with women. They would never admit it and I guess it is the same for women too."

"So you are saying that as a gay man I could also fancy women?"

Tristan laughed, "Yes, of course."

The following Saturday evening James drove to Jasmine's home in town. Jasmine had given him detailed directions and even drew him a map. Her flat was the ground floor of an old house at the edge of the town. He opened the wooden gate and followed the short path to the front door. There was a bell push clearly marked 'De Valle'. James hesitated for a moment, checked that he had the right button and pushed. A few seconds later the door opened and he was greeted by a very different looking Jasmine De Valle than the one who visited Prior's Hill School. This Jasmine De Valle had let her hair down into long flowing locks over a floral print dress. This Jasmine De Valle looked far more feminine than the librarian that James was used to. She was no longer wearing glasses and James noticed that she had applied a fair amount of make-up.

"Welcome, James! How lovely to see you!" Jasmine took his hand and kissed him on the lips.

"Er, Happy Birthday, Jasmine. Just a bottle, and I also thought you would like this."

James handed Jasmine a bottle of wine and a neatly wrapped package, which contained a book, wrapped in birthday wrapping paper.

"Thank you, that is so kind of you. Do come in and meet my neighbours," she purred.

Jasmine strode into her living room followed by James, who was introduced to an elderly couple sitting together on the sofa.

"These are my neighbours from upstairs," beamed Jasmine. "Mr and Mrs Woods. They have lived here for years, haven't you, dears?"

Mr and Mrs Woods stood up, with some effort, to greet James.

"Good to meet you. How long have you lived here?"

"Oh, it must be thirty-six years now," replied Mrs Woods, a bubbly lady with a rosy red face. "We used to own the whole house, but it got too much, so we turned it into flats and sold them off. It's good for us. We have a nice view, but Jack does miss his garden."

"That I do," intervened Jack, "but Jasmine lets me do a bit in hers. It keeps my hand in."

"He certainly does," laughed Jasmine. "I don't know what I would do without Jack. He cuts the grass, weeds and trims the roses. I would never have time to do that."

"We must be going now, dear. We just wanted to pop in to wish you a very Happy Birthday. Now your young gentleman has arrived we will be off."

Jasmine didn't try to stop the couple from leaving and led them to the door. "Well, thank you for coming, and thank you again for the chocolates. They are gorgeous!"

Jasmine waved the couple goodbye, watched them walk down the path to their own staircase and closed the door.

"Well, it's just the two of us now, James. Let me get you a drink."

"A glass of wine would be lovely, Jasmine. I thought you were having a number of friends over for your birthday?"

"Oh, did I say that? No, just Mr and Mrs Woods and yourself." Jasmine paused as she poured the wine. "The truth of it is, James, I don't have that many friends."

"Oh, I'm sure you are mistaken, Jasmine."

"No, really," giggled Jasmine. "Not close friends, anyway. You see, people can find me a bit annoying. I talk too much."

James smiled, but said nothing. The comment about "close friends" disturbed him, particularly as he recalled his conversations with both Doris and Tristan a few days before.

"I'm sure that's not true, Jasmine. Maybe you should have asked them?"

"No, I am quite happy with just one guest," replied Jasmine, sitting on the sofa and looking at him. How James wished that Mr and Mrs Woods had stayed longer.

"Maybe open your present?" began James. "Should I get you some scissors?" He remained standing.

"No, James, I don't need scissors. It is just wonderful that you have given me a present. So thoughtful."

"I hope you like it. I wasn't sure what you liked as you are surrounded by books. This has just been published so hopefully you won't have seen it yet." James now made a point of sitting on the chair at the side of the sofa, nervously sipping his wine.

"Oh, James, this is perfect," exclaimed Jasmine as she ripped open the wrapping.

"It's a new one about the local area. I met the author last week, and look, he has signed it for you," replied James, beaming with a mixture of both pleasure and embarrassment.

"James, this is perfect and I shall treasure it always!" Jasmine stood up, swept across to James' chair and firmly planted another kiss, longer this time, on James' lips.

"Would you prefer to come and sit by me? This sofa is much more comfortable," said Jasmine.

"No, I'm fine here, thank you," replied James, quickly adding, "I think I sat in a draught. It has given me a stiff neck and so it is easier for me to talk to you from here."

"Poor baby," oozed Jasmine, in a voice that set James' teeth on edge. They were right, he was being seduced.

For the next few minutes, and for what seemed like hours, Jasmine and James talked about a whole number of things; books, music, the economy, politics and film stars were all covered at breathtaking speed. James was beginning to realise that he was fast running out of topics to talk about and so he decided to revert to his favourite subject, school and education.

"Oh, don't let's talk about boring old school," purred Jasmine. "Let's talk about other things. We have so much in common, don't you think?"

"Er, yes, certainly. How do you get on with your assistant, Carol?"

Jasmine gave a mocking laugh. "Oh, dear me, that girl! She makes me so annoyed, but she means well, I suppose. Now, don't let's talk about her either. Another glass of wine, James?"

"No, not for me, thank you, Jasmine. I'm driving."

"Oh, don't worry about that. Have fun, James, you can always stay here for the night. It's time you relaxed."

Jasmine poured James another large glass of wine and sat on the arm of his chair.

"Has anyone ever told you what gorgeous eyes you have? So determined and so...masterful."

"Er, no, look, Jasmine, I really do appreciate..."

"Don't keep thanking me, James," Jasmine purred. "I just look at it as if it were divine intervention. That day we met was not by chance, you know."

"Look, Jasmine, there is something that you should know."

Jasmine laughed. "You'll be telling me next that you are gay, James." She placed her finger over his lips. "Sshh, don't spoil the moment."

"Well, that's just it," said James. "I am."

"I know you are," laughed Jasmine, "but that doesn't stop you having a good time, does it? Who knows, you may rather like the company of a good woman who knows how to love. Just relax and let's see what happens."

Jasmine suddenly started gently stroking James' hair and began to loosen his tie. James felt sick and suddenly put down his glass.

"Look, Jasmine. I'm sorry. I must go. Er, I think I have left the car lights on."

James drove home as fast as common sense and his sports car would let him. He burst into the flat and into the living room where Tristan lay sprawled out on the sofa watching a film.

"Good evening, Jay?"

James poured himself a large drink and offered one to Tristan.

"No."

"What happened?"

"That woman, that woman. She is a man-eater! It was dreadful and I didn't know where to put myself!"

"I bet she had some ideas!" grinned Tristan.

"You're laughing at me?"

"No, of course not. Would I?" giggled Tristan. "Go on, what happened?"

"I'm not telling you."

"Did she try and seduce my James?" whispered Tristan in James' ear, still giggling.

"Yes, she did."

"And did he enjoy it?"

"No, he didn't. It was one of the scariest moments of my life. It was awful!"

The two sat in silence with their drinks.

"You knew this was going to happen, didn't you, Tristan?"

"Well, it looked pretty obvious to Doris and me that something like this was going to happen, Jay. We tried to warn you."

"You've been talking to Doris about me?"

"Yes, we do a lot."

"Why did you go behind my back? I must have provided a good laugh for both of you."

"It's not like that, Jay."

"Huh, it sounds like it to me."

"It's because we love you, James. We are both looking out for you."

"How was your weekend, James?"

"Alright, Doris, thank you. What about you?"

"Did you enjoy Jasmine's party?" Doris tried to keep a straight face as she asked the question, but James could see that behind Doris' owl-like glasses lurked a bright twinkle and a laugh waiting to explode.

"OK, OK, what's Tristan been saying?"

Doris let forth a giggle. "Well, he did say that it wasn't quite as you expected."

"No, it wasn't and, if you don't mind, I would rather not talk about it."

"Sorry, James, but I wonder if we will see Miss De Valle again."

"I don't know and I don't care because I shall not be available," snapped James.

James needn't have worried, because neither he nor Prior's Hill School saw Miss Jasmine De Valle for some considerable time.

Chapter 12

Tristan's Story

James had finally come to a decision about where he and Tristan would live. It had not been an easy decision, and although Tristan had raised the subject many times before, James had always found some way of avoiding talking about it. It was not that James didn't want to create and share a new home with Tristan or move closer to the school, but he had been so wrapped up in recent events that he felt that it was yet another thing to worry about. He was tired of the long journey before and after school and the long drive to Tristan's flat was particularly tiring after evening meetings. Tristan was always worried about the long drive to and from school. The narrow hillside roads approaching Abbotsford could be treacherous at night and in foggy conditions. Indeed, James had sometimes stayed overnight at the village pub. He didn't care for that too much either. The landlord, Les, always made him welcome, but he hated the smell of stale beer that seemed to pervade every room in the building. Neither was he too comfortable with Jill, the landlady, either. "A right moody bitch" was how Tristan had described her after their first meeting and James saw no reason to disagree with this seemingly harsh initial judgement.

James did not like staying away from home nowadays either. He missed Tristan, and James had quickly got used to their life together at Tristan's flat. He knew that Tristan felt the same and although Tristan raised the subject of moving now and again, James was not ready to make a decision just yet.

Tristan knew that James had more than enough on his plate at the moment, but also knew James well enough to know that he would overcome these temporary difficulties. However, Tristan had his own problems too. The ex-soldier was not happy with his current security job at the supermarket. Despite earlier problems, he missed the companionship, discipline and order that he had found in the Army and sometimes wondered if had made a mistake in not renewing his term of service. He admitted to James that he was finding adjustment to civilian life difficult. Tristan was just sixteen when he had signed up for the Army. His mother had died several years earlier and his father had discovered the love of a new woman in his life. He had little time for Tristan after that and although he continued to provide a home, he was rarely there and it was unwelcoming. Once the new baby was born Tristan felt pushed out of the home life that he had known and found some consolation with his older sister who understood what he was going through.

It was James who provided the support and comfort that Tristan so desperately needed when his mother died, and Tristan had never forgotten James' kindness. It was during this time that Tristan had realised that James had become more than just a friend in his life. Both were little more than thirteen when Tristan's mother had died, and it was James and his family that always seemed to be there for him. It was James who always made sure that Tristan was included in outings, parties, shopping trips and even holidays together.

Later, the closeness of this friendship seemed to cool as James developed other interests and mixed with a different group of people, both at school and later at university. James had always wanted to be a teacher, whereas Tristan was completely undecided as to what the future held for him. For a time, Tristan felt lost and a little hurt as the close ties that bound the two as boys seemed to be breaking apart.

Tristan was not academic and he had struggled to pass the few O-level exams that he had finally achieved, but he was good with his hands, fit and could turn his hand to most things. After he had left school, Tristan busied himself as an odd-job man, repairing windows and bicycles, and doing plumbing and electrical work and even some basic building jobs for neighbours and friends. He had to make some money because Grant, his father, was rarely at home and, since his mother had died, had shirked away from the responsibilities of providing for his family. As a long-distance lorry driver he earned good money, but it provided Grant with endless opportunities for overnight stays with a succession of girlfriends and to spend most of his money on all the booze that he could manage to drink.

Word soon got around the neighbourhood and Tristan began to make enough money to make a generous contribution towards his own and his sister's upkeep. Grant, in turn, realised that his own contributions were no longer needed, and found more and more excuses to stay away from the family home for long periods, as he was developing a serious relationship with a young woman, nearly half his age. Tristan and Patsy ran the home together and Tristan gave little thought to his future. All he knew was that he missed his friend, James.

Patsy at this time was courting a young Asian man who worked at the same supermarket. Tristan liked Puneet and was happy for Patsy, but he was wise enough to see that Patsy too would soon be leaving him for a new life with Puneet and he would be alone.

A life in the Army seemed to be what Tristan needed at that time because, in a way, it provided a new 'family' for him. One day, on an impulse, he went to the local recruiting office to sign up. It looked tempting and Tristan was impressed with the opportunities that the Army had to offer.

James was shocked when he heard what his good friend had done. Even though they had not met up or spoken together for several weeks he could not understand why Tristan had done this and remonstrated with him over the telephone one evening.

"What's it all about, Tris? I thought we were moving away together once I get my place at teacher-training college? I thought we were going off together to make a new life? I don't want to go without you."

"Jay, you must go and do what you need to. We will always be good friends, but I cannot just follow you around. I have to get a job or a career for myself as well. We will still be in contact and when I get leave, I will come over to see you. Once you meet up with all those other student teachers you won't even notice that I'm not there."

James bit his tongue. He knew what Tristan was alluding to, but Tristan was too kind to say what he really meant. James hated himself for having had so little time for his friend recently. They talked for a long time and the pair would have talked for longer together if it had not been for an old lady banging angrily on the door of the telephone box and waving her hands furiously.

"I've got to go now, Tris. Some old bat wants to use the phone."

"OK, we can talk again tomorrow."

"Tristan?"

"Yes, James?"

"Don't forget me when you go away, will you? You mean a lot to me."

"Don't be crazy, Jay. Of course I won't. You know you mean a lot to me as well."

Over the next few years, James and Tristan had been in constant contact. James had sent him weekly letters and Tristan had found this an enormous comfort, particularly during his posting to Northern Ireland. Tristan was no letter writer, but he made sure that he sent James postcards from everywhere he was posted, as well as small souvenirs. James kept every one.

When Tristan had leave, he would travel to James' college in London and stay with him for as long as he could before going to see Patsy and Puneet at their new home. He loved going to see Patsy as well, but following her marriage to Puneet, their relationship had changed. Tristan was pleased to see how happy the couple were together, but longed for the time when he too would be in a long-term relationship.

Tristan was a very attractive young man and he had no problem in attracting girls when he was away. His golden blond hair and fit physique was always a hit with the girls and he had a lively sense of humour that made him popular with other soldiers. Boozy nights out chasing the local girls was what they all did – and it was expected of Tristan. However, as with many of the soldiers' conquests these liaisons were rarely treated as serious or, indeed, lasted for long. Then one day, Tristan met Maria in Belfast and his life began to change.

Maria was the daughter of the landlord where he and the other lads drank on their nights off. Maria was just twenty, two years younger than Tristan, and the two immediately felt a close bond when they first met. Maria was helping her father in the bar and Tristan had called in on his own early one evening. Maria was a pretty girl with a ready smile and a light, infectious laugh that Tristan had described to James as like "the sound of rippling water". She had long, dark hair, wore little make-up and relied almost totally upon what nature had given her. Pete, Maria's father, liked Tristan and approved of the relationship, although he would have preferred Tristan not to have been in the Army.

The couple dated for about eight months and James regularly received increasingly enthusiastic comments from Tristan on his many postcards home. One Saturday afternoon, Tristan had telephoned James in great excitement. "James, she is adorable. I love her and I think she's the one for me. You must meet her."

James surprised himself at the negativity of his own response. He knew that he should have been pleased for his friend, but instead had said, "It's very quick, Tris. Give it a bit longer. You may meet someone else. Anyway, you are too young to think about settling down. Give it another couple of years when you have got some money together."

Tristan too had been taken aback at the negativity of the response from James.

"I thought you would be pleased. You must come over and meet her. Come over next weekend. You can be my best man when it happens, Jay."

"Tristan, you know I have exams at the moment. I cannot possibly take a few days off. Just wait until your next leave and we can talk."

Maria had plans of her own. She adored Tristan, whom she felt was the boy of her dreams. She felt safe when his strong arms were wrapped around her, guarding her as if she were the most important treasure in the world. She adored looking at him and stroking his, now short, blond hair. When they kissed it was if her world was complete. She wanted more.

It was late one Sunday evening and she and Tristan were alone in the lounge together. Pete and Dawn had finished their work for the evening and had retired, exhausted, to their bed. Tristan had taken Maria for a meal out at the local Chinese restaurant and the couple had settled down after a few drinks on the sofa together watching television. Tristan wrapped his arms around Maria and the two sat contentedly together. Maria gently stroked Tristan's hair, unbuttoned his shirt and began stroking his chest. It was a sensation that Tristan had not experienced before and his loins began to heave with pleasure at this newly discovered sensation.

Tristan gently unbuttoned Maria's blouse, feeling her warm rounded breasts as he did so. He had often wondered what her breasts would be like to touch and after he had unclipped her bra he now had the pleasure of massaging them softly, taking her firm nipples and stroking them gently. He removed her blouse and started licking the tips of her nipples. Maria moaned gently as he did this, as Tristan knew that what he was doing instinctively was giving her great pleasure. Maria began to stroke Tristan gently between his legs and squeezed his manhood. He threw off his shirt as Maria gently but determinedly unzipped his trousers.

"Tristan, I want you, I want you, I love you so much," she moaned.

It was all moving so fast. Much faster than Tristan had anticipated. It was if his world was spinning out of control.

"I, I don't have any rubbers, Maria. I didn't think this would happen tonight."

"Just take me, Tristan, I don't care. We are as good as engaged now, aren't we?"

"Maria, this isn't right. Your father will kill me if he knows what has happened. I can't do it, I just can't do it. I'm so sorry." Tristan began to cry.

Before Maria could make any more demands of his body, Tristan had untwined himself from her wandering arms, zipped up his trousers, grabbed his shirt and fled out of the pub as fast as his legs would carry him.

James hadn't heard from Tristan for many months. He was busy with teaching practice and final exams and assumed that

Tristan had been posted somewhere else at short notice. Even though Tristan would send postcards each week, sometimes the post took a while to come through. It was after about a month that James became very concerned and telephoned Tristan's sister, Patsy.

"Patsy, have you heard from Tristan recently? I've not heard from him for about a month."

"Me neither, James. I think he is very wrapped up with that girlfriend of his, Maria. I'm a bit worried about him. He even forgot little Carl's birthday. It's just not like him."

"Hmm, yes, I know. That was the last thing we talked about. He seems to be getting very serious about her."

James agreed to keep Patsy informed if he found out anything. He telephoned some of their mutual friends and his parents to see if they had heard anything from Tristan. No one had heard anything in weeks and James was by now very worried. He tried calling Tristan's house, but later remembered that his father had not paid the bill and it had been cut off.

At the weekend, James caught a train back to his old home town and immediately walked round to Tristan's home. There was a lorry parked in front. His father was at home. James banged loudly on the front door. The door bell had never worked. After what seemed like an eternity, the door eventually opened and an unshaven, but not unattractive, middle-aged man stood by the door in his vest, zipping up his trousers.

"Well, Mr College Boy, what do YOU want?" He glared at James.

James and Grant had never got on and James hated the way Grant had neglected Tristan and Patsy.

"Have you heard from Tristan?" enquired James politely.

"And what if I have? What's it to you anyway?" came the not unexpected reply.

"I haven't heard from him in a while and just wondered if he was OK," continued James.

"Huh, you should know better than anyone that young runt doesn't talk to me anymore. I'm not good enough for him now. He's got ideas way above his station and I guess he has you to thank for that, Mr College Boy."

Grant had been drinking and James knew better than to argue with him. He had seen the results before when Tristan had argued with his father and he was never backward in launching his fists.

"Who's that? Come back to bed, Sugar Plum," came a female voice from upstairs. James suddenly realised that he had disturbed Grant in his lovemaking.

"I am sorry to have disturbed you. If you hear from him would you ask him to call me urgently, please?"

"Why should I, you young whipper-snapper? Just because you've gone to college, you think you are above everyone round here. Even your parents don't talk to me anymore."

After a weekend of fruitless searching for news of his friend, James decided to return to London and to call the regimental office. James didn't know where to begin and couldn't even remember the name of Tristan's regiment. He called the Army Information Office and was told politely, but firmly, that unless you were a relative they never gave information about their recruits or where they were – because of security issues, and particularly if a posting to Northern Ireland was involved. James began to fear the worst. What if Tristan had been killed in action somewhere?

After a sleepless night of restless dreams where Tristan appeared to him lying dead in a ditch in some far off land, and another where he had been court-martialled and was facing the firing squad, James awoke from his restless sleep, hot and troubled. He remembered their last telephone conversation, and the frosty way with which he had greeted Tristan's news. He felt ashamed and sick in the very pit of his stomach. It seemed that he had always known Tristan – their lives had grown together and he couldn't picture a future without his friend.

James made up his mind that he would travel to Northern Ireland to find out more – the very last place where he had heard from Tristan. He knew the name of the pub that Maria's parents ran, The Black Dog, and he would ask and keep on asking until Tristan was found. Surely this Maria would know something and be able to help to find him? The more James thought about it, the more he was convinced that something dreadful had happened to Tristan.

"James, there's a phone call for you," yelled one of the other students from outside his door. "It's a guy called Rupert on the line."

James ran to the door and down the stairs to the communal phone in the students' lobby. He had spoken to Rupert a few days ago. Rupert was one of their mutual school friends, and he had promised to call James if he heard anything about Tristan.

"James, it's Rupert. You were asking about Tristan. I'm very worried about him as well and I mentioned it to a few friends at my drama group. One of them has just called me. He says that he saw Tristan, or someone very much like him, sitting outside a bar in Cooper's Road last night. He said 'Hello' to the guy, thinking it was Tristan, but he didn't seem to know him. He just nodded, got up and wandered off. Scott is sure it was Tristan, but thought he was behaving very oddly. He was unshaven and looked really down on his luck. Scott was shocked and has just called me when I got home from work."

"Rupert, I'm getting the next train home. Something is badly wrong. Can you get Scott and some of the others to go out tonight and try and find him again? Keep him talking. Get him to my parent's house, anything. Just don't let him go until I've seen him."

"Yes, of course, James. This is a bit cloak-and-dagger, isn't it? Maybe he is escaping from the Army or a mad passionate love affair. Oh, I can just see it now."

Oh dear, thought James. Rupert was well-known for his dramatic tendencies, and was off on one again. Now was not the time for joking, and James needed to get to the station quickly.

"Thanks, Rupert. Look, I'll see you in a few hours. I'll call my parents now and please call them if you have any more news."

"OK, James, will do. Just look for a man in a dark raincoat and sunglasses and that will be me."

"Sure, Rupert. See you later."

Several hours later that evening, James arrived at his home. He was pleased to see Rupert waiting for him. Rupert, who was not one to withhold news for long, was bursting to talk to him.

"We got him. We got him, James!"

"Thank God, Rupert! Is he OK, where is he?" cried James, hugging the delighted Rupert enthusiastically.

"He's OK, well, I think he is. I think he has had some kind of breakdown, James," whispered Rupert conspiratorially.

"What do you mean, Rupert?"

"Well, he won't say much. He keeps asking for you and saying he's sorry. He has been drinking and I don't think he has washed or shaved for ages." Rupert pulled a disapproving face of disgust. "Giles and Stu found him wandering by the train line. I tell you, James, you don't get away with much around here. He won't go to his dad's place and he won't go to your parent's either. Giles and Stu booked him into a hotel room in town. He was happy to go there, but only if you go to see him."

"Just try to keep me away."

James knocked on the door of the hotel room that Rupert had taken him to. There was no answer and James opened the door quietly and stepped inside the gloomy room. It was not the most up-market of hotels and certainly Giles and Stu had not pushed the boat out on this one. James' eyes adjusted to the dim light and in the darkness could see Tristan curled up on the bed. He was still wearing his outdoor clothes and his shoes.

"Hello, Tris! What are you doing here?" said James, gently placing his hand on Tristan's head.

Tristan stirred and looked upwards to James. James could smell alcohol on his friend's breath. Tristan smiled and put his hand on James' arm.

"James, thank God. I am so pleased to see you. Please help me." Tristan sobbed like a child.

James cried too. "Tristan, what has happened, what has happened to you? I have tried so hard to find you." He swallowed hard and tried to keep back more tears from flowing.

"I am so tired, don't leave me. Stay with me please. Please don't leave me. I am so afraid."

Tristan's pleading eyes met James' eyes and James was shocked at the sadness that he saw within.

"What has happened to you? I'll look after you. I will help you. I won't leave you as long as you need me, Tristan. I promise."

James lay on the bed beside his friend and wrapped his arms around him to comfort him. Very soon they both fell asleep.

The next few days were difficult. They decided to stay in the hotel – it was clean and cheap. At first, James was planning to take Tristan to stay with his parents, but Tristan was not in a good state of mind, and James felt that they wouldn't understand and that it may make matters worse. Tristan didn't say much at first, but by the end of the second day together he began to talk to James and a few times even managed to smile at some of

James' feeble jokes. James was a poor joke-teller – he usually started the joke off well enough but, more often than not, forgot the ending or got it confused with the ending of another joke. Tristan had always teased James about this deficiency, and it was good to hear Tristan teasing him once again.

James had decided to take Tristan out for a walk in a nearby park. It was one he was very fond of and he remembered playing on the slides and swings there as a child, often with Tristan and his sister Patsy. James was doing his best to be light-hearted and talking about childhood memories, when Tristan turned to him and blurted out, "James, you do know I'm gay, don't you?"

James laughed. "Of course I do! Anyway, if I hadn't known before, I sure knew you were the other night!"

Tristan giggled, and took James' hand in his. They sat down together on a nearby bench.

"Well, I guess that would have given you a clue, but that wasn't just a one-off, James. I think I have always been gay."

"What happened in Belfast? Did you meet someone?"

"Well, in a way, yes, but it was a girl. I liked her very much as I told you and I thought that somehow by being with her, it would cure me of this." Tristan paused. "It didn't, and it only made matters worse. Maria became my close friend and in a way I loved her, but she wanted more than I could give her."

James nodded, but said nothing.

"It was only when we were really close and she wanted sex that I realised that it was not what I wanted. I wanted something else and it was not with a girl."

"I see," said James. "Did she cause problems for you afterwards, then?"

"Yes, she was really upset and told her father. He made a complaint to the base and told them that I had taken advantage of his daughter. It was nonsense, of course – she couldn't get my pants off quick enough – but she told some of my mates that I couldn't get it up. That part was true enough. It just wasn't going to happen for us. They started calling me a queer. It was dreadful. This went on for several weeks and I would only just have to walk into the mess before everyone started laughing and calling me names. One of them started a fight and I got hauled in for unseemly behaviour. I broke the bastard's nose!" Tristan added with satisfaction.

James smiled, he could well imagine who got the worst of it, once Tristan started fighting. He had seen Tristan scrap once or twice before in the school playground. Tristan was not easily provoked, but once he started, he fought to win.

"Then I started drinking heavily. I didn't want to, but it happened and I was growing more and more like that good-for-nothing father of mine. That scared me. I got caught one night after I had been thrown out of a nearby pub. They called someone from the base and I was disciplined. Later, I had to see a doctor and he said that I was suffering from depression. They gave me pills and they confused me. I didn't know who I was any more. One day I was told that I had to leave for a few months, and get some mental health treatment in a hospital. I am still not sure whether I have been thrown out of the Army or not. It's all such a mess. In the end, I discharged myself and came back here. How I missed you, James."

"I can see what happened now," said James. "But why didn't you call me? I could have helped. I am your best friend and you should have called me."

Tristan looked down at his shoes. "I was so ashamed of the mess that I have made of my life. I have upset one poor girl and her family, all my mates are poking fun at me, my career in the Army is ruined and my family won't want to know me. I am gay, I am a fag – how can I go through life like this?"

James paused and spoke softly to Tristan.

"Just listen to me. You go through life in just the same way as I do, Tristan. We don't talk about it, we don't announce it to the world, but we just get on with our lives and make the best of it. People may guess, but they won't know for sure. I am pretty sure that I am gay, or maybe bisexual. I just don't really know. In the end, we are still who we are. Does it really matter who we love?"

"You didn't seem surprised about me, James."

"Well. I always thought you lingered a bit too long in those showers after sports, Tris," laughed James. "I did too. There were some stunners in the sixth form, weren't there? Funny how we were always the last out!"

"Yes, but I didn't know for sure that you were too. Not until the other night anyway."

James looked lovingly at his friend. Yes, he was a shadow of what he had been, but James knew that he could make him better again.

"Anyway, you look really sexy when you haven't shaved. You must do it more often."

Tristan grinned and held James' hand tightly.

"Well, if that's the effect it has on you, I won't ever shave again, Jay."

"I didn't say that," laughed James. "It's just that the Army has turned you into a really handsome guy."

"And broken me inside, in my head."

"Maybe for now, but we are going to fix that. Just like you used to with all those old bikes people brought you."

Tristan laughed. "Oh, yes, I had forgotten that. I made quite a bit of money at the time doing that."

"Do you remember that ring I gave you, Tris? The one I gave you after you told me the news of your signing up?"

Tristan held up his hand to James, revealing the gold ring that James had given him some years earlier.

"I promised you then that I would never take it off. It is the only thing that has kept me going, James. Sometimes I would fall asleep holding it, wishing that we could be together again."

James smiled and the boys hugged.

Now, some years later, it was Tristan's turn to be concerned for James and to look after him. He knew he worked long and stressful hours, and did his best to try to ensure that James had a good meal and relaxed when he got home. Sometimes he didn't arrive home at all. James always remembered to call Tristan, but usually long after he was expected home. Tristan hated the nights when James stayed away at Prior's Hill, but he knew that sometimes there was no choice. No, they had to move closer to the school and it would also give Tristan the opportunity to look for another job. Tristan was bored with his work as a security guard and longed for something more challenging. When he had finally been discharged from the Army and, with James' care, had fully recovered, Tristan worked as a security guard in several stores. The first was working in a very rough inner-city supermarket, quite close to James' first teaching job in Manchester, and later in an up-market store in the city centre, before moving to rural Bridgehampton. The plan was that James would move south to join him as soon as his stint as a classroom teacher and deputy head teacher were completed.

For the first few years, it was not possible for Tristan and James to live together, but they spoke on the telephone each evening, and every weekend James and Tristan would be together. Security work was the kind of job that many of his mates had gone into when they left the services. It was a job, quite well paid, but now Tristan wanted something that would challenge him. He was now in his late twenties and still had plenty of time for a new career, but he had no idea what that would be.

Tristan had so enjoyed the last few weeks with James. Above all, he had enjoyed living with him and sharing the things that couples do together. Small things like shopping, cleaning the cars, and watching television and football together – although he knew that James did so under sufferance. For the first time since Tristan's mother had died, he felt that he was now part of a family once again and that he had someone to share his life with. Tristan also admired the work that James was doing at Prior's Hill. He knew that his friend had very strong views about education and he was proud of the way in which James had tackled the many challenges that faced him. Tristan had enjoyed the challenge of helping James during those difficult first few weeks, and had surprised himself with how well he had managed some of the practical work that had been needed in painting and plastering walls in the stock-room, as well as sanding and varnishing the old desks in James' classroom. Yes, he had really enjoyed doing it.

"I really don't mind moving closer to Prior's Hill, James. I can easily get rid of my flat and we can find something closer. It will give me a chance to get a new job as well."

The last time that Tristan had shared his thoughts, James had said nothing, but had continued reading his weekly copy of *The Times Educational Supplement*. Tristan realised that he would just have to wait until his friend came to the same conclusion.

James was not insensitive to Tristan's concerns. He too was worried about the future, but he had to be cautious for fear of letting down his friend and making him ill again. What would happen if he couldn't make a success of Prior's Hill? If they did move and find a new home and Tristan had a new job, how could he then leave Prior's Hill? No, he had to be sure that this would work. Mostly, James felt happy and fulfilled, but on some days he felt that he had taken on too much and wouldn't be able to see it through. He didn't want to expose Tristan to that kind of uncertainty. He had been so much better in recent months. He was no longer on medication and James wanted to keep him that way. James was also worried about money. He had no capital behind him and with the way that mortgage interest rates were rising, it would be many years before he could afford to buy a property. It would have to be something rented, but it could not be too expensive. He knew that Tristan didn't earn much and there would probably be a gap before he found another job.

It was after one particularly difficult day at school when Emily had been at her most objectionable and Vanessa had been at her most talkative. James had just endured yet another lengthy Governor's meeting, when all that they seemed to talk about was money and not education. He had not eaten and he arrived home too tired to eat. Tristan was already in bed as James crept in alongside him.

"Fancy moving home, Tris?" he whispered, wrapping his arms around him.

Chapter 13

Ambulances and Bodies

"Did you mean what you said last night about moving, Jay?" asked Tristan excitedly as he poured the orange juice.

"I certainly did. If you want to, that is. I cannot cope with the long journey any more and I am dreading the winters. Apparently, it gets really bad over there and Doris was telling me the other day that sometimes the previous head teacher had to stay in school overnight as he couldn't get out to go home. Just imagine that, Tris!"

"Well, I'll start looking in the papers today for a job for me and somewhere for us to live. Let's get on with it right away. I can't wait to leave that supermarket. Sometimes I think I am just a glorified trolley boy, Jay."

"You're much more than that to me, Tris," said James, giving him a big hug as he got up to leave. "Anyway, I'll mention it to the staff today as well. They may know of somewhere. I don't want to live in the village, but somewhere within five or ten miles would be nice."

James lost no opportunity in talking to the staff about what he was planning to do over coffee that morning.

"About time too, James. You can't keep doing that long journey each day. It must be costing you a fortune in petrol. All those late nights as well. Think what it's doing to that lovely little car of yours. You'll run it into the ground if you carry on like this." Doris shuddered at the very thought. She hated night-time driving and anything beyond the town was too far for her. She left any long-distance driving to George.

"Why don't you mention it to Sir Toby, James?" suggested Anne helpfully. "He has lots of properties he rents in the area – not just in the village either. I know most are short holiday lets, but he might just have something available for you. You two seem to get on well, don't you?"

James grinned. "Yes, we do, and he's a big improvement on the last Chair of Governors."

"That's true," laughed Doris. "I now hear you two giggling like schoolboys sometimes when he comes over. Not like those dreadful silences you used to endure with our good Reverend!"

"You could also try asking Jack Sparrow," added Vanessa. "He knows everyone and I know he would help if he could. He is such a gentleman."

"Yes, good idea," agreed James. "I'll have a word with Sir Toby at lunchtime, as well as Jack. I may even suggest it to the Rector. Maybe he could mention it from the pulpit on Sunday."

The bell rang – playtime was over and Emily burst in to the staff-room, taking off her coat and throwing it on the chair.

"It's chilly out there. Trust it to be my duty morning," she complained.

"James is moving closer to the school, Emily. Do you know anywhere locally that he could rent?" asked Doris.

"No, I don't," snapped Emily, as she shot out of the room.

"Well, really, that woman..." began Doris.

"Don't worry about it," interrupted James. "I don't quite know why, but she has made it clear she doesn't like me at all. I sometimes wonder why we gave her that extra day each week. She thinks that she's doing me a favour, I suppose."

It was lunchtime, and James decided that he would take a stroll to the Manor to see Sir Toby rather than to call him on the phone. He liked Sir Toby and they could talk easily together. James always listened to and respected what he had to say about the school and the village, and Sir Toby, in turn, listened well to James' problems and ideas for improving the school. He had some papers from County Hall for him anyway and he would, at the same time, just mention that he was looking for rented accommodation in the area.

"Good morning, James," came a voice from the other side of the privet hedge. It was Lady Lotitia. James was surprised to see her so shabbily dressed in well-worn jeans, torn blouse and a very old and battered straw sun hat. She looked quite a sight.

"Good morning, Lady Lotitia," said James warmly as he strode over to the gate in the hedge to greet her.

"Just trimming some roses, what?" muttered Lady Lotitia, wrestling with a particularly vicious thorned variety in her gloved hand. "Damned things. I do it myself because I cannot trust Nick to do it properly. He cuts off all the buds and we cannot be having that, what?"

James watched for a few moments as she busied herself with the last of the snipping. He knew better than to interrupt her.

"Now, what can I do for you?" She paused in her ministrations and stared at James. "Would you like a drink? I always have one about now, what?"

Without waiting for an answer, she strode over to the large iron table and indicated with a wave of her hand that James should sit beside her. She rang the bell on the table. A few seconds later, James saw Peggy's familiar form scurrying past the side of the privet hedge and into the garden.

"Yes, ma'am?" curtsied Peggy, and upon seeing James gave him a warm "Good morning, sir," and curtsied to him as well.

James hated this kind of thing and, flushed with embarrassment, stood up and shook Peggy's hand. "Good morning, Peggy. It is good to see you again. Are you keeping well?"

"My usual, Peggy, and whatever James would like," interrupted Lady Lotitia, impatiently glaring at her maid.

"Just a cup of tea, Peggy, please."

Peggy curtsied and James watched her scurry past the privet hedge towards the kitchen.

"More papers for Toby, I see," began Lady Lotitia. "One day, we will all drown under a sea of paper, what? Toby comes back with so much from you, James, and here you are bringing him more, what?"

James wasn't sure whether Lady Lotitia was angry or just teasing him. You could just never tell.

"Well, I thought it would keep him busy," replied James a little cheekily. "But there was something else that I wanted to ask you both. A personal matter."

Unsmiling, Lady Lotitia looked closely at James as he continued.

"As you may know, I have been travelling each day from Bridgehampton. I would like to move closer to the school and wonder if you know of any properties in the area that I could rent. I don't want to be too close to the school, you understand, but if you know of anywhere that is not too expensive, I would be very grateful."

Lady Lotitia looked at James carefully through her steely grey eyes and nodded slowly.

"As it happens, I do. It may be just the thing for you. Thank you, Peggy, just put them down over there."

Peggy had returned with the drinks and was arranging a small silver tray with a gin and tonic for Lady Lotitia, a pot of tea for James and a plate of delicious-smelling biscuits.

"Cook made these today. I thought Mr Young would like one." Peggy smiled at James and returned to the house.

"We do have a small cottage that is available. It is called Apple Tree Cottage and used to be the home of Jock, the dairyman, and his wife, Nora. They moved to Brighton last year when they retired and it has been empty ever since. It is a bit too remote to use for holiday-makers, but it may be ideal for you. It has two bedrooms, but it will need some redecoration before you could move in though, and it may be a bit damp as it has been empty for quite a while. I think it would suit you very well."

"It sounds lovely," replied James excitedly. "But where is it?"

"At the bottom of the next lane – Duck Lane. You could come and see it after school on Friday if you wish."

Lady Lotitia took a large mouthful of gin and tonic and placed the glass beside her.

"May I ask how much you would be charging in rent?" asked James anxiously.

"Oh, really, James. I leave all that sort of thing to Toby. I never talk about money. It is just so vulgar, don't you think? What?"

It is if you haven't got any, thought James to himself.

"I quite understand and, yes, I would love to come and see the cottage after school on Friday."

"Good, that's settled then. I'll come and pick you up in the Land Rover at around half past four. You can have a good look around and then tell me what you think."

James was teaching all afternoon. He was very excited about the possibility of Apple Tree Cottage and couldn't wait to tell Tristan when he got home. He told Doris about what Lady Lotitia had said when he returned to his office.

"Yes, I think I know where that is. It is a bit remote, James, but at least you won't have the children coming to see you after school!" Doris laughed. "Go and have a look, but if it isn't right you must say so, and Tristan ought to see it as well first, remember?"

Doris already knew how impatient James was. He wanted everything doing right away. Doris admired the get-up-and-go of this impatient young man, but also was already well aware of how it could easily get him into trouble. She also had an uneasy feeling that James, unthinkingly, could easily rent somewhere for Tristan and himself without Tristan seeing it first. It was wise counsel.

James laughed. "OK, OK, I know where you're coming from. I bet you two have been talking about me again, haven't you? Tristan's told you to slow me down!"

That's not too far from the truth, smiled Doris to herself, but said nothing more.

Later that afternoon, James had settled the class to a history lesson about the Tudors. The class had watched a short TV film and were talking about it afterwards.

"But why didn't he like Catherine the Arrogant?" asked Neil. "She was his wife, after all. They had a baby and everything. Why did he want to get rid of her so soon?"

"Well, maybe he just got tired of her, Neil. Anne was younger and maybe she was prettier. It's 'Aragon' and not 'arrogant'," replied James.

"My dad did that to my mum," called out Sally in disgust. "He went off with a younger woman. I wish we could have chopped his head off and hers as well, come to that," she added as an afterthought. "My mum says he tossed her aside like an old jacket."

"I'm sorry to hear that, Sally, but things were a little different in King Henry's day," continued James, trying to bring the conversation back on track to the Tudors.

"Yes, Simon?"

"Anyway, Sally couldn't chop her dad's head off nowadays. It's against the law and she would be tried for murder and then she would be hanged."

"I could if I wanted to, Simon Cook," hissed Sally, not in the least daunted by Simon's legal intervention.

"Hanging was abolished long ago, Simon," interrupted James.

"Now, just have a look at your time-lines and you can see what else happened at the same time as Henry was marrying and divorcing all those ladies."

"Well, I think it's dreadful. It shouldn't have been allowed," interrupted Sally.

"Sally Watson?"

"Yes, Mr Young?"

"Get on with your work. That's enough."

Sally muttered something underneath her breath, which James wisely ignored, gave a loud sigh and resigned herself to continuing her work.

"Now, Neil, bring your books over here and we will get you moving on this as well."

Neil trotted over to James' desk with his exercise book and took the worksheet that James had prepared for him the previous evening. James was pleased with the progress that Neil was making. The boy was not unintelligent, but he did have a problem with writing his letters. Many of his letters were also written back to front. James had seen this before and remembered a lecture that he had had at college about something called 'dyslexia'. Apparently, many experts said it didn't exist and it was just an excuse for bad teaching, but James wasn't so sure. Something was wrong. Neil was of at least average intelligence, and James wasn't too sure of the best way of helping him.

After a difficult meeting with Neil's parents and a heated argument with Neil's father, who had thumped the table angrily before James had insisted that he either calm down or leave the building, they had finally agreed for Neil to see a psychologist. James' battle had not ended there, because although he had asked for an appointment with the psychologist right away, so far no one had contacted him. Meanwhile, although James was working individually with Neil, and he had stopped Emily sending him to the infant class, James knew that he was groping in the dark for something he didn't really understand himself. He had even asked the local bookshop to order a new American book for him on the subject. Educationalists in the States seemed to be far in advance in their research and James wanted to know more.

Suddenly, the classroom door burst open and Zachary from the infant class ran in. The small boy ran to James and pulled him by the hand.

"Come quick, Mrs Sprigg's dead."

It took a moment for James to understand the impact of what Zachary had said.

"What did you say, Zachary?"

"She's dead."

"Neil, ask Mrs Cole to call the ambulance and then to go over to the infant class. Sally, please ask Mrs Armstrong to come in here right away. Please tell her we have an emergency in Class 1."

"But, Mr Young..."

"Now, Sally, please," shouted James as ran out of the classroom with Zachary still clinging to his hand.

James ran up the steps to the infant classroom. Mrs Sprigg sat slumped, lifeless, over her desk. A group of children stood around her still form looking very concerned. Others continued with their drawings and playing with their Lego and Stickle bricks.

"She's dead," said Zachary.

"She ain't moved," added Lisa.

"She's dead," said Zachary.

"No, I don't think so, Zachary. She is probably having an after dinner nap," lied James. "Children, just go back to your drawings and I'll look after Mrs Sprigg."

James felt helpless. He thought he detected breathing, but it was very faint. He loosened the clothes around her neck and made her as comfortable as he could on the chair with some old dressing-up clothes acting as a pillow. He wanted to move her to somewhere more comfortable, but remembered from his college first aid lecture that he should not do this. How he wished he had listened more carefully to the whole lecture and also taken a more recent first aid course.

Doris suddenly appeared at his side. James was so pleased to see her.

"I called them and they are on their way. Neil didn't say much and so I assumed it was a child who was ill, not Vanessa. They won't be long, James. What do you think is the matter with her?"

"She's dead," said Zachary, reappearing by the side of the desk.

"Sit down, Zachary. She is breathing, Doris, but it seems very shallow – just look at the colour of her lips."

"I knows she's dead," said Zachary.

After what seemed like an eternity, they could hear the ambulance siren. Doris stood by the gate to lead them to the infant classroom. The children ran towards the window when they heard the siren and shouted with excitement. The two ambulance men came into the classroom with Doris. Briefly, they examined Vanessa and within a few minutes, she had been placed on to a stretcher and fitted with an oxygen mask. By now, groups of villagers and parents had gathered outside the school gate, anxiously watching the goings on through the iron railings.

"This lady's had a heart attack. We need to get her in the ambulance to begin treatment and then on to hospital quickly," one of the ambulance men said quietly to James. "Is there anyone who can go with her to the hospital? We will need more information."

"I'll go with her if you like, James," said Doris.

James agreed. "It's better that I stay here with the children. Can you please also tell the crowd at the gate that everything is alright, and that we will tell them more later when we know what's happening?"

The children settled quietly at their tables and were now focused upon their new interest of drawing colourful pictures of ambulances and ambulance men, doctors and nurses.

Zachary was busily drawing a picture of a dead body.

For the next few hours James waited in the office for the telephone to ring. He had called Richard, Vanessa's husband, but there was no reply. Eventually, he had managed to track Richard down to the accounting firm where he worked and told him the bad news.

"I'll be right over. I'll go straight to the Abbotsford Hospital. Is anyone there with her?"

"Yes, Doris is there, Richard. I'll be in touch with you again later."

Anne knocked at the door and came in. She sat down on Doris' chair. She looked pale.

"What a day, James. What a dreadful day. No news yet?"

"No, not yet, Anne. Richard is on his way to the hospital now and Doris went off with Vanessa. Has she been ill recently, Anne?"

"Well, she does have narcolepsy, James. You did know about this, didn't you?"

"No, I don't know much about Vanessa. I'm sorry, Anne, but I don't even know what narcolepsy is."

"Well, I don't know much either, but it is a condition that Vanessa has had for years. It means that sometimes she just falls into a deep sleep."

"You mean during the day?"

"Yes, she does sometimes. Haven't you noticed it sometimes during staff meetings, James?"

"Yes, several times, but I thought it was because I was boring. I was getting a bit of a complex about it."

"No, it wasn't you, James, it's her condition."

"And we let her have a class of young children on her own in an outside classroom?" cried James, shocked at the implications of what he had just heard. "Why didn't you tell me, Anne? Why didn't someone tell me? I would never have put her or the school in that position if I had known."

Anne went bright red and James thought she was about to burst into tears.

"I'm sorry, James. I just thought you knew. I raised it with Peter once and he said that if she was fit enough to be in school, she would have to go where she was needed and that was that."

"But that's grossly irresponsible," cried James, banging on the desk sharply.

He calmed down a little. "Look, I'm sorry, Anne. I'm not angry with you, but I am angry with myself. I have been so preoccupied with other things I forgot one of the most important things – the health of my staff!"

"Well, yes, James, but hindsight is a wonderful thing, isn't it? The important thing is, what can we do about it now?"

"I promise you this, Anne," said James calmly. "When she comes back, Vanessa will not be in that room on her own ever again. We will either move her into the main school or get a full-time classroom assistant to be there at all times with her. We don't even have a telephone in there! I'll speak to the Governors about it tomorrow."

The telephone rang.

"Prior's Hill Primary."

James listened to what Doris had to say for a few moments and then quietly put the phone down. He paused for a moment before he turned to his deputy.

"It's bad news, Anne. Doris says that Vanessa passed away a few minutes ago."

James was in school early the following morning. He went directly to Vanessa's classroom carrying a large suitcase. Gently, he opened the drawers of Vanessa's desk, took out her personal possessions and placed them in the suitcase. As he opened the drawer, he caught a strong smell of Vanessa, or rather the perfume that she used. James swallowed hard. This was one of the most difficult things that he had had to do at the school so far. He removed her little bag with the orange flowers containing her lipstick, perfume and all the things that women like to have with them. He spotted her distinctive wooden pencil case from Majorca, and her toy frog that she used so often with the children, and placed those in the suitcase. Personal books, pens and anything that looked as if it were her personal property all went inside.

James opened the door of her large walk-in cupboard and found Vanessa's PE shoes, coat and silk scarf. One of the most poignant things that he found was a Tupperware sandwich box containing a round of uneaten sandwiches, a chocolate biscuit and an apple. Vanessa hadn't eaten her lunch the day before. Maybe she had not felt well enough even then? Why hadn't she said something to him? Maybe he could have stopped this nightmare from happening?

James already felt guilty that his skills as a first-aider were not up to scratch. He had shared these thoughts with Tristan the evening before when he had arrived home tired and drained of energy.

"I didn't know what to do, Tris. I just didn't know what to do," he sobbed.

Tristan said nothing, but just comforted James in his strong arms.

James had driven to Abbotsford Hospital as soon as he had received the news from Doris. He met Richard, Vanessa's husband, for the very first time. Now a broken man and with his life now in tatters, Richard had arrived at the hospital a few minutes too late to see his wife alive. He had been taken to the ward to see Vanessa for a few minutes alone. James had intended to speak to him when he was about to leave the hospital. Instead, when he saw Richard's distressed face, he just went up to him and held his hand. Although they had never met, Richard knew who James was and nodded appreciatively. James had offered to drive Richard home, but he had declined, knowing that his daughter would already be waiting for him.

"James, what are you doing here so early this morning?"

James turned and saw Doris standing outside the cupboard with a black plastic bag in her hand.

"I see you are doing what I came in to do. I was going to take away Vanessa's personal things before you came in."

"I think I have just about done it all, Doris, thank you. I wanted to put it away before the children came. It really is such dreadful news, Doris. How long had she been at the school?"

"About fifteen years or so, I think. I need to check it in the log book. She was certainly here when my boy was and he is twenty-five now. What do you want me to do to help, James?"

"Well, we need to get a note out to the parents today. I will write one later. We need to call all the Governors and tell them what has happened, as well as Paul Jones and Dawn Edwards from the Diocese."

"Do you think we should have closed today as a mark of respect?"

"I wondered about that, Doris, and I spoke to Sir Toby last night. We agreed it was too short notice for the parents and I really do need to talk to the children and explain what has happened. The young ones were here alone when it happened, remember. Goodness knows what they saw."

"Do you want me to get Emily to take this class today?"

"Well, call her, Doris, and ask if she will take Class 3 for me today. I'll teach this class today. I feel I should be here with them."

"Right you are, James. I will start right away. What about assembly? Should I cancel it? People would understand."

"No, not at all, Doris. We are having one this morning especially for Vanessa. Tell anyone that you see that they are welcome to be there as well, but goodness knows what I shall say."

James need not have worried. There is a saying that strength comes out of crisis, and by the end of the day, James knew exactly what that meant. The young head teacher had faced death before when his brother, and then later when his parents, died, but he had never been quite so close to it as he had been on the previous day with Vanessa. He had not planned what to say, he had no music, no prayers, no Bible readings, nothing.

He remembered Tristan's words as he had left the flat that morning.

"James, you will always be given the strength to do whatever you have to do. Just have a little faith."

The comment had surprised James. Tristan was a good person, but he had little time for religion or church-going.

James looked at the sad faces in front of him. The children sat quietly on the floor waiting for him to start. The infants usually chattered, but not this morning. The hall was full of parents, Governors and friends of the school. Through tear-filled eyes he could see Jack Sparrow, Bert and Eddie, as well as Lady Lotitia sitting in the corner. Doris and Anne had drawn the glass screen to one side to allow more space for seating. It looked as if the whole village had turned out.

"Just have a little faith, James," Tristan's voice echoed in James' ear.

James stood up to begin. "Good morning, children. Good morning, everyone."

James told the story of the butterfly who lived for only one day. He told them about the beautiful flower, and the little tree frog that was sad to see the butterfly die, and the caterpillars that continued to live after the butterfly had died. James had forgotten all about this story until the very moment that he was retelling it. Here in the silence of the hall, and if James had been aware, he would have seen children sitting silently with their mouths open listening to the story in wonder, parents sitting quietly brushing a tear or two from their eyes, and even Lady Lotitia snorting loudly into her handkerchief.

When James had finished retelling the story he made up a prayer, and children and adults together sang a hymn, his own favourite as a child, 'All Things Bright and Beautiful'. He heard strong tuneful singing from Bert and Eddie and he smiled as he tried to imagine them in the school choir many years earlier. He spotted the Rector standing in the corner of the room and asked him to say a closing prayer and to give a blessing. Eventually, the children quietly filed out to their classrooms. James was about to follow the infant children to their classroom when the Rector began to walk alongside him.

"James, that was inspirational. It was just right. I could not have said it better myself. I really felt that Vanessa was with us in the school hall this morning, James. She would have been delighted."

Zachary tugged James by the hand. "I knows she was dead."

Chapter 14

Facing Issues

The next few days were particularly difficult ones for James and the staff at Prior's Hill. Although James didn't know Vanessa very well, it was clear that she was well-liked and respected by parents, past pupils and the community alike. There had been a private family cremation and the Governors had agreed that the school should be closed the following day as a mark of respect to Vanessa, and to allow staff, parents and pupils to attend the memorial service in Vanessa's hometown a few miles away.

The service was well-attended and James was surprised to see so many of Vanessa's past pupils from the local secondary school at the service, together with the head teacher and several members of the Ledger's School staff. James was touched when Vanessa's husband, Richard, asked him to read a lesson.

"I would be honoured to, but I didn't know her that well, Richard."

"I know you didn't, but she was always talking about you and one of the nicest things that she said about you a couple of days before she died was that at last she had a head teacher who knew what infant pupils really needed."

This was one of the nicest things that Vanessa could have said about James, and he had appreciated Richard telling him.

James had now lost one third of his teaching staff and that had immediate implications for the school. During this period of crisis, at least Emily had been co-operative and had agreed to cover James' class for as long as it was needed. Although James was grateful for her help, he felt a little sad that he would lose the daily contact and routine that he had established with his class. Already he had noticed some changes that he didn't like; for example, the new carpet had been rolled up to one side and the desks had been re-arranged. Still, he told himself, these were small things that would be easily rectified once things were back to normal, and he now had Class 1 to think about.

Although James was trained as a Junior teacher, he had always been fascinated by younger children, never more so than at Marion's school when he had asked whether it would be possible to spend a little time in the infant classes as well. Marion was delighted and readily agreed, because James would be the first ever male teacher in an infant classroom at her school and she was already convinced that both men and women had a part to play in early-years education. Initially, for just one day each week, James had spent time in two of the school's infant classes, as well as in the nursery, of which Marion was very proud. This period in James' professional life had been both an eye-opener and a delight for him. It was difficult and tiring, much more tiring than he had thought possible, but he had enjoyed every minute of it. Marion had been very complimentary and had told him that he should consider refocusing upon this age range in the future.

James stood in Vanessa's classroom wondering where to start. It was far too early to make substantial changes, but already he felt uneasy about the layout of the classroom, as well as the overall shortage of equipment. Both he and Vanessa had discussed this and there was a long list of items to be ordered from the educational supply catalogues sitting in Doris' tray. It was only waiting for the next tranche of capitation money to come through from County Hall and then she could order it. He decided that it would be best, for the time being at least, to follow the existing routines and timetables that the children were used to. He busied himself setting out mathematics equipment for the children to use that morning, when Doris crept into the classroom.

"Sorry to disturb you James, but I have Lady Lotitia on the phone. She is asking if you are still interested in Apple Tree Cottage."

"You bet, Doris. Please give her my apologies, but I am sure she will understand that because of Vanessa, I had other things on my mind on Friday. I felt that going to see it the other day was inappropriate. I did send a message over with Bert to say that I could view later."

"Yes, she knew all about the message and wonders if you would like to see it this afternoon at half past four?"

"Perfect, Doris. Tell her, yes please!"

"James?"

"Yes, Doris?"

"There was also a message from someone called Miss Jean Flickersmill. Apparently, she is the Early Years Inspector for the area. She would like to come and meet you for a brief visit on Friday morning."

"That's all I need this week," groaned James. "Yes, tell her she is welcome, but she will have to take us as she finds us. I am not taking time off class to see her or getting a supply in this week. Class 1 is my first priority. Tell her what happened to Vanessa, please, Doris."

It was half past four and James was waiting for Lady Lotitia's Land Rover to appear outside the school gate as promised. He knew that she would probably forget or be late, as was her reputation, so he busied himself with trying to tidy up what there was in the way of equipment in the sports shed in the playground. Old flat footballs, knotted skipping ropes and broken hoops greeted James when he opened the door. Poor kids, he thought, fancy having to use this rubbish. Most of it needed throwing away and replacing. He smiled when he saw a large yellow plastic box of nearly new netballs sitting in the corner of the shed. Well, Emily had certainly managed to fight her corner, he thought. James started to make a neat pile of items to be disposed of when there was a loud toot on a car horn. It was Lady Lotitia.

After a brief greeting, James climbed into the battered old Land Rover beside Lady Lotitia and the trusty vehicle lurched forward and into the lanes beyond the farm. James held on to his seat as best he could as Lady Lotitia hurled the old vehicle through the dirt tracks that she regularly used in order to make her journey quicker. She said nothing and James was content to let her focus upon her driving. He wondered how many gin and tonics she had drunk already that day.

"Duck Lane, here we are, what?" she exclaimed, screeching to a halt in the empty courtyard of a small farm.

"Apple Tree Cottage is just over there."

Lady Lotitia waved a gloved hand in the direction of a small, very pretty cottage tucked in at the end of the farmyard. Outside the red-brick building stood a group of four large and very old apple trees, their gnarled bark giving away their ages. Apple Tree Cottage was joined to the last of the farm buildings. The walls were adorned with climbing roses, many of which were still in bloom. Neat net curtains were hung in the four tiny-framed windows. Lady Lotitia fumbled with the catch on the gate that led down a small path to the front door.

"Watch your head. These buildings were not built for tall young men," she commanded, as she turned the large key in the old lock and swung open the front door.

"Wow, this is great," exclaimed James as he stood in the hallway leading to a small narrow staircase. Lady Lotitia opened the doors to the left and to the right of the hallway, one side revealing a small dining room and the other a large sitting-room. James walked into the dining-room and surveyed the scene before him. It was true that the building had been empty for some time, and James could see yellowing white paint flaking off some of the walls. However, it was mainly cosmetic and he could see that it would be easily rectified with some sealer and a fresh coat of white paint. There was a clean but old floral carpet on the floor and the dining-table and chairs looked old and dusty, but were in good condition. James rubbed his hand across the surface of the table. The previous occupant had clearly polished the furniture regularly.

"We can get you a new carpet and you don't have to keep the furniture. We can easily store it in one of the barns outside, what?" said Lady Lotitia, opening the door leading to a small, but well-equipped kitchen.

"This is perfect. Tristan will love it!" exclaimed James.

"Tristan? Who's Tristan?" questioned Lady Lotitia.

"He's the friend I live with. Tristan has helped me a lot in the school and he wants to move here as well. He is looking for a new job."

"Ah, is he the young man that disposed of that wretched stage?" queried Lady Lotitia.

"Yes, that's right. I don't know what we'd have done without him. He's very good with his hands. Yes, he will love it, I am sure!"

James wandered around the pretty little cottage picturing where he would put his bookcase and where Tristan would put his beloved stereo unit. Tristan had quite a lot of furniture already and James had a few pieces of his own that his parents had left him. Between them, the place would be more or less furnished. One of the two small bedrooms already had a double bed, although the second room would also take a double bed, ideal if friends came to stay, thought James. They would need to get some wardrobes, as Tristan currently had fitted cupboards in his flat. After a few minutes James went downstairs and found Lady Lotitia waiting for him in the sitting-room, lounging on a comfortable floral sofa, and she immediately got up as if to leave when James reappeared.

"Thank you so much. This is perfect. May I bring Tristan over on Saturday to see it, and then we can talk to Sir Toby about the rent that he is looking for?"

"Quite so, James. Quite so. Now we must go, because I have a dinner party at eight this evening, what?"

Lady Lotitia appeared to be in a great hurry to leave Apple Tree Cottage, and she and James said no more until they were back at the school.

James burst into Tristan's flat in great excitement.

"We've got a cottage! We've got a cottage!" he yelled loudly to the surprised Tristan as he met him at the kitchen door. "Well, I say we've got it, but only if you like it as well and the price is right," he added, greeting Tristan with a big hug.

"It's good to see you in such a good mood, Jay. All I can say is that you need to get one of these cottages every day. It seems to have taken your mind off that school, anyway!" Tristan chuckled.

Over a large drink, the boys sat, laughed and chatted about their future plans together. James could see that Tristan was just as excited as he and was asking many questions.

"Is there somewhere to put the cars, Jay? I really must look after my Mini."

"What? That battered old thing?! Yes, bags of space in the yard outside, and yes, and there is somewhere really good for your stereo," he added with a laugh, guessing the next question forming upon Tristan's lips. "You will be able to play your Beatles tapes as loud as you want."

"Sounds ideal, Jay. How much is it?"

"Not sure yet. I said we would both go over on Saturday morning and have a word with Sir Toby. He's a fair old boy, he won't rip us off, I'm sure."

"Well, I haven't found a job yet, Jay. It will have to be a good price, because I haven't got much in the way of savings left. I shall still have to pay the mortgage on this place until we can sell it."

"My, you are a dark horse, Tris. I thought you rented it! I didn't realise that you owned the flat!"

"Well, I own a tiny bit of it, I guess," laughed Tristan. "I thought I told you. I put the money that the Army gave me into it when I left. I thought it would be a good investment for the future."

"Well, it goes to prove that I'm not with you just for your money," grinned James. "Come on, let's go out for a meal. We've got something to celebrate at last!"

Tristan quietly went back into the kitchen and, without a word, turned off the meal that he had been cooking for James.

By Friday morning, James was getting into the routine of his new class. They were a good class and he had already arranged for a rota of parents to help him with the larger groups of children, particularly in the mornings. Penny Skinner had offered to come and help on her morning off, even though her daughter was not in Class 1.

"You could do with some help, Mr Young. You have helped Carol so much and now I am going to do what I can to help you."

Indeed, it was Peggy's contacts in the village and her gentle arm-twisting that had led to James' provisional rota being filled quickly. Some mothers had offered to help for an hour here and there, whilst others had signed up for a whole morning or afternoon. Both dinner ladies, Gloria and Anna, had agreed to stay after their usual lunchtime work on two afternoons each week to help as well.

James had remembered that Miss Flickersmill was due to visit that morning. He had experienced visits from advisers and inspectors before and was not particularly fazed by the forthcoming visit of this one. He had asked one of the local head teachers about her.

"Bad luck, old boy," Colin said with a guffaw as soon as James had called him. Colin Treader was the head teacher of Coombe School, in a small village about fifteen miles away from Prior's Hill. James had met the older man at one of the meetings for head teachers and the two had immediately got on well together. Colin had been very helpful to him and had let him borrow books, equipment and even a set of old goal-posts that he no longer needed. Colin had been the school's head teacher for many years and took no hostages. He was blunt, had a dry sense of humour and always went straight to the point.

"She's trouble, there's no doubt about it. She's only been in the job for a few minutes, but she's here to make a name for herself. She's already got all the women head teachers in the area dancing to her tune – 'The Flickersmill Babes', we call them. They are all training to be clones of the wretched woman! I've had a few brushes with her already. Paul Jones cannot stand her either!"

James laughed. “Thank you, Colin. I knew I would get a straight answer from you. Anyway, she’s due here sometime this morning. She couldn’t have picked a worse time. By the way, Colin, thank you for coming to Vanessa’s service. It was good to see you there.”

“Dreadful business, James. I was so sorry for Richard and all of you down there. Shocking thing for the children to witness as well. Anything I can do to help?”

“Well, we shall soon be looking for a good Infant teacher, Colin. If you know of anyone, just send them my way.”

“Yes, I will, James. In fact, there is someone I think you would like. I’ll check with her first and give you a call. By the way, when are you going to join the National Association of Head Teachers? You keep saying you will!”

“I promise you, the form is in the post, Colin. Yes, I know I’ve been saying the same thing for ages, but it really is this time!”

Colin was the local secretary for the Association. It was a good professional association and many of James’ colleagues in the area were members, but James had just not got around to joining, despite constant nagging from Colin.

“It better had be, otherwise I’ll be over to see you again, young man. Goodbye, James.”

It was mid-morning when Doris entered the classroom, together with the amiable Paul Jones, and accompanied by Miss Jean Flickersmill. Miss Flickersmill was a tall, unsmiling woman wearing a tweed suit adorned with a single string of pearls. James noticed that she had been a little overgenerous with her lipstick that morning and had forgotten to ‘dab’. It made her lips look thicker than they should have been. James gave his visitors a smile of welcome.

"Good morning, James. It is good to see you again. I was so sorry to hear of your recent troubles. Had Vanessa been ill for long?"

James briefly explained the circumstances of Vanessa's death to Paul, and then turned to the unsmiling Miss Flickersmill.

"Good morning, Miss Flickersmill. It is good to meet you."

"Good morning, Mr Young, and, may I ask, what exactly is a man doing in an infant classroom?"

This was to be the beginning of a strained relationship between the local Inspector for the Early Years and James.

"I don't understand what you mean, Miss Flickersmill. I am here because the class teacher, Vanessa, died last week. I usually teach the older children, but I felt that my priority was to give the children in this class some stability, and with someone that they already know, as quickly as possible."

"Quite so. However, in my experience, men should stick to teaching the junior pupils. They do not have the understanding of what is needed in an infant classroom, unless they are very good and have been thoroughly trained, that is." Miss Flickersmill glared at James and then gave the disorganised classroom a distasteful glance.

"I'm sorry that you disapprove, but I disagree, Miss Flickersmill," argued James, angry at what he had just heard. "I believe that men as well as women have a part to play in early-years education. The world is full of men and women, and young children need to see men in a positive caring role, just as they see women. With all the family break-ups nowadays, many children do not have a positive male role model in their lives. This is why we need men as well as women in the infant classroom."

Miss Flickersmill looked taken aback, said nothing for a moment, and then spotted Zachary drawing his usual death picture. She walked over to him and picked up Zachary's unfinished picture. It was not one of his better ones, although James was relieved to see that he had not scribbled on it just yet.

"Hmm. Why is this child using colour pencils? They are far too thin for him to hold. He is a small boy and so he needs crayons or maybe lots of paint and a thick brush."

"Zachary chooses whatever he wishes to use at the moment, Miss Flickersmill."

"Yes, but you should be guiding him in his choices, Mr Young."

"Should I? Well, I have my reasons, which we can discuss at another time," said James, biting his tongue. "If you will excuse me, I am needed with another group of children. I must get on. Will you be staying for coffee?"

"No, we must be getting on, James," replied Paul Jones. "We won't hold you up any more. We just wanted to see that everything was alright since last week's tragedy, and Miss Flickersmill wanted to meet you. I hear your Governors are making a fuss about getting a classroom assistant in here?"

"What, you are on your own over here?" intervened Miss Flickersmill, frowning deeply.

"Yes, we have never had a nursery nurse or classroom assistant in here," replied James. "The children were on their own when their teacher died."

Miss Flickersmill looked taken aback, held out her hand to James, and said coldly, "That's disgraceful. I will be seeing you again very soon, Mr Young."

James was deeply worried about Zachary. The small boy had seemed preoccupied with death since Vanessa's passing. James thought this was understandable for a few days, but Zachary would say very little and was happiest when he could draw or paint. James let him draw as much as he wanted, believing it to be a good way of expressing whatever he had to get out of his system. James would watch Zachary thinking, sucking one of his crayons or coloured pencils, and then he would scribble furiously. When he had finished, minutes later, he would appear at James' side and thrust the picture into his hand.

"Thank you, Zachary. Well done. Now, come and tell me about your picture," James would say kindly as they sat together at a nearby table and talked about Zachary's latest picture.

"She's dead," Zachary would say, over and over again. "I knows she was dead."

James tried to encourage Zachary to draw flowers, aeroplanes, rockets, spacemen, and once even brought in a model of his sports car for Zachary to draw. However, the result was always the same – a body. Sometimes it was detailed with a face, other times it was not. Sometimes, when Zachary was angry, he would scribble furiously on top of his drawing or painting in black crayon before presenting it to James.

James talked to Anne and Emily about his problem during lunchtime one day. He was concerned.

"I'm just not sure what to do next," he said, as he arranged a selection of Zachary's disturbing drawings and paintings on the staff-room floor.

"You have seen his parents?" asked Anne.

James nodded. "Yes, several times. They are also concerned. One thing Mrs Lloyd said was that he started doing this before Vanessa's death. I had thought it was Vanessa's death that started it all, but apparently not."

"Is that the little tubby boy with the red face?" asked Emily.

"Yes, that's him," nodded James. "Mrs Lloyd did say that it began a week or two after his grandfather died in the summer, but that was in hospital and Zachary did not see any of that."

"So it seems that poor Vanessa was the trigger for all this?" mused Anne.

"Well, if you ask me, that boy needs help and quickly," blurted out Emily. "This is not normal for a five-year-old. He needs to see the psychologist."

"I think you are right, Emily," agreed James. "I'll call him later this afternoon."

Doris came into the staff-room. "It's Sir Toby," she said quietly. "He wants to see you right away. He does seem a little agitated, so I thought it best that you see him now. I can always keep an eye on the infants until you get back."

"Thanks, Doris. As it happens, I have Gloria and Anna in there this afternoon. They are brilliant, and it won't matter if I'm a few minutes late back."

James greeted Sir Toby to the door of his office. Doris was right, Sir Toby did seem agitated. Not unpleasant, but he looked as if he had something important to say. They sat down and James asked his Chair of Governors if he would like a cup of coffee.

"No, thank you, James. I cannot stay for long today as I have another meeting at Ledger's School later. Two things I wanted to see you about. Firstly, have you ordered a telephone for the outside classroom yet?"

"Yes, it is being installed next week, Sir Toby. I am not sure how to pay for it, though."

"Don't worry about that. I will pay for it myself if necessary, James. That was such a dreadful thing that happened to poor Vanessa. I have also raised the issue of a classroom assistant with Paul Jones at County Hall. He says he will back us on this one. However, whatever happens we cannot get ourselves in that situation ever again. It is not fair for the children or staff. I am determined that we will have a classroom assistant in there at all times. Either that, or they can build us a new classroom attached to the main school." He gave James a faint smile.

"Thank you, Sir Toby. I am very grateful for your support with this."

"There is another, very difficult matter that I wish to raise with you, James." Sir Toby now looked serious and seemed to be fumbling for the right words to use. James wondered what he had done.

"It is a personal matter. About the cottage, James. I am not sure how I'm going to put this."

"Don't worry, I shall quite understand if we cannot see it tomorrow," said James helpfully.

"No, it's not that. Look, James, without beating about the bush further, Lotitia tells me that it is not just for you."

"No," began James, puzzled, "it's for me and my friend Tristan. You have met him."

"Yes, I have indeed. A nice young fellow. It's just that we thought the cottage was for you and for you alone."

"No, we live together and Tristan wants to find a job in this area as well. Is that a problem?"

"Look, James, it would not be a problem if it were just for you. Neither would it be a problem if it were for you and your wife, if you see what I mean. It just that..."

James suddenly realised the significance of what Sir Toby was about to say and a chill shuddered throughout his whole body.

"What you are really saying, Sir Toby, is that it is a problem because I am not married and that I live with a man."

"Er, yes, that's about the long and the short of it, James. I'm sorry."

Sir Toby looked down uncomfortably at his well-polished brown shoes.

"I have tried my best to be discreet about my relationship with Tristan. I rarely talk about him at school. I never bring him to school functions. We never shop or are seen together in the area, and yet he is the most important person in my whole life and the best thing that has ever happened to me. I have done my very best to fit in and not to offend anyone, although I don't see why I shouldn't be myself, and you treat us like this? As village outcasts!"

Sir Toby listened in silence and looked very uncomfortable with what James was saying. The two men had never argued before and Sir Toby genuinely liked and respected James. It distressed Sir Toby that they were having this conversation in such a heated manner.

"You see, James, I have nothing against homosexuals personally, you understand. It's just that Lotitia and I cannot be seen as promoting a dubious non-Christian lifestyle in the village. In my position, I have to consider the villagers' moral welfare as well, you know."

"Moral welfare? How dare you! I cannot believe what I am hearing, Sir Toby," exclaimed James angrily. "Just because I am gay and living in a happy and loving relationship with my partner, you are condemning us as promoting a dubious lifestyle! Do you think we will be out at night raping all the men in the village? How do you work than one out?"

Sir Toby looked very embarrassed, shifted uncomfortably in his seat and began to stand up. "I don't think I have any more to say on the subject, James, except that I am truly sorry that I cannot let Apple Tree Cottage to you and your friend."

James thought for a moment and then said calmly and quietly, "Now that I know your true feelings about Tristan and myself, I wouldn't dream of renting anything from you. You will have my resignation on Monday morning, Sir Toby."

Chapter 15

Clearing the Air

James returned to the classroom and tried to forget what had happened at lunchtime with Sir Toby. The true professional that he was meant that he had to carry on as if nothing had happened. His pupils came first. In truth, James felt sick with worry. What had he just done? Whatever his fine words, aims and principles, he had let the school, children, staff and the village down. He had let Tristan down and, above all, himself. What was he going to say to everyone?

"Mr Young?" came a small voice at his side.

"Whât is it, Susan?"

"Tilly Clarke has just wet her pants."

It was half past three and James was relieved to see the children going home. After he had given the children their reading folders and word tins, he walked out with them to the busy playground. It was amazing how quickly children adjust to their new circumstances, he thought. It was the time of day that he always enjoyed, seeing the children reunited with their parents and chatting to them about their busy day. Young children seemed to make progress so quickly, and there was always something new to share with their parents. They were a good group of parents and many would make a point of waiting to tell James something special about their children or to ask him a question about an issue that was troubling them at home. James was usually a good listener and he would always do his best to help when he could. He could see the older children with Emily walking out of their end of the school building and he smiled to himself. At least Emily was backing him up on how the children should behave in and out of school. It used to be a mad hurly-burly of bodies at the end of the school day, and now the children seemed to be showing some consideration for each other.

"I've made the posters, Mr Young. Had them printed in town – in colour too this year," said Mrs Sparks, proudly holding a large sheet of paper advertising the forthcoming Barn Dance for James to see. "This is always a popular night and it should raise a lot of money for the school. You'll be coming as well, Mr Young?"

James nodded and smiled. "I wouldn't miss it, Mrs Sparks. I've heard a lot about it."

"And Mr Tristan too?"

"Er, well, I'm not sure about that yet," replied James, not expecting the last request.

Mrs Sparks nodded and gathered Jack's lunchbox, reading-bag and coat in her arm, grabbed Jack by the arm and turned towards the gate.

"Thank you for taking the infants, Mr Young. We all miss Vanessa, but you have helped the children so much this week. Jack is always talking about you."

When the last of the children had finally left the premises, James stood alone in the school playground beneath the old horse-chestnut tree where he had stood so many times before since he had arrived at the school. In a strange way, James thought that the tree seemed to understand his troubles. There was a wisdom, a timeless quality that transcended the day-to-day worries that he had. The tree had seen it all before and seemed to understand. He looked up at its magnificent apron and sighed.

"You have seen many changes here, haven't you? So many people, so many children, happy times and sad times. I had hoped to be part of your story for a little longer than this."

He wandered to the very edge of the playground and sat on the dry stone wall that surrounded the old building. There was something magnificent about this building at the end of the day. The sunshine was still gently bathing the rugged stone with a warm golden glow. James looked across at Jack Sparrow's cottage. He could see the old man brushing his dog in the corner of his yard. Jack spotted him and waved. James waved back. How he would miss these good people and this place. He loved the silence at the end of the day too.

"James? Are you alright?" It was Doris. "What are you doing here?"

"Oh, just getting a breath of air after a busy day. I like this spot, it gets the last of the sun here. Did you know that? Everything alright in the office, Doris?"

"Yes, I've just got a few letters for you to sign. They're on your desk waiting for you. You also need to call Dr Tipper – I think he is the psychologist. It seems you have managed to get an appointment for him to see young Zachary. His parents will be pleased."

"Well, that's good news, at least, Doris. I am worried about the little lad, but he did draw me a cow wearing a pearl necklace today. Did I tell you earlier?"

"That's an improvement, James. You must be pleased," laughed Doris. "I wonder who gave him that idea?"

"Funny thing was, he drew it right after Miss Flickersmill left this morning. I just wonder if that was a coincidence, Doris?"

Doris giggled. There was then an awkward silence between them.

"You coming in now, James?"

"Not just yet. I'll be in later. You go when you are ready. I'll post the letters on my way home."

"James, I heard."

"Heard what, Doris?"

"You and Sir Toby. I'm so sorry, James, I wasn't really eavesdropping. I was waiting for him to finish with you, so that I could get my notepad. I heard what he said before he left. I'm so sorry, James."

James bit his lip.

"Don't worry about it, Doris. Everyone will know soon enough."

"James, you know no one really cares about you and Tristan being gay, don't you?" said Doris.

"Sir Toby doesn't seem to think so."

"We all know anyway. It's not the secret that you think it is. I just wanted to tell you that. It might make it easier for you."

"Thanks, Doris."

"I don't want you to go. I like you, I like Tristan. You are the best thing that has happened to this school for many years. I cannot believe how much you have done in such a short time."

"Oh, that will be quickly forgotten, Doris. I have to leave. Sir Toby thinks I will be a bad influence if I live in the village."

"Did he say that?"

"Well, perhaps not in so many words, but that's what he meant."

"Look, James, it has been a long and difficult day. Just you go home and talk it through with your Tristan. That lad has his head screwed on alright. He'll give you good advice. Make sure you phone George and I, or come over and see us if you need to talk. Don't do anything hasty, James."

The little woman pulled him down to her height and she gave him a quick peck on the cheek. "I believe in you, James."

"Thanks, Doris. Thank you for listening. Yes, I think I will go home now. I've had enough for one day."

"It will all seem clearer in the morning, James."

"Doris?" asked James.

"How did you know?"

Doris giggled wickedly as she walked towards the door. "Maybe it had something to do with the cut of your jeans, James."

It was with a heavy heart that James locked the main door of the school, gathered up his workbox and briefcase, and headed towards the little car parked outside the gate. He caught a glance of the old horse-chestnut tree. There was now a strong breeze and its branches were moving furiously. The tree looked angry.

"Yes, I feel like that too," said James as he started the engine.

"Hello, you're home early," said Tristan, as James unlocked the door to Tristan's flat. Tristan walked over to James and gave him a big kiss.

"What's that for?"

"Since when have I not been able to kiss my partner when I want to?" laughed Tristan, stopping when he saw James frown. "Hey, what's the matter?"

"It's been a bad day, Tris. I've resigned."

Tristan looked at James, speechless for a moment.

"You've done what?"

"I've resigned, or least I will on Monday morning. We cannot live there, Tristan. I cannot work there and I need to get as far as I can from Prior's Hill School." James looked truly shaken.

"I'm sure Sir Toby didn't mean to say that, James. You must have misunderstood him."

Later that evening, when Tristan had gone to bed, James sat alone in the living-room trying to watch television. He couldn't concentrate and so after the news had finished, he switched off the TV and sat in silence reflecting upon the day that had turned their lives upside down. He had hardly touched the delicious meal that Tristan had cooked for him in a bid to cheer him up. It was James' favourite, yet he hadn't even noticed. He had told Tristan all about his day and the visit from Sir Toby. Tristan had listened in gloomy silence when James told him what Sir Toby had said. He had nodded and said he understood when James said he had to leave and that they would need to move away and find another job in another part of the country.

"I liked Prior's Hill. It was a good place and I felt at home there too. You have done so much, Jay. It is your life."

"You are my life, Tristan. I'm not staying anywhere where we cannot be liked, respected or just live our lives in peace. After all, what have we done wrong?"

James was only just picking at his food and Tristan decided to clear it away and start washing up.

"You're not hungry, James. Let's have an early night and talk about it in the morning."

James walked quietly into their bedroom.

"Tris, you asleep?"

"No, I'm just thinking."

"You know what you said earlier?"

"What did I say, James?"

"You said that Sir Toby didn't mean to say that. I didn't tell you. How did you know that Sir Toby came to see me? I only told you that later."

"Oh, I just guessed," smirked Tristan.

"I always know when you are lying, Tris. You are a terrible liar, you know. It was Doris who told you, wasn't it?"

"Yes, I guess it was Doris, James. She called me earlier. She and George are very worried about you," grinned Tristan as he threw a pillow at James. "You cannot hide much from Doris and me!"

James eventually climbed into bed beside Tristan and turned off the light.

"Jay?"

"Yes, Tris?"

"You know what you told me all those years ago when I had that trouble in Belfast?"

"I don't remember now. It was a long time ago. What did I say? Some rubbish as usual, I expect."

"You said that we should not talk about our love, that we shouldn't announce it to the world, and that we should just get on with our lives and make the best of it. People may guess, but they won't know for sure. You were right then, James, but you are wrong now."

"What do you mean, Tris? I don't even remember saying that."

"Oh yes you did, Jay. I remember every word as if it were yesterday. It was that and other things that you said that saw me through those terrible few months."

"You mean that I am wrong now?" asked James, sitting up in bed and switching on the light.

Tristan sat up and James could see his smooth, fit chest glistening in the light of the two small lamps at the side of the bed. Tristan held his hand.

"We cannot hide anymore. Times have changed and are still changing fast, Jay. With all this AIDS and HIV business, things are looking really bad for gay men everywhere. We are getting a really bad press, yet most are just like us, ordinary blokes who are just trying to live their lives in the only way that they know how."

James sat in bed astonished at what Tristan was saying to him. Tristan was not a great talker, but when he did, he often had some very wise things to say.

"I've been reading a lot about this recently. Why should we hide? You are a head teacher, for goodness' sake, doing a brilliant job that everyone values. You are an intelligent man, Jay. Why should you hide away your true feelings about what is right and what is wrong? You should be setting an example by your actions and not hiding away as a hypocrite."

"For the simple reason that whatever all this so-called equality business is about nowadays, I would be sacked. Governors would always find a way of getting rid of me. Maybe they wouldn't be explicit about it, but that would be the result just the same. There is no equality for people like us and won't be for many years."

"Yes, but that's my point. People listen to you. It is people like you and I that should be helping to fight this appalling hypocrisy. Just ask yourself why your predecessor left?"

"Well, it was because he couldn't keep his flies zipped up, Tris, you know that. He had affairs with any bit of skirt in the village. Several families were destroyed because of him."

"Well, that's my point, Jay. Who is our love hurting? Why are we running away, James?"

Monday morning finally arrived. James had made his mind up. Despite Tristan's protestations and a long phone call from Doris and George on Sunday morning, he was going to give Sir Toby his resignation letter first thing that morning. He would agree to stay on at Prior's Hill until the new school year or, if the Governors wished, until his successor had been appointed. James wanted to avoid any more turbulence than was necessary for the school, particularly as Anne and the part-time Emily were now the only permanent members of staff remaining. That would give the school plenty of time to advertise, interview and appoint a new head teacher. He had no job to go to and James felt that was the best that he could do for the school, given the circumstances.

The little blue car headed onto the well-worn route between Bridgehampton and Prior's Hill. James was sometimes shocked to realise that he often arrived at the school without even being aware of driving the car. The journey usually took just over an hour and yet it just seemed to drive on its own, without any effort from James. This was another reason why Tristan had wanted to move closer to the school, because he feared that James may have an accident one day if his attention lapsed. Still, at least he wouldn't have to worry about that any more. What was he going to do? James had decided that it was now Tristan's turn to do what he wanted. Tristan had supported and followed James' wishes in everything that he had wanted to do so far, and now it was James' turn to allow Tristan the freedom to do the same. He would go anywhere that his friend wished to go and try to get another teaching job or maybe go into journalism. This was something that James had thought about before he went to college, but he always came back to the idea of teaching – it was, after all, his first love. How was he going to tell everyone? What would he say to them? He just didn't know. Tristan had tried to make him see reason over the weekend and he could see that Tristan had said that they must stay and stand up for what they believed, but it was, oh, so very difficult. James had resigned himself to thinking that he was taking the coward's way out. Yes, but it would hurt fewer people this way.

The little blue car swept into Prior's Hill and, this time, didn't stop outside the school, but instead continued down the winding lane until it reached the Manor House. James drove through the large iron gates and onto the gravel driveway, parking his car just outside the main door of the imposing building. As he got out of the car, clutching the important white envelope in his hand, the door of the Manor House opened. It was Sir Toby. For once the elderly man was not wearing a tie.

"Good morning, James. I thought it was you. Come this way."

James shook hands with Sir Toby and offered him the envelope.

"This is what we were speaking about on Friday, Sir Toby. My letter of resignation."

Sir Toby shook his head.

"I am not prepared to accept it, James, not until you have heard what I have to say. Come inside. Do please come inside to the breakfast-room."

This time James was led, not into the grand living-room that he had entered a few times in recent months, but into a small, homely breakfast-room. This bright and airy room had a small circular table in its centre with six highly polished wooden chairs surrounding it. On the far side was a small dresser with breakfast cereals, a jug of fruit juice and a chrome electric toaster. Even though the patio doors were wide open, a log fire was blazing in the fireplace.

"Tea or coffee, James?"

"Nothing for me, thanks. I really must get on. I have much to do today."

Sir Toby paused and looked at him sadly.

"James, despite our conversation last Friday, do please remember that we are friends and not enemies. I need you to listen to me, as I have tried to do for you on many occasions in the past. Please stay for a drink."

James felt ashamed of his earlier cool response. Despite their differences, he was genuinely very fond of the distinguished old man.

"I'm sorry. A cup of black coffee would be lovely, Sir Toby. Thank you."

Sir Toby busied himself with pouring the coffee.

"Would you like some toast? Or maybe some eggs and bacon?"

James smiled, realising that the old man had forgotten that he didn't eat meat.

"I had breakfast before I came, Sir Toby, but don't let me stop you finishing your breakfast. What a wonderful outlook this room has," continued James, trying to engage in small talk. Tristan had often told him he was not very good at this kind of conversation.

"Yes, the patio doors are a blessing in this small room," agreed Sir Toby. "Sometimes with the sun, it gets so hot in here. Lotitia feels the cold and so we usually have a fire in here in the mornings."

James glanced though the open patio doors and onto the terrace, and saw that it was crammed full of large potted green plants, as well as a large selection of flowering plants.

"Lotitia loves that terrace. She spends ages growing plants from cuttings and seeds. They seem to do so well there. Just like your little cuttings at the school, James." Sir Toby smiled, gently stirring his coffee. "They thrive and grow. You have done a lot over there, you know. Helping to make little cuttings grow."

There was an awkward silence between James and his Chair of Governors. James didn't know what else to say, and Sir Toby was clearly carefully gathering together his thoughts and words.

"James, I am so sorry for what I said on Friday. I hadn't intended for you to be so upset. You took it badly, and I can now see why." He paused for another sip of coffee.

"I told Lotitia what I said when I returned home and she was appalled. Indeed, she hasn't stopped being angry with me all weekend," he added sadly.

James began to feel very sorry for Sir Toby as he tried to imagine the scene. The wrath of Lady Lotitia Peatwhistle would not be pleasant to witness or endure.

"Lotitia thinks I have been insensitive and cruel. 'Foolish' was the word I think she used," he shook his head sadly. "Yes, maybe I have been a foolish old man."

James sat in embarrassed silence, sipping his coffee.

"You see, James, I do have my reasons. You see...you see ...my son..."

The old man turned away to the sideboard with his back to James as he tried to continue. He poured himself another cup of coffee.

"More coffee, James?"

"Just a top-up, please."

"You see, James. Oh dear, this is so difficult. We haven't told anyone on the estate." By now, the old man was perspiring heavily.

"James, our son Giles was a homosexual." The voice came from outside the patio doors, and Lady Lotitia swept inside. "Good morning, James. Yes, I see you have coffee already. Contrary to popular village gossip, I don't touch gin until after eleven. Only coffee."

Lady Lotitia smiled and sat down.

"What my dear husband is trying to say so feebly is that our dear, dear son, Giles, was gay, I think you call it nowadays."

"I see," said James, sipping his coffee still unaware of the implications of this statement.

"We knew he was a homosexual since he left boarding school. Indeed, his housemaster told us after a very unpleasant and sordid incident one sports day afternoon."

James nodded, and Sir Toby sat shaking his head.

"Oh, he was usually very discreet – he had to be around here, but it troubled his father deeply. We sent him away to be cured when he left school, but it didn't work."

"Cured?" questioned James. "It isn't a disease, it cannot be cured. We are born like it."

"That's as may be," interrupted Lady Lotitia, "but the point is that it didn't work."

James decided that it would be better to sit in silence and nod occasionally.

"Anyway, James, Giles fell madly in love with, would you believe, one of the estate workers. A highly inappropriate match if ever there was one. Oh, don't misunderstand me, he was nice enough, but not in our class, you understand. I wouldn't have minded if it had been that nice young doctor we had in the village at that time or someone from his university, but a farm worker? Oh no. Can you imagine the gossip, the scandal? He was very handsome, though," she added as an afterthought.

"But if he was in love, did it matter?" James blurted out, suddenly feeling very sorry for Giles Peatwhistle.

"In our position, of course it matters, James," snapped Lady Lotitia, giving James the benefit of her harshest stare.

"We sent him away," Sir Toby began once again. "Lotitia and I thought it would be a good idea to send him away – to America. At least for a while, until he met a nice American girl, we thought."

"Giles moved to San Francisco, James," interrupted Lady Lotitia. "One month later, our young estate worker suddenly left as well and the next thing that we knew was that he had gone to America and that he and Giles were living somewhere in San Francisco together."

"When I heard that, I cut off his allowance," said Sir Toby slowly.

"Yes, and that was the last we heard of him, wasn't it, Toby?" snapped Lady Lotitia.

Sir Toby left the room. James could see tears running down the old man's cheeks.

"The next thing we knew was that he was dead. His ashes were flown home in a laboratory-sealed container. That farm worker brought them to us one evening," she sobbed.

James stood up, now alarmed at what he was hearing, and put his hand on Lady Lotitia's shoulder. It was all now beginning to fit into place.

"They didn't even let us have his body, James. To give it a proper burial in the family plot." Lady Lotitia sobbed quietly.

"I, I don't understand, Lady Lotitia. What happened? Did he have an infectious disease or something?"

Lady Lotitia paused and rang the bell.

"My usual, Peggy. An early one for me this morning."

Peggy looked alarmed when she saw her mistress crying, but was immediately waved out of the room. When the door closed, Lady Lotitia continued in a hushed voice.

"James, he had AIDS. My son, Giles, died from AIDS."

James had stayed at the Manor House for much longer than he had anticipated. He heard the school bell chime to mark the beginning of the school day. He should really be there, but he knew that Doris would realise that something was wrong and would sort something out.

Sir Toby reappeared and sat in the corner in silence whilst Lady Lotitia continued with their heart-breaking story.

"I have not been a good mother, James, but I loved Giles, although I sometimes wondered if he knew. I didn't understand what was going on. I wish I had done things differently and he might have lived. At least we could have helped him to die in peace," she added.

“So what happened to the farm worker?” asked James, wondering if he should have asked.

“He died a year or two later of the same thing,” replied Lady Lotitia. “I went to the funeral – for Giles, you understand. We paid for a memorial and Toby gives his mother a monthly pension to help her. No one knows why, of course. You are the only person we have told, James, and we would expect you to maintain our confidentiality. Yes, as far as everyone else is concerned, Giles is still alive and living in America making a fortune and will not come home. It will stay that way until we pass on. Then the Peatwhistle estate will pass on to one of his cousins. He was an only son, you see.”

“That is irrelevant to this conversation, Lotitia,” snapped Sir Toby. “Let’s keep to the point, for James’ sake. The boy has to get on.”

“As for your resignation,” continued Lady Lotitia, “that was the reason why Toby behaved so appallingly on Friday. We don’t want you to leave and, on the contrary, we want you both to come and live in the village – at Apple Tree Cottage, the one I showed you last week. It may help a little to make up for what we did to Giles.”

Recent events had now become much clearer to James.

“So why didn’t you want us living in the village? Did you think that somehow it would start people talking and maybe guessing what has happened to Giles, Sir Toby?”

“No-one will ever know about Giles,” interrupted Lady Lotitia.

“I don’t know enough about it, James,” sighed Sir Toby. “I guess an intelligent man like you will know the answers and do the right thing. I think it was just that I didn’t want to be reminded of what had happened every time I saw you both together in the village. It was selfish and I was wrong. I am so sorry. Please forgive me and reconsider.”

James stood up. “Thank you for being so frank with me. I really do appreciate it and thank you for your honesty. Your secret is safe with me. Thank you also for your kind offer of Apple Tree Cottage, but no, thank you. Tristan and I have other plans for where we will be living. However, as far as I am concerned Friday never happened.” James took the letter from his inside pocket, tore it into small pieces and threw it onto the blazing fire.

James returned to the infant classroom with a strange mixture of feelings running though his now very confused mind. He ran up the wooden stairs to the classroom to see that the children had just returned from assembly and were now gathered together upon the carpet for registration. Doris appeared to be very firmly in charge.

James crept in behind her.

“Good morning, Mr Young,” chanted the children, happy to see their head teacher.

“Good morning, children. I see that Mrs Cole has been looking after you. I hope you looked after her as well?”

“Yes, Mr Young,” they chanted.

“Doris, I am so sorry I’m late. I had to see Sir Toby,” whispered James in Doris’ ear.

Doris looked up anxiously from the chair where she had installed herself in front of the children.

“Everything is fine here, James. I guessed what was happening. Anne took assembly and even Emily offered to do your playground duty for you. Don’t worry, I haven’t said anything, but I think Anne and Emily sense that something is wrong. Anne asked me this morning if I thought you were a bit off-colour recently.”

“Everything is just fine now, Doris. No, I won’t be leaving you just yet. It’s all been sorted and apparently I can be as gay as I wish!” he whispered.

Doris jumped up from her chair, beamed an enormous smile and gave him a big hug.

“Not in front of the children, please, Doris! What will the parents say? Now what exactly did you mean about the cut of my jeans?”

Chapter 16

The Barn Dance

It was the first week of May. It was one of those 'good to be alive' weeks when the weather was perfect and there was a feeling that summer had at last arrived. It had been a long and difficult winter and James was getting tired of leaving home for school and getting home again in the dark. The first few weeks of spring had been disappointing and brought with them a great deal of rain. Anyone working in schools will recognise the misery that this brings for children and staff alike. Children quickly became frustrated that they could not go out to play, outdoor games were cancelled and they arrived at school wet. Inadequate drying facilities in school meant that their clothes stayed wet for much of the day. The smell of damp clothes seemed to go on for weeks.

Now all that seemed long ago. The majestic old horse-chestnut tree stood bathed in bright sunlight against an almost cloudless blue sky and there was hardly a rustle from its branches. James stood at the school gate for a moment, his critical eye falling upon the flaking paintwork on the door and window frames. "We must get something done about that before winter," he muttered to himself.

James was relieved that the problems of the past week were behind him. Doris had been delighted that he was staying on at the school and brought in a huge chocolate cake the following day to celebrate. Anne and even Emily seemed to sense that a burden of some kind had been lifted from the school, and the conversation in the staff-room at lunchtime was almost one of celebration.

"It's the Village Barn Dance next weekend, James. Are you coming?" enquired Anne, tucking into a large slice of chocolate cake.

"Yes, I certainly will. I've been hearing a lot about it. I gather the profit goes into school funds. We could certainly do with it. Yes, I'll be there and I will try to get Tristan along too. I've never been to one before. What is it?"

Doris giggled. "Well, it's a sort of a large village party in one of Sir Toby's barns. His men clean it up and put fresh bales of straw everywhere. There is a bar, lots of food and we have a folk group playing the night away. It's an event that has happened for years."

"Yes, and it's The Ploughboys again this year as well," said Anne excitedly. "Have you heard of them, James? They are a local group, but are doing really well nationally at the moment. They play country-and-western, folk, Irish and all that sort of thing. I know the lead singer, Bill," she added proudly. "That's why we get them to come and play here cheaper than anyone else."

"No, I cannot say that I have, Anne, but then again I'm not really in touch with that sort of thing. To be honest, it's the dancing that worries me most. I have two left feet. I don't know any country-and-western dances either."

"Well, from what I hear from the children in Class 3, James, they really enjoyed the few country dancing lessons that you did with them. They keep asking me when we can do some more, and I tell them that they will have to wait for you to come back," added Emily.

James laughed. It was good to hear Emily was taking part in staff-room banter at last, and was talking to him almost normally. Although Emily was usually very critical of James' ideas and changes, there was now an acceptance that he was the boss and that he was here to stay.

"Well, that's because I'm using the BBC radio tapes, Emily. I play them over and over in the car and I can more or less get through it. I usually dance with Sally. She keeps me right."

Emily laughed. "Well, if you have Sally Watson leading you, I am sure you will be fine. She is a good dancer, but she is growing into a proper little madam, don't you think?"

"Yes, she certainly is. I can see her in a few years' time, bossing her own children around in the playground."

"Well, I taught her mother and she was just the same at Sally's age, James," added Emily, pulling a face.

"Wasn't that the girl that flushed Neil's father's head in the girl's toilet?" laughed Anne. "I remember that. I forget what he did, but he upset her in some way. She was a big, strong girl too, just like Sally. I know the Head didn't know whether to laugh or be cross when he saw poor Richard dripping with water. He could be a very annoying boy."

"Yes, that was the one. Richard was a nice boy, but just as slow as Neil at reading and writing. He did tease the girls, though. Did you have any joy with the psychologist, James?"

"Yes, as a matter of fact, Dr Tipper is coming to see both Zachary and Neil next week. There are a few others I would like him to see as well. Maybe we should make up a list before he comes?"

"Good idea, James," said Anne. "I know we mustn't swamp him on his first visit, but we have been without a psychologist here for so long. There are a few of mine I think he should see as well."

"Getting back to the Barn Dance, James. It's not a suit-and-tie affair, you know. Just a country type shirt, jeans and, well, basically, model yourself upon a cowboy. You may not want to go home afterwards as you will want a few drinks. You are welcome to a bed at our place."

"Thank you, Doris. I'll have a word with Tristan."

Tristan too had been so relieved when James had called him with the news that he would be staying on at Prior's Hill. However, he had news of his own. When James got home that evening, he poured James a large drink and the two sat together on the sofa. James could tell that Tristan was bursting to tell him something important.

"I went to the estate agent today, James, after you called, and said that you would be staying at Prior's Hill. I know you didn't want to live in the village in Apple Tree Cottage, so I called in at Bennetts' – you know, the one in the High Street next to Woolworths?"

James nodded. "Go on, I am intrigued. Surprise me, Tris."

"Well, it seems that this place is worth a lot more than I thought. I paid a large deposit into it when I left the Army, and the mortgage is not too bad. If we sell this at a good price, I can repay the mortgage and have quite a lot left over – about five thousand quid, I think. That is if we get a good price for the flat. Mr Bennett is confident about selling it, and says it is in the right place and at a price that new buyers can afford."

"That is good news, Tris. I guess that means the pressure is off for you to get a job and we can find somewhere to rent nearer the school, but not in Prior's Hill, please."

"No, I didn't mean that at all, James. It means that we can buy a place of our own if we want to," grinned Tristan.

"Buy? How would we do that? I don't have much money saved."

"Well, with my deposit we can get a mortgage together. You have a good job, in regular employment and all that, and I will get another job as well. It won't be as well paid I dare say, but with the two jobs and the deposit, we can easily do it. Mr Bennett says he will help us to find somewhere in the Prior's Hill area as well. He has colleagues with estate agencies in the area and he is going to put the word out for us. Think of it, James. A place of our own!"

The news initially stunned James. Until that moment he had assumed that a place of their own would be right out of the question for several years to come. Tristan's news certainly excited him.

"Tris, that's brilliant! Well done! What about you, though? You cannot put in all that money yourself. I cannot match it."

"Don't be silly, Jay. Don't you see? You earn more than me and will probably do so for quite a while until I find something new. That will be your contribution. You will pay more of the mortgage than I can afford, so its quits really, isn't it?"

James suddenly realised the implication of what Tristan was saying to him. He hugged Tristan and held him close.

"You mean that you want us to stay together? That we are a couple and that we will always be together, don't you?" James added slowly.

"Yes, Jay, I do. Since we were children, I have always known that we would be together. I have always loved you."

It was Saturday evening and James' little car drove up the muddy lane to the largest of Sir Toby's barns. The barn was very close to Apple Tree Cottage and James pointed out the pretty little cottage to Tristan as they drove into the yard. This time the farmyard was full of badly parked cars, vans and trucks. They could hear the sound of loud music blaring from one of the barns at the furthest end of the yard.

"It is lovely, Jay, but I am sure we can find something similar, if that's what we want. Maybe a flat in town with no maintenance would be better? Let's keep an open mind and see what turns up."

"Well, if we had lived here, we wouldn't have had far to travel, Tris."

"As it has turned out, I think it is for the best, Jay. You would always have been on call if we lived here. There would be no privacy and you would always be going back to the school. I would probably see even less of you than I do now!"

James and Tristan followed the sound of the loud thumping music and wandered into the Old Barn. It was still quite early, the idea being for the village children to come to the first part of the evening and to dance to recorded pop music. Later, when The Ploughboys arrived it would be the start of the evening for the adults. Already the barn was looking very busy inside, and James recognised many parents and children from the school. There was much laughter and it was clear that everyone was intent upon having a good time. James wandered around the barn talking and laughing with the children from the school. He nodded to many adult faces that he recognised, but couldn't put a name to, as well as engaging in small-talk with parents and Governors that he knew rather better. James felt awkward. Although he was good with children, he always found engaging in small-talk with adults he didn't know tiresome and annoying and he wasn't very good at it. Tristan, on the other hand, was a real people person and could talk to anyone about anything. Everyone found Tristan charming and amusing, and he was always very good to have at a party. James remembered that he had always liked going to parties with Tristan, because it took the pressure off him. He looked around. Tristan had gone off in another direction. James knew why he had done this, because they rarely attended anything as a couple and Tristan would always do his best not to cause embarrassment for James. He spotted Tristan in the far corner talking to Doris and George. He seemed to be enjoying himself and already had a glass in his hand.

"Hello, Mr Young. You look really good. I have never seen you in denim jeans before," giggled Sally. Sally appeared with a group of other giggly girls from Classes 2 and 3, and Sally was clearly the leader. "I like your hat too," she added.

James smiled; it was strange to see his pupils in such grown-up clothes and make-up at such a young age.

"Thank you, Sally. Are you all having a good time?"

"Yes, but the music is boring," complained Sally. "They think we are little kids and have put on this stuff. It is so old."

James smiled. He was rather enjoying the music as he remembered it from a few years earlier. Yes, that was probably why Sally thought it was old-fashioned.

"Maybe they will have something on later for you. Have a word with Mr Driver. He is the DJ this evening."

Sally groaned and James realised that somehow Mr Driver wasn't regarded as modern in her eyes either.

"Will you dance with us later?" enquired Sally.

Oh dear, thought James. This is just what he was dreading.

"Er, yes, probably, if you are still around by then, Sally," nodded James.

"Oh, I will be. We'll get the kids home and I'll come back later with my mum," announced Sally proudly, adding a wink for good measure.

"Evening, James. Are you having a good time?"

"Hello, Jack," replied James, grateful for an excuse to leave the girls. "It is good to see you. This looks quite an event."

"Oh, 'tis, young sir," smiled Jack Sparrow. "Every year we has this. Ever since the war. It started with the VE-Day celebration party and we have had one in here every year since. It brings us villagers together and raises money for the pool."

"My goodness, it is well-established," said James, frowning at the thought of the pool. "So it is really fund-raising for the pool?"

"It is," said Jack proudly. "Expensive things is pools. This helps to pay for the heating and all those chemicals you have to use."

James nodded, remembering that it was time to bring the pool back to life again. It was supposed to be used for three or four months each summer, and getting the thing up and running again was his job next week. He was already dreading it.

"You had some of Sir Toby's cider yet, young sir? I'll get 'ee a glass. Real tasty stuff 'tis."

Jack wandered off towards the bar, returning soon after with two large glasses of a dull yellow liquid. He handed one to James.

"Comes from Sir Toby's own orchards right here in Prior's Hill," said Jack proudly. "Now you taste that and tell me if you ever tasted anything like that before."

James could quite honestly say that he had never tasted anything quite like it ever before. It was smooth and sweet, and still had bits of apples floating on the top. He dreaded to think how it had been made.

"Made the traditional way," nodded Jack, but forgetting to say what the traditional way was.

"It is unique," agreed James. "No, I've never had anything quite like this before."

"I tolds you, young sir, but take my advice, don't you go drinking too much of it. Gives 'ee a right bad headache in the mornin!"

Jack gave James a broad toothy grin and wandered off back to the bar with an empty glass in his hand.

It was a good evening and James thoroughly enjoyed himself more and more as the evening went on, and particularly after he had a glass or two more of cider. From time to time, when he spotted that he was alone, Tristan would come over and keep James company, and introduce him to people that he had met during the evening. Doris came over to join them as well.

"Good band, aren't they, James?" she commented, nodding towards The Ploughboys.

"It is infectious music," agreed James. "I cannot stop myself jigging about and tapping my feet."

"You two coming back with us tonight, James?"

"Thank you, Doris," said James looking over at Tristan. "We will if it's still OK. We've both had a few drinks. I don't think we should drive."

Doris laughed. "Well, we cannot have you being done for speeding again, can we, James? It was bad enough last time, as I remember, with young PC Parker pulling you in."

"Don't remind me, Doris," laughed James, shuddering slightly. "I'll never live that one down, will I? He still teases me about it, you know. 'Young hooligan', he called me!"

"We'll let you know when we are leaving and George can drive us all back to our place. George doesn't drink, which is probably just as well."

"Great, Doris, thanks."

"You coming on the floor with me, gorgeous?" interrupted Tristan, grabbing Doris by the hand and pulling her over to the dance floor. "See ya later, Jay."

James laughed as he saw Tristan leading a reluctant Doris on to the dance floor firmly by the hand. He watched his friend and felt very proud of him.

"That Tristan's quite a one, James," laughed George. "She's not danced since our engagement party, you know. I like dancing, but Doris always says no to me. You two get on well, don't you?"

"Yes, I adore Doris," nodded James. "I don't know what I would have done without her over the last few months."

"I don't mean Doris, James, I mean Tristan. You seem so good together. He's such lively young man. You two seem to work so well together. How long have you known each other?"

"Most of our lives, George. We went to primary school together and always got on."

"Treasure him, James. It is rare that in life that we meet our soulmate so early. Treasure him."

"Mr Young, are you going to dance with me?" Sally appeared as if from nowhere.

"Er, yes, Sally. I did promise, didn't I? Where's your mum?"

"She's over there. She says she is going to ask Mr Tristan to dance with her. I think she fancies him. He's gorgeous, isn't he?"

"Really, Sally," laughed James, not knowing quite what to say.

Fortunately for James, The Ploughboys suddenly announced, 'The Circassion Circle', a dance that James was familiar with. This dance involved everyone holding hands in a big circle and he felt that this was ideal for dancing with Sally. He had taught his class this from the BBC Radio programme a few months earlier.

"There we are, Sally! Do you remember this one?"

Sally groaned; it was not what she had in mind at all. Soon nearly everyone in the barn was holding hands and trying to form one large circle. In the end, there were far too many people wanting to take part and the Master of Ceremonies divided the group into three, still large, circles, but each within the other. James could see that Tristan, Doris and George were in the inner circle whilst he, Sally, Carol and Anne were in the middle one. On the outside circle he caught a glimpse of Emily. He was pleased that she had come to the dance as well.

"No sign of Sir Toby and Lady Lotitia, Anne? Will they arrive later?"

"It's unlikely, James. They used to, but after their son went to America they seemed to lose interest in village events and stopped coming to most of them."

The dance seemed to get faster and faster and by the time it had finished James' head was spinning.

"I don't remember us doing it that fast at school, Sally?" he commented breathlessly.

"No, this was very fast. I liked it. Maybe we could do it like this at school?"

"Maybe Sally, but it's too fast for me. I'm going to have a sit down," said James, making an excuse for a quick get-away from the determined schoolgirl.

James found an empty space on a bale of fresh straw. He sat enjoying the scene in front of him. It had been a wonderful evening and James could not remember the time when he had had such fun, and with Tristan in the same room too. Usually they would never go to school events together for fear of gossip. Since that meeting with Sir Toby and Lady Lotitia last week, James now cared less about what people would think and he was pleased and proud to be at an event with Tristan. He liked the people he was with and he felt at home in their community.

"Mind if I sit down, Mr Young?" came a familiar voice. It was Peggy Skinner.

"Hello, Peggy. Good to see you. Come and sit by me. Have you been here long? Young Carol seems to be enjoying herself."

"Oh, that she is," smiled Peggy. "No, I've just got here. Carol came down with Sally and her mum earlier. I have been working at the big house."

"You been working until now?" exclaimed James, glancing at his watch.

"Well, they are having visitors staying tomorrow. I didn't have to, but I like to help Lady Lotitia when I can. She's been very good to me and my sister and she's not always very well."

James nodded. "Yes, I like them too. They have both been very kind to me and Tristan," he added. "Will they come over to the dance as well later?"

"I doubt it, Mr Young. When they were younger they used to be the life and soul of any party going, but since young Mr Giles left for America they seemed to lose interest. I think they came mainly for him."

"I see," said James. "When did he leave?"

"Oh, it must be about ten years back, maybe more. I can see Mr Giles now. He was a good-looking young man, tall yet well-built. I guess he has turned into a handsome man."

James wished that he had never asked the question and was beginning to feel uncomfortable with the way in which the conversation was going. He thought it was time to leave Peggy, but suddenly spotted young Sally heading towards him.

"Fancy another dance, Mr Young?" she began.

"Thank you, Sally, but I am talking to Mrs Skinner at the moment. Maybe later?"

Sally shrugged and wandered off with Carol at her side.

"I have been watching that friend of yours, Mr Tristan," began Peggy.

James chuckled. He thought it was odd how the villagers who had met him referred to him as 'Mr Tristan'. Tristan certainly had a way of attracting attention, and particularly from older women who always fell for the 'little lost boy' look that

Tristan would cultivate under certain circumstances. He certainly did look handsome in his new pair of tight denim jeans and open-necked checked shirt that they had bought together. Tristan's long, blond, wavy hair seemed to glow like a beacon in the dimly lit barn.

"He is a good-looking, young man, isn't he? It is so strange, but I can picture Mr Giles here all those years ago – the last time that the Peatwhistles were all here together. He was with my nephew, Sam. Mr Tristan looks so much like poor Sam. Lively, good fun and the same cheeky mannerisms too!"

James' heart missed a beat. His attention was drawn back to the conversation at the Manor House a week earlier.

"They were such good friends – just like you and Mr Tristan. They grew up together," she added. "Sam was a brilliant cricketer, they both were. They were both in the village team. He looked so much like Mr Tristan," she mused.

"Maybe it's the cowboy outfit," James said quickly, trying to change the subject.

"Maybe. Sam was a real looker, just like Mr Tristan, and almost as blond. He went to America as well, you know. I don't know if they ever saw each other again. He was killed, you know. His mother never got over it."

James nodded, feeling himself colouring up, as he did when he was embarrassed.

"Giles? What happened?"

"Oh no, not Giles, he is still out there somewhere making lots of money, I shouldn't wonder. No, it was poor Sam who was killed. He had only been there a few months. He went out there with hardly any money and he got a job as a deliveryman, somewhere in New York, I think. I don't know the details, but I gather he got into a fight when someone tried to take his money, and he was stabbed."

James felt very uneasy. A few parts of Peggy's story were not linking up with the story that the Peatwhistles had told him. Maybe it was the drink that was causing the difficulty in understanding what Peggy was saying.

"Rita, my sister, was heartbroken. She couldn't even afford to get the body back. He was buried over there, I think. She's not been the same since."

"Did they catch whoever killed him?"

"No, I don't think so. We tried to find out more through the police, but as we didn't know anyone over there we couldn't do any more."

"That is very sad, Peggy. I am very sorry. Is Sam's mother still alive?"

"Oh yes. The Peatwhistles have been very kind to her. Rita lost her mind over this, and they still pay for her to be looked after in a nursing home over in Castle Point. It's run by nuns, you know. Rita isn't a Catholic, but Lady Lotitia is and they managed to get her in. Sir Toby and Lady Lotitia even paid for Sam's memorial stone too."

James nodded, by now quite lost for what to say to Peggy.

"They even gave me a job and I have been there ever since," laughed Peggy. "Some good came of the tragedy, I suppose. Now please forgive me for rambling on. It's just that seeing your handsome friend triggered a few memories. Now where is Carol? Still with that Sally, I guess."

"Hi, Jay, you having a good time without me?" beamed Tristan, appearing with yet another glass of cider for James. "I've had a proposal!"

"Hello, Trouble, good to see you back again. Go on, who from this time?"

"Young Sally," laughed Tristan. "Says she wants to marry me when she grows up! She says I'm handsome!"

"Tris, be careful. She's only eleven and you'll have me struck off," replied James, looking very worried.

"Don't worry, I just told her she couldn't afford to keep me in the style to which I have grown accustomed!" giggled Tristan. "Come on, Jay, dance with me!"

"You didn't? You're drunk, Tris! No, you know I cannot dance with you in public. Just you wait until I get you home," he laughed at his friend, now realising that he was being wound up.

"Mmm, I shall look forward to that," whispered Tristan seductively into James' ear.

James and Tristan awoke late the following morning at Doris and George's home. Both had headaches, and were feeling the results of too much of Sir Toby's cider. They had a quick mug of coffee before saying goodbye to Doris, and George drove them back to Prior's Hill to collect their car from the farmyard. The balloons, banners, trestle-tables and chairs were all still there from the night before. "It will take a small army of villagers to clear up all that rubbish," thought James.

On their way back to Bridgehampton, James told Tristan all about his conversation with Peggy.

"It just doesn't tie up. First, I'm told that both boys died from AIDS and yet the villagers are told that Giles is still alive. Then I find out that Sam was living in another city altogether, and that he was stabbed. Apparently, Sam's body went missing."

"You may have misunderstood the conversation, Jay. We both had a fair bit to drink last night, remember?" replied Tristan.

"Maybe, but I wasn't off my head either. I knew what was going on and I know what Peggy said. This bothers me, Jay. Is Giles alive or dead? Is it some great cover-up? Maybe we have stumbled upon something really important? Maybe a crime has been committed!" persisted James.

"Come on, Jay, don't get too dramatic about it all. I'm sure there is a sensible explanation. If you are that worried, just go and have a word with the Peatwhistles. You seem to be getting on alright with them now. Just ask them. I am sure it is nothing to worry about."

Tristan sighed. He knew that James would have to have an answer, and that he would have to have an answer quickly. Although Tristan didn't want to add to James' concerns, he too thought that it all sounded very strange.

Chapter 17

The Rose Garden

James had serious matters on his mind. After talking the problem over with Tristan, he decided that he would go and speak to Lady Lotitia, alone preferably. Tristan had offered to come with him, but in view of the supposed similarity between Sam Rivers and Tristan, James decided that it would be better not to stir up old memories too much. He was unsure of how Lady Lotitia would take to this interference, as she was always, even at the best of times, highly unpredictable. James decided to ensure that he was with her before eleven, judging correctly that he stood a good chance of seeing her sober at that time of the morning. He also chose a Thursday morning, knowing it was Peggy's morning off, and that there would be little chance of interruption. He pulled at the heavy doorbell of the Manor House. Eventually, the door opened and Lady Lotitia appeared.

"Good morning, James," she said breezily. "What can I do for you this fine morning?"

She led James into the breakfast-room where, this time, the breakfast items had been cleared away and a young servant girl was busily polishing the already highly polished table.

"That will be all, Sylvia, thank you. Coffee, James?"

James was waved to a chair next to the open patio doors. James noticed that the open fire was burning in the fireplace, despite the heat from the morning sun.

"Did you enjoy the Barn Dance, James? I heard that you were there. Peggy told me."

"Yes, it was a wonderful village event, thank you. I wondered if we would see you both there."

"No, we rarely go to village functions nowadays. I find them so tedious. What? We meet the same people that we meet every day, so what's the point?"

James decided not to argue the point.

"I am sorry to disturb you, but it was the Barn Dance that I wanted to talk to you about. You were very kind in telling me all about Giles and Sam last week. It is a very sad story and, to be honest, it has been on my mind ever since you told me."

Lady Lotitia stared at James with her usual fixed, unsmiling glare.

"Well?"

"It's just that at the Barn Dance, someone commented that Sam looked very much like Tristan. One thing led to another, and they said that Sam was stabbed in a mugging incident in New York. I must reassure you that, as promised, I have said nothing to anyone about what you told me. However, I think you ought to know that they said that Sam's body was never returned home. It seems very strange."

"And who was this person, James?"

"I cannot say. That too was told to me in confidence. It's just that the story you told me doesn't tie up."

Lady Lotitia kept her eyes firmly fixed upon James. James was feeling very uncomfortable at this point and wished that he had not raised the issue.

"Are you calling me a liar?"

"Certainly not. It's just... it's just that I thought you may be a little confused and may have forgotten something, or something else may have happened."

"How dare you question me in this way? I have forgotten nothing. What right have you to challenge me like this?" snapped Lady Lotitia.

There was a tap at the door, and Sylvia entered with a large pot of coffee. There was silence as the young maid carefully poured out two cups of steaming hot coffee and offered James milk and sugar.

"No, just as it comes for me, thank you," said James, grateful for the interruption.

The pair sat in silence until Sylvia had left the room and closed the door.

"Come with me," ordered Lady Lotitia, as she swept to the open patio doors leading to the rose garden. "Just come with me. I have told you this much, you may as well know the rest."

Lady Lotitia strode into the rose garden. It was certainly a beautiful sight. Although not a gardener himself, James could fully appreciate the beauty of what he saw. An array of statues, water features and lush green shrubs mingled with roses of every shade imaginable. The perfume from the roses was heady and James realised that this garden was a creation more of love than of duty.

"Over here," Lady Lotitia commanded, pointing to two large Greek statues in the centre of a circle full of deep-blood-red roses.

"They are here, in the centre beneath the statues." Lady Lotitia spoke softly and almost gently to James.

"So this is where you buried Giles' and Sam's ashes? Right here in the rose garden, and not in the family plot," whispered James with reverence.

Lady Lotitia and James sat side by side on a beautiful white wrought iron bench opposite the poignant memorial.

"I... I still don't understand," began James.

"Well, it's quite simple, really," replied Lady Lotitia breezily, her eyes fixed upon James. "We buried young Sam's ashes here as well as Giles'. It is true that he died from AIDS and not from an attack, as you were told. We told Rita and others that story about the stabbing, as that was best for all to understand and, above all, it caused least embarrassment. There was no one else left in Sam's family to care anyway. He was such a handsome boy, and I now know that Giles loved him deeply. He told me so in the many letters that he sent when he was away and was taken ill. He wouldn't let us go to see him, but he always wrote me letters and one day they stopped coming."

Lady Lotitia paused and blew her nose in the tiny handkerchief that she had retrieved from her sleeve.

She continued, "Toby and I were actually very fond of the boy as well. Sam was always here playing in the garden with Giles when he came home from boarding school. Sam went to your school, James. As they grew older, they played a lot of cricket and were both in the village team. They were always together when they were here. Inseparable."

James sat looking at the two statues in the midst of the garden of blood-red roses and he could feel tears welling up in his eyes too. He swallowed hard and did not reply, but for once he could feel a little of Lady Lotitia's deep pain.

"We built this garden of remembrance so that the boys could be together in death. Maybe one day we shall be forgiven for the appalling way that we treated them. Meanwhile, let us hope and pray that they rest in peace."

"Thank you for telling me the story and letting me share some of your pain, but tell me, why have you told me all this? You don't know me that well, Lady Lotitia."

"Well, James, I think it may be that you and your friend remind Toby and I so much of Giles and Sam. We made a dreadful mistake with them and we nearly made the same mistake with you. I hope that we prevented it just in time. We'll say no more about it, except one thing."

James nodded and he shook Lady Lotitia's outstretched hand. For once, he felt almost a warmth in the words that this much misunderstood woman was saying.

"Just love one another, James, and be true to yourselves. Do that for me, please."

"Bad news, James," exclaimed Doris, as she entered James' classroom and caught him stapling some of the children's paintings to the wall. It was lunchtime and the children were playing outside.

"What is it, Doris? Don't tell me Dr Tipper has cancelled yet again."

"No, not as far as I know, but Miss Flickersmill's office has just called. Apparently, we are due for a County inspection next week."

"Oh, no," groaned James. "That's all I need. I knew that wretched woman had it in for me the last time she came. I knew she would be back, but maybe not this quickly."

"It's going to focus upon the infants, although there will be some coverage of the other classes as well. It will last for one day."

"When is it?" enquired James, now stapling the walls harder than ever.

"Monday morning. She will be here in time for the school assembly and would like to speak to the staff at lunchtime, and you after school, alone. It's not just you, James. Apparently, they are working through all the schools in the county, as there will soon be a lot of changes coming and they want to know what's going on in the schools on their patch."

"Hmm. Damn, damn, damn!" exclaimed James, stapling the wall with venom. "Miss Flickersmill, and the swimming pool to be sorted next week!"

It was Monday morning. James was in school early preparing for the inspection of the infant class. Tristan had talked him out of going into school over the weekend, and at the time James had reluctantly agreed with him.

"If it's not right, I need to know. I just cannot do any more," he had said on Saturday evening after a few drinks at their local.

James was now regretting not having spent time in school over the weekend. Although he was well prepared for the week as usual, he was concerned that he had spent little time preparing the school in general and Emily in particular.

"Miss Flickersmill says that it is the Early Years that she is interested in, but she is coming with Paul Jones, so I guess he will be taking a general look at the other classes as well," James had announced to the staff at Friday lunchtime.

James could hear the familiar sound of Doris running up the steps to the classroom.

"Good morning, James, you are an early bird this morning!"

"Good morning, Doris. Did you have a good weekend? I hope you are on top form this morning."

"Bad news, I'm afraid, James. I don't like to tell you this, but Emily has just phoned in sick."

"She's what?" exclaimed James. "I need her in today of all days!"

"She says she's been ill over the weekend. Look, shall I call Mrs Storey and see if she's free?"

"This is a nightmare," muttered James. "Wretched woman is never around when I want her. Yes, see if Sue Storey is still alive and breathing. She's never very lively, but I guess it's needs must, Doris."

Doris laughed. "She's not that bad, is she?"

"Well, the only reason that the infants are quiet when she is in here is that she bribes them with sweets. I caught her last time she was in here. She brought in a huge bag of toffees. The poor kids couldn't talk because their teeth were stuck together! So much for our dental hygiene policy!"

"You are joking, James? I'm never too sure with you," laughed Doris.

"You just check her basket when she arrives. I can guarantee that she has a huge bag of toffees with her. Goodness knows what the inspectors will say."

"Who is taking assembly?"

"I am, Doris. It's all about the Bible story, 'Fishers of Men'. I heard that Miss F is an atheist! I thought it would annoy her to start with and then it can only get better."

"James, you on a suicide mission or something?" laughed Doris. "Let me know if you need me. Good luck!"

"If you could just help me to dress them, Doris, please?" asked James. "The dressing-up clothes are just over there. I had to buy twelve tea-towels on Saturday as I ran out!"

As usual, James was understating what he had already planned in detail. The infant children arrived in the school hall, dressed in a motley array of tea-towels, dressing-gowns and all manner of props to represent the important Biblical story that they were retelling though mime. James told the story beautifully, and the children were attentive. His class played their parts to perfection and the assembled group of doting parents, inspectors, teachers and children clapped heartily when the performance had finished.

James was delighted that it had gone well, and it was only Ben Stringer who had let the side down as chief fisherman when he announced, in mid-performance, that he had to go to the toilet. The assembled crowd of adults roared with laughter, and James heard from Anne later that most thought it was part of the ongoing drama anyway.

"Parents can be so forgiving when their own children are performing," thought James.

The assembly having finished, the children, accompanied by an unsmiling Miss Flickersmill and James, walked back to their classroom.

"Good morning, James. An interesting assembly, but tell me, don't you think you are putting these children under enormous pressure by asking them to lead school assembly when they are so young?"

"No, I don't agree, Miss Flickersmill, otherwise I wouldn't do it. We are part of a family here and the children, having watched the older children over the last few months, know that one day it will be their turn. They have been looking forward to it. I think it is good for them. Did you see anyone upset?"

"Well, I did see one young boy who was so upset that he had to go to the toilet in a hurry."

"Ben has a bladder infection, Miss Flickersmill. That is why he had to go to the toilet quickly. If you doubt me, just ask him what he thought of taking part in it. I think you may be surprised at his answer."

James was determined to behave as normally with an inspector in the classroom as he would at any other time, and he tried to ensure that his day also ran as usual. The children, of course, had other ideas and rather liking the idea of another adult in the classroom to talk and show off to, took the opportunity to interact with Miss Flickersmill as much as they could get away with. In fairness to Miss Flickersmill, James was impressed to see that she was very good with young children. She listened carefully to them and helped them where she could, but James couldn't help but notice that she was continually writing notes on her clipboard and entering a series of small, neat ticks in boxes inside her folder. It was all very off-putting.

"What's yer name." enquired Danny Small.

"Miss Flickersmill, what's your name?" asked Miss Flickersmill pleasantly to the freckly boy picking his nose in front of her.

"I like your beads," said Danny, grabbing Miss Flickersmill's pearls rather tightly around her neck.

"Well, thank you. They are rather shiny little things, aren't they?" replied a flustered Miss Flickersmill, gently removing the freckly boy's fingers from her neck and deciding to get up from her seat and move hastily away from Danny's clutches.

"Tell me about your lovely picture."

"It ain't lovely, I dropped it. I want another bit of paper."

"Well, if you say 'please', I'm sure Mr Young will give you another. That's a lovely pond that you've painted.

"It ain't a pond. It's an ear."

Fortunately, James spotted Danny tormenting Miss Flickersmill and suddenly feeling sorry for her, decided that the poor woman had had enough and went to rescue her from the persistent Danny.

"Maybe you would like to see what the sand-tray children are making this morning, Miss Flickersmill?"

Miss Flickersmill smiled benignly, grateful to James for allowing her to escape from Danny's attempts to throttle her with her own necklace.

"Good morning, children," beamed Miss Flickersmill to the sand-tray children, who were busily weighing, moulding, tracing sand letters and having great fun in the sand tray that James had recently bought for them.

"Sarah Lou," whispered a tiny girl in Miss Flickersmill's ear.

"Hello, Sarah Lou, it is good to see you. Tell me what you are doing."

"Sarah Lou," said Sarah Lou, whispering more loudly in Miss Flickersmill's ear.

"Yes, I know your name is Sarah Lou, dear. Such a pretty name too. Do tell me what you are doing?"

"Sarah Lou," shouted the small girl, pointing to the door. Suddenly, she burst into tears and a flood of liquid appeared around her dress and trickled rapidly down her leg.

"My goodness, Sarah Lou, you should have told me," exclaimed a flustered Miss Flickersmill. "I think you need to go to the toilet quickly, my dear."

"She did," said Danny, appearing from the painting area. "Sarah kept telling you she wanted to go to the loo. I heard her," he announced with pride.

During a relatively quiet moment, Miss Flickersmill sidled up to have a quiet word with James.

"Tell me, Mr Young. Why was that small boy, Danny, I think he is called, painting an ear? It looked very much like a pond to me."

"Oh, it probably was an ear, Miss Flickersmill. Danny's father went to prison last week for biting off someone's ear during a pub fight. Just watch he doesn't grab you by the neck, though. He tends to do that when he's angry, just like his father, sadly."

It was a shaken and chastened Miss Flickersmill that left James' room at lunchtime, together with her sheaf of notes. James spotted her leaving the school premises before he could speak to her and she was seen heading towards the village pub, accompanied by Paul Jones.

"So much for the planned meeting at lunchtime," muttered James to himself. "What a complete waste of time."

After lunch, Miss Flickersmill and Paul Jones reappeared.

"Sorry about that, James," grinned Paul. "I think your children gave Jean quite a rough time this morning. She is a bit of a delicate flower, but she really knows her stuff, James. I know you don't suffer fools, and I can guess what you may be thinking. A word of advice from a friend, James. Just give her a chance. She could be a useful ally, but a very bad enemy. She has the ear of Miss Partridge, the Director of Education, and I know that she is very impressed with Jean."

"Thank you, Paul. Of course, I will give her a chance. It's just that I have had so much to do here, with little in the way of resources, and I could really do with some practical help to get things moving. I know what needs doing. Just help me to do it, please, Paul."

"Well," said Paul, slapping James on the back. "My reasoning was that if she had a bad time, you did too. I thought we would give you all a break at lunchtime. It will be a light touch this afternoon and, no, we won't be looking at Class 3. I can imagine what you would say if we did."

James nodded, pleased with the reassurance that Paul had given.

"By the way, James, why are your Governors giving me such a hard time about another classroom assistant? You have one, so why do you need another in a school of this size? Are you putting them up to this?"

"Certainly not! We don't have even one classroom assistant, Paul!" exclaimed James. "That is why the Governors are making a fuss. We desperately need one in the infant classroom. Look what happened a few weeks ago when poor Vanessa died. I now have a child requiring psychotherapy as a result."

James had learned long ago the art of exaggeration from Marion, in cases of emergency, and he deemed this to be one of those occasions.

"I see," reflected Paul slowly. "You see, James, you have always been entitled to one classroom assistant and I don't understand why you have never had one appointed here."

"You mean we have been without an extra member of staff to which we are entitled for all this time, and no one has ever thought to tell us? That is ridiculous, Paul."

"I quite agree, James, I quite agree. I suggest that you appoint one sooner rather than later."

It was a very happy James who floated back into his classroom that afternoon. There was so much he could do with a classroom assistant in Class 1. There might even be time for whoever was appointed to work with children throughout the school who have special needs, such as Neil. His head was buzzing with ideas.

"Mr Young?"

"Yes, Polly?"

"Why are you smiling?"

"I feel happy, Polly."

"Is that because of us, Mr Young?"

"Yes, Polly. It most certainly is."

The afternoon went quickly and James was soon walking out of the classroom with a line of infant children trailing after him into the playground. It was the end of yet another busy day, but he still had the interview with Miss Flickersmill to come.

"How did you get on, Anne?" he asked as his deputy walked towards him, smiling.

"She's not a bad old stick, is she?" laughed Anne. "She was a bit serious at first and then I told her about you removing the stage. I don't think she believed me. She sat with her mouth open when I told her. I think she approved, James."

"Well done, Anne," beamed James. "I owe you one."

"I know you have your interview with her now. Just be careful how you handle her, James. I don't think she likes men."

James sat in his office facing Miss Flickersmill. Paul Jones sat at her side, but it was clear from Paul's demeanour that Miss Flickersmill was firmly in charge of the interview and final feedback.

"Well, James," she began. "Thank you for your hospitality today. I have mostly enjoyed being in your school, although I have to say that some of your children are challenging."

"How do you mean?" responded James, feeling the hairs on the back of his neck standing to attention in the childrens' defence. "These are some of the nicest and most straightforward children that I have taught."

"That is as may be," replied Miss Flickersmill coldly, "but I see them as challenging and requiring more help than they are getting now. One example of this was that I saw at least four children in your class this morning who have special needs. They require additional support."

"Well, I wouldn't argue with that," agreed James. "We need someone else in the classroom who can give that additional support."

"Quite so, and this leads me to the next point. The equipment that you are using is grossly out of date. Some of the reading material would be better placed in a museum than a modern-day classroom."

James nodded. "Again, I agree. I inherited a school with no money and although we have done our best to borrow from the library and other schools, it is not enough."

"However, I am most impressed with the materials that you have made for the children to use, James. They are imaginative and well constructed. I don't feel that your children are suffering in any way because of the individual materials that you have made for them. Well done!"

James appreciated her kind words. He had received few professional compliments as head teacher, and he glowed within at this favourable comment.

"I also like the way that you are involving parents with the learning process. You are sending home books and word tins, and you are also bringing parents into school to work with their children. Again, very well done."

James recalled the comment from Lady Lotitia at his first interview relating to cheap teachers. He caught Paul's eye, who winked and smiled broadly at James. Yes, Paul had remembered the comment as well.

Miss Flickersmill read the remainder of the report relating to Class 1, and finally closed her notepad and smiled.

"James, your practice as an infant teacher is outstanding. Rarely have I seen men able to work in the same way as you. I would like you now to develop what you have started. I will be making a special development allowance of one thousand pounds immediately available to you. Secondly, I know that Paul has spoken to you about immediately recruiting a classroom assistant. I would suggest that you consider a trained nursery nurse in view of all the toilet problems that your children seem to have."

She smiled again. Not a warm smile, but a smile nevertheless.

"Thirdly," she continued, "I would like you to have some time made available to you so that you can work alongside Anne as well. She is not particularly good, but I suspect that she is a willing work-horse and may get better if you work with her, and give her the support that she needs to get better."

"Anne is a good teacher," protested James. "She just needs greater confidence, support and decent equipment."

"Quite so," glared Miss Flickersmill, not appreciating the interruption to her carefully planned presentation. "Well, as her head teacher, you must make those resources available to her right away, don't you agree?"

James nodded, whilst biting his lip.

"Finally, I would like to invite you to attend my monthly meeting of Early Years' teachers. You will be the only male and so it could be quite a challenge, James. However, it will help you. I believe that they are known locally as the Flickersmill Babes!" She smiled at her own joke.

Paul could contain himself no longer and guffawed loudly with laughter.

"Well, that's a new one, James. I shall enjoy telling my colleagues that you are now one of the élite Flickersmill Babes. Er, so sorry, Jean," said Paul glancing apologetically at his colleague, who was glaring coldly at him.

"A delight to have met you. Thank you again."

Miss Flickersmill held out her hand and James felt that he really ought to kneel and kiss it. He just didn't dare to look at Paul Jones again, because he knew that Paul might well be thinking the same.

The trio walked to the gate. They had a general conversation about the school building, the village, and its community.

"Such a charming little place. I guess you don't get much trouble from these kind of people," said Miss Flickersmill as she reached the gate.

James didn't even consider telling the inspectors what exactly had been happening in recent months.

He smiled and said diplomatically, "Yes, in the main, they are very supportive of the school."

"Quite so," agreed Miss Flickersmill, whilst Paul Jones looked heavenwards for assistance in controlling his pent-up laughter.

"Oh, by the way, James, well done in removing that dreadful stage. Very well done!"

James almost floated rather than drove home to Tristan that evening. He bounced in carrying a large bottle of sparkling wine.

"Hey, someone's in a good mood," shouted Tristan, as he appeared out of the kitchen and gave James a big hug. "You had a good day, I see."

"Brilliant," said James, laughing, and for the next half hour or so, over a glass or two of wine, James entertained Tristan with all the goings-on of the day.

When he had finished, Tristan looked admiringly at his friend.

"James, you do so deserve this. I am so very proud of you, and I love you very much," he said, giving James a big kiss.

"I love you too," said James, "and there is more!"

"Go on."

"The old girl has asked me to join her élite club of Early Years' teachers. It's for the rising stars in Early Years' education in the area," James joked.

"Brilliant."

"They are known locally as the Flickersmill Babes," announced James proudly. As soon as the words left his lips, James immediately regretted telling Tristan this part of the story. It was to be a while before Tristan stopped calling him 'Babe' with great glee, and a twinkle in his eye!

Chapter 18

Swimming Pool Blues

The issue of the swimming pool had to be tackled eventually. James knew that. However, after all the furore over the school stage, James was diplomatically biding his time and waiting for the right moment to consider his next step. After scrutinising the school accounts with Doris, it soon became very clear to James that the swimming pool was a real drain, literally, upon precious resources. All the chemicals, replacement liner, swimming pool cover, as well as heating, had been paid from school funds in recent years. Discussions with Sir Toby and George Cole revealed that the pool was an odd combination of Local Education Authority, village and private funding. The pool was built on a plot of land at the edge of the school grounds and had been given to the school some twenty-five years earlier by Sir Toby's father. The pool itself had been paid for by village fund-raising as well as a generous cash donation from the Peatwhistle family. The school, in turn, had paid for ongoing maintenance, including the heating bill that seemed excessively high during the previous year.

In theory, the Prior's Hill villagers paid for a season ticket that gave them ready and free access to the pool whenever they wished after school. All they had to do was to collect a key to the gate from Jenny in the village Post Office or from her cottage when the Post Office was closed. However, a quick calculation soon drew Doris and James to the same conclusion – an annual season ticket of five pounds per adult and three pounds for children went nowhere towards the cost of providing the facility – the rest was being covered from the school's own funds. In short, James felt that he was dealing with a case of misuse of the public funds that were allocated to the school.

"If this ever came up in an audit, Doris, we would be for the high jump!" exclaimed James one morning, after he had scrutinised a detailed income and expenditure sheet that Doris had prepared for him the previous day.

"Well, I suppose we could try putting the subscriptions up? That may cause a problem though," Doris added as an afterthought. "I remember Peter Wright tried to do that just after he came. It caused a lot of problems and people wouldn't pay it."

"Well, they will or they will lose it," snapped James.

Doris smiled, confirming to herself once again that James Young was a very different character to his predecessor.

"I am also concerned about safety," continued James. "Do you know that anyone can just collect the key from the Post Office and come on to school grounds and use the pool? There is no one on duty. There should be a qualified life-guard around, according to County Hall guidelines. Besides, there could be dozens of copies of the gate key cut by now."

Doris nodded. "Yes, and we have had some vandalism during previous summer holidays. It was a group of local lads that used the swimming net pole as a punt for the canoe that they tried out in the pool. It was that that tore the lining. It had to be replaced. Peter was livid."

"Yes, and that cost a fortune to sort out," exploded James. "Do you know that when I was working in school last Saturday, a group of girls arrived to swim in the pool? There was no adult with them. The eldest was about thirteen or fourteen, I guess, and the youngest was a toddler. They were from the village, I think, but none of them came here. I sent them away and told them to come back with an adult when the pool is ready. The older one swore at me when she got to the gate!"

"I expect that was Alison Park and her sisters," explained Doris. "No excuse for that kind of behaviour at all. Anyway, Colin Park would be the first to create a fuss if one of his girls had an accident in the pool."

"That's only part of the problem, Doris. You know who has to maintain the pool, don't you?"

Doris nodded; she did know. It was James' job.

No one had mentioned it before and James had always assumed that the caretaker would be responsible for maintaining the swimming pool, but Angela had other ideas.

"I don't do pools," she announced one morning after James had tentatively raised the thorny issue. "It's your job. Peter always did it morning and night. It's quite easy, and I can show you what to do."

James had many talents and skills, but checking pool chemicals, cleaning and maintenance were not on the list.

A few weeks later James found himself standing with Angela at the edge of a very murky-looking swimming pool early one morning, wearing a blue overall and with a swimming pool test kit before him.

"Best to wear overalls, James," announced Angela, brightly. "You are dealing with some nasty chemicals here – acid and things. This stuff could easily burn a hole in your jacket and trousers if you are not careful."

Angela then proceeded to explain all about acid and pH levels and how if one reading was down he was to add a little of this and if the colour changed to pink he would need to add a little of that. She talked confidently about skimming the pool for debris and cleaning down the sides of the pool with a brush, as well as using a 'Hoover' to vacuum the bottom of the pool. She went on to explain that this process would need to be carried out twice each day – morning and evening, and maybe even lunchtimes if the weather was hot. James nodded, but he was totally confused by the explanations and instructions thrown at him.

"Well, that's as may be during term-time, but what happens at weekends and in August? I am certainly not driving over here twice a day to do the pool check."

"Oh, I do it then," replied Angela breezily, handing James the pool skimmer.

"Well, I am sure I have missed the point somewhere along the line, Angela," began James. "If you look after the pool during the holidays, why can't you do it during term-time as well?"

"Oh, I'm far too busy during term-time, James. Besides, I get paid extra for doing it during the holidays."

James decided not to pursue the conversation further. He felt far too angry, but he had every intention of raising the issue with the school Governors at their next meeting.

The week before the pool was due to open was a busy one. James had arranged with Simon Tucker from the Parent-Teacher Association to gather a group of volunteer parents to clean the pool thoroughly before the start of the new season. James was horrified, but not surprised, to learn that the water was never emptied from year to year on the grounds that it would be far too expensive. Simon, who now seemed to have forgiven James over the school stage incident, added helpfully, "I guess changing the water doesn't matter really. All those chemicals soon kill off any germs that may be in there. It will keep your water bill low."

James had forgotten to add the cost of water in his calculations. The question of what went into the pool water was the main reason why James hated public swimming pools so much. He was convinced that over a number of years, a school swimming pool, particularly when used by young children, contained nothing more than pure urine. He was also convinced that all the chemicals that were added were not good for the body either.

Simon laughed when he heard James' theory.

"Well, it didn't do me any harm, James. I swam in this pool for six years of my life. Maybe a drop of urine does us good!"

James was pleased with the group of six volunteer parents that Simon brought along to help on the following Saturday morning. They were a motley group and although James knew most of them, they all looked so different in their flowery shorts or swimming trunks. Simon explained that usually the group worked in the pool first to clean and vacuum away the debris. It was only after this had been done that more water was added and the first batch of chemicals poured in. The group spent the day cleaning the sides, scrubbing and painting. It had quite a party atmosphere, with the radio blaring out pop music and the comings and goings of other villagers to watch and sometimes help. It was clear that it was an annual ritual and village event, and Doris had thoughtfully warned James the day before that all he had to do was to provide a large box of wine and an endless supply of cakes and biscuits.

"Well, James, it's over to you now," beamed Simon, as he handed James the keys to the swimming pool store later in the afternoon.

"All you have to do is to add the chemicals and it should be ready for the children to use from Monday. I think we shall soon need another bubble cover though. This one seems to have rotted through again."

“I thought we bought one for it last year,” said James, looking worried. “It cost a lot of money. Surely we don’t need another so soon?”

“Well, they only last a short time, but I think you will find that Peter only got around to paying for the last one a couple of years or so after it was fitted. I think he lost the bill – by mistake of course, if you see what I mean.” Simon gave James a broad wink and laughed knowingly.

James nodded, making a mental note to ask Doris what had happened. Was this some deliberate ploy of his predecessor to try to avoid paying the bill on time? He certainly would not be going down that route.

“Not sure how long the boiler and pump will last either. I know the PTA picked up the bill for a major repair a couple of years ago. It’s not going to last much longer.”

“How much is that likely to cost?” enquired James, looking worried.

“I doubt there will be much change from five thousand for the boiler. The pump needs looking at as well. I guess it is all due for a major renovation.”

“Will the PTA pay for that?”

Simon laughed. “You must be kidding, James. We only raise a few hundred each year, mainly from the Barn Dance, so that will have to be paid by the school, I’m afraid. Unless you can get Sir Toby to cough up, that is.”

The beginning of the new week saw James arriving at school even earlier than usual to complete his swimming pool duties. He donned his overalls and then made his way to the pool. After the big clean on Saturday and the ‘shock dose’ of chlorine that Simon had added, James was impressed that the water now looked very clear; indeed, it looked sparkling. James began to think that, yes, it might be possible to use the pool right away, but he would need to check it first. He opened his notebook and read once again a summary of all that Angela and Simon had told him. He took a sample of the pool water, added the required tablets and watched the colour change to match a strip of colours on the side of his test kit. No, it looked as if he had to add more acid to get the balance right. James opened the pool store and removed the lid from one of the large drums of chemicals and immediately closed the lid again. As soon as he opened the lid he felt a burning sensation in his nose, eyes and mouth. It was the fumes from the acid.

James hadn't realised that the chemical was so noxious, even in its dry state. He made up his mind to buy some gloves on the way home, as well as goggles and a facemask for the future. Meanwhile, he tried again, lifting off the lid very gently before he poured a substantial dose into the pool. He checked the temperature. It was still cold – far too cold for the children to swim in. He would have to leave the pool for another day.

Each morning that week, James went through the same tedious and time-consuming process. He was now fully kitted out with gloves, mask and goggles, and by the end of the week he no longer had to add any chemicals, although the temperature of the pool was still cooler than he would have liked. However, he was already getting a lot of pressure from pupils, parents and indeed the staff about when they could start swimming.

"I just don't understand why it cannot be used yet. The season will be over before we can start using it," began Emily one morning.

"As I told you, it is still far too cold," replied James, getting tired of Emily's constant complaints.

"Well, I think you are treating them like softies," sniffed Emily. "They will warm up once they have been in for a few minutes. Children don't notice the cold."

"That's as may be, but I have also had a problem getting the chemicals right. I have never done it before, Emily. Maybe I should have asked you to do it instead of me?"

"That's not my job. I am only here part-time and besides, I have to prepare when I get to school."

"What do you think I have to do, Emily?" replied James quietly.

Emily didn't answer, but strode out of the staff-room, slamming the door behind her.

"That's a fair point, James. She is supposed to be in charge of PE. She used to do it when Peter was here. I don't see why you should have to do the job every day. You have enough to do," said Doris. "What about a rota? I am happy to give it a go."

"Well, thank you, Doris. I wouldn't mind some help from time to time," agreed James. "Maybe we could talk about it at the staff meeting?"

By Friday, James had had enough. Parents were continually asking him about the pool whenever he appeared in the playground and, indeed, the children were also very excited about when their swimming lessons were due to start. James had a brief word with the staff and they all agreed that swimming would start for Classes 2 and 3 that afternoon, but that the infant swimming would start the following week, when it was warmer and when parents had been recruited to go in the pool with their children. It was only Emily who disagreed with James' suggestion.

"I think it is ridiculous for parents to go in with their children, James. We have never done that before. Just let them splash about a bit and give them some floats. They will soon learn. 'Sink or swim' is the best way. Better that than parents in the way."

"Thank you for your opinion, Emily. I completely disagree with you. The infant children will not be going in the pool without adults, and that is final."

After lunch on that sunny afternoon, even James, who was not a great admirer of swimming pools, had to admit that it was a wonderful experience for the children. He watched as Emily took the first group of junior children into the pool. A number of children shrieked and shivered as they first got into the water, but after a few minutes most were soon enjoying floating, swimming and splashing. Indeed, James was surprised at how many of the older children could swim. Most were confident swimmers and James had to admit that this was no doubt due to annual lessons in the pool.

Later, when they had finished their lesson, James took the older children back to their classroom for a music lesson, whilst Emily concentrated upon the non- and weaker swimmers. Emily reappeared just before the end-of-school bell with a group of happy and talkative children. The lesson had obviously been a great success.

"Thank you, Emily," said James, as Emily reappeared in the classroom. "The afternoon seems to have gone very well. The children have enjoyed it."

Even Emily seemed pleased with herself.

"Yes, they did. The pool was lovely this afternoon. I wouldn't mind going in myself after school."

James shuddered at the thought.

Swimming lessons at Prior's Hill became the focus of the next few weeks. James, together with Simon from the PTA, were both putting together plans for the annual swimming gala which, James learned, was a major event in the village. Even Sir Toby and Lady Lotitia usually attended this event and gave out the collection of silver cups that were dumped in a box in James' office. James made a mental note to get the cups polished and displayed properly before the event, but it had been the least of his priorities so far.

The junior classes managed to swim every day although, for the infants, it was usually twice during the week, assuming that James could find enough volunteers. Even the youngest and most timid of children happily went into the pool and James was careful to ensure that at least three adults were also in the pool with the children. He had also bought a number of new attractive floats and equipment for the pool and the children enjoyed playing with these, even though Emily had dismissed them haughtily as "just beach toys."

"That's as may be, Emily, but I want the children to look forward to and enjoy their experience in the pool. After that, we can focus on teaching them to swim. First of all, we need them to be happy and confident."

As far as James could see, the only problem was after-school use of the pool. Occasionally he had found empty beer cans and bottles at the side of the pool on Monday mornings. The main problem was litter, crisp and sweet packets left around the pool, and sometimes left floating in the water. There had been no major damage and for this James was grateful. However, he was concerned about the lack of supervision and the possibility of vandalism to the school and its grounds by youngsters other than local teenagers. He had mentioned this to Sir Toby during one of his regular meetings, but Sir Toby dismissed this as unlikely.

"We get very little trouble here, James. It would be such a pity to spoil the enjoyment of the majority by the thoughtless actions of the few, don't you think?"

Tristan had surprised James by suggesting that he join James at the school one evening for a private swim.

“It could be fun, Jay,” grinned Tristan, as they were relaxing together after their meal one evening. “It has been a hot few days and I would love to cool down in a pool. Maybe I could come over one afternoon when school has finished, or maybe we could drive over together at the weekend?”

James pretended to be shocked. “We cannot possibly do that in the school pool, Tris. I don’t allow skinny-dipping by the staff or their partners. What would the children say, and what if Emily should turn up? She would have a fit!”

“Forget that old bag, James!” whispered Tristan in James’ ear. “I bought some new Speedos especially for the occasion. Would you like me to put them on?”

James eventually gave up and one warm Saturday evening they drove to the school to enjoy the pool. It had been a hot and sticky day in Bridgehampton, and they were pleased to get out of the city and feel the wind in their faces. James and Tristan arrived at the pool with Tristan carrying a large car rug, a cool box and a large sports bag.

“We are having a picnic, Mr Headmaster. I have prepared a special treat for us and we are going to enjoy it. You go ahead as I have something to do first. Don’t ask questions.”

James laughed and went round to the swimming pool gate and unlocked it. The pool looked good in the setting sun and James sat on one of the picnic tables at the side waiting for Tristan. It seemed an odd place to spend a Saturday evening. When Tristan came back, he removed his outer clothing, and James noticed that Tristan was sporting his new blue-and-white Speedos. James had to admit that Tristan looked fabulous in them. Tristan could swim like a fish and immediately dived into the pool. He enjoyed tormenting James about his dislike of swimming pools and splashed him.

“Come on in,” yelled Tristan, as James sat by the pool, just dipping his toes in from time to time.

"In that filth, never!" shouted back James. "Remember, I know what goes into it and it's not nice."

"Stick in the mud, stick in the mud," laughed Tristan, as he swam a few lengths, seemingly without any effort. James watched his friend and remembered how much he loved him.

"If you don't come in, I will come and get you," yelled Tristan.

James laughed. It did look tempting and as he watched Tristan in the pool, he suddenly had an urge to be with him. James took off his shoes and socks, removed his shirt and trousers, and jumped into the pool in his underpants. He surprised himself.

"Well, I didn't think you would ever do that willingly, Jay," whispered Tristan, as he swam over to his friend and hugged him. "You're not such an old stick-in-the-mud after all, are you, Mr Headmaster, or should I say, Flickersmill Babe?"

"Right, you've asked for it, Trouble," yelled James. "I may not be as good a swimmer as you, but I am determined. Just you wait till I get hold of you."

"Can't wait, can't wait," teased Tristan, and James could see little more than the gleam of his friend's brilliant white teeth in the darkness.

The two friends enjoyed fooling around in the pool, just like James' pupils, and James began to understand the pleasure that it gave them as well as to him.

"I brought a picnic," announced Tristan, as they sat together on a car rug that Tristan had brought to the edge of the pool, "and a bottle of sparkling wine. Do you fancy a pool picnic with your lover, Mr Headmaster?"

"I'm wet. I haven't got a towel and I don't have another pair of pants."

"Well, I do have a towel, but I don't have a spare pair of pants, and so you will just have to take them off, Mr Headmaster!" announced Tristan seductively.

James giggled. It had been a long time since he had felt quite so relaxed. Tristan had brought with him an amazing picnic. Sandwiches, salad, crisps, cakes and fruit – an endless supply of food seemed to appear from Tristan's cool box. He had even brought two wine glasses, carefully wrapped up in a tea-towel!

James laid his head in Tristan's lap. "I have really enjoyed this, Tris. I didn't think I would, but thank you for making it so special. We are a good team together, aren't we? I'm just so pleased no one else has come here tonight. I shudder to think what the parents would have said."

Tristan chuckled. "No chance of that, my naive little friend. Guess who locked the gate as we came in?"

"Well done," laughed James. "I wouldn't have thought of that. Whatever will those season ticket holders say?"

"Well, I guess it's just one of the few headmasterly perks. Let's face it, you don't get much out of this job, do you?"

"It has its compensations, Tris. Right now, I'm thinking that I'm the most fortunate head teacher in the world. Should we think about going home soon?"

"No, Jay, let's stay here for a while longer. Just look at the moon glistening over that beautiful tree. It's a full moon as well. I want to watch it. It is a perfect evening and we will never forget it, will we?"

"That's my special tree, Tris," whispered James. "I sit under it when it all gets too much for me. It sounds silly, but it has become a sort of friend. It has been here forever and I think it looks over and guards the school and everyone in it. It sounds silly, I know. It has been here for me ever since I first arrived."

"No, it doesn't, Jay. I feel it too," said Tristan, rubbing his finger up and down James' naked torso. "It's been quite a year, hasn't it?"

"I couldn't have got through it without you, Tris. I know I am not always easy to live with and I get preoccupied with school, but I do love you, you know."

"Yes, I do know, and you need to know that I have always loved you. Maybe ever since the first time we met all those years ago as children. I knew that we would be together one day."

James and Tristan sat silently together, reflecting upon their lives, where they had come and what they had achieved.

"Tris, let's make a priority of getting a home together. A proper home that we can create together. I have been preoccupied with Prior's Hill, but now it is time for us."

"How I hoped you would say that, Jay. I agree!" laughed Tristan excitedly, leaping up. "When do we start?"

"Right away. I said, let's make it a priority, didn't I?"

"Great, then I can get a new job as well as a new home! Jay, this is what I have always wanted. Jay?"

"Yes, Tris?"

"Why don't you keep the pool cleaner, Jay?"

James leapt up and playfully pushed Tristan over to the side of the pool.

"How dare you! I spend half my life looking after that bloody pool!" he yelled.

"I give in, I give in," laughed Tristan, as James wrestled with his friend and pinned his arm to his back. He also knew that, had Tristan wished, he could easily have overpowered him.

"What do you mean, keep it clean?"

"Seriously, James. Don't you think the water looks cloudy?"

There was a shriek from Tristan and a loud splash as James pushed Tristan back into the pool.

It was another Monday morning and James made his way to the swimming pool. How he hated this part of the job. James' head was buzzing with the lessons he had planned, parents to see, as well as Sir Toby later in the day. The last thing that he wanted to do was to spend half an hour on pool duties. James opened the gate to the pool and was horrified with what he saw. No longer was the water of the sparkling clarity that he had come to be rather proud of, but it had now turned into a murky shade of green. He checked the pump – yes, that was running. He remembered the conversation that he had had with Tristan during that Saturday evening. Maybe Tristan wasn't teasing after all? Maybe the pool really was cloudy and, in the moonlight and headiness of that evening, he just hadn't noticed? James didn't even bother to test the water, but grabbed a large tub of acid from the store and poured it into the pool. There would be no swimming today.

Just before school assembly, Doris came into the classroom.

"It's Simon from the PTA on the phone for you, James. I wouldn't bother you normally until break time, but he does seem very anxious. It's about the pool. He's muttering something about it being a health hazard. I can keep an eye on things here if you want to take the call, James."

James nodded. "Thanks, Doris," he added appreciatively, "Yes, I think I know what this is about. I'd better take the call. John here was just showing me the model dinosaur that he made at home over the weekend. Isn't it great, Mrs Cole?"

James left the classroom realising yet again what a treasure he had in Doris. She would always do anything to help him out. There were few people that he could rely on, but he could certainly rely on Doris.

"James, we have problem" said the voice at the end of the phone.

"Good morning, Simon. Yes, I know. Is it about the pool? I have just seen it. Yes, it has gone green. I don't know why, I am no expert."

"Yes, James, it is. We came round on Saturday evening to swim, but the gate was locked. Strange that, as we could see lights on at the back," Simon added.

James could feel himself blushing with embarrassment as he recalled that wonderful Saturday evening with Tristan by the pool.

"Er, yes, Simon. That must have been me locking the gate by mistake. I was working in my office until late," James lied.

"Ah, that explains why we saw your car parked down the lane then. Well, we couldn't get in, so we gave up and tried on Sunday morning instead. The pool was an awful colour, a sort of milky green."

"Yes, I know, Simon. I put some more chemicals in this morning. It has been so hot over the last few days, maybe I should have given it a higher dose before."

"The pool should be checked twice a day, you know, James. I thought Angela was looking after it?"

"I wish she were, Simon. Angela will only do the weekends and I just don't have time to do it more than twice a day. I try to check in the evening, but I certainly cannot manage lunchtimes; I am far too busy with other things. I suppose she did check it on Saturday?"

"I very much doubt it, James. She went to London for the weekend, I think. She told us when we saw her in the supermarket on Friday."

"Well, she didn't tell me she was going away, Simon. So I guess that was the problem. No chemicals on Saturday or Sunday."

"We need to be careful, James. The last time that this happened, in Peter's time, it got very nasty. The villagers have paid their subs and they expect unrestricted use of the pool, you see."

"Well, they will just have to put up with it until I can get it sorted, Simon. Now, if you will excuse me, I have a class waiting for me."

James put the phone down and ran back to his class. It was going to be one of those weeks, he could tell.

During morning break, Doris appeared in the staff-room just as James was pouring himself a coffee.

"James, we have a visitor. He wants to see you urgently."

"Right you are, Doris. Just coming. Who is it?"

"It's a Mr Toris, from the Public Health Department. I told him the pool was closed, but he wanted to see it anyway. He has been carrying out tests on the water quality and is not at all happy."

"Mr Young, I presume?" said the pompous grey-suited man waiting in James' office. My name is Toris, the Public Health inspector for this area. You are responsible for the operation of this swimming pool, I presume?"

"Good morning, Mr Toris," said James warmly, as he shook the limp hand outstretched before him. "Can I get you a cup of coffee?"

"No, thank you. I always provide my own, just in case," came the unexpected and unusual response.

James would like to have asked "in case of what?" but thought better of it.

"You've come about the pool, I guess. Yes, we have a problem with the water today. I added extra chemicals this morning and it should be alright in the next day or so. Until then it will be closed, of course."

"I don't think you realise the seriousness of the problem. It is a health hazard, Mr Young. Not only is the water quality poor, as you say, but it is not just a question of adding chemicals. The filtration and pumping system is inadequate. You appear to be operating a public swimming pool facility here and different rules apply for such facilities. You are contravening a number of public health requirements. I have no alternative but to close the pool until further notice."

"Surely you can come back tomorrow and check it again. The water will be clear again then and it will be safe to use."

"As I said, Mr Young, this pool is a public health hazard and will remain closed until further notice. Good morning to you."

"Just a minute. We have our swimming gala in the next couple of weeks. Surely you will be back again before then."

"Well, that rather depends, doesn't it, young man?" replied Mr Toris in an increasingly patronising manner.

"Depends upon what?" snapped James.

"Whether or not you have completed all the requirements in my report."

"And when will I be receiving a copy of your report?" enquired James.

"In the next week or so, I should think. Then you will have to fulfil the requirements reported therein," Toris added pompously.

"So what you are really saying is that we cannot use the pool until we have received and carried out all the recommendations in your report?"

"No, I said requirements, I did not say recommendations."

"So the pool will probably have to remain closed for the rest of the season. The swimming gala will have to be cancelled!" spluttered James, hardly containing his anger towards the grey suit standing in front of him.

"Precisely. Good day to you, Mr Young."

Chapter 19

Cedric Parsons

Simon was right: the sudden closure of the school swimming pool did cause great annoyance in the village. Initially, the villagers' anger was directed towards James who was blamed for "not looking after our pool properly." For the first few days, James received both the cold-shoulder treatment from some parents and villagers, as well as thinly disguised anger from others. Two parents asked for their swimming pool subscriptions to be returned as they would now be using other swimming pools in the area. James said nothing – he was getting used to the political ups and downs in this small village.

It was a telephone call from Lady Lotitia that began to put matters right. Doris appeared in James' classroom at the end of the morning's lessons.

"It is her Ladyship for you," curtsied Doris, smiling broadly.

"Oh God, what have I done this time?" exclaimed James. "Is she sober?"

"From our brief conversation, I can tell you that she has not been drinking yet. We had a perfectly normal and acceptable conversation. She is concerned about you, James. It really is unusual of her to take such an interest in anyone."

A few minutes later, James had reached the office telephone.

"Good morning, Lady Lotitia. What can I do for you?"

"James, what is all this I hear about the school swimming pool? Apparently, you are getting the blame for it being closed."

"Er, yes, it appears so," replied James. "I did what I could, but it obviously wasn't good enough."

"From what I hear from Peggy Skinner, this isn't your fault at all. Peggy tells me that your caretaker, Angela, is really the one who should be blamed. By all accounts she abandoned her post and went to London for a few days without telling you. How were you to know that it would be left for the weekend, if you weren't told?"

"Thank you for your concern, Lady Lotitia. It is true that I didn't know, otherwise I would have made alternative arrangements for the pool to be checked."

"I know the trouble that can brew if our villagers get the wrong end of the stick, James. They are mostly kind and warm-hearted people, but sometimes their ignorance can turn into mob rule. I suggest that you just tell them what really happened."

"I can't do that. If I do, they will turn their venom onto Angela. I don't want that, nor do I want to lose a caretaker. I have been through other storms, I shall just have to weather this one."

"Not if I can help it, James. Jack Sparrow tells me that you have attended to the pool meticulously since the season began. Maybe you should get another caretaker?"

"Angela is alright. She just tends to do what she wants, when she wants. I know she has a few family problems."

"Stuff and nonsense, don't we all?" interrupted Lady Lotitia. "We have to still carry on with our duties. James, you are being far too generous with the woman, and now you are taking the blame for something that is not your fault. Angela is totally unreliable and self-centred. Don't forget that she is also a Governor and should be supporting you. Since she was appointed, she has done very little and rarely attends meetings nowadays."

"Well, I will speak to her. Thank you for your concern," replied James, taken aback by the venom in Lady Lotitia's words.

"Make sure you do, James. Make sure you do. Goodbye."

By the end of the day, relationships between James and the parents and villagers appeared to be back to normal. Parents came and chatted with him in the playground at the end of the day as usual, and nothing further was said about the pool. James commented to Doris about the sudden and surprising change in attitude at the end of the day.

"As you have already discovered, this is a strange village, James. It tends to look after its own. I think you will find that Lady Lotitia has had a word in the right ears."

"Well, I wish she would let me fight my own battles. Whatever will Angela think if the villagers now turn upon her?"

Angela had made a point of avoiding James since the swimming pool incident and although her work was always done, she was careful to do it late at night or first thing in the morning before James arrived at school.

Two days later there was a note on James' desk. It was a letter of resignation. Angela's note was polite yet brief, stating that, due to family circumstances, she could no longer be a reliable school caretaker and had resigned with immediate effect. James was saddened and also angry. He spoke to Doris about it when she arrived that morning. He handed the letter to her, which she read and passed back to James without comment.

"This is obviously Lotitia's doing. Why couldn't she leave well alone? I was dealing with it in my own way."

"Maybe this was just the tip of the iceberg, James? It's not for me to spread gossip, but Angela had other problems, you know. I hear that she has left Tony and has moved to London to stay with her sister. Apparently she wants to train as a social worker."

James nodded. "I see, Doris. I guess that makes sense. She is quite a clever woman and young enough to train and start a new career, I suppose. What I don't understand is why Lotitia was so much against her."

"I don't really know the details, James, but Angela knew more about the Peatwhistles than most. Remember that she used to work at the Manor before their son went to America. She left after that and then the Peatwhistles turned against her for some reason. Lady Lotitia, in particular. They tried to stop her becoming a Governor, but she was clever enough to appeal to the Diocese, and they supported her nomination."

"I see," replied James, his mind turning over recent events and conversations with Lady Lotitia. He decided that he ought to change the subject.

"Well, it leaves us without a caretaker or cleaner. How do I get one at short notice? Presumably they are expecting me to do that job as well, Doris?"

During the lunchtime break, James asked Doris to place an advertisement in the local newspaper for a caretaker. He typed out a large notice advertising the job, covered it in clear plastic and stuck it to the school gate. As the situation was desperate, James also called the local employment office and asked if they had anyone suitable. They did not.

"Well, it's me and a mop tonight, Doris," laughed James, as he began to put on his swimming pool overalls after school. "My old colleagues just would not believe what happens here. This job is certainly one of variety, isn't it?"

"Don't worry, James. This has happened before, you know. Angela was off quite a bit last year. We all helped out. I will be down to help in a few minutes and you will find that Anne is already there. Who knows, we may even get Emily to help. It's great for team-building, James."

"Pigs might fly, Doris," chuckled James, as he quickly drank his mug of coffee. "Here goes."

Doris laughed as she handed James a new mop, retrieved an old yellow overall from the stock cupboard and tied a headscarf firmly around her head.

"Don't just stand there with your mouth open, James. Let's get on with it and then we can all go home."

The next two hours saw James, Anne and Doris mopping the floors, emptying waste bins, and cleaning sinks and toilets. Doris was firmly in charge of operations and, on this occasion, James was happy to let her tell him what should be done and how.

"I don't know what to say. I am just grateful to you both. I thought I would be here all night," began James.

"What, and deprive the lovely Tristan of your company, James?" giggled Doris. "It's what happens in schools like this, James. We all pull together when the going gets tough, and sometimes we have to do things that we wouldn't do normally."

"Well, thank you both," nodded James, spontaneously giving both Doris and Anne a big hug.

Anne giggled. "Pleased to help, James, but have you thought about what we can do until we get someone to take over from Angela?"

Doris interrupted. "I have. I hope you don't mind, James, but I just happened to mention it to Sir Toby when he came by earlier. He says he will ask Bert and Eddie to do the job for a few weeks until we get someone. He couldn't get anyone for tonight, but Bert and Eddie will be here after school tomorrow."

"Doris, you are truly wonderful," laughed James. "From now on you are in charge of cleaning and caretaking issues. Isn't that right, Anne?"

Doris blushed. "Well, it is good of Sir Toby to help us out. This way we have time to get the right person for the job. It's not an easy job, but the caretaker is very much at the heart of the school."

Anne agreed., "It is wonderful. I didn't fancy doing this each night. All I want to do now is to go home for a nice long, hot bath."

"Me too," said James. "Let's get out of here and go home."

Like many couples, James and Tristan had fallen into an easygoing routine that suited them both. During weekdays, when James arrived home from school, the couple would usually enjoy a glass of wine together on the sofa before Tristan began to prepare the evening meal. James would then spend the next hour or two preparing lessons and materials for the following day. Over dinner, they would relax together and talk. It was by now a well-established routine, but it was time that they both valued. Sometimes it was Tristan who had news to tell but, more often than not, it was James who had much more news to share. Although James was bursting to tell Tristan about his day and the problems with the caretaker, he sensed that it was Tristan who should share his news first.

"Jay, did you really mean what you said about us getting our own place? You know, the other night by the pool. Do you remember?"

"How could I ever forget such an erotic evening with my lover?" grinned James, pulling Tristan closer towards him. "Of course I did. I remember every word."

"Jay, I think I have found just the place for us. It is a beautiful cottage in Coombe, a small village about fifteen miles from Prior's Hill. It has two bedrooms and a small garden. I went to see it today, together with a few other places. It looks ideal. Look at this!"

Tristan thrust a piece of paper into James' hand. It was details from the estate agent. Although a very poor quality black and white photo graced the top of the piece of paper, James could see that it was indeed a very charming cottage.

"Yes, I know Coombe a little. I know the head teacher there. This looks great, Tris. When can we go and see it? This weekend, maybe?"

"I was hoping you would say that. Yes, I think so. I will make an appointment with the agent tomorrow for Saturday. You haven't asked me the price, Jay."

"No, I forgot that. How much is it?"

"Well, that is the best bit. It is in a bit of a state and needs a lot of work doing to it, so they are only asking fourteen thousand pounds for it and the agent thinks they will take less to get it sold quickly. An old lady lived there until she died a couple of months ago and her son wants to sell it as soon as possible. I am sure we can do it with the money that we will have left from the sale of this place, once I have paid off the mortgage, and then maybe you could get a mortgage for the rest?" It was a long time since James had seen Tristan quite so excited.

"Sounds good, but if it needs a lot doing to it will it cost more than we have to put it right? I don't have much in the way of savings, Tris."

"Well, that's what I thought and then I had an idea. I will be looking for a job as soon as we move there but, if we get the place, why don't I take a few months off and do the work myself? It will save us a lot of money and we can get it just as we want it and as we can afford it. I can get some part-time work to help finances as well."

"Brilliant idea, Tris. Are you happy doing all that, though? I will do what I can, but I don't think I could face doing much in the way of building work after school."

"I think most of it is cosmetic, Jay. Needs redecorating and some re-plastering, but I can do that. It will also need rewiring, a new kitchen, a new bathroom and the conservatory roof is leaking."

"Well, Tris. I am not at all sure about that. This requires someone who is good with his hands," said James, looking very serious towards his friend.

"What do you mean, Jay. I am good with my hands!" exclaimed Tristan, suddenly looking very hurt.

"I know, I know you are! I'm only teasing!" laughed James, and yelled as Tristan tried to smother him with a large cushion.

Sir Toby was as good as his word and for the next two weeks, Bert and Eddie arrived as regular as clockwork just as the children were leaving to go home. James liked the two men. They were reliable and worked hard to get the school clean for the following day.

"How's young Mr Tristan?" enquired Bert. "I haven't seen him for a while. I hope he is alright."

"Yes, he is thank you, Bert. Actually, he is a bit busy at the moment finding us a new home. We are looking at one in Coombe on Saturday."

"Coombe, yes, I haven't been there in years. I used to court a young woman from Coombe, but that was many years ago, long before my Jill came on the scene," replied Bert. "Anyway, you give Mr Tristan my best regards."

"I certainly will, Bert. Thank you both for coming in and helping us like this."

Bert nodded, and he and Eddie headed for the hall, with Eddie wheeling the heavy floor polisher.

"Doris, I think the school is the cleanest it has been since I've been here. Have you seen the shine on that hall floor? I could see my face in it when I took assembly this morning," commented James one morning over coffee.

"Yes, I was going to say the same thing. Emily was saying how nice everything looked only the other day."

"Praise indeed!" laughed James. "Even Emily looks happier nowadays. I must be doing something right at last."

"I think it helped by putting her in charge of the swimming gala, James. She thought you would use it as an excuse to cancel everything once the pool was closed, but she has really appreciated the trouble that you have taken to make sure it goes ahead elsewhere."

James had worked hard to ensure that the junior children still had access to a swimming pool. He had managed to make arrangements with Colin Treader, the head teacher of Coombe Primary School, who had willingly agreed to let James bring two classes of children to use his pool once a week, as well as agreeing to host Prior's Hill swimming gala at his school. James was deeply grateful and offered to make a payment to Coombe School.

"No, James. I wouldn't hear of it," replied Colin. "I know how hard it has been for you this year and I think it is a miracle that you have nearly got through it. I only hear good things about Prior's Hill nowadays. You will have to pay the transport costs yourself, but nothing else. Just don't pinch any more of my kids, will you?"

James glowed at Colin's comment because he knew that he didn't give praise easily. Colin Treader was a well-respected head teacher in the area and had a lot of influence with the Local Education Authority. A number of pupils that had previously attended Prior's Hill had drifted to Coombe School during his predecessors' time, but were now returning to Prior's Hill again. James and Colin had sometimes joked about it, but James knew what Colin meant. Parents could be very fickle and would easily change schools at the drop of a hat if the school upset them in some way. Small schools were particularly vulnerable when this happened as it could make a significant difference to the amount of money that the school received and could even make the difference between gaining or losing a teacher.

"I'll try not to, Colin, but thank you for helping us out this year. Maybe there are more things that our schools could do together? Perhaps football and netball competitions, or a school trip? By the way, we are looking at a cottage in Coombe. It sounds ideal for us."

"That's good news, James. We could do with some more professionals living in the village. It is a good village and not too close to Prior's Hill, so it will give you a bit of distance. Look, if you do decide to go ahead with it, why don't you come over one evening for a meal? I can show you around the village and give you some gossip about the place! Maybe we could also have a chat about your ideas for our two schools working closer together. What you have said is similar to my own thoughts. I tried once before with Peter, but it didn't work out, and because of his amorous antics thought it best to distance ourselves from him. We get on well, so why not work closer together?"

"I'd love to, Colin, thank you. Just say the day and I'll be over."

"OK, I will have a chat with Belinda, my wife, and will call you in a week or two when you have made up your mind. By the way, do bring your friend with you. Tristan, isn't it? He would also be welcome."

James had been hoping Colin would ask Tristan as well. "Thank you, Colin, I really do appreciate it."

There had been very few applications for the caretaking job. Despite James and Doris' best efforts to advertise in newsletters to parents and the local newspaper, as well as by word of mouth, there had only been two applications. One was from one of the mothers – a frail-looking young woman with three young children whose husband had left her. James had felt very sorry for her and, despite Doris' warnings, had almost decided to offer her the job.

"James, Rosie's just not up to it. She will let us down. Can you see her heaving those cleaning machines around and shifting furniture? Anyway, what will she do with the children when she is here? She cannot afford a baby-sitter, so I guess this will become a crèche as well."

James knew that Doris was right. A day before James had arranged to see Rosie Butler he received a note pushed through the letter-box. It was from Rosie, withdrawing her application as she had decided to live with her parents some distance away from Prior's Hill. As well as losing a prospective caretaker, James would also be losing pupils.

"It's for the best, James. Anyway, we still have Cedric Parsons to see."

James was not too sure about the second letter of application. It was a very badly written and smudged letter, written on a scrap of paper. Obviously the writer was no scholar, but, as Doris pointed out, that was not what they were looking for. There were few clues as to Cedric's past other than that he used to clean the drains for the local council. Doris agreed to put George on the case, as he knew many people who worked at County Hall.

The following day, Doris reported back what George had found out. Cedric Parsons, by all accounts, had been made redundant due to the current financial cutbacks at County Hall. He lived with his sister in the nearby town and, according to George, had been a reliable and loyal worker.

"George says Cedric is a simple soul. Honest as the day is long, works hard and is reliable. He likes a drink and a flutter on the horses, but George thinks we should give him a try."

James took an immediate liking to Cedric when he arrived for his very informal interview. Cedric was not quite what James had expected. He was a portly, short man, but James could see from the build of his arms that he was no stranger to physical duties. James took him on a tour of the school, pointing out areas of interest and commenting upon things that he was hoping to change. Cedric nodded, but made few responses to James' questions and comments.

"Well, what do you think of it?" asked James after the tour and when they had returned to his office.

"Very nice, sir," nodded Cedric with a smile. "Very nice."

"Do you think you could do the job?"

"Wazat? I have a few problems with my ears," grinned Cedric, pointing to his two hearing aids and shaking his head.

"I quite understand," said James, speaking loudly and clearly. "Do you think you could do the job?"

"Yes, no problem, sir. I would like it. It's not too heavy for me and it would fit in nicely with my gardening. I have an allotment, you know."

"When could you start?" enquired James.

"Oh, not today, but I could do it tomorrow."

"Well, Cedric. I am pleased to say that the job is yours. We look forward to seeing you tomorrow, and I will go round the school with you again and tell you what needs doing."

"Right you are, sir," replied Cedric, standing up.

James shook hands with Cedric as he was about to leave. "We are pleased to have you on board, Cedric. By the way, do please call me James."

"Right you are, sir," said Cedric, as he shook hands with James and closed the door behind him.

Cedric was something of a phenomenon. He always arrived for his duties, not always on time, but at least he did arrive. The school was always maintained in a reasonably clean condition when James checked in the mornings, but certainly not of the same high standard that Bert and Eddie had established. James reasoned that Cedric needed time to settle in and that he ought to spend a little more time with him, telling Cedric what needed doing and the priority order. Cedric always listened carefully to what James had asked, nodded and said, "That's right, sir."

One afternoon, James had a meeting with Cedric to discuss what needed doing in the infants toilets. The pair walked over to the classroom and James pointed out that the room smelled heavily of urine. James had had enough of the foul smell which had now reached a level where it invaded the classroom and even the children were commenting.

"That smell makes me feel sick, Mr Young," Timothy had commented to James during story time.

"Yes, it does the same for me as well, Timothy," James had said. "Let's see if we can get something done about it, shall we?"

"It's the floors, Cedric," James pointed out. "The pans are clean enough, but urine has soaked into the floors. It needs more than just a quick mop to put right."

"That's right, sir," responded Cedric.

Another time, James led Cedric into the hall and pointed out that the hall floor looked dusty and worn. It was clear that it needed not only a coat of polish, but some hard work with the polishing machine.

"That's right, sir," said Cedric.

"Doris, can you hear what I am saying? Am I mumbling, or do I have some kind of speech defect?" exploded James one break time.

Doris turned around from her typewriter and laughed, "Perfectly, why do you say that, James?"

"Oh, it's Cedric," complained James. "I like the man, but he does annoy me. I talk to him, tell him what to do and nothing, absolutely nothing goes in. He just nods and says, 'That's right, sir' and 'Wazat'!"

Doris nodded. "You do realise that Cedric has a hearing problem, don't you, James?"

"Yes, of course I do. That's why he wears his hearing aids, isn't it?"

"Yes, but did you know that in windy weather he keeps them switched off? He doesn't like the whistling noise they make."

Suddenly, James realised what had been happening. The source of his frustration had now become very clear.

"Yes, I see, Doris. That makes sense because..."

"For the last two weeks, it has been very windy," laughed Doris. "He hasn't heard a word that you have been saying!"

The next few weeks were exciting ones for James and Tristan. The following Saturday morning they drove to see the cottage that had recently become available in Coombe. It was called Lavender Cottage and its very name conjured up a chocolate-box scene for James. As they got close to the village, Tristan stopped the car and pointed from the car to the village below.

"Come on. It's just down there, Jay," Tristan said excitedly. "Let's get out and look at it from here."

James and Tristan left the car at the side of the narrow road and walked to the broken iron fencing that lay between the road and the fields beyond. In the distance, James could see a small village church and what looked like a small school at the side. Between the church and the school, James could see a small playing field, at the side of which was a cluster of pretty whitewashed cottages. Coombe was indeed a very pretty village nestling in a lush green valley dotted with groups of cows and horses grazing in the fields.

"Lavender Cottage is one of those," announced Tristan, proudly. "I think it's that one on the left. The one with the green railings."

James squinted his eyes, wishing he had brought binoculars with him.

"Yes, I can see. It's beautiful. What a brilliant setting, Tris. If the cottage is anything like it looks from here, I can see that it would be perfect for us."

"Yes, it is beautiful, isn't it? A perfect setting, and not too far from Prior's Hill either."

Tristan and James stood together, focused upon what they hoped would be their new home. The little white cottage seemed to glow in the morning sunshine, its profile set against a perfect blue and almost cloudless sky. It was indeed a picture postcard scene that belonged to another age.

"You really do think we can afford it?" asked James.

"Yes, I think so. We have had to come down a bit on the price of the flat, but we are getting a good price for it. I am sure you could get a mortgage for the rest."

"Well, let's go and see it," shouted James, as he was already back at the side of the car. "Tris, I am just so excited about this! It feels right. Hurry up!"

James and Tristan stood outside Lavender Cottage, waiting for Mr Trill, the estate agent, to appear. It was indeed a very pretty cottage, in need of some attention, but the possibilities were immediately obvious to both of them. Although the white cottage was showing signs of neglect and decay, most of the work that was needed appeared to be superficial.

"A coat of paint would soon smarten up the outside," began Tristan.

James nodded. "Yes, and maybe we could put a door here, in the porch?" added James, outlining his idea with his hands.

There was a small porch leading directly onto a narrow winding lane, beyond which was the playing field. The couple peered through the small pane of glass in the doorway.

"Bit of a mess in there," said Tristan. "I guess it would be all cleared out before it is sold."

"Look at all this lavender!" exclaimed James. "Now we know why it is called Lavender Cottage."

At the side of the cottage was a small patch of garden covered in little else but clumps of lavender. Some had outgrown their shape and looked untidy and unkempt, but the perfume was unmistakable.

A bright red Ford Escort suddenly appeared and parked at the side of the railings at the front of the cottage. A smart young man holding a clipboard leapt out of the car.

"Good morning, I am Christian Trill. Sorry if I am a bit late."

The smiling young man shook hands with James and Tristan.

"No, we haven't been here very long," replied Tristan. "It has just given us a few minutes to look at the outside."

"Well, as you can see it does need a bit of work. It is structurally sound, but you would have to spend some money on it to bring it up to modern-day standards. An old lady lived here for many years and didn't have anything done. She lived here with a very big dog and so it does smell a bit doggy in places, I warn you."

James nodded. "Does this road get very busy, Christian?"

"I don't think so. Maybe in the morning and late afternoon you get a few cars passing, but it is mainly used by farmers taking their cattle to and from the milking parlour."

"Yes, I thought that judging from the manure on the road. It doesn't bother me. We are in the country, after all."

"Look, let me go ahead and unlock everything and then you can come in through the front door. I like to do my tours following a certain route. I don't get the details mixed up if I do it like that."

Christian disappeared around the back of the cottage. Tristan grinned at James and whispered, "He is rather cute, isn't he?"

James laughed. "Yes, he is, but don't forget that we are looking at the cottage, and not the lovely Christian Trill!"

The front door opened and Christian led the excited couple into the cottage. Immediately in front of them was a narrow flight of stairs, to the left was a small dining-room, and to the right a slightly larger living-room. The floors of each of the rooms were covered in worn and mostly torn sheets of faded and cracked linoleum, although the bare boards on the staircase had been painted with a yellowing white paint. The living-room contained an attractive dresser and a worn suite in front of an open fireplace. Tristan and James wandered into the dining-room. A modern Formica covered table stood in one corner, together with two plastic dining chairs.

"The family have taken out some of the furniture already," explained Christian. "What is left will be removed before the sale. As I explained to Tristan on the phone, the relatives want a quick sale and will co-operate as much as they can. By the way, is it alright to call you Tristan?"

"It certainly is, Christian," grinned Tristan, "and this is my partner, James."

Christian gave an understanding nod. "You, you are a couple then? Will you be buying the house together?"

"If we like it, yes, we certainly will," replied James.

Christian led James and Tristan into the kitchen and on to the bathroom and toilet. It was not an attractive sight. The kitchen units were of poor quality and reflected an age long gone. Some of the doors on the kitchen units were missing or were hanging sadly on one hinge. Drab kitchen tiles, an old metal sink and an antique electric cooker completed the scene.

"Try to imagine this room with new kitchen units, new tiles, a new cooker and maybe a vinyl floor covering," announced Christian, desperately trying to think of something positive to say about the room, which he too thought was ghastly.

"I see what you mean about dog smells," sniffed Tristan, pulling a face of disgust.

"It's the carpet in here," replied Christian. "Once that is taken up and the floor has a good clean, the smell will go. The old lady had a huge dog that she adored, but thankfully it now has a new home and doesn't come with the sale."

"Well, at least it has a separate toilet and bathroom," began James, feeling sorry for Christian, who was now looking a little dejected. "We could easily fit a new bathroom suite and a coat of paint would make all the difference."

"Now you are sounding like Christian the estate agent, Jay," laughed Tristan.

Christian laughed. "Well, I am new at all this. I try to look at the positive side, but I am certainly not blind to what needs doing. It is a dump inside, to be honest, but I think that if you spent a bit of money and were prepared to do most of it yourself, you would soon turn it around. It would make a nice home for the two of you. Come and have a look at the bedrooms."

The young estate agent led James and Tristan up the narrow staircase to the two bedrooms. Apart from an old iron bed in each room, they were empty and looked almost liveable. The views from the bedroom windows were breathtaking. From the larger of the two, James could see the church and school set against the hillside – it was a perfect village scene. From the small bedroom, there was a glorious view of some woodland and the fields beyond.

"There's no bathroom upstairs," began Christian. "But if I were you, I would consider an extension in the future and turn the large bedroom into one with an en-suite bathroom. They are all the rage nowadays and would save you going downstairs after a night out!"

James and Tristan spent a long time looking around the cottage revisiting each room in turn, as well as looking at the small garden outside.

"We could have a small shed here and maybe even a dog," exclaimed Tristan excitedly.

"It's just perfect, Tris. Yes, I would like a dog – a small one, but only if one of us can get home at lunchtimes to look after it. Maybe we can get a cat as well?"

"You like it then?" said Christian. "You spend as long as you like, but I should warn you that I have another couple coming to look at it in about fifteen minutes."

"I think we have finished for the moment, thank you," replied Tristan. "We will chew it over and get back to you first thing on Monday morning."

"Do you mind me asking? Will you require a mortgage?"

"Yes, we will," replied James. "Can you help with this?"

"Well, that's why I mention it, James. The truth is that if I can sign you up to a mortgage as well, I get a commission. It's as simple as that. We do have some good deals and we can also offer endowment mortgages as well as repayment."

"Fair enough," nodded Tristan. "So will we need to come to your office?"

"Just as you like. I think you said that James is a local head teacher. I could easily come to your school, maybe after work one day, to complete the paperwork, if that would be easier for you?"

After an anxious weekend of talking, calculating finances and pretending to each other not to be too excited, Tristan and James agreed to make an offer for the cottage. Christian had called at Prior's Hill the following day and was able to arrange a suitable mortgage for them. They now had a firm offer on Tristan's flat and it was now just a question of waiting for their offer to be accepted before submitting their mortgage application. James and Tristan had decided to make an offer for one thousand pounds less than the asking price, as so much work needed doing.

James returned home one evening to an excited Tristan.

"James, our offer has been accepted! I had to raise our offer by an extra five hundred though, as that other couple were also interested. The other bit of good news is that Christian says that our mortgage application has also been accepted!"

Chapter 20

A Moonlight Parting

The beginning of July was the beginning of a very busy and happy time for James and Tristan. They had both fallen in love with Lavender Cottage and it looked as if their purchase would proceed smoothly. The sale of Tristan's flat appeared to be going ahead as well, and Christian, the estate agent, had called to say that James' mortgage application had also been accepted. All was going well and, with a bit of luck, completion of both the sale of the flat and the purchase of Lavender Cottage would take place during August, an ideal time for James because of the school holidays.

Meanwhile, there was much to do and James' head was now full of planning for the forthcoming Sports Day, Parents' Evening and the Leavers' Service. James loved this time of the year, despite it being hectic, but he dreaded having to say goodbye to the older pupils as he had grown very fond of them. Emily had surprisingly agreed to plan the swimming gala, for which James was very grateful. She had even asked James about his opinion on several matters and was keeping him fully informed of developments. There were also reports to be written, as well as the usual preparation for the new school year. James and Tristan had agreed that it would be Tristan who would take charge of the sale of the flat and the move to Lavender Cottage.

"Look, Jay, just leave it to me. I know how busy you are and this is a bad time of the year for you to start worrying about the fabric for curtains and the colour of paint. I'll keep you fully in touch with what I am doing, but let me do the worrying until the end of term."

James was grateful for this offer and, as he was driving to school on 'automatic pilot' yet again, he recalled how close he and Tristan had become over the last year. The move to Coombe would really give them an opportunity to build a new home together, as well as giving him much more free time to spend with Tristan. James was tired of the journey to and from school, and Tristan was always reminding him to be careful on the narrow hillside roads, particularly in foggy winter weather. Despite the many difficulties of the last year, it had been one of the most challenging as well as rewarding times in James' life and he was very happy.

"Pupil numbers are up again, James," announced Doris one morning. "It looks as if they will hit ninety in September and we will be well on our way to getting another teacher. I had the office on the phone last week checking our forecast numbers. It really is amazing what you have achieved in less than a year, James."

"That is such good news, Doris," beamed James. "We can do so much more with another teacher. That and the extra money will make a real difference to us."

"You are looking happier as well, James," added Doris. "The move to Coombe will be good for you both, won't it?"

"I really am excited, Doris. We had dinner with Colin Treader and his wife over the weekend. He was so kind to us and made Tris really welcome as well. He showed us around Coombe. It really is a lovely village. Do you know it?"

"Yes, Colin is a good man," agreed Doris. "Some years ago we used to go there quite often with the football and netball teams. Then it all got difficult as children started leaving here and going to Coombe. Peter was very angry, but I cannot say I blamed the parents for voting with their feet."

"Well, we are hoping to restart that, as well as some kind of joint school visit. It would be good for our year groups to combine now and again for some of the activities. As it stands there are so few in some of the year groups. There is only one third-year junior girl, for example. It's not good to have so few."

"Didn't you also say that you may be able to get some extra money from County Hall to do this?"

"Yes, apparently it's all the rage now in some counties. Linking groups of schools of a similar size together and giving them extra resources. I was reading in the *Times Educational* that they do this a lot in some rural counties. Sometimes schools even get another teacher to share between them for curriculum development. They call it 'clustering'. Think what that could mean here, Doris!"

"Can we cluster Cedric with someone do you think?" interrupted Doris, laughing. "I do like him, but he is such hard work!"

"Tell me about it! The other day I asked him to paint the sports shed with preservative when he had time. I even offered him overtime. He came back to me later with a bottle of insecticide for the roses. He thought I had asked him to spray the roses!"

"Yes, he does seem to be on a different planet, but I guess he means well. He seems happy enough here and the children seem to like him. He is such a gentle old thing."

"Yes, that's true. I caught young Neil helping him the other day. That lad is so much more confident nowadays. The strange thing is that Cedric seems to understand what the children are saying, but not me!"

"Maybe it is the pitch of the voice," mused Doris. "Or maybe it's just us!" she added as an afterthought and returned to her typing.

"Christian says that I can borrow the keys to Lavender Cottage tomorrow afternoon to measure up and make a plan of what needs doing," said Tristan excitedly as soon as James arrived home and had settled down with a much-needed glass of wine. "I thought I would drive over in the Mini and take him out to lunch. He has been so helpful and he is very cute!"

James laughed. "He certainly is. Yes, good idea, he has been very helpful to us and I think it is due to him that things are moving so smoothly. I really feel that we are getting somewhere with this. I cannot believe just how smoothly this is all going, Tris."

"I can't wait for it all to happen, Jay. I hate you doing that journey twice a day. It is such a long one and I am always worried that you will drop off to sleep when you are driving, particularly after a late night at school. The fog on that hill is lethal. I just don't know how you do it each day!"

"Don't you worry about me, Tris. My little car always looks after me. More or less drives itself nowadays."

"Yes, that's just what I am afraid of. By the way, Jay, the couple who want this place phoned today as well. They would like to come over on Saturday morning. They seem interested in buying the sofas and curtains as well. I said that would be alright, because they won't fit Lavender Cottage anyway. We may as well let them have them."

"Oh, Tris. I shall miss these sofas, we have had such a good time on them!" grinned James.

"Don't you go worrying your pretty little head about such things," teased Tristan, ruffling James' hair. "I shall think of something else. Just you leave it to me! I thought maybe a pretty floral little number, maybe even chintz!"

Tristan knew how much James hated floral patterns on furniture, wallpaper and curtains. It was now his turn to be hit by the two large cushions that flew across the room.

The following morning James was up earlier than usual, as he was hoping to get some more reports written before the school day started. He got out of bed quietly, so as not to wake the sleeping Tristan, showered and dressed, and made himself a cup of coffee. He wondered about making one for Tristan, but decided to let him sleep on. Tristan always got up early and so the rest would do him good. James remembered that Tristan would be following on later in the Mini to go to Coombe and Lavender Cottage. Maybe he would call at Prior's Hill on his way back? He would leave Tristan a note. Just before James left the flat he returned to the bedroom and peered around the door. Tristan was still fast asleep. James loved looking at Tristan when he was asleep. He always looked so young and so handsome, with his long, blond hair spread on his pillow. James tiptoed to Tristan's side of the bed and gently kissed him. Tristan stirred gently and turned on his side. James stood for a moment watching Tristan sleeping peacefully. James turned towards the door and as he did so he heard a mumble from the bed.

"I love you, Mr Headmaster, and don't you ever forget it."

James just smiled. Usually he would pretend to be very hurt when he was called 'Mr Headmaster', and then he would catch Tristan when he was least expecting it and tickle him until he shouted for mercy, but this time he let him sleep.

It was early afternoon and James was standing on the school football field attempting to coach the football team. Tristan always teased James about his sporting efforts and he would often volunteer to come to Prior's Hill to coach the boys, particularly if they had a match against another school. James really hated football, but he knew how much it meant to the boys and went along with it. Simon, his brother, had once tried to teach him the offside rule, but he never really understood. Mostly James would run up and down the pitch, blowing his whistle and encouraging the children on. It was good exercise yet he was always pleased when his afternoon of torment was over. Emily had protested strongly when he had included Becky in the football team. "Come off it, James. Football is for boys and netball is for the girls. Becky should be playing netball, not football. What will her parents say?"

"But she loves football, Emily! She is always asking me to put her in goal. I tried her out last week and she is better than any of the boys. Anyway, why shouldn't she play football if she wants to? Maybe I could interest you in a few boys for the netball team, Emily. Neil, for example? He is always saying he likes netball, so why don't you let him have a go?"

"Over my dead body," snapped Emily.

"Well, if that's what it takes." James had roared with laughter. Anne and Doris were also laughing, knowing full well that James was winding Emily up. Emily had gone pink with embarrassment and had left the room.

"I do believe that the old girl is finally learning a few lessons," James concluded, as Anne and Doris suppressed their laughter.

Doris stood at the edge of the playing field waving her arms furiously. James, who was not blessed with the best of eyesight, waved back equally furiously. He then saw that Doris was running towards him from the far side of the pitch. He blew his whistle for the children to stop playing and walked towards her.

"James, James, come quickly," shouted Doris.

Doris reached his side. The short, stocky woman gasped between breaths.

"James, come quickly. There's been an accident. It's Tristan."

What seemed like hours later, although it was, in fact, only minutes, James and Doris arrived at the entrance to Abbotsford's modern hospital. James headed for the reception counter.

"I've come to see Tristan Peters. He has been involved in an accident."

The young woman at the desk looked at James and asked, "What is your name? Are you a relative?"

"I'm James Young. I'm a friend of Tristan Peters. A good friend."

"Well, I'm afraid that won't be possible. A young man by that name has just been admitted as an emergency. It's relatives only, I'm afraid, until we are more certain about his condition."

"You must let me see him. I'm his partner. He has no relatives living in the area. I must see him."

"I'm sorry, Mr Young, but those are the rules. We just cannot let anyone come in to disturb patients."

"Anyone? Didn't you hear me? I'm his partner. I insist on seeing him now."

"Calm down, James," intervened Doris, gently. "How can we find out how Tristan Peters is?"

"If you wait over there, I will find out and let you know if there is any news," said the young woman, pointing to a row of steel-framed grey chairs at the side of her desk.

"This is crazy," shouted James, banging loudly on the counter with his fist. "I need to see him now."

"If you continue to shout and make a fuss, Mr Young, I shall call the police and have you removed from this hospital."

As good fortune would have it, and this was something that James would reflect upon in the weeks to come, Doris suddenly spotted the Reverend Hubert Langdon-Hobbs, James' old adversary, walking from one of the corridors. He had just come from the wards. Doris ran over to him.

"Good afternoon, Doris. What are you doing here? Not one of the children, I hope?"

"Thank goodness you are here, Rector. We have a problem. Tristan, James' partner, has had an accident and they won't let James see him because he is not family. Can you do anything?"

"Oh yes, I remember Tristan. Nice young man, golden hair, as I recall. Doesn't he help to coach the football team from time to time? The boys speak very well of him."

"Yes, that's him. Can you have a word and let James see him? We don't know what has happened."

The Rector walked over to James, who was by now shaking with both fear and anger, and put his hand kindly on his shoulder.

"James, I will do what I can."

With that, the Rector walked to the desk and had a quiet word with the receptionist, who nodded and picked up the telephone.

"Mr Young? I have asked Sister to have a word with you and then she will take you to see Mr Peters."

"Thank you. I'm sorry for the fuss," was all that an emotional James could say as he made his way down the stark corridor with Doris and the Rector at his side.

"I'm afraid it is very serious," began the Sister. "It was a road accident, I believe, and Mr Peters had to be cut out of his vehicle. The car had been hit by a lorry and rolled partly down a bank before it caught fire. He has multiple injuries and burns. The doctors are with him now and we are trying to make him comfortable."

By now James was as white as a sheet. Doris led him to the chair in the Sister's office.

"Will he, er, will he be alright?" choked James.

"Mr Young, it is too early to say. All I know is that it is serious and all we can do now is hope."

"And pray, James," added the Rector. "And pray."

James nodded.

"I have told you too much already," added Sister. "Reverend Langdon-Hobbs has told me who you are and of your close relationship with Mr Peters. Nevertheless, you are not his next of kin and I should really be speaking to them. Do you have any contact details?"

"He has a father, but they have not spoken in years. There is also a sister living nearby. I can call her, if you like?"

"I'll do it, James," interjected Doris. "Just give me the number and I will call her."

"I don't have it with me, Doris. I think it is in the back of my diary at school. In my briefcase, maybe."

"I'll go and get it now. Will you still be here, Rector?" added Doris, knowing what she had to do, but also realising that this was the time that James needed her most.

"Look after him," she added as she left the room.

"I'll stay with James until you get back," said the Rector, sitting at James' side.

"Thank you," said Sister Mason. "No, please wait here and I promise to come and see you as soon as there is any news, and you can then see Mr Peters."

James nodded. Never in his life had he felt so helpless and so much in despair. All kinds of things were racing though his head and he suddenly realised, despite their previous differences, how grateful he was to the Rector and for what he had already done for him.

"Thank you, Rector, for sorting this out. They wouldn't let me see him."

"I know, James. It can be so unfair. I have come across this sort of thing before."

"They will let a father see him who has not seen him in years, but not his partner. I love Tristan with all my heart. I should be the one with him now."

"And so you will, my boy. Leave it to me. Let's just sit and pray quietly together until we have some more news."

After what seemed a considerable time, Doris returned with the all-important phone number.

"I phoned Tristan's sister, but all I got was an answering machine saying that they were away on holiday. I gave the number to Sister Mason. Do you have his father's number anywhere, James?"

"No, I don't know where that is. It may be in Tristan's things. He and his father are not close and have not seen each other for many years. I have not seen his father for years, either. We were not the best of friends and he doesn't like me very much."

The door opened and Sister Mason entered the room, accompanied by a serious-looking doctor. James stood up, but the doctor beckoned for him to sit down again. The doctor also sat down at the side of Sister Mason's desk and addressed James.

"I'm Dr Webb. Sister Mason tells me that you are Mr Peter's partner?"

"Yes, that's right. I'm James Young. How is he?"

Dr Webb paused for a moment and looked James straight in the face.

"Not good, I'm afraid, not good at all."

He stood and walked to the window.

"Mr Peters was badly injured in the crash. Not only has he suffered considerable burns to his body, but there is also considerable damage to his internal organs."

"Yes, but surely that can be put right? He is young and fit."

Dr Webb sat down again. "Mr Young. It is not as simple as that. You see, he has also suffered some brain damage although, as yet, we are uncertain how extensive that damage is. We need to carry out more tests; however, at the moment he is too sick for that. All we can do is to try to stabilise his condition, make him comfortable and... hope."

James felt tears welling up in his eyes, and he could not swallow. He felt Doris gently take his hand in hers and he was aware that the Rector too had put his hand on his shoulder. He sat in stunned silence.

Dr Webb finally stood up and walked across the room to James and said quietly, "May I call you James? James, I think it would be better if you were to stay here tonight. We have put Mr Peters in a room on his own and you can maybe get some sleep in the chair. We may need you later."

James stood at the doorway of Tristan's hospital room staring at the still form that lay before him. Machinery buzzed in the background and between the blur of tears in his eyes James could see a number of tubes attached to Tristan's broken body. Two nurses busied themselves around the bed. Tristan's golden hair lay spread around his pillow, just as James had seen it that morning before he left for school. He looked like an angel. James looked and wept.

"James, I am going to leave you and Tristan alone now," said the Rector, quietly. "I'll be here for you if you need me. Remember, James, whilst there is life there is always hope. May God bless you both."

"Thank you, Rector, thank you for helping me," cried James as the Rector placed his hand on his shoulder and left the room.

Doris slipped her hand in his.

"James, I will be just outside the room. Call me if you need me. You and Tristan need to spend some time together alone."

Doris and the Rector left the room and eventually the two nurses also left.

"Just press the button if you need us. Mr Peters is being monitored very closely at the main control and we will know immediately if his condition worsens. Remember that we are only a few steps away."

The next few hours were the worst in James' life. The constant buzz of the machinery, the sucking and shuddering noises of the pumps and equipment attached to Tristan's unmoving form, seemed surreal. This was not happening, maybe it is a nightmare? thought James. He sat by the bed, sometimes stroking Tristan's golden hair and other times just looking at his handsome face. Through the transparent mask he could see Tristan's mouth and lips. He imagined those generous lips teasing, tormenting and loving him. From time to time the nurses would reappear and carry out further tests, check the equipment and leave the room without saying a word. Occasionally, a doctor would enter the room and leave shortly afterwards. As evening came, James was aware that Doris would come into the room, sometimes with a cup of tea or a glass of water.

"Can I get you a sandwich, James?" she asked on one occasion.

"No, thank you, Doris. I feel so sick in my stomach. I cannot eat anything. Anyway, it's time you went home to George. He'll be wondering what has happened to you. Thank you for all that you have done for me this afternoon."

"No, James, as you are here and Tristan is so poorly I am staying as well. I will be just outside. I'm not leaving you until things improve. Give him a kiss from me as well, won't you?"

Evening slipped into night-time, and James walked to the window and peered outside. The window looked out onto a near empty car park. Occasionally James could see and hear ambulances coming and going. Hospitals were busy places and could never sleep, he thought. James wondered about the accident. How did it happen and where? He had so many questions to ask. He didn't dare think of more now. He just looked at the moon and prayed for his friend, lover and soulmate to get better. How he prayed. He stared at the moon. It was so bright and filled the car park with an intensity so bright that James couldn't recall the last time he had seen the moon like this. He remembered the last time that he and Tristan had sat together looking at the moon. It was by the school swimming pool, that wonderful evening they had spent together. He remembered the picnic that Tristan had prepared and how he had wickedly pushed Tristan into the pool. He remembered their deep love for each other. A faint groan came from the bed. James rushed to the side of the bed.

"Tris, it's me, Jay. I'm here. You are in hospital. You had an accident, but I am here. You will be alright, Tris, I know you will be alright."

The moonlight shone brightly on Tristan's bed and onto Tristan's face. James turned out the central light in the room and the moonlight shone brightly on Tristan's golden hair. James sat by the bed once again and gently held Tristan's hand.

"Tris, it's me. Can you hear me? Tris, I love you so much. Please hear me. I love you."

Tears were streaming down James' face and onto the bed.

"Tris, I need you so much. Don't leave me alone. I love you and I will always love you."

James felt a tiny squeeze from Tristan's hand. The moonlight faded and the room darkened.

Chapter 21

Saying Goodbye

The following few days were the worst that James had known. After Tristan had died, Doris and George insisted that James stay with them for a few days. James was relieved, because he could not imagine returning to Tristan's empty flat alone. For the next two days, James sat in stunned silence in Doris and George's guest bedroom. He would not eat and refused to go to bed to sleep properly. Doris was so concerned that she asked Dr Jackson to call and see him. James knew Dr Jackson quite well because Clifford Jackson, his eldest son, was in Class 3 and his youngest, Susan, was in Class 1.

"Good morning, James. Doris asked me to call to see you. I was deeply saddened to hear about Tristan. Clifford spoke well of Mr Tristan, as he calls him. You must miss him dreadfully."

James nodded.

"Am I right in thinking that you were a couple? You were more than just good friends?"

"Tristan was my life, my reason for living," replied James. "There is just no point in anything anymore. I have lost everything I have ever cared about. First my brother, Simon, then my parents, and now my partner and best friend."

Russell Jackson nodded and sat on the corner of the bed, looking at James.

"Look, James. I can only imagine a little of what you are going through. I can give you some pills to help you get some sleep. That will help, but that is all that I can do for you. Take some time off work and I will come and see you again next week. You will find the strength to get through this. You have a lot of friends at the school, and I know that Doris and George will do all that they can to help you through this. They say that time is a great healer, James."

James sat in silence, but when Doris reappeared later with a cup of tea, he finally agreed to take a couple of sleeping pills.

Death is often followed by a period of intense activity for those that are left behind. In most cases, this is a welcome distraction from the immediate effects of grief. There are arrangements to be made, papers to sign and funerals to organise. However, for some, and for most gay men and women, they are even denied this slight easing of their grief. In the worst cases, relatives move in and take over the organisation of the final arrangements for their loved one, and the partner is often denied the dignity of being involved as much as they should or wish to be. This was partly the case for James. He had first experienced the injustice of not being able to see Tristan after he had been admitted to hospital because he was not officially the next of kin. It was only after the intervention of the Rector that James was allowed to be with Tristan during those last precious hours. Indeed, as James had no legal status in Tristan's life he was, at first, denied access to the flat that was their joint home, as well as not being allowed to make the arrangements for his funeral.

Within a day of Tristan's death, Tristan's father, Grant Peters, had instructed lawyers in Bridgehampton to telephone James at Doris and George's home. James was asked to return his keys to their offices within the next seven days. He was also asked to remove all his own personal belongings and to make arrangements to move out of the flat immediately because it would be sold. George, who was by nature a gentleman in the true sense of the word, became very angry and James could hear him shouting at the caller before the phone was finally slammed down. Later in the evening he and Doris came into James' room.

"James, we need to talk," began George. "This is a terrible thing to ask you now, but we need to get you to Tristan's flat as soon as we can tomorrow morning. His father's lawyers have been on the phone and they want you to vacate the flat and remove your things at once. The rest is to be sold as soon as probate comes though. Apparently, you can now only have access to the flat under the supervision of his lawyers. For goodness' sake, James, that was your home. We will go tomorrow and get your things, lawyers or no damned lawyers. Do you know if Tristan made a will?"

James shook his head. He had never seen George so angry, and neither had Doris, for that matter. This mild-mannered man very rarely lost his temper.

"I understand, George," nodded James, "but his father hasn't seen him in years. There was a big family upset and Tristan never forgave him."

The following morning George, Doris and James made their way to the small yet tidy flat in Bridgehampton. James unlocked the door and immediately burst into tears. This time there was no cheery greeting from his beloved Tristan, nor a glass of wine shared together on the sofa. James walked into the bedroom. Even the bed had been made before Tristan had left on that fateful last journey. A pile of James' clothes had been neatly ironed and placed on his side of the bed.

"James, you must tell me which are your things. I will pack them for you," said Doris, who was also trying to hold back the tears.

In the next hour or so, James' life had been packed into two suitcases and a number of black bin-liners that Doris had thoughtfully brought with her.

"James, is there anything of Tristan's that you would like to take?" asked George. "If so, take it now because you may never be able to do so again."

James looked around. "No, nothing, just a few photos."

James went to the drawer at Tristan's side of the bed and removed a small plastic photo album. He flicked through it and put it in his suitcase. He went into the living-room and took a small photo in a brass frame from one of the shelves. It was a black and white photo of a young and very handsome Tristan in his soldier's uniform the day that he had joined up. James stroked his hand across the front of the frame and gently placed it also in the suitcase, wrapped carefully between his neatly ironed shirts. Finally, James went to another drawer and removed a small leather case. In it were all the mementos and postcards that Tristan had sent him when he was in the Army. How James had treasured them.

"That's about it," said James, handing the keys to George. "I don't belong here anymore. Let's go."

The following day there was a telephone call from Tristan's sister, Patsy. Although they had got on well together in the past, it was several years since Tristan had seen his sister and they had grown apart. James and Tristan had tried to see her several times, but she was always busy.

"May I speak to James, please?" she had asked Doris, between sniffs.

"Yes, but only if you are not going to upset him," answered Doris.

James agreed to take the call. "Hello, Patsy. It is good to hear from you after all this time. Yes, it is dreadful news, isn't it?"

After an initial explanation of what had happened on that fateful afternoon, Patsy asked a question that chilled James to the core.

"James, what are you doing about the funeral?"

"I don't know, Patsy. It has been worrying me, but your father's lawyers told me not to get involved as your father is the next of kin. I have been waiting to know what is happening. I want to be there."

"Nothing's happening, James. Dad is always boozed up to the eyeballs nowadays and couldn't organise anything. He says it's up to you to organise it. He says he doesn't care whether Tristan is buried or cremated or what you do, as long as you pay for it."

"Will he be coming to it?"

"No, but I gather he is coming down the week after for the sale of the flat. I'll be there though. We can talk more then."

Once again, George exploded with anger as James retold the essence of the telephone conversation with Patsy.

"He was quick enough to get you out of the flat, James. This is disgraceful. Of course you won't pay for the funeral. That will come out of Tristan's estate. What a horrible man."

"Of course I will pay for it, George" said James quietly. "I am happy to. It is the last thing that I can do for my Tris."

Later that day Doris had arranged for Mr Brown from the local undertakers to call and see James.

"I don't want Tristan to be cremated," said James firmly. "I would like him to be buried. We talked about this some time ago and Tristan hated the idea of cremation."

"Of course, Mr Young. Do you have anywhere in mind for his final resting place?"

James hadn't thought of this before. He thought of Tristan's home town, but decided against it as few people would still remember him. He thought about Bridgehampton, but apart from

Tristan's work colleagues there were few links to the city. Another idea flashed into his mind.

"Do you think the Rector would agree for Tristan to be buried in Prior's Hill churchyard, Doris?" asked James quietly. "I know he wasn't a villager, but he loved the village and the school, and he knew quite a few people there."

Doris smiled and nodded. "Good idea, James. I'll call the Rector now."

Doris returned a few minutes later. "The Rector says he would be pleased to arrange this for you, and has agreed to take the funeral service as well. He says he will call here later to discuss the arrangements with you."

From that moment, everything became a little easier for James. The undertakers were very understanding and liaised between James and Tristan's father, who once again made it clear to Brown and Co. that it was James, and not he, who was picking up the bill. The Rector called and discussed a simple yet dignified service for Tristan. James was happy for him and Doris to work out the details, and was touched with the compassion and thoughtfulness that the Rector showed. The funeral date was agreed. It was to be the following Friday morning, although James wished it was earlier.

"The school Governors have agreed with me that the school should be closed for the day as a mark of respect to Tristan," said the Rector gently. "We all liked Tristan, and you and he have become very much part of our village community. This way anyone who wishes to attend can do so."

James later discovered that Doris was arranging an after-funeral buffet in the school hall. She was doing it herself, with the help of Mrs Hilary, the school cook, and the other staff to help James to "save some money."

"Oh no, not ham sandwiches, Doris. I hate the idea of that sort of thing after a funeral. It's not a party. There's nothing to celebrate, whatever the Rector tells me. Is it really necessary, Doris?"

Doris assured James that it was necessary as, presumably, some people may have long journeys and would require some refreshment. On this occasion James was happy to concur with Doris.

It was the day of the funeral at last. James had felt in a state of limbo throughout the week and now wanted it all to be over. James had spent a lot of time walking the nearby hills with Trigger, the neighbours' dog. The old dog seemed to have bonded with James and sensed his unhappiness. He waited patiently by the gate for James to collect him at the same time each day.

"James, Mr Brown called earlier. He says that Tristan is in the Chapel of Rest. Would you like to see him again before Friday?"

James nodded, biting his bottom lip. He did so want to see Tristan again. After a few moments thought, he turned to Doris.

"Doris? Will you...Would you mind...?"

"James, I am coming with you. I want to see our angel again as well."

Later that day, James and Doris arrived at the funeral parlour. Mr Brown led James into a back room where taped music was playing gently. He pointed to the side of the room and nodded. "Go ahead, he's just over there. Take your time."

James walked over to the coffin and looked at Tristan lying there peacefully. It was not like the broken, burnt and cut body that James had last seen in hospital, but a Tristan as beautiful as ever, with his golden hair neatly gathered around his tanned face, and now at peace. James kissed him for one last time and left the room.

The church was packed with people. Mr Brown led James, Doris and George to the front pew of the pretty village church. James glanced around and was amazed by the number of people in the church. Indeed, some of the villagers were standing at the back of the pews. There were some of James' older pupils and their parents. Sally Watson spotted him and waved. Sir Toby and Lady Lotitia were at the back of the church, sitting next to Peggy Skinner. James could see Jack Sparrow, Cedric, Anne and Emily sitting together a few rows behind him. Mrs Hilary and Jean Sparrow, her kitchen assistant, as well as Anna and Gloria were there too. He was touched to see Colin Treader and some of his staff from Coombe School sitting in one of the side pews. There was no sign of Tristan's sister, Patsy, or of his father.

Despite the seriousness of the occasion, James smiled when he heard the strains of 'Love Me Do' hissing loudly from the church's ancient speaker system. Although James had agreed to everything that the Rector and Doris had suggested for the service, James had insisted upon one thing. He had asked that the Beatles be played at the beginning or end of the service. Tristan adored the group and James often caught him dancing and singing to a Beatles tape in their kitchen.

"Tristan hated sad music. Just play a couple of tracks from a Beatles album and also that song that the Liverpool team always sing, and Tristan will be happy," he had said.

James turned to see Tristan's coffin slowly entering the church, poignantly carried by Bert and Eddie as well as by two pallbearers from Brown and Co. He tried to hold back the tears, but found it impossible to do so. Doris squeezed his hand tightly and George put his arm on James' shoulder.

"This is the worst bit, James. It will soon be over," she whispered.

The service went well and although James had been asked to give the eulogy he had declined to do so, but he had given the

Rector plenty of information about Tristan. The Rector was magnificent and James now saw this seemingly pompous man in a new light. He was so grateful to him for all that he had done for them both.

Tristan's simple coffin was carried out of the church to the strains of 'You'll Never Walk Alone' and, behind the tears, James smiled as he thought of what Tristan would have said. Tristan would have pretended mock surprise that James had even heard of Liverpool FC and his teasing was bound to have ended in their usual cushion fight.

Standing by the open grave, it was hard for James to throw a handful of soil onto the coffin. Later, he stood alone by the graveside until all the mourners had left. Suddenly he heard a voice behind him.

"It is so hard, James. I am so sorry for you."

It was Christian Trill, the estate agent.

"Look, James. I don't want to intrude upon your grief. I just wanted to pay my respects to Tristan and to see you. We met a few times to discuss the cottage. Do you know how much he was in love with you?"

James nodded. "I think so."

"One day when you feel better, I want us to meet up for a coffee. During Tristan's last visit we went out for lunch together. He had so many plans for the cottage, and everything he said began with 'James would like this' or 'I want James to have that'. He simply adored you. I want to share all those plans of his with you. I think it may help."

James smiled. "It sounds like my Tris. He was so thoughtful."

"You are a lucky man, James. You may not think so now, but to have been loved like that for such a short time is more than many people experience in a lifetime."

James thought for a moment. “Thank you, Christian. I really appreciate you telling me that. Come over to the school and have a drink with me.”

James and Christian walked down the churchyard towards the church.

“Look, I’m sorry, Christian. I shall have to pull out of Lavender Cottage. I cannot afford it and besides, I couldn’t live there without Tristan anyway.”

“I quite understand, James. Look, I didn’t come here to raise that with you. The vendors will understand and I shall get your deposit back to you next week.”

James nodded. “Thank you, Christian. I wasn’t looking forward to telling you.”

“Are you going to stay here?” asked Christian after a few moments.

“No, I don’t think so. It’s time for me to move on and start again,” began James.

“Is it because you have lost your home?”

“Yes, partly. It is true that I now have nowhere to live, but I see Tristan everywhere.”

“Isn’t that good? The memories, I mean.”

“Maybe.”

“I heard that his father has snatched the flat and left you with nothing. It really is terrible, James. Life just isn’t fair for people like you and I.”

“Well, you can certainly forget equal opportunities for gay men and women, Christian.”

“Well, maybe it will happen one day. I really do hope so.”

“I doubt it. Not in our lifetimes, Christian, not in our lifetimes.” James shook his head sadly.

Patsy was waiting for James outside the church porch.

“James, may I speak with you?” asked Patsy, hesitantly.

"I'll see you in the school later then, James?" asked Christian, and walked down the lane towards the school building.

"Well, you finally made your brother's funeral then?" snapped James.

"I was here. I came late, but I was here, right at the back. Didn't you see me?"

"You should have sat with us in the front. You are his sister, for Christ's sake," exploded James. "I don't suppose that lazy bum of a father managed to get here either, did he?"

"I haven't been a very good sister, have I, James?" wept Patsy.

"No, not really," agreed James, and then, feeling sorry for her, held her hand tightly.

"Look, Patsy. I'm upset. I could have done with you here as well. I just need to be close to Tristan and you are the only thing I have left."

"No, Dad couldn't come. He's not well, James, but I also found out that he has turned you out of Tristan's flat. That's a dreadful thing to do. Where will you go?"

"Well, we never got on," replied James, avoiding answering the question. "He told me once when I was at university that I was out of my station," he chuckled. "Maybe he was right. I don't seem to have achieved very much, do I?"

"James, never, ever say that," interrupted Patsy. "You gave my brother so much happiness. I know how much he loved you. He told me once. You were always together, right from being children. I remember it very well. I used to think that you were my big brother."

James and Patsy held hands and walked to the end of the church path. Patsy stopped and opened her handbag.

"James, I nearly forgot. I wanted to give you this."

Patsy thrust a small brown envelope into James' hand. Carefully, he opened the envelope and retrieved a gold ring. It was Tristan's signet ring.

"The hospital gave it to me and I wanted you to have it. I know you haven't got anything of Tristan's, so I thought this might help a little. Don't tell Dad you have it though," she added.

James slipped the gold ring onto his own finger, his eyes once again filling with tears.

"Thank you, Patsy. You couldn't have done anything better for me. Do you know the history of this ring?"

"No, I think he bought it when he was in the Army."

"No, Patsy, he didn't buy it. I did. I gave it to Tristan when he joined up. I was so upset that he was leaving. I went to Samuel's and bought the best ring that I could afford and gave it to him before he got on the train. He said he would never take it off again. I think I spent most of my grant cheque on it," he chuckled.

"I don't think he ever did take it off, James. Now you have it once again. It will help a little."

Patsy and James walked into the school hall and James was surprised to see quite so many people there. There was some laughter, but it was mostly a subdued affair. James slowly walked over to the end of the room that had been his classroom. His eyes fell upon the large globe that Tristan had so joyfully presented to him nearly a year before. He remembered Tristan's words of praise for what he had achieved and how he had glowed with pleasure when it was given. Yes, he knew at that moment how much he truly loved Tristan.

"Doris, where did all this food come from?" enquired James, and Doris passed him a very welcome glass of wine.

"Well, I made some, and so did Anne and Emily, of course. Mrs Hilary and Jean made the sandwiches and sausage rolls, and the Peatwhistles provided all the drinks. Mrs Hilary even made a vegetarian selection for you!"

"I am so touched. Tristan would have been overcome by all this. Who are those people over there?" enquired James, nodding towards two burly men standing by the door, looking embarrassed in their dark grey suits.

"I'm not sure," said Doris. "I thought you would know them. Maybe they are from Bridgehampton?"

James walked over to the two men and nodded. "I'm James, Tristan's partner. Thank you so much for coming. I don't think we have met before?" James and the two men shook hands.

"I'm Mike and he's Chris. We worked with Tristan. The store manager, Paul, is over there somewhere chatting up that blonde bird."

James smiled and could see a young man talking earnestly to Patsy. He chuckled to himself. Yes, some things certainly ran in the family and he was struck by how much Patsy looked like her brother from a distance.

"Tristan was quite a lad, wasn't he?" began Mike. "We had some great laughs together and we really liked him. He spoke a lot about you, but we didn't know that he was a poof and lived with you."

Chris nudged his friend and shook his head.

"Oh, don't worry about that," smiled James. "I've been called a lot of things worse than that in my time. By the way, what are you two sweeties doing later when all this is over? I'd like to get to know you both better, much better," he whispered seductively in Mike's ear.

Mike spluttered on his egg and cress sandwich and Chris looked very uneasy and shuffled closer towards the door. James walked away from the two laughing wickedly and caught up with Christian, who was chatting to Anne. Doris sidled up to James.

"James, I saw and heard all that," she whispered, pretending to be shocked. "Behave yourself, James. Tristan would be shocked to see you flirting with his workmates at his funeral."

"No, he wouldn't," laughed James heartily, twisting the ring on his finger. "He would think it was very, very funny."

Doris started laughing as well. "Yes, I do believe he would. I can see that you are feeling much better today, James."

Chapter 22

Journeys and Jigsaws

It was the last day of the summer term. The end of the school year is always very special for teachers as well as for pupils, and James was no exception. Somehow the exhaustion of the long school year and a hectic summer term is put behind them and the thoughts of the long summer holiday ahead is something to look forward to with relish. The last day of the school year is often one of great pride as teachers see pupils whom they have cared for over a whole year move on to the next stage of their lives. It is also a time tinged with sadness as it is often the last time that pupils and their teachers will see each other.

James had not been well since Tristan's death. Doris and George had cared for him in a way that only loving parents could have done. They had both made it clear that James could stay with them for as long as he wished. They both knew a broken heart when they saw it and James would spend hours sitting alone and in silence. Sometimes he would go for a long walk with Trigger, and he found solace in the elderly dog's company. At this time in his life, James often preferred to be by himself, and George and Doris were happy for him to do as he pleased, although they remained very concerned for his well-being.

George had put James' mind at rest when James started to worry about the end of term activities at Prior's Hill.

"Look, James, the doctor has signed you off for a few weeks. You need time to get yourself better again. We talked about it at the Governors' meeting the other evening. They are happy for you to take the rest of the term off. They want to help you and frankly, James, I have never been to a Governors' meeting where everyone was so focused upon one thing and in total agreement. This business with Tristan has shaken the whole village, make no mistake. So many people seemed to know him, yet you have barely been here a year."

James was grateful for George's reassurance and nodded. He felt that he had let the children and the school down.

George continued, "James, I have never known anyone quite as dedicated as you, but if you are not careful it will damage your own health. You can only help Prior's Hill when you are fully better again. Doris tells me that Anne is running the show beautifully, just as you would like it. Emily is in full-time and we have asked Dorothy Sparrow to come in as well. You know Dorothy, I think. She taught here some years ago before her last baby was born."

James nodded. "Yes, Dorothy, I remember her. A good choice. Is she related to Jack, by the way, George?"

George laughed. "Most are, in Prior's Hill. I think Dorothy is Jack's nephew's wife, something like that. Yes, it's certainly a case of Sparrows everywhere, isn't it?"

George laughed heartily at his own joke. James liked George very much. He was a very thin, frail looking man and much older than Doris, but he had a heart of gold and was generous of spirit. Everyone knew and liked George.

James smiled. "Thanks, George. Yes, I know it is in good hands. I do miss it, yet I don't think I can face it just yet."

"What are you going to do today, James?" asked Doris over breakfast.

"I am going to the Leavers' Service this afternoon," announced James.

"Are you sure that's a good idea?" asked Doris anxiously. "Everyone will be there."

"Precisely," replied James. "It really is time that I started making an effort again. I must say goodbye to the leavers. They will expect me to be there."

"Right you are," said Doris, and sighed. She knew 'the look' and was always well aware when James was determined to do something that she did not think was wise.

James walked into the church alone. Sally Watson, who was giving out the Order of Service sheets, was standing by the door with Neil. As soon as she spotted James, she rushed over to him and gave him a big hug.

"I am so pleased you have come, Mr Young. We have all been worried about you and really missed you. We wanted you to be here today."

James blushed. "Thank you, Sally. I am not sure that you are supposed to hug me, but thank you. I am pleased to be here as well. How's Neil, are you alright? How's that reading coming along?"

"Good, thank you, Mr Young," beamed Neil, as James walked over to him and ruffled his hair. "I'm on the next grade now. Mrs Cook thinks I am doing really well."

"And so you are, Neil. I always knew you could do it. Ledger's School will be very pleased to have you. I shall miss you, Neil."

James went to sit in the same row as Anne. She smiled when she saw him in the same pew.

"It's all under control, James," she whispered. "It's just the same as you planned it, so don't worry."

"I have no doubt it will be perfect," smiled James.

The service was a traditional one. James would have liked to have made it livelier and add more of his own ideas, but he felt that rather than to cause more problems for the school and village, he would leave it this year and change it for the following one. The service began with opening words from the Rector, which he boomed from the pulpit, followed by a hymn that James knew well. It was always sung at the end of year service at Marion's school as well. It was 'One More Step Along the World I Go'. The children sang the hymn with gusto and James was pleased to see that Anne had included a small group of recorder players, who more or less kept up with the piano. Anne even had Neil playing a tambourine. Anne glanced at James and he gave her a nod of approval.

For once, James couldn't join in with the singing. He tried, but every time he opened his mouth, nothing would come out. He found his eyes welling up with tears as he remembered the previous time that he had been in this church, facing Tristan's coffin. It was all still very raw for him, but he hummed the music and followed and thought about the words.

James stood up and walked to the front of the pews. It was his job to give a Bible to each of the pupils who were leaving Prior's Hill School. James had carefully written the name of each pupil inside the front cover, together with the date and 'From the Governors, Headteacher and Staff of Prior's Hill Church of England Voluntary Aided Primary School' inside each one. Doris had carefully grouped the children in the correct order and James read each of the pupils' names in alphabetical order. As they approached him, James shook their hands, smiled, and said a few words of encouragement to each pupil and gave them their Bible. It was clear that Anne had briefed the children well, and all knew in which hand to accept their gift and remembered to shake James' hand with the other. Parents clapped each pupil heartily before they returned to their seats.

"Would you like to say a few words to the pupils, Mr Young?" whispered the Rector. "You don't have to. I always have something that I can say. You know me, James!"

"Well, er, maybe I'll say just a few words," stammered James. This was something that he would have found so very easy to do a few months ago. Now it seemed like a huge challenge and a moment that he had been dreading. He stood up again and coughed nervously. He opened his mouth, but nothing came out. He cleared his throat again and glanced at Doris, who was sitting in one of the side pews. She smiled with encouragement. The church, although full to capacity with pupils, parents and villagers, was in silence as they waited for their head teacher to speak.

"Good afternoon, everyone," he began.

"Good afternoon. Mr Young," chanted the children.

James smiled, "Well, it is good that you have remembered my name after all these weeks," he smiled. "I'm sorry that I have not been around for a while and that I missed all of your end-of-term events. I wanted to be here today to say goodbye to you, and especially to our leavers."

Doris nodded and smiled with more encouragement.

"I just wanted to say that we shall miss you all, but we cannot keep you at Prior's Hill forever. You know, life is rather like a journey, a very long journey – just like the hymn that you have been singing. On its path you will meet good times and bad times. Sometimes there will be good times and really good things, and you must remember those to help you to get through the bad times."

James paused for a moment. He had the reputation of being a good public speaker and as he delivered his unprepared speech he began to feel more confident, particularly as the children were listening and not fidgeting.

"On your journey through life you will also meet some good people and some not so nice people. You will meet people whom you love and others that you don't like. Just as you have made friends here you will do the same at your new schools and, later, in your jobs and maybe even at college and university. Don't be afraid, and make the most of your opportunities. Be true to yourself and only ever do what you know to be right in your heart. One day, if you are fortunate, you may even meet someone special who will make your life complete."

A hand shot up. "Yes, Sally?"

"Do you mean like you and Mr Tristan?"

There was silence as James froze for a moment.

"Er, yes, Sally, like Mr Tristan and myself. He was my best friend and I miss him."

"But he died. Will you ever see him again?" blurted out Timothy Blossom, who had been placed in the front row 'to have an eye kept upon him'.

"He's gone to heaven. 'Course he will," added Naomi, pulling a face at Timothy. "I liked Mr Tristan, he played catch with us and he could skip, but not as good as Tina Martin," she added, smiling at her best friend who was sitting at her side.

"Yes, Tim, I believe and I hope so. It's what all Christians hope for, that we will see each other again one day in heaven."

Sally's hand shot up again.

"Yes, Sally?"

"I don't understand. What's the point of life, if you lose people you love? I love my mum, but I hate my dad. My mum will die one day and leave me on my own. It scares me."

"There's no need to be scared, Sally. The point of life, as I said before, is to take both the good and the bad bits. Together it makes the whole picture. It's a bit like a box of chocolates. You cannot eat all those nice strawberry cream ones without having some of the boring ones as well."

"My mum takes all the strawberry ones and leaves the nutty ones for my dad," interrupted Timothy Blossom.

"Shh, Timothy," whispered Emily loudly, glaring at the small boy at her side who was now contentedly picking his nose.

James smiled and walked over to the piano and took out an old jigsaw puzzle in its box from the shelf behind. He walked back to the front of the church and shook the box. The pieces in the box rattled.

"What have I got in here?" he asked.

Hands shot up across the church.

"Yes, Vanessa?"

"A jigsaw, Mr Young."

"Yes, Vanessa, but what is it of?"

"I don't know, Mr Young."

"Why don't you know, Vanessa?"

"I can't see the picture yet, Mr Young."

"That's right, Vanessa, but one day you will. Just look at this."

James held up the lid of the jigsaw puzzle box for everyone to see. It was one showing a seaside scene, complete with sandcastles, donkeys and deck-chairs.

"Each part of your life is like the pieces of a jigsaw. When you fit them together it makes a picture, a wonderful picture of your life, but you cannot see it at the time. Now do you see what I mean, Sally?"

Sally nodded.

As the older children walked out of church with their parents, James stood saying goodbye and shaking hands. He was sad to see the children leave, but was immensely proud of them. Emily and Anne led the way across the road and back into the school where the children would collect their things for the last time.

"I'll be back next year, Mr Young," beamed Timothy Blossom.

"And so you will, Tim," laughed James. "I shall look forward to that."

"Does that mean you will be back with us next year, James?" came a familiar voice.

It was Lady Lotitia, sitting on a bench in the porch. She waited until all the children had left, then stood up and walked over to James.

"A remarkable service, James. Very poignant, and I think it was very brave of you to be here. You said some wonderful things and I hope you took them on board for yourself. Now, will you be back with us next year? Toby told me that you were thinking of leaving us, what?"

"I really don't know at the moment, Lady Lotitia. I am so confused about things."

"James, I know how much you miss Tristan. He was your soulmate and you loved him very much. Everyone could see that. Have you thought just how much that young man meant to people in this village as well? After his accident, people were shocked. It was as if it was if they had lost one of their own. Yet the strange thing is that they hardly knew him. They knew him through you, James. You worked as a team for the school, for the village and, most importantly, for the children. It has been quite remarkable."

James nodded and once again his eyes filled with tears.

"Look, James, I am not very good at this sort of thing, but what I am trying to say is that people admire, respect and like you in this village for who you are. Whether you are gay or straight is no longer important. We have all learned an important lesson because of you and Tristan this year. We have all shared your grief in some way. Doesn't that say something important to you, what?"

"I think there may be too many memories here, Lady Lotitia. A fresh start somewhere else may help me to get over it."

Lady Lotitia paused and sat down again on the bench in the porch.

"Come and sit beside me, James."

"Do you remember my rose garden? Do you remember why I created it? Do you remember what I told you some months ago?"

James nodded.

"I lost a very special son and his lover, just like you and Tristan. As I told you before, Tristan so reminded me of young Sam Rivers..." Her voice trailed off.

"You have created a wonderful place of rest and a place where you could go and almost be with them," said James.

"Precisely, James. I could have moved away, but I get the greatest comfort by being where Giles grew up, played and loved. I know people laugh at me for being a foolish old woman and drinking far too much gin, but I tell you this, James, I would be dead otherwise. My rose garden has helped me to cope with life."

"Does the pain ever go away?" asked James.

Lady Lotitia paused and gently shook her head. "No, not really. It just gets a little easier to live with, James, but no, it doesn't ever really go away. You are young enough to find someone else and, in time, that will help."

"I just thought that if I moved away and started again it would get easier. I don't think I could go through life feeling like this. I feel so empty inside."

"Look, James. You will never escape your memories. Sometimes it is far better to face and embrace them. Do you see what I mean?"

James nodded. "I think I understand. Thank you."

"Well, James, I must be going now. The hunt group are coming over later to discuss the ball. Now try to get a good rest and we hope to see you creating havoc in our village school again next year, what?"

Lady Lotitia stood up, smiled at James, and strode down the church path towards the Manor House.

"Ah, James, I am so pleased you are still here," boomed the Rector. "I wanted to catch you before you went over to the school, but I got held up by Mrs Maggs, the pianist. You don't play the piano, do you James?"

James smiled. "I seem to remember being asked that once before, at my interview last year."

The Rector laughed. "Goodness, yes, it was one of Lady Peatwhistle's trick questions, I believe. Didn't she ask you which hand or something equally obtuse?"

"Yes, she did. Yes, I do play a little, Rector, but very badly, and only on a keyboard."

"It's just that Marjorie Maggs has just resigned. I think I have upset her in some way, but I can't think how," he sighed.

"Well, I will help out if I can, but I wouldn't recommend it," smiled James. "Rector, I just want to thank you for helping me out at the hospital and for all your kindness whilst I have been off sick. I just don't know what I would have done without you."

"Think nothing of it, my boy. It was all very distressing and, if I may say so, so very unfair to you and people like you."

James nodded.

"Look, James, what I really wanted to see you about is this. Do you remember that I asked whether you thought Tristan would have liked funeral flowers or that we should put the money to something more tangible?"

"Yes, I think we said we would buy something for the school, didn't we?"

"That's correct, and we have raised a lot of money. Already it is in excess of five hundred pounds. I thought we could put that towards the new school library. What do you think?"

"Good idea," nodded James. "Yes, Tristan would have liked that. After all, he, Bert and Eddie repainted and replastered the room and he started making some shelving for it as well before he died."

"There's something else as well. It was Bert and Eddie's idea. They wanted to do something special for Tristan – in his memory. Come and see it."

The Rector led the way down the church path and the short distance down the narrow lane to the school playground. James followed, stopping beneath the old horse-chestnut tree.

"Look at this," boomed the Rector, pointing proudly.

Beneath the old tree was placed a new large wooden seat. It was made of a heavy dark wood. The arms and the back of the seat were intricately carved with a pattern. James ran his hand over the smooth wood.

"Bert and Eddie finished it yesterday. It was meant to be a surprise for you today. Look at this as well."

The Rector pointed to a small brass plate that was inserted in the centre of the back piece of wood. It read: 'In loving memory of Mr Tristan. A great friend of Prior's Hill School'.

"Oh, this is beautiful. It is just perfect," said James quietly. "They really made it for Tristan?'

"Oh yes. His death hit them both badly. Strange really, as they only knew him for a short time. They bought the wood themselves and we paid for the brass plate out of the collection. I was a bit annoyed with it actually, because it should have said

‘Tristan Peters’ and not ‘Mr Tristan’. That was their doing. I did tell them to get it done again.”

“No, this is just right. All the children called him ‘Mr Tristan’ for some reason and he rather liked it. This is just what he would have wanted. Why did you put it here?”

“Well, I think the staff commented that you often came over here to think at the end of the day and so we thought from now on you could sit on Mr Tristan’s bench seat. Look, James, I must go. So pleased you like the bench. Thank you for this afternoon and we hope to see you in September, if not before. God bless.”

James went back into the school, visiting each of the three classes in turn to say goodbye to the children. They all seemed to be having some kind of leaving party as there were plates of crisps and plastic cups of cola on the tables. James smiled and walked across to Emily.

“Nice touch, Emily. Thank you for organising this.”

Emily smiled. “I like to do a little something for them at the end of the year, James. I shall miss them.”

“Yes, they have been a good lot, haven’t they, Emily?”

“James, have you got a moment? I need to speak to you privately.”

“Of course, Emily, let’s walk outside for a few moments. Doris is here and so is Anne, so the children will be alright for a few minutes. What can I do for you?”

James and Emily walked over to the horse-chestnut tree and Emily admired the new bench seat.

“This is wonderful, James. You must be very pleased and proud to see it.”

They both sat down on the new seat.

“Now, what can I do for you?”

“Well, James, I know we haven’t always got on very well. We haven’t always seen eye to eye, have we? I just wanted to say that I was so desperately sorry about what happened to

Tristan. I do understand. I lost my husband a few years ago. I know how it feels." Emily squeezed James' hand.

"Thank you, Emily. You have already helped me. I was so worried about Class 3, yet I knew the children were in good hands with you, Emily. I trust you, and I know you are a good, dedicated teacher. No, we don't always see eye to eye, but that is good. I have a lot of new ideas, some are untried and untested. You are an experienced teacher and you challenge me. That is good, although you can be so annoying sometimes," James laughed.

James began to see the elderly teacher in a new light. He now began to understand why she was often so angry with him and challenged his ideas in public. However, he did trust her and always knew that the children were in good hands when they were with her.

"Thank you, James. I guess it is fear of change. By the way, I meant to say, your talk to the children in church this afternoon was very poignant. It made me think and, yes, you are so right, life is like a jigsaw. Anyway, please come back next year. Doris says that you may be leaving Prior's Hill?"

"It is a strong possibility, Emily. I am just not sure what to do yet and I hope the summer holidays will help me to sort a few things out."

"Well, I shall probably regret saying this later," said Emily. "But you need to know that I admire you and your determination in improving this school. We are on our way forward here, James. I know that now. You have put us back on the map. You have achieved so much for this school in just one year. Please don't leave us. You have still much to give to Prior's Hill."

"Thanks, Emily. I appreciate you telling me this and I am sorry if I have been, shall we say, a little clumsy in my approach."

"By the way, James, I nearly forgot to give you this." Emily rummaged in her basket. "I have brought you this."

She handed James a plastic bag in which there was a jar.

"It's just a jar of my homemade strawberry jam. My Martin always loved it. Homegrown strawberries, and I made the jam only a short time ago. I hope you enjoy it, James."

James remained seated on the bench as he watched Emily walk back to her classroom. She is a strange old girl, he thought, but she has given the school stability and is a good teacher, despite the rough edges.

By now, James could see the younger children walking to the gate with Mrs Sparrow, followed by Anne's class and finally Class 3 with Emily. He watched as parents gathered their children and either walked with them down the lane to the nearby cottages or to their cars. The bus children were collected promptly and the battered old bus made its way noisily down the lane to other nearby villages. Eventually, the playground fell silent once again and left James alone with his thoughts.

"You coming home now, James?" interrupted Doris.

Doris, as usual, was laden down with cake tins, bags, boxes and armfuls of flowers and plants. He was also pleased to see that she was carrying a number of presents that the children, presumably, had given her.

"A bit later on, Doris. I want to make the most of this seat. Have you seen it?"

"Yes, it is wonderful, isn't it?" beamed Doris. "It was all Bert and Eddie's idea. I think the Rector wanted to change the wording on the brass plate, but they insisted. It was all getting a bit political and so I stayed well out of it!"

"Typical Prior's Hill, eh, Doris?" smiled James. "I see you had plenty of presents."

"Yes, the children have been very kind to me, but they gave me some for you as well, James. I have put them in the boot of your car, so you won't have to go inside again. You are well liked here, you know. Have you decided what you are going to do? Please don't leave us just yet, James. You can live with George and me for as long as you like. You are no trouble at all."

"Thank you for looking after me, Doris. The truth is that I just don't know. I am hoping that an answer will come to me soon. I know it will, but I just have to wait and see."

"I understand, James. Well, we will see you later. Vegetarian shepherd's pie tonight. Your favourite, so don't be too late, will you?"

James laughed, as he already knew the conversation and endless teasing from George that he would have to endure about vegetarian shepherd's pies.

"Oh dear, George will love teasing me about that!"

Doris laughed, gathered up her basket and bags and wandered over to the school gate.

"You staying on for a bit, sir?" interrupted Cedric.

"Yes, just for a while. I'll lock the gate when I go. How are you getting on, Cedric?"

"So sorry to hear about your friend, sir. I'm alright. I knows what to do during the holiday. Mrs Armstrong tells me the other day."

"That's good, Cedric. Thank you for all that you have done."

"You back with us in September, sir?"

"Maybe, Cedric. Maybe."

The last of the afternoon sun fell between the leaves of the old horse-chestnut tree, lighting up its trunk and falling upon the new wooden bench and also upon James. There was a slight breeze and the leaves rustled and played gently in the wind. James looked at the branches of the old tree above him and thought about the many end of terms and end-of-years that it had seen. There was a timeless and peaceful quality that James always felt when he was beneath its all-embracing apron. James could feel the warmth of the last of the afternoon sun gently bathing his face. He recalled the last words that Tristan had spoken to him. The leaves on the tree seemed to whisper the words lovingly in his ear. "I love you, Mr Headmaster, and don't you ever forget it."

It was now clear what James had to do. He stood up and made his way to the school gate. He took another look at the school building, its golden stone now bathed in the last of the day's sunlight. James carefully locked the school gate and got into his car. The shiny blue sports car sped its way through the narrow, winding lanes and out of the village.